Also by Janet Gleeson

Nonfiction
The Arcanum
Millionaire

The Grenadillo Box

A Novel

JANET GLEESON

SIMON & SCHUSTER
NEW YORK   LONDON   TORONTO   SYDNEY

SIMON & SCHUSTER
Rockefeller Center
1230 Avenue of the Americas
New York, NY 10020

Copyright © 2002 by Janet Gleeson
All rights reserved,
including the right of reproduction
in whole or in part in any form.

Originally published in Great Britain in 2002 by Transworld Publishers

SIMON & SCHUSTER and colophon are registered trademarks
of Simon & Schuster, Inc.

For information about special discounts for bulk purchases,
please contact Simon & Schuster Special Sales at
1-800-456-6798 or business@simonandschuster.com

Designed by Lauren Simonetti

Manufactured in the United States of America

1   3   5   7   9   10   8   6   4   2

Library of Congress Cataloging-in-Publication Data
Gleeson, Janet.
The grenadillo box / Janet Gleeson.
p.   cm.
1. Cabinetmakers—Fiction.   2. Country homes—Fiction.   3. Nobility—Fiction.
4. England—Fiction.   I. Title.
PR6107.L44G74 2004
823'.92—dc22   2003061709
ISBN 0-7432-4686-1

For my children, Lucy, Annabel, and James, with love

Author's Note and Acknowledgments

I have based this fictional story on various elements of truth. Lord Montfort's death after dinner on January 1, 1755, at Horseheath Hall (a Palladian mansion that no longer survives) is described by Horace Walpole. Montfort was one of the original subscribers of Chippendale's *Director,* the book on which his fame is founded. Two albums of original drawings for the *Director* in the Metropolitan Museum, New York, since 1920 were acquired from the collection of Montfort's neighbor Lord Foley, although there is no concrete proof Foley accepted them from Montfort in settlement of gambling debts. Although Alice Goodchild is a purely fictional character, Chippendale did have a journeyman by the name of Nathaniel Hopson. Partridge Wood does exist as described, but the character John Partridge is purely fictional. The description of Chippendale's grand writing cabinet is based upon the Murray Cabinet, by John Channon, in the Victoria and Albert Museum. There is plenty of documentary evidence to suggest that Chippendale was far from incorruptible. He is recorded as having several close shaves with the law (including smuggling chairs from France to avoid paying duty). Though fictional, the character of Madame Trenti is based on Theresa Cornelly, an Italian impresario and adventuress to whom Chippendale loaned or rented furniture and with whom he became mysteriously embroiled later in the century. The account of the opening of the Foundling Hospital is directly quoted from the committee record books. All the details of the children's admission and treatment are based on fact.

In concocting this story I have drawn on the colorful accounts of London inhabitants such as Horace Walpole, James Boswell, and William Hickey, and the researches of numerous eighteenth-century historians. I am particularly indebted to the following sources: Christopher Gilbert, *The Life and Work of Thomas Chippendale* (Studio Vista, Christie's, 1978); Christopher Gilbert and Tessa Murdoch, *John Channon and Brass-Inlaid Furniture* (Yale, 1993); Pat Kirkham, *London Furniture Trade* (Furniture History Society, 1988); James Gaynor and Nancy Hagedorn, *Tools Working Wood in Eighteenth-Century America* (Colonial Williamsburg, 1993); Jane and Mark Rees, *Christopher Gabriel and the Tool Trade in Eighteenth-Century London* (Roy Arnold, 1997); John Gloag, *Georgian Grace* (A. & C. Black, 1967); Christina Hardyment, *Behind the Scenes* (National Trust, 1997); the Thomas Coram Foundation for Children, *Enlightened Self-Interest* (Draig Publications, 1997); Gabriel R. H. Nichols and F. A. Wray, *The History of the Foundling Hospital* (Oxford, 1935); R. K. McLure, *Coram's Children: The London Foundling Hospital in the Eighteenth Century* (Yale, 1981).

In addition, I should like to offer my heartfelt thanks to the following people: to Christopher Little, for believing I could do something I'd always wanted to do; to Lucy Ferguson, for her constructive advice and encouragement; to John Rees, for explaining the intricacies of cabinet-makers' tools; to John and Eileen Harris, for discussing Chippendale and the eighteenth century with me; to Patrick Janson-Smith and Sally Gaminara at Transworld, for giving me the chance to write this book; to Deborah Adams, for the painstaking editing of it; and to my husband, Paul Gleeson, for putting up with me while I wrote it.

J. G

ON CABINETMAKING

The youth intended for this purpose ought to be able to write a good hand, understand arithmetic, and have some notion of drawing and designing. It requires more ingenuity than strength: a nice eye and a light hand are absolutely necessary as he is by far the most curious workman in the wood way. His success as a master must depend on the delicacy of his fancy and the neatness of his work.

From J. Collyer, *The Parent's and Guardian's Directory and the Youth's Guide in the Choice of a Profession or Trade* (1761)

The

Grenadillo

Box

Prologue

London March 4, 1755

Alice,

A thousand pardons when you see this letter and the sheaf of pages it encloses. I hazard you will toss the bundle on the fire—why in heaven's name should you read a line penned by someone who has caused you such havoc? Why give a jot for the protestations of one who frightened you senseless and whose ineptness gravely injured you?

Yet, if you've read this far, Alice, grant me forbearance and read further. Without preamble let me explain my reason for writing. It is a simple one: not anguish at the deaths I didn't prevent, or shame at my stupidity in unraveling them, but rather my mighty hope that if I explain my actions you'll comprehend them and our estrangement will be over.

And so I send you this private history, a candid account of events drawn as carefully as any historian from the journals and papers in my possession. Should these revelations astound or even offend you, bear in mind I embarked on this record for my own clarification, as a means of establishing some semblance of order among the stew of fact, inspiration, supposition, and history fomenting in my brain.

I didn't know then what a hefty task I'd set myself. Remember yourself, Alice, standing in your parlor, before the aged looking glass you once showed me. Remember the image you saw reflected—a distorted, ungainly figure with gaunt cheeks and cavernous eyes. How easily did you discern between this weird specter and the wholesome person you know yourself to be? How speedily did you glance down to reassure yourself you were not this apparition? My perception of what took place was frequently flawed like that image. The conclusions I drew were often fanciful, sometimes ludicrous, rarely just. You will witness occasions where I was no longer master of my own faculties, a prey to wild conjecture and idiotic theory. You will perceive how my imagination made strange parallels between my profession, the objects I create, and these events, which resembled in my mind some strange cabinet of curiosities, like the one made by Chippendale, replete with hidden compartments, chambers, and niches.

You well know that this most precious of cabinets was adorned with marquetry inlays, pictures concocted from timber morsels of various hue, figure, and hardness, each portion separately and precisely cut and assembled to form the design. Thus have I related the story, piece by piece, as we assembled it, until at length the pattern became clear.

I remain yours most affectionately and devotedly,

Nathaniel

Chapter One

Clumsiness rather than cleverness marked the starting point. To put it another way, the discovery happened after two blunders.

It was New Year's Day, 1755, in the midst of Lord Montfort's dinner, when I stumbled first. The platter I was serving tipped and sent a pyramid of oranges madly spinning over the Turkey carpet. Puce with self-consciousness, I squatted to gather them up, threading my way between a forest of silk-stockinged and mahogany legs. But I needn't have worried; no one had noticed. They were ablaze with alarm at the cause of my slip—a deafening gun blast that had rudely interrupted their party. It had reverberated through the building, a truly deafening noise, made more earsplitting perhaps by its unexpectedness; loud enough to make the door shudder and the glass in the window frames rattle; loud enough to ring in my ears several minutes afterwards.

The people assembled in that room cried out, pressing hands to their ears as if to ward off the penetrating sound, but none of them went straight to the nub of the matter. None asked the most obvious question. What had become of their host, Lord Montfort?

The gentlemen strode stiffly about the room or sat erect in their chairs. One (I know not whom, for I was still scrabbling on the floor at this juncture) cried out the only question to which the response was already evident. "What in God's name was that?"

"A gunshot."

"A gunshot, you say?"

"Aye, a gunshot . . ."

In her husband's absence, the mistress of this household, Lady Montfort, should perhaps have taken charge. Yet when the other ladies rose fluttering and squawking like startled pheasants put up by a beater, she seemed oblivious to her obligations. Cowed and silent, she turned a ring with her forefinger, her shoulders twitching with suppressed emotion.

In truth, though I was but a stranger here, I did not think her behavior peculiar. From the outset Horseheath Hall had struck me not only by its air of isolated seclusion—I am well accustomed to city life, and found its remoteness unsettling—but also by its singular character. This was my sixth day in the house; the longer I stayed the more my conviction grew that, for all its studied luxury, the mansion lacked some fundamental quality. Horseheath Hall was devoid of the essential warmth that fuses mere stone and bricks and floors and windows into an entity deserving of the name of home. Its elegant rooms were suffused with shadow. Gilded furnishings and damask draperies and ornaments did not fill the emptiness; nor did sunlight and fires ever warm it.

This oppressive chill seemed also to infect its inhabitants, and in particular its unhappy mistress. Elizabeth Montfort was but a young woman, of perhaps two and twenty years, yet there was no youthful gaiety about her, no liveliness, no freedom of expression or spirit. As far as I had observed, her habitual manner was one of suppressed anxiety and unusual agitation. Her complexion was wan, her face pinched, her eyes pale blue and rather prominent, which only added to her fretful expression. Over the past days, whenever I caught sight of her, whether penning a letter or stitching her embroidery or going listlessly about the house, it seemed to me she started, as if my appearance was somehow fearsome to her.

This evening that nervousness had worsened when her husband's temper grew markedly capricious. His final choleric outburst had caused all vestige of composure to desert her. When he stalked from the room her face turned parchment pale. Afterwards she sat clenching the tablecloth as if terrified to the depths of her soul that at any moment he might burst back and berate her again.

It was Lord Foley, senior guest at the present assembly, who swiftly took command. He instructed all servants to be sent in search of the source of the sound. When I lingered on (not regarding myself as a servant, I didn't feel obliged to follow his direction), my inertia was swiftly remarked; whereupon he clicked his fingers, furrowed his caterpillar brows, and ordered me away as curtly as one might command a dog to follow a scent.

Unable to refuse such a command, I bowed with suitable deference, then turned tail so swiftly I reckon I surprised him. But why dawdle when it was plain to me where to go? Naturally Lord Foley wasn't aware then who he was ordering about, that I was in a sense an impostor here, or that there was only one room in the house that concerned me. Lord Montfort's new library was where I headed.

From the threshold I looked in. The room was blacker than a mourner's coat, not a candle lit, only a blast of January cold, the sound of rattling panes and flapping cloth, and a yawning mouth of chimney where the fire should be. Unthinkingly, without a glimmer of dread, for I was a lusty one and twenty years and knew so little of the world that I could laugh at the indeterminate terrors it held, I retreated, took hold of a candlestick, and plunged back into the Stygian murk.

My flimsy light showed me it was no ghostly presence but an open window on the far side of the room that chilled the air and billowed the curtains. I began to cross the room, my intention being to reach the window and secure it before I ventured further. From the corner of my eye I could see the velvet-clad figure of Lord Foley now picking his way some distance behind me like a strange iridescent beetle. I located the great bookcase facing the windows and began to inch my way along it, with Lord Foley following on a few yards behind. Our lights threw feeble yellow stains over shipwrecked hulks of furniture. We walked forward slowly, footsteps clicking on the polished boards, twirling the candles about our heads as elegantly as dancers do at a summer entertainment in the Vauxhall Gardens.

I had taken scarcely half a dozen paces when my foot came down on an invisible object. I relinquished my grip on the bookcase and skidded forward, only to be halted by a further obstacle concealed in shadow. For the second time that night I staggered. The candle clattered to the ground and went out. An instant later I plummeted alongside it.

As I have said, fear had hitherto been a stranger to me. Until that moment. For as I recovered myself in the blackness and groped around waiting for Lord Foley to find me, I recognized its presence rising spontaneously like a fist in my gullet, dampening my armpits, prickling under my wig. Looking back, I believe I must have had some presentiment of danger. I knew in my marrow, even before I saw it, that something horrible awaited in the shadows.

"What happened, man?" demanded Lord Foley as he drew close.

"I can't see, my lord," said I, sitting up on the floor and rubbing my head. "My foot touched something and I tripped. If you would be so kind as to bring your light here, I will find out what it was . . ."

He lowered his light; I squinted through the jaundiced flame.

It was the body of a man. He lay spread-eagled against a painting, *The Death of Icarus* (of moderate quality, so Lord Foley later informed me), which had been propped against the bookcase ready for hanging.

I say "body," for it was apparent from his distressing condition that the man was dead. His head had slumped forward and was supported by rippling concentric circles of chin. A mess of gore, like maggots feasting in a plum, emanated from a circular wound in his temple. This stew of brain and blood and bone had matted his wig and formed a slimy trail merging with a trickle of saliva oozing from his lips. Stupefied and sickened by this scene, I sat rooted to the floor like an idiot. Even in its mutilated state I recognized the grotesque face with its bulbous pitted nose and thick fleshy lips, the corpulent body clad in silk and lace and velvet finery. It was my patron for the last few days, the owner of this estate, Lord Montfort. In life Lord Montfort's choleric humor and fondness for dissipation had reddened his jowls. In death his color was diminished. Beneath the rivulets of blood that emanated from his wound, once-florid flesh was now pallid and blotchy. How vividly I remember the unnatural hues illuminated by Foley's candle: the white of bone, powdered wig, starched cravat, against which lilac flesh and crimson gore glistened. As I looked I felt any vestige of youthful courage extinguished. Beads of perspiration bulged on my brow. I could hear my own heart palpitate within my breast. How long I stayed rooted thus I do not know, only that at length I became aware of the spindly figure of Lord Foley beside me. He crouched over Montfort, shaking his head incredulously, muttering to himself, "What is this? What is this? I cannot . . . cannot be the cause of it."

The emotion in his voice unfettered me. I raised my head in his direction. His candle was now on the floor, and its light cast a vast distorted silhouette of his profile on the ceiling above—a jutting brow, a great hooked nose, a prominent chin—and called to mind some monstrous gargoyle.

"I am sure you are not the cause of this, my lord," I replied, although I hadn't a notion to what he referred.

"What? Do you know whom you address? How can you conceive of what has happened here? You can have no knowledge of this. It is no business of yours."

His snappish tone should not have surprised me—I was a member of the lower orders (even if I wasn't precisely the servant he believed me to be), and I had presumed to speak to him without the deference he expected. My face flamed at the crispness of his rebuke, but I understood his drift. He was an invited guest in this house, a noble one at that; I would be prudent to adopt a more subservient manner.

I murmured an apology and busied myself as best I could. I relit my candle, pushed back Montfort's head, and probed his neck for signs of life. His skin was already clammy from the bone-chilling air; there was no flicker of a pulse. By now my eyes had become more accustomed to the gloom, and I thought I discerned a lozenge of glistening black, about as long as my thumb, wedged between his fleshy jowls. I screwed up my eyes, pushed his head back again, this time at a slight angle, and leaned forward to examine his neck. Imagine then my surprise when I discovered that the black shape was not alone but one of several. Gingerly I touched one. It fell into my hand, pulsating and slimy, leaving a bead of garnet blood on Montfort's neck.

"Dear God!" I exclaimed, flicking my hand violently to dislodge it.

"What is it?" asked Lord Foley impatiently.

"There are leeches on him."

Scarcely had I uttered these words than a surge of nausea rose in my belly. I became feverishly hot within my costume, my head boiled beneath my wig, yet my face and hands grew cold and clammy as death itself. I began to shudder uncontrollably. This only doubled my distress. I was mortified to make such a pathetic display of myself before Lord Foley, and yet I was incapable of suppressing any of it. And at that moment a further discomforting thought occurred to me. The spectacle I made was no different from one I had witnessed, without comprehension, not five minutes earlier. I was reacting precisely as Elizabeth Montfort, wife of the unfortunate victim, had done when she first heard the gun blast.

Foley lit another light and brought it close. He stared unblinkingly at Montfort's neck. He saw the creatures I'd described, and his lip curled with scorn. "Come, come, man," he said, flaring the nostrils of his hawkish nose, "you are very squeamish. To be bled is a common enough occurrence—a panacea for multiple ills."

I gulped a mouthful of air and swallowed deeply to stem the sickness that was growing stronger by the minute. "I am well aware of the benefits of bleeding, sir. . . . Only the leeches took me by surprise. I had not expected them . . . in these . . . these . . . circumstances."

"I grant you they are unsightly," said Foley, bending low to study Montfort's neck, on which I could now detect half a dozen or more leeches were feasting, "but they are hardly the horror you make them." He glanced at me once more, steely-eyed, and must have read the queasiness in my face. "If you wish to retch, man, go quickly and do it from the window."

Groaning incomprehensible words of apology, I staggered across the room towards the open window. I stooped my head beneath the sash, slumped out over the sill, and the steamy contents of my stomach ejected to the ground below. Thank God I had my back to Foley and he was shielded from the worst of my degradation, though I knew he could hardly fail to hear my spittings and splutterings. The knowledge only compounded my torment. All the while my stomach was racked by spasms and disgorged itself, my mind was snarled in similar turmoil. This was the first body I had witnessed, and as I've said, until the moment I clapped my eyes on it I'd believed myself to be impervious to fear or squeamishness. Now I'd shown myself I'd no more pluck than a rabbit.

Foley displayed not a jot of interest in my plight. He continued his monologue while I vomited from the window, although I was too incapacitated to pay any attention to him until the worst of my seizure had subsided. Even when I listened more attentively, most of his words were no more than indistinct babble. The only phrase I caught quite clearly was this: "What *is* beyond my comprehension, however, is why he should choose to bleed himself during this evening's dinner."

The sound of the closing sash drew his attention back to me. I teetered towards him, sensing an arrow of disapproval let loose in my direction. All at once he addressed me directly. "In any case, as I've already told you, this is no business of yours. Indeed if there's an alien body in this room, I fancy it's not these creatures but you. Who the devil are you? For I swear I never saw you before."

"You are right, my lord," I conceded, gulping to dispel the acrid taint in my mouth. "We have never met until tonight. My name is Nathaniel Hopson, and I do not belong here at all."

I have long prided myself on the quickness of my fists and feet, yet the speed and violence of his reaction flabbergasted me. He gathered his brows to a black line and, placing his candle so close to my chin I fancied he might singe me, pressed my scalp back with his other hand and held it there. I felt my wig slip awry and tumble to the floor. Like a horse at market, I was being prodded and pulled, assessed for teeth and temperament. Yet Lord Foley had already made clear he expected me to be pliant, and I'd no desire to anger him unnecessarily, thus I could do nothing but submit. Eventually the unnerving examination was complete. He released my head and drew back. "Explain yourself, man. This is no time for puzzles or impudence, and besides I detest both."

I retrieved the fallen wig and held it in my hand. "Forgive me, my lord, I didn't intend to muddle you. I'm journeyman to Thomas Chippendale, cabinetmaker, of St. Martin's Lane, London."

Here I should explain, as I knew I must that night for Lord Foley (despite chattering teeth and queasiness still lurking in my belly), the unusual events that had brought me to Horseheath Hall. But first let me also set down something of the awkwardness of my predicament.

Until I stumbled upon the grisly scene I've just described, I'd led a carefree existence. I was born lucky, never troubled by the burden of choice that blights the lives of so many in our complicated modern age. My father was a kindly joiner, as was his father before him. I was his only child. There was never a question that I would not in some way follow him.

According to my mother, I was a gangling fledgling who unfolded from her womb like a bolt of cloth and never quite fitted my lanky proportions, always more limb than loveliness, more appetite than angel. For her part, my mother was a woman of powerful maternal disposition who demonstrated her affection in fondly administered scrubbings and scoldings. (A torn blue coat and a kidney pudding and pigeon pie eaten without her say-so are still emblazoned in my memory and on my rump.) My father was no less mindful of my well-being. By his account, I took to a saw and chisel as easily as I did to breathing and walking, although strangely, he used to say, it wasn't carpentry that was born in me but rather the reverse—the urge to demolish things. Ever since a small boy, I'd a compulsion to unscrew, dismantle, break open, detach. He attributed this to the fact that once, while bathing me in the washing copper, my mother dropped me on my head on the kitchen flags. The sudden gush of water that accompanied me had knocked over a three-legged stool, which had fallen apart. For weeks afterwards I'd tried the legs on every other piece in the house to see if they too could be dismantled. When they could not, I took up a turnscrew and a chisel to assist me. My mother made valiant attempts to starve or scold or beat the inclination out of me, but she never succeeded. My father joined my mother in warming my behind, and when that failed he sought to distract me by teaching me joinery.

In vain did I try to explain to them my preoccupation was not idle vandalism; what drew me was what had gone into the creation of the outward appearance of any given object. My childish eye viewed every lock plate, drawer front, or clockface as a question. How did it turn? What made it operate? Why did it appear thus? I was full of queries, restless for answers, which I believed I'd secure only by inspecting the guts behind each exterior.

I was thirteen when my parents conceded defeat. My hunger for undoing had continued for years, despite reddened ears, bowls of water gruel, and hours of practice in mortise and tenons, the simplest method of joining two pieces of wood. Thus was I dispatched to London to be an apprentice to Thomas Chippendale, master in the craft of cabinetmaking. This was, I well knew, no punishment—an honor rather. Thomas Chippendale was lately settled in St. Paul's Yard, in the heart of London's furniture trade, and ranked high among his fellow cabinetmakers.

Chippendale was a canny Yorkshireman whose reputation permitted him to pick and choose his apprentices as the rest of us select apples at market. He viewed his apprentices as inexpensive labor and a means to profit handsomely. Most masters required £35 for their apprentices' indentures. Chippendale demanded my poor parents pay him £42, a high sum which he claimed was entirely justified by his elevated position. They should understand, he said, that when the time came for me to set up in business, my links with Chippendale's august establishment would enhance my prestige and add to my earnings. Was it not just that this advantage should be reflected in his price? My parents could find no argument. Thus, in the belief they were doing their best for me, they scraped together the exorbitant sum and I embarked upon my new life.

I settled quickly to the city. Within a year or two I left off sweeping floors and carting wood and began to experiment with all manner of construction. I learned to fret and plane fragments of timber no larger than a butterfly's wing. As well as these skills I encountered the distractions of the back stairs and bedchamber. Thus challenged in both quarters, I learned to relish fabricating rather than destruction, to enjoy making caddies and dovetails and amour. Within seven years I had much to crow about. I was journeyman to a master by then the most esteemed in the city, whose newly opened premises in St. Martin's Lane drew gasps of amazement for their grandeur. In my professional capacity I called at the grandest mansions, which frequently led me to the company of the most alluring chambermaids, cooks, and lady's maids imaginable. In short, I enjoyed an existence as busy and lusty as any man.

As a journeyman I am accustomed to visiting fine saloons to hobnob with gentlemen of Lord Foley's caliber, though only on such subjects as the advantages of mahogany over oak, the appropriateness of a cabriole leg over a straight or a carved chair splat over a plain. Yet when it came to general conversation with the upper gentry, I was green as a toad. Herein lay my dilemma. How should I explain my involvement to Lord Foley? How much detail did he require? Should I be frank and open, or distant and brief? How in my present muddleheaded state was I to decide what was relevant and what unnecessary? Even while I wrestled with this concern, I knew I had little time to waste. Lord Foley had demonstrated he was a man of unpredictable temper. Thus, with little confidence in where my tongue would lead me, I hastened to begin.

The events that brought me to Horseheath Hall had started innocently enough, on Christmas Eve, in London.

I'd been out on important workshop business, returning in time to pass some moments in the arms of a fair, high-spirited upholsteress of my acquaintance, Molly Bullock. She was in the feather room filling mattresses in a blizzard of goosedown when I found her. No sooner had I kissed her lips and burrowed my hand in her petticoats than she giggled and spread her dimpled thighs to let me between them. A while later, Molly's mushroom softness still fresh in my mind and feathers still whirling about, the scrawny figure of a young messenger appeared amid the snowstorm. I was summoned immediately to go to the master.

I paused to stoop (I am taller than the longcase clock in the hallway) and examine myself first from one side then the other in a gothic looking glass (price £1 15s 6d) conveniently positioned on the stair. I should say here I've learned the importance of a good suit only since I came to London. This isn't out of vanity—I don't have the means to be showy—but I've learned a well-cut coat and clean linens make amends for a grasshopper figure and a purse that's empty as often as my belly. In short, I dress as well as I am able to disguise my imperfections. Upholstery over horsehair stuffing, you might call it.

That day I was clad with customary modishness: a brass-buttoned coat of blue broadcloth, a frilled shirt, knitted stockings (thanks to my mother's attentions), and in the crook of my arm, my three-cornered hat. I didn't much like what I saw. Like a room furnished with too many large pieces, everything about me looked overcrowded. I was born with arms longer, hands broader, a face more lopsided than anyone else I know. My nose is long and crooked; my lips so wide they skew when I smile; my eyes, neither blue nor gray, are set slanted in a sallowish complexion—at the moment so heightened by my exertions with the luscious Molly I could have passed for a gypsy.

I peered closer to examine my most recent adornment, a crescent scar decorating my left brow. I touched its red surface gingerly, but today neither this nor any other of my asymmetric imperfections dampened my humor. They'd proved no deterrent to Molly, and I'll disclose here, it wasn't only she who'd elated me. I'd had another, earlier encounter of great promise, one which warmed me with anticipation every time I dwelled on it.

But was I not foolish? To dillydally while an urgent interview with my master awaited was to invite his wrath. A couple of stray feathers lingered on my shoulder. I picked them off, retied my hair smoothly, arranged my features in an expression that I intended to signal eager diligence, and thus, with no evidence of my preoccupations remaining, I entered my master's office.

Chippendale was at his desk drawing. His room was dark and cold with a musty smell that made me long to light a blazing fire or throw open the window. "Ah, Hopson, it is you," he observed, before returning to his page. The design—one that had occupied him for several days—was for a writing cabinet containing countless compartments and mechanisms to open, disclose, conceal, and reveal myriad surprises. I waited for some minutes, yet he said nothing.

I knew he was a man who used words sparingly, a dab hand at impressing his thoughts and wishes on those beneath him with no more than a silent gesture or a facial grimace. Somehow I had the feeling he expected me to speak, yet, unusually, I had no idea what I should say.

"The design progresses well, I trust, sir?"

He did not respond. Instead, placing his pen down, he turned his attention to the order book at his side and, with a vague twirl of his forefinger, signaled me to wait. Under the last week's date, the list of entries was inscribed in copperplate script; I knew them all, for it was one of my duties to record them.

For Richard Butler: to wainscot chamber for the housekeeper's room (£16); to supply a mahogany clothespress in two parts with shelves in the upper part, lined with paper and baize aprons (£5 6s), two new locks and repairing a lock and fixing them on a secretary and easing the drawers of same (£1 7s).

For Lord Arniston: a china shelf (£1 2s), a cheese box (£1 4s).

For Sir John Filmer: tassel and line for a bell (£5 17s), a large mahogany card table (£2 1s 2d), curtains with appurtenances for the dining parlor (£5 17s), a pair of large candlestands carved and painted white (£6 7s).

I watched him read. He sat bolt upright, from time to time sucking in his breath, swelling his chest in contentment whenever his eye flickered over a sizable commission. Drawings for dozens of such items were pinned in rows, like hunting trophies, on the walls around him. Yet his knuckles were clenched, his jaw taut. Something irked him. Had he discovered my liaison with Molly, or was there some error in the pages that had made him send for me?

A few minutes later, he snapped the book shut and addressed me as if we were in the midst of a discussion. "A design can contain all the novelties you choose, Hopson, but without the timber to fabricate it, it is no better than a piece of scenery at the playhouse."

Unsure where this was leading, I responded as cleverly as I could. "Indeed, sir, but without an ingenious mind to shape it, wood is only wood."

His brow fretted with annoyance. "I see you will waste my time with your foolishness and tell me nothing useful unless I interrogate you like a schoolmaster. Was the journey to the wood yards fruitful? What did you discover?"

The tightness in his voice made me curse myself for lingering with Molly. A recent survey of his sheds had confirmed a worrying dearth of exotic timber. To be sure, there were indigenous oaks and walnuts and fruitwoods and softwood, deals, balks, and boards in abundance, but these would no more satisfy his clientele than a duchess in need of a ball gown would be satisfied with a piece of cambric in place of damask or tiffany or brocade. Fashionable patrons clamored for mahogany, rosewood, ebony, or padauk. Therein lay his dilemma. Should his supplies dwindle, they might drift elsewhere with their custom, demolishing his reputation more speedily than a master cutter could slice a half-inch veneer. He had earlier dispatched me to the wood yards in search of new stock.

"Indeed I discovered much of interest. A new consignment has recently cleared customs. Mahogany from Cuba; ebony and rosewood as well."

"Where?"

"Goodchild's."

Chippendale looked me up and down with granite eyes. Even at forty he was a well-made man, manicured and wigged as a gentleman. Only his contoured face, resembling a rock lashed for centuries by wind and rain, bespoke the struggles of his origins. "Alice Goodchild flourishes in her father's absence, I understand. But we must be wary or she will attempt to cheat us as her father did. Was it she who kept you?"

Blood rushed to the newly healed scar, which began to throb uncomfortably. "Forgive me, sir. I would have come sooner but presumed you were occupied." Before he could question the lameness of this excuse I hurried on. "As for Miss Goodchild, she struck me as an honest, plain-speaking tradeswoman. She assured me that no one else had yet received word of the consignment. She will grant us first choice should we agree terms within the next three days. But she'll allow us no longer. Seddon is clamoring for mahogany at any cost for Northumberland's library. No other ships are expected, and she says she'll be unflinching as to price."

Chippendale's tone sharpened at this mention of his rival. "Alice Goodchild does canny business; she cannot know for sure what ships will dock. But I will not have Seddon's scraps. He shall have mine. You may send word that I will call on her the day after Boxing Day."

"Shall I accompany you?"

Silence again. He surveyed me darkly, up and down. "How could you? You will not be here."

There was another interminable pause as he picked up his pen, dipped it in the inkpot, added a final curlicue to the cresting of his cabinet. From the downturn of his mouth, I judged the drawing brought him little satisfaction.

Rarely had I seen him as dismal as he seemed today. Was there some new unspoken sorrow in his life with which he had become burdened? Perhaps he was deserving of my solicitude. I knew him as well as any man, yet in truth I knew very little, for he kept himself hidden. Seven years' apprenticeship and a year as his journeyman had taught me only that he was frequently melancholic, always secretive, open only in his desire to maintain the ascendancy of his enterprise.

I responded more gently than before, in deference to what I honestly believed were his wounded spirits. "Forgive me, sir, I will do anything you ask of me. But I don't comprehend your meaning."

Chippendale was looking towards the window, staring morosely into the impenetrable dark, as if observing some demon only he could discern. He turned to face me, and I glimpsed a fleeting expression in his eyes that made me hastily reconsider my sympathy. I understood then it wasn't solicitude I should be feeling but trepidation. For in that instant I believe I discerned something ugly—something cold and ruthless—an unbending will that would never be crossed. A second later and the expression had vanished, to be replaced with his habitual authoritative aloofness. Had I imagined it all?

"The reason I sent for you, Nathaniel—apart from discovering if you'd found me any wood—was to inform you that I have decided that it will be you who will supervise the installation of Lord Montfort's library at Horseheath. It has been dispatched this week. You will follow it directly after Christmas."

I'd played no part in the Montfort commission. All I knew of it was that some nine months earlier Lord Montfort, a wealthy baron with an estate in Cambridgeshire and a fortune made in sugar plantations, had decided upon a furnishing scheme of astonishing extravagance for the library of his country seat. A fellow journeyman, my dearest friend, John Partridge, had been tasked to create the commission—a bookcase of vast proportion, elaboration, and expense.

"Surely Partridge should go? He has worked on little else these past months. He should travel to Cambridge to put the finishing touches to what you must acknowledge to be his finest masterpiece," I said fiercely.

"Partridge has been absent a week."

"He will return." I had been aware of my friend's absence, and indeed I was concerned about it, for I had heard no explanation.

Chippendale glowered at me. "I have today received word he is stricken with a virulent distemper. Montfort is determined to have his library in time for the New Year festivities and cannot be offended."

"If you explained the situation to him . . ."

"He is not a man to view such impediments with sympathy. You will leave on Boxing Day by the six-fifteen carriage from the Bell Savage Inn, Ludgate Hill. Your allowance while you are there will be the usual guinea a week, to be paid by Montfort. That is all, Hopson."

His mouth was a ruled line that forbade further argument. There was nothing I could say to shift him. I might have spent seven years learning my craft, but I was his employee, and as such bound to subservience. If I chose to disobey him, there were scores of other journeymen cabinet-makers as able as I who would willingly take my place. Without waiting for my reply, he gave me a brusque nod of dismissal. Then he buttoned his black coat and went in search of his wife and his supper.

Left behind, I drummed my fingers on the candle box, struggling to contain my frustrations. How could he have failed to see that I was in a fever of excitement? The answer, of course, I realized well enough. Even if he had known, he wouldn't have cared any more than if he'd trampled on a wood louse.

Let me make my agitation properly clear. It concerned the aforementioned Alice Goodchild, who'd taken charge of her father's wood-merchant business a year ago. I'd often remarked her striking figure on the dockside when cargoes of wood were unloaded, yet until today I'd never had cause to address her, for Chippendale doubted her father's honesty and refused to deal with him. I should say here that I'm not usually reticent in such matters, but Alice was unlike anyone who'd previously fanned my amorous flames (and I readily confess to generosity in several quarters). She was tall, almost to my shoulder, with bright auburn hair to match her fiery temper, and none of the curves that usually enchant me. Her chief drawback—or was it this that drew me?—was her reputation for awkwardness. I worried that if I declared my admiration she might scoff, as I'd seen her do on several occasions when offered an unwelcome compliment. She might then grow cold, avoiding my presence thereafter. I'm not timid when it comes to making advances, but neither am I so foolish as to go courting humiliation. And yet, with the swagger of one who's enjoyed more successes than failures, I trusted she would succumb to my charm, provided I picked my moment carefully.

As I said, I knew that Chippendale avoided dealings with the Good-child yard because he deemed them dishonest, and yet when he sent me in search of wood, I reasoned there was little purpose in trying the usual suppliers and decided to take myself there. In truth (though I barely acknowledged this to myself) it was Alice, not her wood, that drew me. But all the while I made my way to her premises my apprehensions mounted. By the time I tried the gates to the front of the building in the Strand and discovered them to be locked, my courage had begun to ebb. When I entered an alley leading to the yard behind, I had determined to concentrate first on the business in hand, and to assess my chances in the other direction as I went along.

Light spilled from a window of a modest Dutch-gabled cottage bordering the far limit of the yard. I knocked at the door and was instructed to enter. In a small, low-ceilinged, astonishingly disorderly front parlor, Alice Goodchild sat on one side of an oak gateleg table, with her account books open. Opposite, busily conjugating Latin verbs, was a young boy. A bright fire burned in the grate, and a smoky tallow candle bathed their faces in a halo of yellow, shrouding much of the chaotic room in sympathetic shade. Nonetheless I could vaguely discern that all about the walls were heaped up piles of ledgers and papers, jumbled together with a broken chair, a pewter kettle, assorted pieces of crockery, and a couple of unlit candlesticks. A pungent smell of burning seemed to emanate from the open door leading to the kitchen.

"Forgive me for calling here, Miss Goodchild," I said, bowing to her. "I had thought to find you at the yard."

She looked a little startled to see me in her private abode, yet she did not ask my business. "Good afternoon, Mr. Hopson. The yard is closed early since my foreman has journeyed home to his family for Christmas" was all she said.

"I should not have called. . . . I see you are engaged." I gestured to the table piled high with papers.

"As you see, I have my books to occupy me." She paused for a moment, glancing into the shadows to the muddle of papers, crockery, and books, before adding with a distracted smile, "My apologies for receiving you thus. My brother and I rarely keep company and, as to the smell, our supper has burned while I was about my figures."

I could not but reflect that the acrid stench and the jumble of papers cascading over every surface could do nothing to detract from the delightful effect of that fleeting smile. Her brown eyes shone warmly, and a few mahogany curls had escaped the cap confining them and fell about her face in attractive disarray. If she had been any other woman I would have made clear my sentiments—complimented her, paid court to her—but her reputation for sharpness kept me wary.

"You have no need to apologize, Miss Goodchild, it is a perfectly charming parlor," I responded courteously. "Perhaps I should return at some other more convenient time, for I come to discuss the possibility of supplies for Mr. Chippendale."

She seemed delighted at the opportunity to do business with my master, and assured me that indeed she did have some stock of interest. A new consignment from the Indies had recently cleared customs and would be ready for delivery the next day. Should I return in three days' time when the stores were reopened, she would gladly show them to me.

"I shall certainly return," I declared, struggling to retain an air of detachment. Discovering her thus in domestic surroundings seemed to have given me an advantage. I detected an unusual mellowness to her manner. Perhaps, after all, her reputation was exaggerated. Perhaps I should seize the opportunity to declare my interest? Before my indecision made a coward of me, I resolved to take my chances.

"May I also make another request?"

"Unless you make it I will not know its nature, therefore I can hardly refuse. What is it, Mr. Hopson?" she replied.

I dithered, realizing even as I did so that this was no time for shilly-shallying. "Why," I replied, as coolly as I could manage, "you have spoiled your supper and I venture your brother is in need of nourishment. Allow me to invite you to the Fountain, where the cook is reputed to be exceedingly good."

Immediately, and I fancied rather hungrily, her brother looked up from his exercises. Alice meanwhile took a step backwards and inspected me suspiciously. "You are most solicitous, Mr. Hopson. But my brother may rest assured there are provisions enough in the pantry to satisfy him and these books must be completed tonight."

Her brother, now downcast, returned to his exercises, and my heart began to sink. Then somewhat to my surprise she continued, "I hope I do not seem ungracious in my refusal. . . . Perhaps you would care for a glass of wine?"

As an expert in feminine ways, I needed no further signal to pursue my cause. I waited as she searched in the shadows of the room for a glass and decanter, and cleared a space for me on the settle by the fire. "Have you visited the playhouse of late, Miss Goodchild?" I asked, as she deposited sheafs of papers in a pile on the floor.

"No, sir, I have much to keep me here as you see."

"Then would you, and your brother, do me the pleasure of accompanying me there on New Year's Day?"

Although her back was towards me, I could see her stiffen. She rose slowly and turned towards me with an expression of—what? Astonishment? Indifference? Indignation? Then, to my astonishment, for I had never seen her lose her composure, she reddened most becomingly.

"I scarcely know how to respond, Mr. Hopson. We have never spoken before today. The speed of your invitations is remarkable."

"Forgive me," I said, still unsure of her sentiment, "I did not mean to presume . . ."

"I believe you did not, Mr. Hopson." Her voice was softer than usual, girlish almost. She paused and scrutinized me again before granting me another wisp of a smile. "I'm only teasing you. But if you are sincere in your offer, we accept with great pleasure."

"Do not doubt the sincerity of the offer, I beg you. And as to the pleasure, madam, it is all mine, I assure you," I replied, gallantly as any gentleman.

Thus had I sipped my wine as slowly as I could, enjoying her conversation for those fleeting moments before taking leave. Thus had I returned to my workplace, after my brief diversion with Molly. (I could think of no other way to alleviate the anticipation of passion sweeping through my veins.) And thus, when Chippendale commanded me to Cambridge, had my hopes been extinguished.

Chapter Two

And so I came to Cambridge, leaving Ludgate Hill on the six-fifteen coach, riding on top as I invariably choose to do whenever circumstances permit. That day I happened to share my precarious platform with two fellow travelers. The first was a lugubrious bonesetter, with a thriving business of mending broken limbs in Fetter Lane, who was journeying to Lincoln to visit a sister not seen in three years. The second was a young knife grinder's apprentice, returning to his home village of Waterbeach for the funeral of his mother. Below, cocooned in the luxury of windows, side panels, and a roof, sat six further passengers, none of whom deigned to speak to the three seated, so to speak, on their heads.

My family lived some distance from London, in the village of Cottenham, some ten miles from Chelmsford in the county of Essex. Consequently since settling in London I had made coach journeys on numerous occasions, though never before had I ridden on top in the depths of winter. My dear mother had expressly forbidden me to travel thus between the months of November and March, and I, in my fondness for her, had always observed the prohibition. Nonetheless, for a man such as I, whose achievements were measured by the fineness of a dovetail or the delicacy of a crossbanding, the position held rare delights. Whenever I sat astride the coach, I become oblivious to mere discomfort. The racing clouds and changing landscape, the sensation of my teeth shaking in my skull as the vehicle lurched over hills and ditches and rumbled through ramshackle settlements, and the impression of prodigious speed far removed from the snail's pace of my daily life never failed to revitalize me.

For my second fellow passenger, the young knife grinder, who had never adopted this mode of transport before, the journey proved a fearful ordeal. The carriage was still stationary, and he had scarcely clambered up to the platform when he developed vertigo and the unwavering conviction that to release his grip on the side rail would doom him to certain death. The vehicle pulled out of the coach yard and began to gather speed past the Shoreditch Turnpike, jolting over potholes, ruts, and boulders. With each toss and sway of the chassis, the boy's face turned more alarmingly pale, and before long, to the chagrin of those below, he was retching profusely over the side. When at length we stopped in Bishop's Stortford, I was struck by the indifference of our fellow passengers. At the first sign of the boy's distress they drew the leather curtains of their compartment, and not one of them expressed any concern for him.

I suppose it was because I am an only child and often longed for the company of a younger brother that I did what I could to assist him. There was no room within the coach—by this stage his misery was such that I would happily have paid the extra shilling to ease it—but I suggested that he might feel more secure riding in the luggage basket. He gratefully agreed, although even there his terrors continued. I had not considered the movement of the poorly secured crates and boxes stowed there, and after half an hour he was half buffeted to death. Hearing his whimpers and mounting distress, I whistled to the driver and postilion to slow down, then lowered an arm to retrieve him from the basket and haul him back on top. For some time afterwards I continued to hold his arm, as much to calm him as to prevent him from falling. He now regarded me as his savior and settled himself close beside me, trembling violently from the dual terrors of death by squashing or falling from which he had so narrowly escaped.

It began to snow at three in the afternoon, around the same time we drew into the town of Royston to change the horses. There the knife grinder's apprentice quit the coach, swearing as he did so that he would never forget my kindness. I ruffled his hair, told him it was nothing more than anyone should have done, and gave him a shilling from the traveling purse Mr. Chippendale had supplied. The snowfall was light, but the driver, anxious to reach Cambridge before the road became impassable, would allow us no more than ten minutes to drink a glass of sack in the warmth.

The bonesetter and I returned to our position while the remaining passengers settled themselves back inside the carriage, burying their feet in straw and covering their knees in blankets the driver provided. We had scarcely set off before the gentle flakes strengthened to a blizzard and my costume revealed its woeful inadequacy. My hat threatened to blow off, so I was forced to remove it. My surtout flapped, allowing the cold wind to pierce me, and my fingertips grew chill within the thin gloves that covered them. Soon I was shivering as violently as the petrified boy had done a few hours earlier, and ruefully recalling my mother's warnings. The bonesetter, who throughout the sufferings of the boy had remained impervious, now loudly lamented his discomfort. His gnarled, gloveless hands had turned the color of damsons from holding the wooden handrail. "I would be happy to be greeted by a cutpurse or highwayman now," he muttered, "for it would mean I could put my hands in my pockets." I felt no inclination to offer him sympathy.

By the time we pulled into the Bell at Cambridge at half past five that evening, we were caked in ice and utterly numbed with chill and fatigue. Since there was no other accommodation in the immediate vicinity, I and all the other passengers were obliged to rest here for the night. I passed some hours with a comely barmaid, who warmed me a little, though she wouldn't sample fully the amusements I offered since I was forced to share my room with the bonesetter. He, meanwhile, chose to obliterate the memory of the journey by consuming quantities of ale while explaining the mysteries of his trade to anyone who would listen. A far from congenial roommate, he fell into bed fully clothed, boots and all, and snored loudly all night, waking only to piss loud and lengthily into his chamber pot.

I rose the next morning to find Cambridge blanketed with snow, and the only means of completing my journey to Horseheath—some ten miles to the southeast of the city—was by the oxcart of a local grocer who, by good fortune, was delivering supplies that afternoon. The driver who transported me this last stretch was an ancient deaf-mute who sat hunched on his driver's seat staring unblinkingly ahead, all the while muttering quietly and incomprehensibly to himself. Beneath a dolorous sky we traversed a landscape made featureless by the snowy blanket. At length, after three hours' silent plodding, we arrived at the village of Horseheath. I say village, but in truth the settlement was no more than a steepled church, an inn, and a dozen or so ramshackle houses strung along the lane, with several dung heaps, sundry miserable-looking animals, and a duck pond.

The entrance to the hall was marked by lichen-covered gateposts garnished with a pair of stone dogs, their teeth bared in fearsome grimace at any visitor who dared to enter. At our approach iron gates creaked open, and an aged porter, leaning heavily on his walking stick, hobbled from his lodge to salute our rickety cart.

We lurched up a potholed drive that traversed a park in which clusters of artfully planted trees led the eye to a lake and a turreted folly on an island. A quarter of a mile or so further on we reached a sharp bend in the beech-lined avenue and Horseheath Hall came suddenly into view. The house was an austere Palladian mansion built of a bilious yellow stone, fronted with a forest of fluted Corinthian columns. My venerable driver skirted the main entrance and followed a path disguised by a tall yew hedge to the rear, where the domestic buildings were located. Outside the kitchen door he clambered to the ground, deposited his delivery—sacks of flour and barley, a side of bacon, a pound of white pepper, a firkin of soap, and two pounds of wax candles—snatched my fare of a shilling, and drove off without so much as a gesture.

I tapped on the door and waited. Some minutes passed. My knock produced no effect whatsoever. Frozen and fatigued as I was by my journey, my patience began to wear thin. I tried the handle: the door was unlocked and opened to a cavernous kitchen, where a dozen or more staff were presently occupied. I cleared my throat importantly.

"Nathaniel Hopson from London bids you a good afternoon. I believe a Mrs. Hester Cummings expects my arrival. Is that good lady here?" I bellowed as loudly as politeness and my frozen jaw permitted.

The cleaning of vegetables, grinding of loaf sugar, buffing of wineglasses, and counting of spoons and plates continued without interruption. Mrs. Cummings, the woman I was soon to discover to be the unquestionable ruler of this domain, was weighing currants on the brass scales, scolding the kitchenmaid for her galling inattention. The girl's distraction was the only result of my speech. She now stood staring at me, eyes as round as shillings, pretty mouth gaping like an open flower.

Mrs. Cummings dusted her hands this way and that over a large pudding basin, clouding her torso with a mist of flour. "What's with you today, Connie? How do you expect to learn if you stare like a half-wit everywhere but at what you're doing? Stop fidgeting and weigh me a quarter peck of flour, put in half a pint of ale yeast, make it to a paste with warm milk, then set it to rise while you wash these raisins. When you've done, there's butter and rose water to add, loaf sugar to sift, cinnamon, cloves, mace to grind—no pinching raisins, mind . . ."

As these complex instructions rolled off Mrs. Cummings's tongue, the girl was gazing at the succulent fruit tumbling into the scales. She licked her lips hungrily but couldn't help glancing back at the doorway where I stood. "It was him. I was looking at him, ma'am. I was asking myself what he was doing."

"Him? What him?" Wrenching themselves away from the sugary mass, Mrs. Cummings's currant eyes followed the maid's gaze and at last registered my presence. She advanced towards me, black dress and starched apron pulled tight over a capacious bosom, skirts rustling, as majestic as a duchess.

I smiled and bowed respectfully. "Madam, I have been sent by Mr. Chippendale of London to install the new library for Lord Montfort. I was told to make myself known to Mrs. Hester Cummings, who would find a bed for me here." I paused, watching as she took in every detail of my features and traveling garb. "I take it you are that lady."

It seemed she was not entirely displeased with what she saw, for I was granted a brief nod and a floury handshake as welcome before she turned back to the kitchenmaid, whose eyes were still fixed on me. "Constance Lovatt, what are you gawping at? Haven't you seen a Londoner before? They are no different from any other. Take him to the servants' hall, hang up his coat, stir up the fire—no delaying, mind. Mr. Hopson does not want his head filled with your gossip, do you, sir? But I fancy he wouldn't say no to a bit of something to eat."

Constance was not at all put out by the severity of her tone. Indeed, I fancy she stifled a giggle as she said, "This way, sir," and led me down a narrow servants' corridor to the appointed room, allowing me ample opportunity to admire the neat waist around which her apron was secured by a plump bow.

I settled myself gratefully into a beech Windsor chair that reminded me of the one in which my father sat at home. Constance crouched to goad the embers to new life. "Will you be staying with us long, Mr. Hopson?" she said.

"I cannot be sure. A few days perhaps."

"I fancy Lord Montfort will want the library finished in time for New Year?"

"I believe so."

"He has guests invited for dinner and will take pride in displaying his newest improvements."

"Hmm."

"Mrs. Cummings is in a frenzy about the dinner 'cos the French chef up and left saying he was going home for Christmas and hasn't been seen since."

"Indeed."

"He's the one who's meant to do the pastries and such fancies as were ordered. Now it will all be left to her."

"Is that so?" I replied without a trace of interest.

Perhaps fearing Mrs. Cummings's wrath, or disappointed by my dullness, she made no further attempt to engage me in conversation. When her duties were done, she left with a bobbed curtsy and a promise to return with refreshments presently.

Had I been in my usual good humor I would not have responded to her overtures with such coolness. You will know by now I have a sociable nature and well realize that pretty girls with such merry eyes as Miss Constance offer all manner of enjoyable distraction. But this day I had no appetite for such flirtation as Constance promised.

It wasn't just the rigors of my journey that made me melancholy. Even with the fire to warm me, my mood remained dark, and if anything I grew more restless. At the root of this agitation lay my reluctance to come here at all. The truth was that I still heartily wished myself back in London, not simply on account of Alice but because of a graver preoccupation. I felt I was here under a false pretext, a second-rate substitute for the ailing Partridge, my dearest friend, who had been responsible for creating the furnishings I was due to install.

As I'd frequently done over the past days, I cast my thoughts back to the last occasion I had seen him, trying to recall any sign of the illness that Chippendale said was now troubling him. My efforts were in vain; nothing came to mind. Of course, I told myself halfheartedly, this didn't mean he might not have had some secret plan brewing. Was he really unwell? I cannot pretend my dear friend was without guile. Partridge was gifted in many respects, particularly in his capacity for conceiving pranks. Etched upon my memory is a skulling race on the river when he fixed my boat to sink in full view of the White Hart at Richmond. I well recall our competition for a place in the bed of the handsome widow at the Fox and Grapes, when he usurped my lead by pouring gin in my ale and leaving me on the floor in a drunken stupor. Nor will I forget the time he set fireworks alight in the courtyard, while I was engaged with Molly Bullock. He cried "Fire!" through the keyhole, and I tumbled out in an unseemly rush with my breeches about my ankles, to the merriment of the craftsmen he'd assembled outside.

Thus when I fretted over my friend, I knew unpredictable behavior was not out of character. But, as a small voice in my head reminded me incessantly, his schemes were usually spur-of-the-moment adventures. He'd never left me out of one for so long before. And in none of his schemes had he ever gone missing.

It was now more than a week since I had seen him at the workshop. By last Sunday I'd become so concerned that I'd called at his lodgings. The landlady hadn't seen him. His belongings had been moved. No, she could not tell me where I might find him. His sweetheart, Dorothy, had unexpectedly returned to Yorkshire. When I questioned Chippendale, he appeared indifferent to the absence of his most talented employee. Indeed, whenever I raised the subject he seemed irked by my curiosity. The day I learned of my journey to Cambridge was the first he deigned to volunteer any information on the subject. Partridge, he told me, had sent a letter explaining that his sudden absence was due to his being stricken by a contagious distemper. Not wishing to infect his workmates, he had exiled himself to a friend's house in Shoreditch, where he was presently recuperating.

My natural inclination was to believe this story. I held my master in the greatest respect; he had no reason that I knew to lie to me. But while I dared not question him for fear of rousing his anger, I could not help but find this explanation implausible. Last time I set eyes on Partridge he was in good health, talking rashly about Dorothy, hinting at their betrothal. I now began to question the reason for Dorothy's precipitate departure as well as Partridge's absence. I asked myself how, if Partridge were ill, had he vanished so rapidly from his lodgings? And as for the friend in Shoreditch, I was convinced it was nonsense. I was close as a brother to him and never heard mention of this person. The illness, I decided, was most probably a yarn spun by Partridge, for some reason of his own. Only I couldn't fathom what that reason might be.

Perhaps it was fortunate that over the days that followed I did not have long to dwell on my worries. It was impressed upon me almost every hour that the library must be finished in time for the dinner Lord Montfort was holding on New Year's Day. Since this involved assembling a vast bookcase and the date was now only four days hence, my time passed in a frenzy of activity. I supervised the transportation of crates to the library. I ensured the packing mats and battens, paper and lay cord were removed without damage to the carvings on which Partridge had labored so painstakingly. Piece by piece I watched each segment emerge, marveling as I did so at the brilliance of the craftsman who conceived and so dexterously executed it.

It is a commonly held misbelief, among those who have never commissioned furniture, that the proprietor of a great workshop must himself draw and cut and carve every object produced under his name. In truth the great London cabinetmakers—John Channon, William Hallet, William Vile, Giles Grendey, and of course, Thomas Chippendale, all of whom do flourishing trade in this golden age of cabinetmaking—have long since put down their tools. Proprietors are transformed by success into administrators and salesmen, their craftsmen's skills forgotten. Their talent must be diverted into lavishing attentions upon patrons in place of tabletops. Thus, in order to supply the fabric of his trade, Chippendale relied upon a host of journeymen in his employ. Without workers such as Partridge, Molly Bullock, and I, scarcely a stick of furniture would have been made in his name.

In this instance it was Partridge who'd created the finished sketches, Partridge who'd carved the most intricate parts and overseen the completion of the whole. Partridge, my friend and ally. I didn't doubt that, if he could see me fretting over his whereabouts while I assembled his great masterpiece, he would have laughed and called me an idiot. But therein lay my concern: I hadn't seen him.

Yet have I learned how distance and time can shift our perception of almost anything. Over the days of frenetic work that followed, when I was removed from London and all that was familiar to me, I began to feel my fears were unfounded. Working in this great room, piecing together Partridge's creation from the fragments laid before me, my worry diminished. There was nothing I could do about Partridge here. I would carry out my instructions to the best of my ability. By the time I returned to London, Partridge would surely have reappeared, doubtless rolling with laughter at some clever scheme he'd carried off.

The library was a long narrow room that spanned the western limits of the house and had recently been redecorated in readiness for the new furnishings. The walls were freshly hung in crimson silk damask; a sumptuous flower-filled Axminster carpet, its pattern reflecting the stuccoed ceiling, lay ready to be unrolled. The ceiling alone had taken a dozen local craftsmen six months to complete. The long outer wall was centered upon a Carrara marble chimneypiece. To either side four sash windows gave onto a formal Italian garden. The view was generally considered delightful, one of the marvels of Horseheath, and in the summer season—according to Constance—numerous visitors came specially to walk in the gardens. To me, however, the marriage of Art and Nature seemed profoundly discordant. Walls of oppressive privet terminated in stifling niches; urns were filled with skeletal plants; and in the center a huge fountain formed the hub of an immense circular ornamental pond. And betwixt every path, white marble statues of nymphs, now frosted by winter, stood frozen in various stages of undress.

Partridge's gargantuan bookcase faced this garden and, appropriately enough, resembled a Roman temple. Ancient architecture had recently become his obsession—how often he lauded its symmetry, its precision, its order. For in the ancient past, he claimed, were proportions and details that had never been improved upon, and therein the fashionable future lay. This notion had been the cause of some dissension within the workshop. Chippendale, though fond enough of meticulous design and classical architecture, preferred a multiplicity of decoration whenever possible. If patrons could be persuaded to festoon their commissions with chinoiserie knickknacks in the shape of hoho birds, dragons, and pagodas, or with ribbons and roses and watery cascades, extra might be charged and the piece would appear suitably sumptuous. Urns and pilasters didn't compare visually or commercially.

Partridge's fondness for antiquity was shared by Lord Montfort, who had spent some months in Italy as a young man. In Rome, like every other youth of his generation and rank, he had studied ancient architecture, acquiring much of the statuary visible from the window as well as the collections within the house. He agreed with Partridge's classical theme—a room devoted to learning demanded some reference to ancient civilization. Yet he was equally obsessed by the need to impress his acquaintances, and fretted that scholarly restraint would be too subtle to be remarked. Thus to Partridge's austere pilasters, urns, and pediment he added Chippendale's suggestions for sundry swags of trailing foliage and flowers. The resulting structure resembled nothing so much as some classical temple relic overgrown with Arcadian vegetation.

It was New Year's Eve, my fifth day at Horseheath, before I made Lord Montfort's acquaintance. He exploded into the room, swirling his hunting cape, a mangy lurcher skulking by his side.

"Hopson, where are you, man, you rascal, you idler?" he thundered. "I come to remind you I expect company tomorrow. Unless they can admire this room and its fittings to my satisfaction I shall be pleased to inform Mr. Chippendale of your tardiness and detain my payments accordingly."

The fact he could not see me, for I was presently perched on top of a ladder ensuring that the plinth of an urn was precisely square to the column beneath, further infuriated him. Like a freak tide with no sandbags to halt it, the onslaught surged forth unabated. "And you may tell Mr. Chippendale when you see him that, under the circumstances, he need not trouble himself to demand the return of his folio. I shall keep hold of it for as long as it pleases me."

I had no comprehension of this reference to a folio, but in any case his fury had thrown me into such red-faced confusion I would scarcely have recognized my own mother.

"Lord Montfort," I exclaimed, hastily folding my two-foot rule into my pocket, descending to his level and bowing. "I am Nathaniel Hopson."

Montfort peered at me through small bloodshot eyes. The lurcher thrust forward, growling, the hair on its back standing up like a thistle. I tried to ignore the dog and fix on the man. He was stout-figured, aged perhaps fifty and five years, wigless, with lank hair and a belly that strained at his breeches. He was sweating profusely, and from his incessant twitching and blinking I judged him to be in a state of high agitation.

"I trust when your lordship examines the progress thus far you will not be displeased. The bulk of the work is already completed. It remains only for me to make minor adjustments that will be accomplished in the next hours." The lurcher sniffed my breeches, its ears pressed back close to its head, its snout pushing insistently at my groin. It was still growling. Ignoring his dog, Montfort took in for the first time the work I had virtually completed.

The scale and magnificence of the room could hardly fail to inspire his awe. He drew short grunting breaths, while registering the extraordinary metamorphoses of mere wood into towering bookcase, library table, steps, globes, and chairs.

"Looks the part, don't it, Hopson? Finest library in the county, I'll wager."

"Yes, my lord."

"A grand setting for a spectacle?"

"Indeed."

The dog retreated beside his master. I breathed more easily. It was weeks before I recalled those words and comprehended their true significance.

Chapter Three

T hus to Lord Montfort's dinner and the dreadful discovery with which this strange tale began. Eight people, in addition to the host himself, took their seats that afternoon at the fine mahogany dining table. Three were family members and residents of the household—Elizabeth, Montfort's fragile young wife, I have already remarked; Robert, his nineteen-year-old son by a previous marriage, was heir to the estate, a handsome, strongly boned man, grandly dressed that evening as befitted the occasion; Margaret Alleyn, Lord Montfort's spinster sister, had run the household for the past two decades. The five remaining guests comprised a pair of neighboring landowners, Lord Foley and Lord Bradfield and their respective wives, and a last-minute addition to the party—Montfort's attorney, a man by the name of Wallace, who had been called in to attend on his lordship earlier in the day and had yet to be dismissed.

My previous description of this assembly, its strange atmosphere and awkward guests, might perhaps have conveyed the impression that the event was from the start ill-fated, that the signs of the impending tragedy were all too evident to anyone with an ounce of sensibility. In truth I must confess that such a view, though easy enough in hindsight, does not give a true appraisal of the situation. I am no different from any man in that conclusions I draw are fashioned from the raw materials of experience and event. If I possess any special talent, it is that my profession has taught me to employ those materials more carefully than most men, for my skill depends upon my capacity for meticulous precision. In this case, however, my materials were sparse. I was unfamiliar with the household. The strained atmosphere did not unnerve me because I presumed it to be the usual state of affairs. In any case how could I judge the household accurately, being so unaccustomed to such grandeur? Devoid of any similar experience, I knew only what I saw.

My encounter with Lord Montfort the previous day had shown me he was a man prone to outbursts of choleric ill-humor, who frequently evoked uneasiness in those surrounding him. Thus it did not seem unusual that his temper, far from improving, showed signs of further deterioration. Yet, as the evening drew on, the extremes of Montfort's moroseness threw a shadow over the proceedings that appeared to surprise his guests and family. Dinner was under way when the first of them remarked it. His neighbor Lord Bradfield, a man of large girth and matching appetite, had interrupted his imbibing of turtle soup to recount a prized fragment of gossip. "The bishop was actually pleased when he found himself to have the itch. Said it was of no concern where he caught it, for it would help him keep his mistress to himself."

Ignoring his wife's glare, Bradfield paused and slurped a spoonful of soup, spilling a large droplet upon his purple damask jacket, which was already much spattered with the residue of good dinners. If Bradfield expected to gather encouragement from his host, he was sadly disappointed. Montfort stared at him bulbous-eyed, scowling, silent. The ladies on either side were equally aloof. His sister, Margaret, seemed preoccupied. Elizabeth, his wife, lowered her eyes and shifted uncomfortably in her seat.

All this while I was standing ramrod-still by the sideboard, waiting for the footman's signal to clear away. I should say here that I'd never waited at table before and had only stepped in when pressed by Mrs. Cummings. She was in a fluster on account of Miss Alleyn, in her capacity as housekeeper, thoughtlessly giving three of the staff the night off. On top of this, the second footman had fallen unaccountably ill (Mrs. Cummings blamed the potency of the ale at the tavern). That left only Connie and a scullery maid to help in the kitchen and the footman to serve. Thus she'd begged for my assistance "just till the dessert is on the table," and foolishly I'd succumbed. Now, standing here in a scratchy wig, squeezed half to death by scarlet livery and gold tassels, like some ridiculous confectionery box in a shop window, I regretted my acquiescence.

How different was this chilly assembly from the raucous jollities at the Blue Boar or the Fountain. Were it not for Partridge's inconvenient absence I should have been there—or, even better, I should have been at the playhouse with Alice. I yearned for the throng, the gaudiness, the cacophony of song, the air thick with the smell of roasting meat, boiling puddings, tobacco smoke, and sweat. I yearned, above all, to distance myself from this dismal gathering.

Bradfield's gawking expression showed me he was taken aback by Montfort's mood, but he didn't inquire the reason for it. Perhaps he didn't dare. Perhaps he already knew what lay behind it. At any rate, not wishing to squander his storytelling talents on an unappreciative recipient, he shifted his attention towards the other end of the table, where he caught Lord Foley's eye. Foley was clad in a black velvet suit that gleamed with the luster of moleskin, untouched by any imperfection. A froth of milky lace accentuated his skull-like face with its great beak of a nose and dark-socketed eyes. He gave Bradfield a vague half smile, all the encouragement needed for that gentleman to hasten on with his narrative.

"I have it on excellent authority his mistress is always vastly good for two or three days after his Sunday sermon, but by the time Thursday comes all the effect is worn off."

Catching the joke, Lord Foley bared his wolfish teeth. Given an instant longer he might have responded with some clever witticism, but Montfort unexpectedly interrupted.

"You do not want to leave your mistress with Foley even till Thursday, for I wager he'll have her himself, itch or no itch. Ain't that right, Foley?" Montfort had turned an ominous shade of puce, and his breathing was labored, his expression thunderous. Sensing his master's mood, the lurcher, until then asleep under Montfort's chair, began to stir.

Foley pointedly avoided Montfort's gaze. Taking a corner of his damask napkin, he dabbed a droplet of soup from his lower lip. He turned to Montfort's son, Robert. "You intend to leave for Italy soon, I understand."

Robert was dissecting a woodcock. Detaching its head and long pointed beak with extraordinary delicacy, he laid it on the edge of his plate like a wreath on a gravestone before responding to the inquiry.

"I hope to depart by the end of the month. I'm filled with as much impatience to be gone as my family are keen to be rid of me. Don't you agree, Elizabeth?"

This last question he addressed to his young stepmother, who was seated between the bulky forms of his father and himself. Her voice was soft and rather high-pitched. She spoke rapidly, as if afraid she would be told to be quiet. "I am sure you will find much to entertain yourself, Robert. As for your family's eagerness to be rid of you, I cannot be the judge of that—but I shall be sorry to see you go."

Montfort glared at his son and his wife. A moment later, wheezing furiously, he heaved himself to his feet, shuffled past me to the windows, and pulled back the curtains. Nothing gave him as much pleasure as the prospect from this room, he declared, and he refused absolutely to have them drawn for the rest of the evening. Catching the nasty set of his mouth, none of the assembled company dared remonstrate that there was nothing to be seen of the prospect since it was dark outside, or that the fierce cold he'd let in caused them unnecessary discomfort. The ladies pursed their lips, shivering in silence as goose pimples rose on their décolletage. The men too fell silent. Montfort, still shadowed by his sleepy dog, lumbered back to the head of the table and lowered himself slowly into his chair.

At the far end of the table, Foley alone was undaunted by his host's foul temper. He rekindled his conversation with Bradfield. The subject matter was inaudible, but to judge from Foley's black brows jerking up and down like startled spiders, it was a question of some drama. A short interval later and the rest of the assembly had mustered the courage to resume a subdued chatter. The attorney Wallace attempted to attract the attention of Miss Alleyn, who was rapt in her nephew Robert's account of his imminent voyage to Italy.

Miss Alleyn, her thin nose reddened by the sudden burst of cold, was trying to question Robert on the details of his journey, but, apparently oblivious to her, he was deep in conversation with Elizabeth on the subject of Rome. In the midst of this exchange he leaned over to her, whispered a confidence, then continued with his description. Soon after that I heard a loud snort and a strange growling sound issued from Montfort's lips. Robert paused and turned to his father, his brow wrinkled in puzzlement.

"Are you well, sir? You appear out of sorts. Does your gout trouble you?" he inquired solicitously.

"If I find myself indisposed, I would thank you not to add to my unease by your interrogation. You may fancy yourself a physician, but that is no more than a flight of your imagination."

Robert was startled by the harshness of this retort. "I did not intend to add to your discomfort. I am merely concerned for your well-being."

"I will choose when and with whom I wish to discuss my well-being, Robert," responded his father bitterly. "And as for you, Elizabeth, I will thank you to remember your guests."

As if she'd been slapped, Elizabeth flinched and lowered her eyes. She was coiffed with an elaborate white-powdered wig interwoven with silk rosebuds and leaves, and her gown was of crimson silk trimmed with black lace. The richness of this garb seemed only to heighten the pallor of her powdered face. A black beauty spot had detached itself from her upper lip and trembled precariously before falling to her breast. She stroked the ringlet of white hair that lay on her shoulder, as if touching something soft in the face of his harshness offered some small consolation. Then, though plainly shivering from the cold, she took out her fan and began fanning herself as if feverish with heat. This evident distress failed to move her husband. Turning to the roast partridge on his plate, he pierced its golden skin with his fork, hacked off a large section of succulent meat, and began to chew.

It was not the first time I'd witnessed Lord Montfort speak roughly to Elizabeth, and I confess his treatment of her rankled with me. Perhaps I was being foolishly unworldly in my distaste; after all, what husband is not masterful on occasion? Is it not a man's God-given right to be ruler in his own household, to demand obedience of his spouse whenever he deems it necessary? Yet in this instance something in the disparity of their ages (she was only three years older than his son), something in his physical grossness and her fragility (I could not help picturing his vast belly crushing her birdlike frame) struck me as profoundly distasteful. How had such an unlikely match come about? I'd quizzed Constance, a fountain of knowledge on such subjects, and learned a little of the sorry tale.

Some five years earlier, aged seventeen, Elizabeth, the youngest daughter of a respectable merchant, had attended a summer ball. Henry Montfort, widower, owner of this fine estate, and father of one motherless teenage son, had clapped eyes on her sweet, innocent form and determined to be the first to enjoy her. According to Constance's enthusiastic account, this was an easy enough challenge. Elizabeth was little match for Montfort's guile. She was swiftly persuaded to drink too many glasses of champagne and to accompany him on a moonlight promenade, which led to her brusque deflowering beneath a marble nymph. Some time later Elizabeth's father had discovered his daughter wandering the gardens in distress. Having established what had taken place, he threatened uproar unless a marriage was hastily effected. Thus within a matter of weeks had the hapless Elizabeth left her comfortable, sheltered childhood and the parents who doted on her, to become the wife of Lord Montfort. Thus ever since, I deduced, had she been bullied and ill-used by her husband.

Connie was less sympathetic than I to her plight. Elizabeth had her consolations, did she not? What were these consolations? I demanded. Connie spelled them out for me: Elizabeth was rich; she was mistress of this grand house; she had friendship tendered to her by Miss Alleyn, who viewed her as the daughter she'd always longed for. And then (here Connie paused theatrically) there were other consolations. "What do you mean," I cried precisely as intended, "'Then there are other consolations'?" Connie winked knowingly, but more than that she wouldn't say.

I was rinsing cutlery and glasses in the urn specially fitted for the purpose (Mr. Chippendale does thriving business in such accoutrements for the well-appointed dining room—the most popular being a matching pair, one lead-lined for rinsing, the other fitted for storing cutlery), when the sound of Foley and Bradfield guffawing at the other end of the table distracted me. Foley's lips glistened with grease, and his cobweb cuffs swirled as he gestured with a drumstick caught between bony thumb and forefinger. He had finished eating, and his plate was piled with white-picked bones. Bradfield listened avidly; suddenly grasping Foley's witticism he was racked with convulsive laughter. Morsels of half-chewed flesh spurted from his lips, adding to the ancient encrustations on his belly. To Lord Montfort the sight of this messy hilarity was insupportable. His face flooded deeper crimson than his wife's garb.

"Foley," he snarled, "you may well jest. You are leaving my house the richer."

There was a long pause, during which I froze, not wishing to draw Montfort's fury by an injudicious clattering of spoons. Montfort's vitriol must have been as unmistakable to Foley as to me, but he ignored it, turning instead to engage his wife in conversation. "My dear Jane, do you catch sight of this picture of the Veduta, is it not quite as ravishing as that of San Daniele I purchased last spring?"

The snub served only to incense Montfort further. "Sir," he spat, "I would ask you to respect my presence. You may make a fool of me at the gaming table but not at my dining table."

"I was not intending to make a fool of you in either environ, Henry," responded Foley suavely. "If your losses are so insupportable to you, I suggest you desist from future play at White's. Take up cribbage in the saloon instead."

"I should desist from inviting you to my house."

"That of course is your prerogative. Provided of course our business is successfully concluded . . ."

"It soon will be," said Montfort. Then he fell silent, his chest heaving as he glared malevolently around in a manner which was, if anything, even more alarming than his voluble rage. Stabbing what remained of his partridge with his knife, he ripped a leg from the carcass and bit into it. Rivulets of pink juice coursed down his chin and soaked his cravat. Slowly he wiped himself with the back of his hand, then turned to his attorney, Wallace.

"The documents are in order, I take it."

"Indeed, Lord Montfort," replied Wallace. His hand trembled as he spooned butter sauce onto his potato. "As they were from the moment of signing, before witnesses, as stipulated—"

"Nothing can be done to alter them. They are all legally binding. Yes or no?"

Wallace's frog eyes blinked rapidly. He dropped the spoon in the sauceboat, where it slid beneath the surface. "They are all sanctioned and viable."

"And should I die this night, would remain so?"

"I sincerely hope nothing will befall your lordship this night, but no, the time would have no bearing. The document would still stand. Unless of course you were physically indisposed . . . for instance as we discussed earlier . . . if for instance you were to take your own—"

Montfort held up his hand to silence him, turning in the opposite direction as he did so. He caught his sister staring intently at him. Embarrassment etched itself across her face as she realized she had been apprehended listening to his conversation. I could not but sympathize with her predicament. Montfort's face ripened from red to purple. He rose unsteadily to his feet. Miss Alleyn was an uncommonly tall woman, towering over her brother by several inches. Yet now, with his barrel paunch looming like a battering ram at her eye level, she was utterly overwhelmed.

"Damn you, Margaret! Do you eavesdrop on my private discussions? Is this behavior to be endured? You are as insupportable as everyone else in this room, even if the subject is beyond your comprehension." His words were slurred from the strength of the emotion he felt.

Miss Alleyn retracted her neck into her bony shoulders and twisted her napkin helplessly, unable to meet his accusing glare. A pulse in her neck throbbed visibly. "Henry, I overheard nothing. I was merely concerned—as we all are—for your well-being."

Her contrition only added to his fury. "Do not treat me like an imbecile! Is it for this I have shown you hospitality these past years? Without me you'd have starved, as you still might if I choose to abandon you."

"But, Henry," she stammered, "I have never forgotten how much I owe you. I depend on you. You have been the most generous of brothers to me. I did not intend to cause you distress. I simply chanced to hear the conversation. . . . It meant nothing, as you have acknowledged. I could not understand . . ."

Montfort lowered over her, mute yet threatening. His eyes seemed swollen with rage, the expression in them wilder. Did I detect a flicker of lunacy? When he spoke it was to spit out his final rebuke.

"What use is exerting myself over such conduct? Your disgraceful actions are no more than I might have expected. I believe you will drive me mad if I remain in your presence. I am leaving now, and understand this, all of you, I mean it when I say under *no* circumstances do I wish to be disturbed."

Then, with the eyes of the entire company upon him, he marched from the room, crashing the door closed behind him.

After the echo of his footsteps had faded, his ill-humor remained in the room like some noxious odor that even a spring breeze cannot erase. The footman and I stood uncomfortably guarding each side of the serving table. Guests and family stared at the food congealing on their plates. At length Miss Alleyn calmed herself sufficiently to signal to John, who signaled to me to clear away the plates. Meanwhile Robert did what he could to break the chill.

"Ladies and gentlemen," he began hesitantly, "I apologize for my father, who as you see is indisposed. He hasn't been well these past days. I trust his ill-health won't intrude upon your enjoyment of this evening."

"But what has caused his indisposition?" demanded Elizabeth, alarm ringing in her voice, distress raw on her face. "This evening was arranged at his desire. The library is completed for him to unveil to his guests as he intended. Yet today he ordered the room to be left dark, the fire unlit. What has changed? Has he taken leave of all his senses?"

"I have asked myself the same question, sister," concurred Miss Alleyn, her pinched face still showing the strain of her brother's verbal assault on her. "I confess I am no closer than you to comprehending it."

Foley and Bradfield looked conspiratorially at each other and nodded. Foley cleared his throat with a small cough. "I believe I may be the cause of Lord Montfort's indisposition."

Miss Alleyn regarded him uncomprehendingly. Elizabeth's eyes widened. "In what way, sir?" they demanded in almost perfect unison.

"Ladies, I cannot—should not—spoil these happy festivities with such discussion—besides it is a matter of confidence between Lord Montfort and myself."

"Come, come, Lord Foley, we have already noted the circumstances are far from festive. And it appears that only Margaret, Robert, and I—his immediate family after all—are ignorant of these affairs," cried Elizabeth.

Whether or not Foley would heed her plea she never discovered, for as in some playhouse melodrama, at that precise moment the servants' door creaked open and Mrs. Cummings entered carrying an array of syllabubs on a platter. Lord Foley suspended his narrative as Connie and the scullery maid followed, bearing similarly delicious burdens. Murmuring something about attending to the kitchens, Miss Alleyn rose and left the room.

Some fifteen minutes later Mrs. Cummings and her entourage had replenished the table with rinsed cutlery and finger bowls, spice cake, compotes, tarts, and port jellies that gleamed like garnets in crystal bowls. But even these delicacies did nothing to alleviate the stifling cloak of ill-humor that lingered over the gathering. I stood there with aching limbs and heavy heart. I longed to remove my wig and shoes and enjoy a glass of ale with my feet up before the fire. I thought of how I'd recount the dismal conversation I'd just heard for Connie to make her laugh. Yes, I confess, at that moment the gloom of the party struck me as so bizarre as to be almost amusing.

Needless to say Mrs. Cummings had no intention of letting me go. How could she? She was still rushed off her feet, she implored me, for heaven's sake, to stay "just till the port was out." What difference could a few minutes make?

What difference indeed!

In the hiatus caused by the arrival of dessert, Bradfield left the table to relieve himself noisily in a chamber pot behind a screen. He replaced it politely in the side cabinet (for the footman or me to empty at our convenience), buttoned himself, and returned to his seat. Only three of the guests—Wallace, Lady Bradfield, and Lady Foley—now remained. The two ladies, avoiding the uncomfortable subject of Montfort's ill-humor, were discussing the niceties of quilling and crewelwork. Which might be the better to cover a sewing box? Wallace sat morosely at the far end of the table, an empty wineglass in front of him.

"What has become of everyone?" Bradfield inquired as he drew his chair closer to the table. He alone appeared relatively unaffected by the emotions of the room and eyed the temptations on the table impatiently.

"Miss Alleyn is attending to matters in the kitchen," replied Wallace.

"And Foley and Robert and Elizabeth? What of them? Have they too vanished?"

"Foley went to the saloon to admire some painting—a Roman scene of which he seems uncommonly fond. Robert went after him, saying he would discover the precise nature of his father's anguish. Lady Elizabeth—in a state of some distress, I fear—accompanied him."

Bradfield shook his head, as if the disappearing diners and foul-tempered host were all beyond him. "Are you aware of the source of Montfort's agitation, Wallace?"

The attorney twirled his glass. "It may have to do with the reason for my presence here. Lord Montfort summoned me this morning to prepare some legal documents. You will forgive me if professional etiquette forbids me to discuss the matter further."

"Naturally I would not wish to compromise you," said Bradfield a trifle indignantly. "Indeed I strongly suspect I know the reason. It was only your corroboration I was after."

Wallace licked his lips but did not respond. An awkward hush descended. The only sounds in the room were a small gurgle as each man refilled his glass from the decanter, the crackling of the fire, and a series of complaining growls emitting from Bradfield's stomach. "Can you think of nothing but food?" demanded his wife crossly. It was that admonition that spurred me, in an effort to provide some distraction, to pick up the platter of oranges. I had half-crossed the room with the fruit when the deafening gun blast exploded.

I went flying with my platter. Oranges cannoned across the floor. I cursed myself and dived beneath the table to retrieve them just as the general commotion began.

From my vantage beneath the table I saw the shoe buckles and stockings of Foley and Robert burst into the room, closely followed by the crimson petticoat hem of Lady Montfort. A few seconds later and I was returning to my position by the sideboard when the servants' door to the kitchen opened and Miss Alleyn flew in like a leaf in a gale. "What on God's earth was that? Did you not hear it?" she screeched.

"We heard but are no wiser than it seems you are, my dear lady," responded Foley smoothly. He gave a cursory glance in the direction of Elizabeth, who was now seated at the table, quivering, and clearly incapable of taking charge. Robert was similarly frozen with inertia. "May I suggest you send the servants to inspect both the downstairs and upstairs rooms, and that they ascertain the whereabouts of your brother, who has now been absent for over half an hour."

Relieved to be told what to do in such a masterful manner, Miss Alleyn bustled back the way she had entered. The footman followed her. Uncertain whether to stay or go—was I a servant? did I belong here? no on both counts—I remained on the spot. Foley meanwhile paced thoughtfully about the room until his gaze came to rest upon me. Now he'd clapped his eyes on my figure they seemed to stick there. He made a disapproving tutting noise while glaring at me crossly as if waiting for me to speak. At length, realizing I would remain silent, he coughed. "You," he said loftily.

"Yes, my lord?" I responded.

"Are you asleep or idle?" He was standing only a foot away from me, and his voice was far louder than necessary.

"My lord?"

"Why do you not respond to my instruction when you plainly heard me direct Miss Alleyn to send all servants to discover the source of that shot?"

I felt myself redden with embarrassment. I was unused to such interrogation from the upper orders and alarmed to find myself suspected of indolence. "Forgive me, my lord, I was unsure whether or not I should stay in case anything further was required."

"Well, now you are certain. You now have directions. From me. *Go.*" The last admonition was shouted so loudly I fancied I felt Foley's breath upon my face. With what I hoped appeared a deferential nod of assent, I stepped swiftly round him and retreated through the servants' door down the corridor.

"Where are you going?" he shouted after my departing back.

"To the library, my lord," I replied without diminishing my pace.

"Why there with such determination?"

I stopped dead in my tracks and pivoted back towards him. Lord Foley only narrowly escaped colliding with me. I was several inches taller than he and looked awkwardly down at the top of his elaborately curled white wig to explain my logic. "Because I judged, from the echo, that the shot originated there."

Without waiting to see if this response would elicit more questions or a further reprimand for boldness, I sped to the door and turned the handle. The brass knob rotated in my hand, but the door stuck fast.

"Locked from the inside," I declared, as I opened the adjacent door to the entrance hall. I stepped niftily through it, not realizing I'd left Foley still in the corridor with the door swinging back in his face.

The entrance hall gave access to the four main ground-floor reception rooms and a grand curving staircase to the first floor. The library was opposite the saloon, adjacent to the dining room. Beyond was the withdrawing room, a passage to further rooms, and the kitchens. I walked to the library door, grasped the handle firmly, and opened it.

An icy gust carried the unmistakable whiff of gunshot to my nostrils. After the brilliance of the other rooms, a wall of blackness confronted me. I blinked and waited. As my eyes adjusted to the gloom, I could discern the windows along the long wall opposite, the curtains of one flapping like unfilled sails in the wind. Any precise terror contained within the room remained, however, invisible in the gloom. I swiveled back in search of illumination. The hall was lit by a large brass lantern, wall sconces fitted to the paneling, and a pair of candelabra on a side table. Lord Foley, by now emerged from the corridor, saw me grasp one of these lights and turn back to the door behind. Determined to shadow my every move, he snatched its pair and followed. Thus with our lights held high did we enter the library.

Chapter Four

At first I was so stupefied by my discovery of Montfort's corpse I didn't question what might have led to his death. As in some martyr's ghastly supplication, his arms lay outstretched at his sides, palms upturned. Close to his right hand lay a small pocket pistol, no longer than six inches, ornately decorated with a fruiting vine design. Both sleeves and cuffs were bloodstained, and clasped in his left hand was a small box about the size of a goose egg. Scarcely had I registered this last detail, however, when I remarked the leeches, and my shock transformed to revulsion which I could not contain. Thus it was only after I'd returned from retching at the window that I drew the candelabra closer and extricated the box from Montfort's hand.

It was carved in the form of a columned classical temple. There was something small that rattled within. Despite the horror surrounding me, I remember I held the box in my palm, pausing to admire its gleaming surface, crisp carving, the irregular whorls and tight figuring of the wood, as only a fellow craftsman can truly appreciate the intricacies of his trade. But while hinges were visible along the apex of the roof, there appeared no sign of a catch.

I was still rotating the box in my hands in search of the mechanism to open it when Foley crouched beside me. He was once again babbling to himself, "I cannot be the cause of this. I will shoulder no blame." He repeated these words over and over as he gazed at the dead man before him.

Then, abruptly, he collected his thoughts and remarked upon my preoccupation with the box. "Let me see that," he cried, snatching it from me.

I stood up. My head swam and my body was beginning to shudder uncontrollably, although whether this was from shock or the bitter temperature, I cannot now be certain. I know, however, that while I felt unable to drag my eyes from the grim spectacle we had discovered, this was no ghoulish fascination. I was looking, even then, for any detail that might explain it.

My curious and inconvenient instinct to dismantle things may have been suppressed by my learning the craft of cabinetmaking, but it has never entirely disappeared. These days, however, the demolition usually takes place in my head. I've learned to observe closely. I've taught myself to *imagine* taking a given object apart, rather than carrying it out in fact. Naturally enough (so it seemed to me) I now applied the same method of scrutiny to the scene before me. Close to the body, leading to the window, I observed a faint pattern of overlapping smudges. Around them perhaps thirty or more papers were strewn. These, I now saw, were drawings from Mr. Chippendale's famous volume, *The Gentleman and Cabinet Maker's Director*, which had lately brought him great fame.

I confess their presence shocked me deeply. I knew that Chippendale greatly treasured his drawings, often displaying them to select patrons prior to publication, as a means of cajoling them into commissioning something grander than they originally intended. It occurred to me that these were the same drawings to which Montfort had referred in his threatening outburst of the previous day. But why Chippendale had given something that was so precious to him to Montfort I could not fathom.

There were sheets of designs—girandoles, daybeds, cabinets, and card tables. I gathered them one by one, intending to place them together on the desk. As I did so I discovered among them a clutch of drawings by a hand I recognized as that of my friend Partridge. The reason for their presence among the Chippendale drawings was equally mystifying. The thought of Partridge made me conscious of how far I was from my familiar surroundings, and how strange was my present situation. What would Partridge make of it if he could see me here holding his drawings? I stepped forward with the bundle of pages, placed it on the desk, then halted abruptly. Montfort's fearsome dog was curled behind the desk chair in the deep shadow. I trod gingerly round it before hastening away to trace the smudges leading from Montfort's body. Halfway across the room the footprints became invisible, but by then I'd decided they led towards the window closest to where Montfort lay.

The sash was already open. I'd left it thus to allow the final coat of varnish to dry. I raised the sash further and peered out to see if there was any sign of footprints continuing outside. The ground floor of Horseheath is raised up some six feet above the garden level. Even from this distance, however, I could make out that there was indeed a trail of heavy prints on the frosty earth below, which seemed to lead off in the direction of the Italian Garden. Leaning out to look more closely, I rested my palm on the sill for support—and recoiled immediately. My hand had touched something sticky and wet. Lowering my light to the sill, I saw a thick pool of semicoagulated blood, wider than my fist. So much blood that it had dripped down the wall, leaving, I now saw, dark streaks on the damask covering. Revulsion and nausea surged again in my belly. I staggered round towards Foley, holding my bloodstained palm outstretched in front of me as if I myself was savagely wounded.

Foley was still occupied with the box. He'd turned it, twisted it, shaken it, and taken a paper knife in an attempt to prize it open. The contents rattled mockingly, but still the catch remained invisible and unyielding. Now, seeing my bloodstained predicament, he placed the box on the desk and addressed me sensibly.

"What have you done? Cut yourself?"

"It is not my blood. . . . There is blood . . . see for yourself," I stammered.

Foley's brows shot up in astonishment at my agitation. "Compose yourself, Mr. Hopson. Take this. Clean yourself." He handed me his silk handkerchief and walked to the window. I was in such distress I wrapped it over my hand, without a thought for the value of such an article. After a minute or two he drew down the sash with an air of finality, before turning back to me. His face was impassive, his voice, when he spoke, dispassionate. "Hopson. Go immediately and summon the family and guests. Do not divulge to them what we have discovered. Request only that they come here immediately."

The coolness with which these orders were issued brought me quickly to my senses. Pushing his handkerchief deep in my pocket—already uncomfortable about staining such an item, how could I return it now it was sullied with blood?—I did as he bade me.

When I returned to the dining room, I found it deathly silent. Six remaining diners were seated around the table fidgeting uncomfortably, avoiding one another's eyes. Only Robert—the new Lord Montfort—

stood, legs braced in front of the dying fire, gazing fixedly at Elizabeth, who was turned to face the window and the invisible landscape beyond.

The grand dinner for which such careful preparation had been made was now a sorry sight. I was oddly reminded of a painting I'd once seen in Lord Chandos's London mansion, by an Italian master, of a bacchanal in which Bacchus and various attending nymphs and satyrs sit frozen around the detritus of their meal. In this case, collapsing custards and melting syllabubs, fractured nut husks and wilting fruit peelings were strewn about like flotsam from the tide.

Six heads turned inquiringly towards me as I entered. "Ladies and gentlemen," I announced, "Lord Foley requests that you join him in the library without delay." As Foley had directed, I gave them no hint of what awaited. Yet by the paleness of my countenance and the faltering of my voice they might easily have suspected some calamity. Nonetheless not one of them was consumed by curiosity about what was happening to them. Docile as children, they rose to their feet and followed me along the hall to the library.

Lady Montfort led the straggling group as I opened the door, thus it was she who first caught sight of her husband's body. I confess her reaction startled me profoundly. I had expected tears, shrieking hysteria, a violent outpouring of emotion. But she betrayed no shock or fright. She didn't tremble, nor did she shiver as I had seen her do earlier. Indeed she displayed no sign of any sentiment whatsoever. For perhaps half a minute she gazed unflinchingly at her husband's corpse. Only when the rest of the group clustered behind her and began to express astonishment and dismay did the full horror strike her. Her legs seemed suddenly to give way, and she toppled forward and would have struck herself had not Bradfield stepped in to save her.

Miss Alleyn's response to her brother's death was as voluble as Elizabeth's was silent. She uttered a shrill birdlike cry, and began manically twirling the fringes of her shawl between her bony fingers. Wallace the lawyer placed a comforting arm about her shoulder, his feet braced, his brow furrowed. After a few moments he mumbled something inaudible.

"What's that you said?" cried Foley impatiently. "Speak louder, man!"

"Only that while I take no responsibility for the present tragedy, there is something I must divulge which may have a bearing upon it."

I couldn't help wondering how it could be that both Foley and Wallace felt that they were somehow to blame for this death. Surely both couldn't be responsible, or were they in conspiracy together? Before Wallace could shed light on this perplexing matter, Robert Montfort pushed his way from the rear. Seeing his father's corpse for the first time, he fell to his knees, and taking a linen kerchief from his sleeve, dabbed at the gunshot wound on his father's head. He then took his father's left hand and pressed it to his lips. "I cannot believe he would take his life. Why did he not speak to me of his melancholy?" he exclaimed, rising stiffly to his feet. "I blame you for this, Foley. You now have an obligation to explain yourself."

Foley met his accusing stare directly but said nothing. The culpability he had voiced earlier seemed to have disappeared. Perhaps I imagined it, but his expression seemed to me more akin to triumph.

"Take his life, what do you mean?" interjected Miss Alleyn.

"See here, the gun has dropped from his hand. Is that not proof enough, taken together with his melancholy and his strange humor this evening?" said Robert.

"I do not believe that your father took his life," I said, realizing Robert Montfort's drift and intending to console him.

He swiveled round and glowered at me. "Hopson the carpenter, is it? Do you presume to know something of this?" He spat.

"I . . . I . . . forgive me, for I do not mean to presume, sir," I stammered. "It is only that when I came into the room I stumbled and I believe—"

"This is a family tragedy, and one that does not in any way concern you, Hopson," he cut in rudely. "I thank you to keep your opinions to yourself. You may remove the leeches from my father's body. Then leave this room immediately. Foley, I await your explanation."

I must have looked dazed by his order, for I did not move until Miss Alleyn came forward and thrust a small stone jar with a perforated lid into my hands. "You may place them in here," she murmured, patting me kindly on the shoulder.

I crouched down before the corpse, pressing my palms against the cool sides of the jar to suppress my revulsion. One by one I plucked the creatures from Montfort's neck—they were as soft as overripe berries—and with a trembling hand dropped them in the jar.

In between removing each beast I glanced up at Foley. I could say it was a way of distracting myself from my horrid task, but it would be more truthful to confess that even though Montfort's death was no concern of mine, I was caught up in it and intrigued to know what Foley would say. His expression surprised me. There was no glimmer of the compassion you might expect a man to feel if his close friend had just died, nor did I see the earlier gleam of victory I'd imagined. His eyes were cold and empty.

"I believe your father's earlier ill-humor was caused by a hefty gaming loss," he said, addressing Robert. "You must already know of his passion for cards. For the past years we—Bradfield, your father, and I—have met at White's for evenings of play. On occasion all of us have been unlucky, but the evening we last met—two weeks ago—was spectacularly unfortunate." Foley paused while I, biting my cheek to control my revulsion, captured the last leech.

"Spectacularly unfortunate for all of you, Lord Foley?" whispered Elizabeth, who had recovered from her earlier shock and was now listening with rapt interest.

"Chiefly for your husband, madam. We were not, I should add, alone. We played faro; I was banker. Half a dozen other gentlemen were present and will vouch for my account. As the evening wore on, anticipating the turn of events, Bradfield and I urged him to be prudent, little knowing that this advice would spur him to follow the opposite course." Foley's dark eyes burned; he paused, seeming unwilling to continue.

"And the extent of his losses, Lord Foley?" demanded Elizabeth.

"Considerable, madam. In excess of ten thousand pounds, and the bills he gave me were due for settlement in a week's time. I fancy that is why he called Wallace here today."

At this information Wallace reddened, but before he could reply Elizabeth swooned and everyone formed a comforting circle around her. Miss Alleyn took out her salts and wafted them underneath her sister-in-law's nose. I took advantage of the interruption to deposit the jar on the desk and depart. I was closing the door when Foley came after me. Catching my elbow, he walked with me into the hall, out of earshot of the others. "I should like you to explain to me your conviction that Montfort's death could not be suicide," he murmured quietly, before instructing me in a louder voice to ensure that word was sent to Sir James Westleigh, the local justice, to come immediately.

Having relayed the instructions as ordered, I washed in the pantry, then anxious for solitude, returned to the sanctuary of the servants' hall. Grateful to find the room deserted—the other servants were still occupied in the kitchen—I replenished the fire, puffing the embers until the flames flickered and burned steadily. Then I settled myself in the high-backed chair and closed my eyes to better contemplate the extraordinary events I had just witnessed.

Why was I so sure Montfort had not taken his own life? Why did Foley think he might be partly to blame for Montfort's death? Plainly he didn't mean he'd killed him directly, yet suicide brought on by melancholy over gambling debts could not explain the evidence in the room. I wondered what it was that Wallace had been poised to disclose when Robert interrupted him. Robert's reaction had not been what I would have expected of a loving son; anger rather than grief had appeared to be his dominant emotion. Thus while he and the rest of the company seemed to assume that Montfort had committed suicide, I was far from convinced of it.

I was still examining these thoughts when, some minutes later, Constance entered with a pint of porter and a slice of meat pie sent on Mrs. Cummings's instruction to revive me. The kitchen staff had greeted the news of Montfort's death with shock but little real regret, for he had not been a popular master. I too felt no real sorrow, only a wish to recover from the shock of my discovery and forget the horrid image of his corpse. I smiled now at the sight of Connie's pretty face and the refreshment she carried. "Constance—angel of mercy—a welcome distraction indeed," I said with heartfelt sincerity.

She greeted the compliment with a brisker smile than usual.

"Is something amiss?" I asked.

"Only Mrs. Cummings going on at me. Her humor's bad since this evening's adventures. She's accusing me of breaking a crystal salt and not daring to tell her."

"It'll pass, I'm sure. She's a kindhearted woman."

"A bad-tempered one more like. Any rate, I thank heaven not to have witnessed what you have done, Nathaniel."

"Indeed, the shock of seeing that corpse has disturbed me more than I thought possible. The terrors of that room, the blood, the leeches … horrors I'll never forget. Feel my head, have I a fever?"

At this she giggled and placed the tray on the table. "I've no doubt the ordeal was fearsome, but I don't believe you're so profoundly distressed *now*. There's no fever to be sure, Nathaniel." She paused, examining my forehead with a quizzical expression. "How did you come by that scar?"

"Which scar is that?"

"Why this one, there's no other I can see," said she, touching my forehead with her soft finger as I hoped she would.

"Ah well, 'tis a long tale, one which would weary you to hear …"

"Tell me or I swear I must go mad!"

"Well, briefly. Some years ago, I was traveling by stage to London when from the rear window I observed a dozen or more highwaymen approaching from the cover of a forest. They were armed to the teeth." I paused dramatically—her eyes were big as saucers. "Did I not warn you this was the dreariest of tales?"

"Go on, Nathaniel—you can't stop now."

I gazed solemnly into her eager eyes and continued, speaking deliberately slowly at first, and then gradually faster, so as to drive her to a frenzy (or so I intended). "The driver was oblivious, and the other passengers were all asleep. . . . Not wishing to rouse and alarm them, I sprang from the window onto the rear postilion's horse . . . then I whipped up the other horses and left the vagabonds standing, but not before one of them hit me with a pistol butt."

I was still looking earnestly at her but was suddenly unable to prevent a broad smile from taking hold of my lips.

She smacked me playfully on the cheek. "You are trifling with me. A dozen highwaymen indeed."

I shrugged, accepting defeat. "And, what of it? Don't I entertain you?"

She lowered her lashes and looked at the fire. "You are entertaining enough for now, but I'll never see you after tomorrow."

I recognized this wistfulness as an invitation and took speedy action. "And the thought makes you sad? Come here and I'll help you forget your sorrow."

I reached for her waist. She giggled coquettishly, shook her head, but not so vigorously as to deter me entirely. "There's more than you to make me sad. Mrs. Cummings says we'll lose our posts before long," she said, deftly removing my roving hand and changing the subject.

"What made her say such a thing?"

"Something she overheard when she took the refreshments to the saloon."

"Tell me what then. I can see you're bursting with it."

She perched herself on the arm of the chair. Her skin smelled of treacle and rose water. I felt my spirits rise. Softly I placed my hand on hers. This advance seemed not to disquiet her, for she continued happily enough.

"Wallace the attorney said the reason for his visit was to make over a large part of Montfort's estate to Foley in settlement of his losses. Wallace says he believes it likely Lord Montfort took his life in despair because much of the estate was mortgaged already on account of his losses. According to Mrs. Cummings, that means there'll be almost nothing left for his wife and son, and they'll have little alternative but to sell the house, and we'll most likely all lose our posts."

I furrowed my brows as I pondered her words, wondering if now was the time to kiss her. "I see their reasoning, but they didn't see what I did in the library."

"You deceive yourself, Nathaniel. They saw the same as you."

"You don't comprehend my meaning."

"Tell me plainly and perhaps I will."

I patted her knee fondly. "There is all the difference in the world between seeing and observing. Moonshine is brighter than fog."

"What is the meaning of that?"

"That someone desires Montfort's death to look as if it is a suicide, and their attempts don't convince me. But while I don't see how it could be suicide, I can't make sense of what *did* happen."

She squirmed on her perch and pushed my hand away again. My evasiveness was beginning to wear thin. If I couldn't pacify her, an opportunity would be lost.

"What makes you believe your observation is better than anyone else's?"

"I recognize you for your peerless attractions. I'll wager they scarcely glance at you. Doesn't that show you I've been trained to observe and they have not?"

From a faint coloring of her cheek I could see she was mollified by the compliment; but my logic didn't entirely convince her. "You're a cabinet-maker, Nathaniel. That's a craft that requires clever hands, not eyes."

I held up a finger to her lips to quieten her, touching them with feathery lightness. "When I was a child, my father—a joiner by trade—took me to the residence of a local gentleman."

"What's that to do with Montfort's death?" she said, tossing her head in annoyance yet doing nothing to prevent me from stroking her cheek.

"The gentleman required a new bureau for his withdrawing room. My father was commissioned to make it. He brought me with him."

Connie smacked my hand away and pursed her lips. "Speak plainly or I'm off."

"We were shown the saloon where the bureau was to stand. I gazed round while my father discussed his commission. I'd never seen a grander room: looking glasses, sofas, commodes, lacquer.

"Afterwards when we returned home my father asked me what I thought of the place. 'Very magnificent,' I replied.

"'Tell me then,' he asked, 'which piece most impressed you?'

"I mentioned a japanned cabinet decorated with chinoiseries that had caught my eye. My father demanded I describe a scene upon it. I could not. Then he asked me to name three other pieces in the room that pleased me. The room had seemed so remarkable, yet all its contents had vanished from my memory."

"And what then did this teach you?" asked Connie.

I looked hard into her eyes. "Vision is a tool to be sharpened like any other."

She followed my analogy. "Then you saw something with your sharpened eye that no one else did. Tell me, what was it?"

"I wouldn't upset you with it."

She pushed my shoulder playfully as if unable to remain cross. "Nathaniel, you are teasing me again. *Tell me,* I beg of you."

"I'm not teasing," I said, widening my eyes. "I'm not even sure myself." I paused and thought back. "The footprints weren't as they should be; there was blood upon the sill, and blood on both his sleeves." I pulled her closer, intending to save myself by kissing her downy cheek. But although she permitted me this favor, I was barred from further progress. The moment I attempted an advance upon her thigh she wriggled free, Montfort's death forgotten. The kitchen and Mrs. Cummings required her more urgently than I.

Despite the fact that he lived only five miles distant Sir James Westleigh, the local justice, did not arrive until two hours later, at midnight. It was I who answered his knock. Since I expected to be required to speak to him on account of being the first person to discover the corpse, I'd undertaken to wait up so Mrs. Cummings and Constance and the first footman might retire to their beds. I asked Constance laughingly to keep a space warm for me. She consoled me with a prettily blown kiss, saying she'd have none of it and that her door would ever be locked against nocturnal interlopers with unexplained scars on their foreheads.

Westleigh was a jovial man whose breath reeked of onions and porter. With all the panache of a regular footman, I ushered him to the saloon and stood at the door awaiting further instruction. He was an old acquaintance of Miss Alleyn's. Seeing her pallor and realizing he had been called out on account of some calamity, he shook her hand vigorously, inquiring, "My dear lady, tell me what has upset you so. Not a family matter, I trust?"

To spare Miss Alleyn the ordeal of an explanation, Foley interrupted. "Come this way if you would, Sir James. I believe Miss Alleyn is about to retire." Then as an afterthought he gestured to me. "Nathaniel, perhaps you would accompany us also, since you were the person who stumbled on the corpse."

Foley led Westleigh into the library, where the body of Montfort still lay spread-eagled as we'd found it. Westleigh peered briefly at the cadaver before settling himself in a thronelike armchair. I wondered to see the still-dormant dog behind the desk chair, but Westleigh appeared not to remark it. He looked expectantly at Foley, who cleared his throat before beginning to speak.

"It is the view of Montfort's attorney Mr. Wallace, of Lord Bradfield, a fellow guest here, and of Robert, Lord Montfort's unfortunate son, that Henry Montfort shot himself in despair at his gambling losses, which were due for settlement a week from today," he began gravely. "I was his chief creditor. He called in Wallace to make documents in my favor. However, I believe that Hopson here has other views upon the matter. He tells me he's certain the death isn't one of self-murder."

"And you, Lord Foley? You counted yourself a friend and neighbor. You were the second person to see him dead. What is your opinion?" inquired Westleigh.

"My mind as yet is uncertain. I am curious to hear what light Hopson can shed for us," he replied.

In a firm but amiable tone Westleigh then demanded that I explain myself.

I felt myself redden to the roots of my hair as I opened my mouth to speak. "It is my conviction—or rather my view," I replied hesitantly, "from what I observe in this room, that the death of Lord Montfort couldn't have been suicide."

Westleigh looked at the prostrate figure and frowned. "Explain yourself properly, Mr. Hopson. What precisely do you perceive that makes you so certain?"

I flushed deeper—I was beginning to burble, and I could feel my embarrassment worsen under this examination. Clenching my fists, I walked towards the cadaver and forced myself to speak clearly and plainly.

"First the pistol. I believe I trod on it, and it was that which made me fall. I remember distinctly having the impression of traveling forward before I fell. I estimate I skidded a distance of some three feet, and surmise the pistol was under my foot when I did so. Thus, although we found it close to his right hand, I believe that was misleading. The pistol was beyond Lord Montfort's reach."

"But the pistol might have fallen some distance away after he fired it," said Foley, tapping his shoe impatiently on the floor. "I don't see that that is proof of anything at all, Hopson."

I tried not to feel humiliated as I continued. "Second, examine his body if you will, sir." Both Foley and Westleigh directed their eyes towards the side of Montfort's head at which I pointed.

"You see blood not only on his right side, where he was shot, but also several stains here." At this juncture I moved round the corpse and pointed to the clearly visible blood on his left arm and cuff. "It is this I find inexplicable. Admittedly there is less blood on the left than the right side. But the fact is, there shouldn't be any at all." I stopped and looked at Foley and Westleigh, waiting for their response, waiting to see if they would draw the same conclusion as I.

"How would *you* explain it, Mr. Hopson?" questioned Westleigh, a note of irritation creeping into his tone.

"The possibilities are plentiful."

"Name them."

"The one that springs most immediately to mind is that someone else attempted to shoot him as he tried to wrest the gun away with both hands. Then there *would* be blood on both sleeves."

Foley gaped. "Are you suggesting, Hopson, that some other person entered the library, held a gun to Montfort's head, and shot him *while we were at dinner?*"

"That might explain the physical evidence before us, sir," I said, "and moreover the theory is supported by the leeches and the footprints on the floor."

"Footprints?" echoed Foley, from which I divined he'd never even remarked them.

"Leeches?" interjected Westleigh.

"We found several on his neck," Foley explained impatiently. "Hopson has since returned them to their jar. But what footprints are you talking of, Hopson?"

I addressed Westleigh's query first. "Lord Foley has already posed this question: why would a man about to commit suicide choose to bleed himself? The answer it seems to me is simple. He would do no such thing. The leeches are therefore another significant indicator that Montfort *did not* shoot himself." I turned to Foley. "Furthermore there are the footprints to consider. They are difficult to see, but they are present nonetheless."

Here I waved towards the faint smudges I had earlier remarked on the floor. They had dried now and were almost invisible on the polished boards.

"What do you make of them, Hopson?" asked Foley.

"They are certainly made from blood. Yet Montfort could not have formed them himself. There's no blood on his slippers. We must presume therefore they were made by his assassin, with his victim's blood."

Westleigh scratched his chin. "These are grave accusations." He looked uneasily at the blue morocco slippers on Montfort's feet, on which no trace of blood was visible.

"I do not make them lightly, and they are only a hypothesis," I said, worried now that he would chastise me for audacity in disagreeing with the prevailing view. "But suicide cannot explain what we see here. Indeed even the theory I have just posed doesn't answer everything."

"What d'you mean?" said Foley.

"I cannot fathom the pool of blood on the windowsill. Or the fact that the prints on the ground outside appear quite different from those in here."

"What!" exclaimed Westleigh, heaving himself to his feet and marching to the window. "More blood and more footprints?" Having paused to examine the stains on the sill, he opened the sash and leaned out. Foley followed close behind. "How can you be sure?" demanded Westleigh.

"Observe the shape of the footprint and the space between the paces," said I. "Those inside are made by a narrow square-toed shoe, a fashionable shoe I daresay. One such as a gentleman might wear. They are positioned strangely close, no further apart than a foot, while those outside are heavy-booted and widely spaced. Even from the window I'd put close on a yard between them."

"What does that signify?" asked Westleigh.

"That they were made by different people, or, less probably, by the same person wearing different shoes. Perhaps whoever killed Lord Montfort had an accomplice, or perhaps the assassin changed his shoes, though I cannot for the life of me fathom why he would do such a thing. And that still would not explain why so much blood came to be spilled under the window when Lord Montfort was shot over here, nor why the footprints disappear as they lead towards the window, where there seems to be most blood."

At this moment Robert Montfort burst into the room. His complexion was dark, and his eyes bulged in a manner that reminded me uncannily of the previous day when I'd first encountered Lord Montfort in this very room.

"I think it most discreditable," he fumed, "that a tradesman's word should be given credence above those of distinction who know something of the matter."

I began backing towards the door. Westleigh was pressing his fingertips delicately together as he contemplated my argument. He looked up and, seeing me retreat, signaled me to stay.

"Mr. Hopson is here, sir, at Lord Foley's suggestion, and as one of the first witnesses to the scene. I am giving his evidence no more weight than that of any other person, although it seems to me that his eyes operate remarkably efficiently regardless of his middling rank. Perhaps I should also remind you that I am the justice of this district; as such if I am called in by an interested party—in this instance your aunt, Miss Alleyn, and Lord Foley here—I am duty bound to investigate such a sudden and mysterious demise as your father's. It is my task to ascertain whether or not a felony has been committed, and if so who will bring the appeal and who will be prosecuted. Mr. Hopson is assisting as he too is obliged to do."

"Felony be damned! The death may have been sudden," retorted Robert, "but there was nothing mysterious in it, and no need for any investigation. My father mentioned suicide to Wallace this very evening. His apothecary treated him for melancholia yesterday. What more do you need by way of evidence? And what reasons has Hopson for his outlandish postulation?"

Westleigh repeated that he was duty bound to proceed with the investigation, that I was only doing as I was bidden; then, sensing my embarrassment, he outlined the gist of my argument for me. Robert Montfort remained skeptical.

"The position of the gun means nothing. It was dark, Hopson is only guessing that he stumbled on it some distance from the corpse. The footprints are easily explained. We have only his word that he saw them when he discovered the body—and he could be mistaken. All those present saw me in my grief take a handkerchief and wipe my father's brow. Then I'm sure I must have walked to the window. Does it not seem plausible that in so doing I inadvertently caused the footprints?"

"And what of the blood on the other arm?" demanded Westleigh, "and the blood on the sill and the footprints outside? Were you inadvertently responsible for those too?"

Robert snorted. "There will be a plausible explanation for all these details if you bother to look for it. I find it quite peculiar that you give such an excess of credence to the suggestions of this creature Hopson. For instance, it would not be beyond the realms of possibility for my father to have used two hands to fire the fatal shot."

This was more than I could bear. I nervously opened my mouth to point out that I was forcing no one to listen to me, but Westleigh interrupted. "Before we proceed any further may I see the soles of your shoes, sir? If you stepped in wet blood there will be stains on them. If the blood was already dry there will be none."

As if searching for an objection that he was unable to find, Robert hesitated for a fraction of a minute. Then, scowling, he slumped heavily in a chair facing the justice, lifted his feet on the desk between them, and stretched a pair of narrow black calfskin shoes garnished with diamanté buckles towards his inquisitor's nose. The buckles sparkled in the candlelight.

"What do you see?" he demanded insolently.

"Nothing," replied Westleigh.

"And nothing is proven by nothing." Triumphantly he replaced his feet on the floor. "For there could have been blood on my shoes two hours ago that has since been wiped clean on the carpets."

Westleigh raised his hands as if conceding defeat.

I could scarcely believe my eyes. "Sir James," I stuttered, "this still does not explain the blood on the window, or how Lord Montfort could have held the box in his hand."

"What box?" asked Westleigh.

"I saw no box," said Robert.

"Why, the one in the shape of a temple that was clutched in his fist," I said, mustering my wavering courage. "I tried to open it but did not succeed. Lord Foley took it from me and put it on the desk."

The three men now turned to look for the box and, finding nothing in the place I indicated, turned back to me accusingly.

"Perhaps Lord Foley removed the box after I left the room? Ask him, for I'm sure he can explain it."

Westleigh looked expectantly towards Foley, who wrinkled his brow as if wrestling with his memory. "I was confused," he replied, shaking his head vaguely. "I believe I do recall taking the box from Hopson. And I believe I did put it down but I really do not recall where, nor have I the faintest idea where it is now."

He took a large gold snuffbox from his waistcoat and proceeded to enjoy a leisurely pinch while the eyes of the room rested upon him. At length he replaced it in the same pocket and turned to us again, as if he'd only just noticed our presence.

"Perhaps Mrs. Cummings or Miss Alleyn removed it? They have both retired, I believe. We shall ask them in the morning," he suggested.

"Perhaps Hopson stole it," said Robert.

I began haltingly to protest my innocence, but Foley interrupted. "I can vouch he did no such thing," he said. "I definitely recall seeing it after he left the room. In any case he would hardly draw attention to the box if he was trying to run away with it."

Robert looked fiercely unconvinced. Westleigh sighed. I sympathized. I was grateful of course for Foley's defense, yet vexed at his vagueness regarding the box. How could he possibly have forgotten such a significant detail? And Robert Montfort's crass dishonesty shocked me profoundly. His suggestion that he had made the footprints after the body was discovered was ludicrous, as was the theory that his father had used two hands to shoot himself.

It was only much later that I thought to ask myself why, when self-murder is well known to be a crime against God, and might lead to the confiscation of his father's entire estate by the king, Robert Montfort should be so insistent his father *had* killed himself. But for now I was heavy-eyed and yearned for my bed and solitude. Westleigh clearly shared my fatigue. "I must talk with the rest of the family," he said with a yawn. "But it will wait till morning. Hopson, you may call my carriage."

I bowed and hurried away, grateful that I would not be present for the next day's interviews. I was due to leave Horseheath the following morning at six and could scarcely contain the desperation I felt for that hour to arrive. What fueled my sense of urgency wasn't just that I'd witnessed the first (extraordinarily gruesome) murder of my life—for there was no flicker of doubt in my mind that Montfort *had* been murdered. It wasn't just that Robert Montfort doubted my testimony, or that Westleigh and Foley failed to comprehend the evidence before them. How rigorously Westleigh performed his duty and what note Foley took of my assistance or of Robert Montfort's ridiculous notions were no concerns of mine. What bothered me was a gnawing disquietude that I was incapable of dispelling. I had become unwittingly caught up in this matter. I had been forced to express opinions that I would have preferred to keep to myself. If Montfort had been unlawfully killed, then his assassin was most likely to be someone *in this house*. Everyone here already knew or would quickly hear of my lone insistence that Montfort's death was murder. Including the murderer. Which led me to the inevitable question: might my outspokenness have cast my own life into jeopardy?

Chapter Five

The sky was dark as mussel shells when I rose from my attic bed. According to Mrs. Cummings, a carter from the village was leaving for Cambridge market at five-thirty. I had only to present myself at his cottage and he would allow me to ride with him. From Cambridge I would take the coach and arrive (God and the turnpikes willing) in London the same evening.

My eyes ached and my limbs were leaden. I had slept fitfully all night, fretting that some mysterious maniac might assault me in my sleep. No such assault had come, but far from consoling me this had only fueled my conviction that my attacker was watching and waiting for the moment my eyes drooped. Eventually, when I dozed, it was a restless sleep disturbed by dreams of drowning in an icy sea, watched by Chippendale, whose only assistance was to tell me to swim harder. Thus it was with relief that I counted the fifth chime of the landing clock and roused myself. I dressed hastily, turned back the press bed to the wainscot, and gathering my few belongings, descended the back stairs to the servants' corridor. Ignoring the doors leading to the kitchen, china room, pantry, and servants' hall, I reached the milk house doorway. I threaded my way past wooden pails and tubs and marble-topped tables. I was tempted to sample a tumbler of milk but resisted, telling myself I'd do better to wait for hot ale in Cambridge and not risk missing my ride. At the far end I unbolted the door to the kitchen garden. Buttoning the cape of my surtout about my neck, I walked out.

Frost crusted every blade of grass and tree in sugary white. The air felt more penetrating than the previous night, and each intake of breath seemed to freeze my nostrils until, like some mythical beast, I exhaled to cloud the blackness with steamy breath. I planned to shorten my walk by circumnavigating the northern side of the house and crossing the Italian Garden. I walked briskly, enjoying the crunch of my boots on the frozen path, relishing the distance growing with every step between myself and that ill-fated house. Soon I would be far from the unhappy Horseheath Hall. Soon my grisly discovery and the mysterious killer responsible for Lord Montfort's death would be no more than a distant memory.

With this thought my spirits began to lift. I admired the marble nymphs splashed in pearly moonlight. I imagined Constance in similar dishabille warm in her bed, then remembered that next day I might call again on Alice. I felt no qualms to be banishing Connie thus from my conscience. She and I had whiled away dull moments together, though neither of us had deceived the other into thinking that our friendship was anything but a pleasant interlude. But the nature of my sentiments for Alice was as confused as ever in my mind.

I quickened my pace, all the time drawing closer to the central pond. I could see it now, glazed with luminescent ice. And then, as I came nearer still, my eye was drawn by a dark, indeterminate form emerging from the frozen water. I stopped and peered hard. The object was lumpish and silvered with granular crystals; its furrowed surface jutted unevenly from beneath the ice. I racked my brains as to what it could be. A branch from a tree? A fallen statue? My curiosity was aroused, but with it returned my earlier jitteriness. I was aware of a pounding sensation starting up in my breast, a pulse surging in my veins. Part of me knew this was something unwelcome, that I should ignore it and turn and run. Yet my damned inquisitiveness was determined to be satisfied. Time was short, I was filled with trepidation, but I couldn't leave the object without examining it.

The pond spanned some twenty feet, and a low stone wall rimmed with flagstones bounded the water's edge. I leaned out over it and found I could now reach the object without difficulty. The instant I grasped the object, I realized it was covered by cloth of some kind, and either I'd grabbed more roughly than I intended or the cloth had been weakened by the frost. In any event the fabric had ripped, and beneath it a small white patch now lay exposed to my scrutiny.

I stared bemused for a moment, then shuddered with realization. A human body lay facedown, its limbs sprawling below the pond's frozen surface. From the size and the nature of its clothing, I perceived it to be a male. In my attempt to seize him, I'd unwittingly torn his jacket and exposed the base of his spine, where a crescent of flesh now gleamed pallidly in the moonlight.

Feeling unaccountably discomfited by this sliver of nakedness, as if I had assaulted him, I replaced the fabric as best I could and withdrew. I was panting audibly as I tried to determine what further action I should take. With the shock of discovery my heart and lungs raced. The awful images of my previous discovery returned to haunt me. What was it about this place that seemed to doom me to chance upon corpses? Why, even now, hadn't I the wit to leave the body alone, pretend I'd never seen it, and go on my way? But it was as if my mind had become a battlefield between fear, which told me to leave, and my wretched curiosity, which bade me stay. Some minutes later and dread was temporarily vanquished. I fashioned a plan of sorts: I'd examine his face and thus gain some impression of his age and demeanor, then I would return to the house, report my discovery—and be on my way.

Three-quarters of his skull lay below the surface, embedded in ice. I tried to raise the head by clutching the hair, then by clamping my hands either side of the crown and lifting with all my strength. Numerous attempts at this gruesome task numbed my fingers and had me once again gasping for breath. But the ice did not yield. Refusing to allow my emotion to get the better of me, I leaned forward, took two wide grips on the torso, and pulled firmly. Nothing.

For several minutes I stood there helpless, numbed hands shaking uncontrollably. I became conscious that I was all alone in a dark landscape with a dead body. Was the murderer of Lord Montfort responsible for this death too? Perhaps I was still in jeopardy; perhaps even now he was watching me, waiting for his moment to strike. With this thought I felt the last of my faltering courage drain away. Telling myself the task of releasing the dead man was impossible, I scurried away in search of assistance.

The first glimmer of dawn was visible when I returned with a party of three laborers who, at my instruction, had brought with them picks and chisels and half a dozen scaffolding planks. I cannot pretend that terror was not still reverberating in my breast, yet I did my best to disguise it, and the presence of other living bodies and the sound of their voices comforted me a little. I would not allow myself to dwell upon the horror incarcerated in the pond, or the danger lurking in the shadows. I would concentrate on directing the men.

The ice cracked audibly as the first man placed his foot gingerly onto the surface. Uncertain how deeply the water was frozen, and with no desire to witness another tragedy, I halted him and demonstrated a means of positioning the planks across the rim of the pond and thus creating a support for his weight. A second man assembled a similar structure while the third stood on the wall between them, holding a flaming torch aloft to illuminate their task. The men raised their picks and slowly let them fall. Whirls of ice splinters glowed yellow like showers of fireworks at some pyrotechnic display.

I stood and watched them, unable to tear my eyes away from the body they were releasing, unable to banish the sensation of the icy flesh I had touched. It was only the voice of the torchbearer that shattered my delirium.

"The tragedy is that if it were not for our work yesterday he might never have stuck fast," he observed, adjusting the angle of his flame so it shone more directly upon the corpse.

"What do you mean?" I asked, still transfixed by the activity before me.

"This is the first good freeze of the year. Yesterday we removed a wagonload of ice from the pond to fill the icehouse. Had we not, the ice might have been thick enough to support him."

"But instead it broke up with his weight and he drowned in freezing water. Is that what you're saying?"

"Aye, sir."

I shuddered as the blade of one man's pick fell within inches of an arm. "You may be right," I replied, thrusting my hands deeper into my pockets in a hopeless attempt to warm them, "but we don't know how he came to be here, or whether his death *was* by drowning. Until he's been extracted from the ice it's too early for such reflection."

"It's not the only curious matter though."

"What else then?"

"I walked past here last evening. I fancied I caught sight of someone here. Slumped over, they were."

"Did you come and look?"

"I'd no lantern, but I came a little nearer. And as far as I could tell they'd gone."

"What time was this?"

"Seven, eight maybe. I don't rightly recall."

I thought for a moment. This was around the time Lord Montfort left the dining room and entered the library. "Did you hear a gunshot just before you saw the figure?"

He shook his head. "Don't recall that neither."

"More likely the ale deceived you, not your eyes," jeered one of his companions. The first man grinned, shook his head again, and gave his friend a rueful wink. How could they bait each other at such a time? I dismissed the story as nonsense and crossly gestured that they should waste no more time in completing the task at hand.

They made rapid advances. With the dexterity of sculptors, they were now taking chisels and mallets to chip away the last fragments. Soon after the two men set down their tools and positioned themselves to retrieve the body. Each of them bent down and, bracing himself, grasped an armpit and a thigh and heaved. There was a small crunch as the ice ceded and the body came away, leaving a pool of water beneath as black as death itself.

Naturally since my discovery of the dead man I'd given more than a passing thought to his identity. It crossed my mind that he might well be involved in some way with Montfort's demise, a second victim or the killer himself. Failing that, I presumed he might be a village trespasser met with some misadventure, or perhaps an ill-fated member of Lord Montfort's household. Certainly I felt sorrow for the victim, but the shock of finding him had by now subsided a little. Thus it was with detached curiosity—and certainly no inkling that he might be known to me—that I waited to see his face.

The men edged their way along the planks, hauling the body still face-down between them. At the wall they stepped slowly to the ground and lowered him along the path. It was only when the body touched the ground that they turned it over and the torchbearer drew his light close.

How can I describe that awful moment of recognition? A shudder convulsed me—horror, dread, sorrow, fear all mingled into one. I gasped and blinked, hoping I was mistaken. Yet another look confirmed the dreadful truth. I was not. How could this be? It wasn't possible, and yet evidently it was true. I was dimly aware of the voices of the men, floating on air as though I were overhearing a conversation in another room.

"Never seen him before. A stranger."

"I heard there was someone came calling in the last days."

"He's in a poor way, that's certain."

Still I said nothing. I dropped to the dead man's side and gazed more closely at his face. Tears pricked my eyes as I acknowledged there was no mistake, no misjudgment on my part. Before I knew it, I was blinded by grief, unable to speak or move as tears coursed down my cheeks. The man holding the flambeau looked down. He was waiting for further instruction, and caught the misery on my face.

"Did you know him, Mr. Hopson?"

I stayed there, staring down at the corpse. "Indeed I knew him well. He was a good friend of mine."

"Who was he then?"

"His name was John Partridge," I replied in a whisper so brittle I barely knew it as my own.

I did not, could not, add that the man lying before me, staring upwards as if contemplating infinity, was almost unrecognizable as my friend. His lips were blue, his face blanched of color, his flesh spongy and plastered with a shell of ice-coated hair. On one side of his temple was a small purple bruise. Despite his manhandling from the pond, his right arm had stayed bent and stiffened, with his hand still thrust deep in his pocket. Looking down at him, I suddenly yearned to ease whatever agony he had felt at the moment of death. Ignoring reason—which told me that he was beyond any help I could give him—I tugged at the arm to take out his hand from his pocket and hold it.

But what was this? I lurched back with an involuntary cry. Horror and revulsion overwhelmed me. Even as I relive that moment, my hand begins to shake, my pen wavers, and I am swamped with doubt at my own capacity to describe the desecration I witnessed. And yet I acknowledge that no record of these events can be complete without these awful details. I must write what I saw.

Where his fingers should have been, there remained only four mutilated stumps. The fingers had been hacked or ripped off, leaving only sinews and bone and pale, waterlogged flesh, from which all the life's blood had drained.

What could I do in the face of this terrible violation? How would anyone react to finding his dearest friend in such an appalling condition? The truth is that in such moments, when we are overburdened with horror, reality ceases to have meaning. We are insensible, we no longer know what we are or what we do. We do not behave as we ought. I began to shudder more violently than before. A taste of bile rose in my gullet. My throat burned, tears pricked. And yet I was unable to retch, unable to cry, mute, immobile. It was as if this last discovery had been too much for my natural responses to bear, and I was frozen, like my surroundings, into inertia. I wanted to weep and rage. Yet I did not, could not, for within my breast there was nothing but numbness.

The men, to whom Partridge was but a stranger, were more straightforward in their response to this brutality.

"Good God," said one, "that's murderous cruel. Worst thing I ever saw."

"Must've been chopped with a cleaver, like jointing a pig."

"No, look at the tears to the flesh. Those wounds aren't clean—more like the fingers have been twisted off, or wrenched by a pair of monstrous jaws . . ."

"Who could have done such a thing?"

"Foxes or badgers . . . or Montfort's dog. God knows he never fed it. Delighted in keeping it hungry."

I could bear it no longer. "Heaven spare us!" I shouted. "Have you no respect, no feeling for the dead? This man was my friend, the dearest friend I had. I don't wish to hear a word more!"

Realizing my torment was worsened by their speculation, they grew silent, standing awkwardly about, stamping their feet on the gravel in futile attempts to ward off the cold, looking down on my crouching figure and Partridge's prostrate one, saying nothing. Of course I had no wish to keep them there. I wanted more than anything to be alone in my wretchedness. Yet I realized that unless I addressed the men, gave them direction, we would all remain unhappily together. Thus I forced myself to my feet and attended to the practicalities of the moment. We had to bring Partridge back to the house, I told them. No more could be done for him here.

The men formed a rough stretcher from two planks and some twine and placed Partridge's body upon it. I removed my coat and laid it over his poor face and walked behind. In this unhappy procession we moved off.

We laid him in a vacant storeroom, and while I kept vigil word was sent to the house and to Justice Westleigh. An hour later I heard the crunch of carriage wheels outside and Westleigh bustled in. With only a cursory nod in my direction, he began his examination of Partridge's body. He looked at the mutilated hand and then at the other, which was untouched, showing no more sign of emotion than if he were gazing on haunches of mutton on a butcher's block. Next he rifled through the pockets of the dead man's jacket. He placed the contents in a neat line on the table beside the corpse: three silver shillings, a single gold sovereign, a handkerchief, a penknife, a folded paper. The last he opened and examined, but it had been submerged so long in water that any writing it once bore was indecipherable. There was nothing to offer any answer to Partridge's presence at Horseheath, let alone in the pond. Nothing to explain his death.

After some minutes Westleigh turned abruptly to me. "You knew him, did you, Hopson?"

I nodded my head and explained that we were fellow journeymen from Chippendale's workshop. Partridge had fallen ill before Christmas; had he not, he rather than I would have installed the Horseheath library. In view of his recent absence I could make no sense of why Partridge might have come to Horseheath. Nor could I offer any explanation as to how he'd met his untimely death.

Having listened to my short dialogue without comment, Westleigh ordered me to join him in the library within the hour. There were other matters concerning Partridge he wished to clarify, for they might have a bearing upon the death of Lord Montfort, and he wished to write a record of my account.

When I went in, Westleigh was seated at a large leather-lined desk, a sheaf of paper, ink, pounce, and quill laid on the table before him. Lord Foley had somehow heard the news and come immediately to offer his assistance. He sat some distance off, in front of a blazing fire. His head was concealed behind the wings of a large armchair, leaving only his elbow propped on the armrest and his legs visible. With some relief I saw that Montfort's body had been removed—presumably in preparation for the undertaker's arrival.

"This is a strange business indeed, Mr. Hopson," said Westleigh, looking searchingly at me before he indicated a chair facing him. "Tell me something of this man, your friend John Partridge. How did you become acquainted?"

"Our friendship stretches back eight years. He arrived a week after I had started my apprenticeship in Chippendale's workshop."

While Westleigh recorded my testimony, I began, reluctantly at first, to trace our joint history, endeavoring to control my confusion, to put the gruesome spectacle of his damaged body from my mind as I spoke. I pictured poor Partridge when we first met: a miserable specimen, scrawnily built, puny of stature, with a pair of penetrating blue eyes that were perpetually downcast.

"Partridge was a foundling," I told them, trying to control the wavering of my voice. "He had been discarded as an infant on the steps of the newly built Foundling Hospital, to be raised by charity to become a useful citizen."

I did not add that, having been brought up in the distant countryside, I had been utterly ignorant of the preconceptions associated with that institution. I soon learned, however, of the ignominy attached to its inhabitants. Foundlings were conceived in sin, abandoned without name by their parents, who would not or could not raise them. Without the hospital they would almost certainly have died in the streets. With it they were saved, but the shame of their birth would never be forgotten, for they represented the physical evidence of their parents' failings.

"Is it not unusual for foundlings to be apprenticed to cabinetmakers? I had thought them suited to more lowly occupations—as befitted their origins?" demanded Westleigh abruptly.

Although his remark was not ill-founded, I felt anger rising in my breast. What right had he to speak so disparagingly of my friend? How cocooned are the privileged from the harshness of city life. How little he understood. "As you say, most boy foundlings are enrolled in far less prestigious occupations or sent to sea. To be apprenticed to a cabinetmaker such as Mr. Chippendale was thus uncommon, but then Partridge was uncommonly talented." My voice was cool and sharp. I tried to contain my desire to be insolent, telling myself that rudeness wouldn't help poor Partridge. Unless I cooperated there was no chance of discovering how he came by his appalling fate. "The apprenticeship happened, so Partridge told me, because he was singled out by the hospital's benefactor, William Hogarth. Partridge was sent to assist the craftsmen working in the hospital's new chapel, where he showed the first signs of his remarkable talent. Mr. Hogarth thus approached Mr. Chippendale, who agreed to take him in."

"Was that not most philanthropic of your Mr. Chippendale?"

"It was," I replied, still struggling to contain my irritation at his manner. "But Mr. Chippendale benefited greatly from Partridge's skills." There was no point in telling him what Partridge had told me: that our master had accepted him only in the expectation of gaining favor with the polite society in which Hogarth mingled.

"And yet you say this most fortunate of foundlings was woebegone? One might justifiably ask what is the point of philanthropy if it is to be greeted with such ingratitude. What d'you say, Foley?" blustered Westleigh.

"What does Mr. Hopson say?" replied Foley, thoughtfully kicking a log further into the grate so it exploded in myriad sparks.

"Partridge was not ungrateful, and the reason for his unhappiness is easily understood," I said sharply. "His origins were no secret, and certain of the other apprentices tormented him for it."

While I waited for Westleigh's scratching pen to catch up with my account, I returned to the days when our friendship began. I'd helped Partridge get the better of his tormentors and turn their contempt to respect, but I'd done so unwittingly. Finding myself in need of a companion, on the spur of the moment I'd invited Partridge to go rowing on the river and afterwards to dine at the Castle Tavern in Richmond. You'll recall I knew nothing of the prejudices attached to foundlings. I'd noted he was a little miserable but saw no reason why he shouldn't make me a suitable friend. So I'd filled him with burgundy, oyster pies, cabbage farced, and marchpane cake, which he'd eaten as hungrily as if it was his first proper meal for a month. The sustenance, or the day itself, seemed to effect a remarkable transformation. With a bottle of wine he became a little more lively; another bottle and he was transformed into a boisterous accomplice. There was no restraining his onslaught on a third. Then we had grand entertainment with a couple of pretty milliner's apprentices we encountered. After such an auspicious beginning, we repeated our excursions (until one of the milliners slipped a shilling from my purse). Partridge's smallness didn't worry the ladies, who were enchanted by the quickness of his wit, the gap between his teeth, and the eagerness of his embraces. I recall there were several who took it upon themselves to teach him gentler skills, which he learned as readily as I. Our weekend diversions gave him a new assurance in the workshop. He flung a few punches at the worst of his tormentors and floored them, for they never expected him to retaliate. With this the ribbing from the others dwindled. By the time our apprenticeship was complete all animosity had faded, for not only had Partridge surpassed them all (apart from me) in stature and in his appetite for revelry and mischief but it had also become clear that Hogarth was correct in his judgment; Partridge was peculiarly gifted.

Westleigh had covered several sheets with his laborious script when his progress was unexpectedly interrupted by a hesitant knock. Miss Alleyn hovered on the threshold, eyes flitting between Westleigh, Foley, and me. She was dressed in mourning black, twisting the fabric of her dress between her forefinger and thumb as I'd seen her do when she first saw her brother's corpse the previous night. "Forgive me for interrupting," she faltered, "but I have seen the body of Mr. Hopson's friend and have something to say that I believe may have a bearing upon his death."

At this Foley shifted forward in his chair a little and gave a vigorous thrust to a large terrestrial globe on a stand, rotating it so fast that the seas and continents blurred into one. Westleigh smiled comfortingly. "Madam, in that case there is no need for apology. Enter. We are all ears to hear it."

He drew up a chair for her, and she sat upon it, shoulders hunched, sinewy neck jutting forward. Looking at her, I was reminded of nothing so much as the bats that used to shelter in the rafters of my father's work-shop.

"Some days ago this same man, John Partridge, called upon my brother, Lord Montfort. It seems Partridge had fallen on hard times and had formed the impression my brother was of a philanthropic bent. I was present during this conversation and witnessed Partridge ask my brother for money to establish his own business."

Westleigh was staring directly at her, his lavish gray eyebrows uplifted in curiosity. "What made him form this opinion? And how did Lord Montfort respond to the application?"

She looked away, apparently distracted by the still-twirling globe, which was making a faint grinding sound. Foley halted its rotations by jabbing his forefinger on Italy.

"I can't say why he thought my brother might assist him. And in any event my brother refused, with a rudeness and violence that I'm sorry to confess was entirely characteristic of him. He wasn't an easy man, Sir James . . ." As she said this her lip trembled, and I feared she might break down entirely.

"I had gathered as much," replied Westleigh soothingly, "but don't trouble yourself with your brother's character now. His ill-temper is common knowledge, and I see it distresses you. Tell me instead, what was Partridge's reaction to this refusal?"

"Far from equable. He took out some drawings and presented them to my brother, hoping that they might verify his talents."

"And what did your brother say to this?"

"He laughed derisively. "You are nothing but a chancer. I want no more to do with you and will have you leave the premises immediately," he said, tossing the drawings on the floor."

"What happened then?"

"Partridge grew agitated. He said he had a further gift for my brother that would prove his talent, and more besides, and that he would bring this proof next day. This made my brother's temper rise even more. "I have no intention of accepting such a gift, or examining any proof. I say again you are no better than a grasping opportunist. Never do I want to catch sight of you on my property again." Then he took hold of Partridge by the scruff of his neck and thrust him out of the house."

There was a lengthy pause, interrupted only by Foley opening and closing the lid of his snuffbox. I confess I was astounded at the information. That Partridge had taken this course and journeyed to this house so far from London came as a profound shock to me. There must have been dozens of other patrons he could have approached. Why had he chosen Lord Montfort? Why had he not told me of his predicament? I searched my memory to see if I could recall Partridge mentioning Montfort. But while I well remembered his enthusiasm for the design of the Horseheath bookcase, I didn't recall him mentioning Montfort by name.

I thought back to the last days when I'd seen Partridge. Yes, he'd seemed animated, exhilarated even, but I'd presumed he was fired by love. He'd hinted he hoped to marry in the spring, the object of his affections being Dorothy, Chippendale's younger sister, of whom he'd grown fonder than of any other woman. Now I began to question my assumption. Had he brimmed with passion for Dorothy, or was there some other sentiment or ambition he'd kept hidden from me?

Suddenly I began to feel less sure of our friendship. Partridge, someone I'd always assumed I knew intimately, who didn't have secrets from me, had surprised me. The thought came to me that there might have been more to him than I knew, that he might have deliberately deceived me. I tried to suppress the sentiment, but at heart I felt a worm of doubt.

Westleigh scratched his chin thoughtfully. "One more question, madam. The pistol in your dead brother's hand. Did you recognize it?"

She answered without hesitation. "Of course I did. It was his own. One of a pair he always kept loaded in his drawer."

Westleigh pushed back his chair, leaped to his feet, and strode about the room. "Madam," he declared portentously, "it seems that you have given us the key to begin unlocking this tragic conundrum."

Foley replaced his snuffbox in his pocket and stretched out his feet so his silver buckles glinted in the flames of the fire. His eagle profile jutted forward. "Tell us then what you make of it, Westleigh."

"Wait, wait. I haven't straightened it entirely in my mind, Foley," said Westleigh, holding up a hand. "Very well. Let me at any rate begin, and we'll see where it takes us." He drew a deep breath, steepling his fingers beneath his chin as he paced in front of the bookcase.

"It seems to me entirely probable that after his unsuccessful interview with Lord Montfort some days ago, Mr. Partridge returned to Horseheath yesterday night. His intention was perhaps to deliver his drawings and his gift and, I would hazard, to beg once more for the money he required, for reasons known only to himself. Yes, Mr. Hopson," he cried as if some great revelation had just occurred to him, "I now believe you may be correct in your hypothesis that Lord Montfort was murdered."

"Go on," said Foley impatiently.

Westleigh paused as he marshaled his theory. "It is my conjecture that Partridge caught sight of the family seated at dinner. I believe you told me Lord Montfort himself opened the curtains?"

Foley nodded.

"Perhaps then he also saw Montfort storm from the room and enter the library. And here was the moment he'd waited for. An opportunity to accost Lord Montfort. He entered this room through the window that had been left open earlier in the day to allow the varnish to dry. Left open by you, I understand, Mr. Hopson." Here he turned to me and, though I already had a fearful inkling of the turn his thoughts were taking, I could do little but nod.

Westleigh tapped his chin triumphantly. "We cannot be certain why Lord Montfort came into this room in the dark. But we can imagine his surprise to find himself once again pestered by the young interloper Partridge. There must have been some heated exchange, which led to Montfort taking out one of his own pistols. A struggle ensued, during which Partridge received the small wound I observed on his head, and yet was able to wrest the gun away from Lord Montfort and shoot him . . ."

I could contain myself no longer. "The very idea of Partridge shooting Montfort is ludicrous," I exclaimed. "In any case you ignore the small matter of illumination. The library was unlit. How could Partridge see Montfort enter, accost him and shoot him, and all this in the dark?"

Westleigh halted and looked at me as if I were no better than a common thief.

"Hopson, I'll thank you to keep your opinions to yourself until you're asked. Be reminded I am the justice in these parts. It is usual for a justice to appoint a suitable officer to assist him in his inquiries. I have decided in this instance that Lord Foley, as interested party, will be that officer. It is our responsibility to seek out the truth. Truth is not always as clear as the pimples on your chin. It is often a complex matter that requires a little probing. There is no better way that I know to do this than by discussion. Therefore if you impede our debate, I'll have you apprehended for unruliness."

I flushed with anger. Foley glanced in my direction and perhaps read the look of fury, dismay, and incredulity upon my face. Even though Westleigh's theory was obviously ridiculous, I was aghast at the speed at which he'd assembled it, and fearful of how he might twist the facts to develop it further. Was I too to be implicated as an accomplice to my friend for leaving the window open? I knew whatever I said would be turned and molded to suit his purpose. Better to remain silent and fume.

"But perhaps we should heed Hopson," interjected Foley. "For he has a point, does he not? The room *was* dark. Thus Partridge could not have seen Montfort enter. Furthermore, your theory does not explain why Montfort's body was arranged to look like suicide, nor the blood at the window, nor how Partridge came to be frozen in the pond without four of his fingers."

Westleigh nodded his head encouragingly. Clearly he could accept criticism when it came from the great Lord Foley, but not from a cabinet-maker of middling birth. "Agreed. What then is your solution, Foley?"

There was a brief silence while Foley mustered his thoughts. "You may be right about Partridge's surprise entry to the library during dinner, but I don't believe he expected to come upon Montfort. I believe he intended to leave his gift—the box, I presume and return later on, once Montfort had examined it and been won round by its quality. It's my conjecture that Partridge was killed by Montfort. That the wounds to his hands were administered by Lord Montfort himself *in this very room*. You recall the bloodstain at the window? That would explain it."

Westleigh furrowed his brow. "In that case, where is the weapon he used, and where, pray, are the missing pieces of his anatomy? And how did Montfort come to be shot? Partridge could not have shot Montfort without his fingers. Montfort could not have dissected Partridge's hand if he was shot, nor could he have done so without a knife of some sort. Your argument is no less flawed, Foley."

Foley shook his head helplessly but made no response. Westleigh continued. "We may all hypothesize, but before we can discover beyond doubt what took place we must hold an inquiry. We must search the grounds, we must find Partridge's lodgings, we must have his body examined by a medical practitioner."

"A wise decision," conceded Foley, lifting his gaunt head to gaze out at the icy wasteland beyond the window, rapt in thought. "Have you considered that the two deaths could be entirely unrelated? Or that a third party could be involved? The footprints were different outside from in, remember that, Westleigh. The third person might have seen Partridge murder Montfort, followed him, attacked him, and left him for dead."

Westleigh was unconvinced. "But where's the motive, Foley? Would not such an avenger of Montfort's murder declare himself? It is my observation that in sudden deaths coincidences are rarely as they seem. I'll wager this was no quirk of fate or act of God but some evil of man's invention. And I fancy that Mr. Partridge, far from being the blameless innocent Mr. Hopson paints, is at the heart of the depravity. As to a third person's involvement—I should doubt it, for was not the entire household assembled in the dining room or occupied in the kitchens at the time of Montfort's death?"

By now I was unable to hold back my fury. How could he vilify my friend, whom I knew to be a man of principle? I didn't know why Partridge had come here or why he'd seen fit to keep it a secret from me, but I knew enough of him to be sure he would never slaughter a man. I owed it to our friendship to defend my defenseless, murdered companion. "Sir, I don't wish to be disrespectful, but I beg you to construct another theory, for I'm certain you are mistaken in this one. You can bend the evidence to suit your argument, but it will not alter my belief—and more than my belief, my certain knowledge of my friend's character. Partridge was not a violent man. He would never have entered here clandestinely to thieve, let alone attack Lord Montfort. Why, I doubt he'd ever held a pistol in his life. He'd certainly never fired one."

"He was eager for financial support, Mr. Hopson. And in a state of agitation. You have heard Miss Alleyn vouch for that. And, as *you* have testified, he was of unfortunate birth. Such men will often, in my experience, deviate from their usual character. Or perhaps—since we know nothing of his origins—*return* to his true character. Virtue reverting to villainy."

I shook my head vehemently. "I still believe you are wrong, sir. I remain convinced of his innocence in all this. In the meantime, with your permission, I must return to London."

I gave Westleigh an assurance that he could contact me whenever he wished, and that if he desired it I would return to Cambridge, and with this undertaking he saw no reason to prevent my departure. I made my way to the servants' corridor. I had been anxious before to distance myself from this unhappy place; now I was filled with desperation to be gone. I craved time alone to contemplate the death of my dear friend, to fabricate my own theory as to how it might have happened, for I confess I was no closer to understanding it than Foley or Westleigh.

I stood for a moment in a doorway in the passage, my eyes closed tight, my head pressed hard to the wall, yielding to the ferment of shock, fear, and dismay swirling in my heart. I felt as if I was tumbling down into a vortex of darkness, in which each horror I discovered was overshadowed by another more dreadful uncovering. If it had shaken me to stumble on Montfort's corpse, how much more rocked had I been to find the body of Partridge. And then further devastation—I'd confronted his gruesome injury. Were my ordeals still incomplete? Was I now to discover that this dear friend of mine was a common murderer? No! I knew I must refute the suggestion. The issue of Partridge's culpability should not even arise in my mind. Yet how was I to resolve the barrage of other questions his death posed? How was I to make sense of it all?

And still solitude eluded me. I'd stood for scarcely two minutes in the passage before I heard Foley calling after me. "Mr. Hopson, you are on your way to Cambridge, I believe. Allow me to offer you a ride in my carriage, for I have volunteered to go there immediately to summon the apothecary physician to examine Mr. Partridge."

Until now Foley had seemed aloof, and I knew that if he offered me a ride there must be something he wanted from me. But I had no other certain means of making the journey to Cambridge in time to catch the midday coach, and I was consumed by eagerness to be gone. I grasped the offer gratefully, no matter what its hidden motive.

I did not have long to wait to discover it. The coach and four pulled past the sentinel dogs, the driver whipped up the horses, and Foley addressed me.

"Mr. Hopson," he said, "I would speak freely to you and ask you to do the same with me. Do not stand on ceremony. I want your honest views."

"As you wish, my lord."

"I have no doubt, Hopson, that you are asking yourself what I want with you."

Emboldened by the informality of his tone, I responded candidly. "I confess, my lord, I'm too overcome with sorrow and the traumas I have witnessed to worry greatly about it."

Perhaps he was shocked by my stark riposte, for his mouth twitched, as if there were an answer he wished to make but he was restraining himself.

At length he continued. "It's a rare thing to be as percipient as I believe you to be, Hopson. I've confidence your knowledge, your observations, might assist me."

"My knowledge and observations of what, my lord?"

"Of Partridge."

Was he trying to lull me into trusting him, only to use the information I gave against me? "Forgive me, my lord, but I'm intrigued to know why Partridge—a penniless foundling—should concern a gentleman such as yourself."

"His relationship with Montfort is what concerns me, in the bearing it has upon his death. Yesterday morning Lord Montfort drew up a document in my favor in settlement of his gaming losses."

"I'd heard as much from the servants' hall."

He snorted. "I'm sure such a private matter was the talk of the household. What you don't know perhaps is that my entitlement is not clear-cut. It could be affected by the manner of his death."

I was so baffled by this that for a moment I forgot my misery. "Surely if Lord Montfort made over his property to you, in the proper manner, it now belongs to you?"

"It's not straightforward. Wallace advises me that if Montfort is found to have taken his own life, he'll declare him *non compos mentis*—mentally deranged—in order that the entire estate is not confiscated by the crown, for according to the law as it stands, self-murder is a crime and thus punishable. But should Montfort be declared unsound of mind, the document settling our debt might be declared invalid, and my entitlement called into question. If, in contrast, Montfort was killed by another hand, the document of debt stands, and I will benefit."

"But even Sir James Westleigh believes it was murder."

"His mind is undecided. You heard his vague theories. They will undoubtedly change. You may have remarked how anxious Robert Montfort was that his father's death should be declared a suicide. Did you ask yourself why? The reason is plain enough. He wishes to contest my claim, and there's no one to oppose him. Elizabeth, Montfort's widow, stands to share the estate with Robert and will follow his direction. Westleigh is a family friend, and will give weight to their opinions. You've rightly observed there's much that's questionable in these deaths. The scant facts in our possession will be easily misconstrued. The matter of Partridge is a mystery that none of us begins to understand. None of us—neither you nor I nor Westleigh—has formulated a theory that bears scrutiny."

He hesitated, twirling the knob on his silver cane, as if he was waiting for me to respond. I didn't know what to say. I didn't want to ponder the matter now, or share my opinions and thoughts with someone I had no reason to trust. All I wanted was to be gone. In any event, why open my mouth when my comments might be misinterpreted against Partridge? I clenched my jaw and said nothing.

Foley accepted my silence without demur. "That is why I'm happy to assist Westleigh. I'll act as his officer and steer him in his investigation," he added quietly.

Against my better judgment I was curious. "And where would you begin?" I asked suspiciously.

"I'd return to Montfort's death. One peculiarity we have not explored is the box discovered beside the corpse. Do you believe that was the gift of which Partridge spoke to Montfort? Did the handiwork reflect your friend's capability?"

I recalled the exquisitely carved temple box which had so mysteriously disappeared. "I thought you'd forgotten it. Have you found it yet?"

He shook his head. "I never lost or forgot it. I chose not to leave it where it might fall into the wrong hands."

I was incredulous. Robert Montfort had accused me of filching the box. Granted, Foley had defended me from his accusation, but he had denied he knew where it was. "You mean you took it?"

"Yes, for I wanted to know what was inside before Robert or Elizabeth or anyone else tampered with it. Certainly it must have a bearing on all this." He rummaged beneath his greatcoat, pulled out a package wrapped in a calico bag, and handed it to me. "The box is inside," he said. "I want you to take it with you to London. Open it, find out what you can about its contents, and discover what you can of Partridge's actions since last you saw him."

I looked at him, dumbfounded. "I'm honored you trust me with it, but I fail to see how this can help you."

"Neither can anyone until what is inside has been revealed. As to Partridge, the more I can find out about him and the reason for his visit to Lord Montfort, the more likely I am to discover the truth behind their deaths."

"But you said earlier that they could be unconnected."

"And so they might be, though I doubt it. But what I need, Mr. Hopson, is fact, not supposition. You haven't answered my question. Do you believe this box was made by your friend Partridge?"

I took the box, unwrapped it, and held it in my hand again. The wood gleamed richly in the soft winter light. The skill of its carving and the ingeniousness of its design once again struck me.

"It could be."

I folded its cover back over it, still holding it in my hand. I made him no promises and felt no obligation, but his conversation puzzled me. Was the outstanding debt at the root of his interest in these deaths? He didn't strike me as someone to whom money was of paramount importance. His manner was too proud, too detached for that. I remembered his outburst when we'd discovered the body, the guilt he'd voiced, yet even then something had been missing. Montfort had supposedly been a close friend of his. Yet there was nothing in his expression that revealed the terrible emotions of loss and horror that I'd experienced on my discovery of Partridge. Surely there was some deeper motive that he was keeping hidden. Dare I test him a little to discover what it was?

I looked out of the window, as if I were mesmerized by the scenery flying past. "And if I refuse to assist you?"

"I could remind Westleigh that the window was left open on your instruction, which suggests that you aided Partridge in his entry, and are quite possibly an accessory to murder. I don't wish to threaten you, Mr. Hopson, but you must see it's in your interest to cooperate."

"And then you will prove Lord Montfort's death was not suicide and profit handsomely?"

"That is not my chief concern. It's the quest for the underlying facts that inspires me—as I fancy it does you. Assist me in this and you shall be rewarded."

"Rewarded with money?"

I caught a wry smile as it flitted across his face.

"With money certainly. But chiefly with what will bring you far greater satisfaction. The truth."

Chapter Six

Chippendale was in the garret when I returned. This to him was the treasury of his emporium, the drying store where most days he came to admire his timber. Providence had smiled since I'd been gone. The racks were now piled with the jewels of his trade: mahogany and padauk, rosewood and walnut, ebony, pigeon wood, fustic, and countless others besides.

I watched him yank out planks of mahogany, deciphering the annual rings, signal of changing seasons and thickening sap, as easily as reading a letter. He emerged from one stack to continue his inspection elsewhere and glimpsed me at the head of the stair. Without a word of inquiry as to why I'd returned a day late, and before I could tell him my terrible news, he disappeared in the shadowy depths. His mood was jubilant. "Can anything compare with the beauty of this timber? Is it any wonder every patron in the land demands it?" he exclaimed more to himself than me.

"I am delighted to hear it's so laudable, sir," said I weakly, before adding in a firmer, more solemn tone, "unlike my stay at Horseheath, which was tragic."

Chippendale seemed not to hear; his attention was all on his wood. "I believe it is the superiority of tropic timbers that makes them produce more than one ring a year. See here, Nathaniel, this is not any Spanish wood, but the finest of Cuban timber. Regard the richness of it, consider the span—wide enough to construct a table for a dozen from a single

77

board." He gave a further snort of delight. "And look here, I believe this is an oversight on Miss Goodchild's part for she didn't charge me for it."

I stooped my head, threading my way through the rafters after him. I was uncomfortably hot. The wood store was situated beneath the roof, above a well-stoked German stove, and the moisture leeching from the drying wood made the air as stifling as Calcutta. Yet it wasn't only heat that reddened my cheeks and quickened my pulse but rage kindling within my breast. How could I muster my enthusiasm for a plank of wood after all that had transpired? Was Chippendale blind not to see I had a matter of urgency to communicate? I was muddled and fatigued and frustrated, in need of a little tranquillity, a place to mull over the events of the past days, to disentangle the fearful images of blood and gore in my mind's eye and then lay them to rest. Yet since I'd left Cambridge I'd had not a moment to reflect. No sooner was my interrogation by Foley over than I'd been pressed into a coach between strangers whose meaningless chatter had distracted me for the duration of my journey back to London. I'd passed a fitful night, disturbed by the raillery of drunkards, and then been obliged to rush to Chippendale's workshop to avoid incurring his wrath. Was this not enough to throw any man into despondency and confusion?

Beads of sweat seeped from my forehead. I wiped my face with my sleeve. The more I dwelled on my frustrations, the more insistently a small voice in my head sounded. Was there some other reason for my muddled despair? Was I really so anxious to think quietly, or was I actually glad of these distractions for staving off the moment when I had to face myself and decide what my course of action should be?

Even now I couldn't bring myself to confront this question. Pushing it from my mind, I leaned forward to squint at the board Chippendale was showing me, before straightening myself and stepping back. "What of it?" I said brazenly.

"What of it?" he repeated incredulously. "Why, what d'you think of the grain, Nathaniel? Have I taught you nothing in all these years? D'you not see that this has been taken from the fork of a branch? Cut and polished, the figuring of it will be as meandering as a serpent. I shall guard it for my cabinet."

Suddenly he glanced at me and perceived that I was standing as rigid as the boards all around me. "Well," he said, replacing the wood in the stacks and turning towards me, "you return late, Nathaniel, and evidently in ill-humor. I trust you acquitted yourself well at Lord Montfort's, and that your tardiness has some explanation?"

"It was a tragedy not negligence delayed me," I declared, brushing a damp forelock from my brow.

"So," said Chippendale, waving his hand loftily, as if signaling a carriage to drive on, "explain yourself."

And so I outlined, in a rather garbled fashion, the awful events I'd witnessed. I told him how I'd installed the library bookcase in time for the dinner, but that Montfort had been out of sorts. I told him that during the dinner I'd found Lord Montfort's dead body in the library surrounded by drawings taken from his book. I told him that there was a question over the nature of Montfort's death: some believed he'd killed himself; others, myself included, held that he was murdered. And finally, my voice shaking, I told him how the next day I'd been on my way back to London when I'd discovered poor Partridge, mutilated and frozen to death in the pond.

For several minutes after hearing this sorry tale, Chippendale said nothing. When at length he spoke, it was to express his chagrin, not for Montfort or Partridge but for his drawings. It was their fate that concerned him most deeply. He seemed visibly to tremble when I mentioned I had retrieved them from the floor around Montfort's corpse.

"What became of my designs, Nathaniel? Were they damaged? Why did you not return with them?"

"I did not know under what circumstances the drawings were at Horseheath. How should I think to seize them? For all I knew you had sold them to Lord Montfort."

"Would I sell something so precious? Something that is the keystone of my success?"

I shrugged noncommittally, although I seethed at his callousness. Was there to be not a word of regret for Partridge?

"Where are they now?" he barked.

"I am not entirely certain. I presume them to be either at Horseheath, where I left them, or seized by Lord Foley as part of his debt."

He shook his head slowly. "This is indeed a tragedy beyond compare."

I knew he meant the drawings, not poor Partridge. He'd yet to make a mention of his name.

"Let us discuss it further, for there is much I would tell you," said Chippendale. "Come with me."

As he issued this command he sighed deeply and regarded his hands. Wood dirt had lodged itself beneath his fingernails in several places, sullying his flawless manicure. Observing this simple gesture, I was reminded vividly of poor Partridge's mutilated hand and felt sickened to the core. Chippendale might be able to pass over such a death without comment, but I was haunted by it. I would never forget the icy pond, the frozen body, the blood. I saw it even now as I watched Chippendale. What manner of monster could perpetrate such an atrocity on a fellow man? What manner of monster was Chippendale to show no glimmer of pity for Partridge's suffering?

But was I any better than he? I ruefully recalled my own reluctance to cooperate with Foley, my taciturn response to his questions and request for assistance. It seemed to me now there was little logic to my hesitancy. I was honor bound to seek justice for my dead friend, yet like a coward I had resisted Foley. There was but one reason for my reluctance. Fear. My instinct for self-preservation. I had expected that once I left Horseheath I would feel safe, that the evil I had witnessed would remain within its boundaries, leaving me to go back to my carefree ways. And yet returning to London hadn't lightened my spirits or lessened my sense of peril one jot. The oppressive atmosphere of Horseheath Hall and the danger I had sensed there remained with me. Uneasiness shadowed me; any attempt on my part to probe into the events of the past days might draw down on me the attention of the killer. The two corpses I'd witnessed were harrowing enough. I couldn't bear to contemplate another death, let alone my own.

Yet I had to acknowledge that this cowardly apprehension didn't tally with my steadfast loyalty to Partridge. I had told Westleigh and Foley that Partridge couldn't be Montfort's killer, but how could I be sure when I hadn't the first notion who his killer was? Both deaths were complex, and it was obvious that Westleigh with his Montfort family allegiances and Foley with his financial interests were hopelessly ill-suited to the task of unraveling them. Thus, despite my reservations, fears, and doubts, my mind was driven helplessly towards the inevitable conclusion. Whatever the dangers to my own person, I had no choice but to remain involved with the investigations. Not to do so would be a final betrayal of Partridge.

Chippendale led the way down the dingy staircase, which opened into the bustle of the upholsterers' shop. Here, amid sacks of horsehair and bales of webbing and canvas, a dozen women were busily engaged in stuffing and combing and gossiping and stitching. Chippendale strode in saying nothing to any of them. His broad-shouldered physique and coal black hair seemed to cast a cloud over the entire room, and the chatter within subsided. The master was present: all could see his knotted brow and chiseled expression, and no one wanted his foul temper to fall on them.

Only Molly Bullock, who was tacking sky blue moreen to a chairback, failed to notice Chippendale's arrival. I was stepping neatly over a mound of hair when she raised her eyes and smiled straight at me. Like sunshine in a leaden sky, for an instant her smile lifted the gloom in that room. I winked back. Her companion spied this boldness and couldn't stop herself from nudging Molly sharply in the ribs. "Your cheeks are redder than holly berries, Molly Bullock. Is it fever or the oven that warms you? Or perhaps you have some other malady," she whispered loudly.

The sound of nervous giggles drifted out of the upholstery shop and followed us to the muddy yard outside. We skirted the cabinetmakers' workshop, feather rooms, storerooms, and chair rooms, making our way towards the front of the premises. The yard was shaped like a decanter, broad at the rear, narrowing to a long covered passage at the entrance to St. Martin's Lane, where stood three adjacent premises leased by Chippendale. Two made up the showroom. The third was his private residence. It was towards this building that he now directed his steps.

We came in through the side entrance, where a cramped corridor led to a small dark hall. Chippendale opened a door to an oak-paneled room. "Wait for me in the parlor," he said. "I must go to my closet before speaking with you."

I suppose Chippendale's extraordinary reaction to the news of Montfort's and Partridge's deaths shouldn't have startled me. I knew his work was all to him. I was aware he viewed all softer passions as mere distractions. Partridge and I had often heard him across the street in Slaughter's coffeehouse, where he'd expound his views on his profession to any man who would listen. He was at the pinnacle of his career, yet the middling state of his craft irked him. "What unjust arbiter decreed that artists and architects, silversmiths and clockmakers and makers of porcelain pots should be the pride of monarchs, while cabinetmakers are accorded only cursory consideration? Why is wood inferior to metal or stone or canvas or clay? Furniture making is an art as noble as any, and equally worthy of the attention of men of discernment. For what use are noble architecture and inspiring paintings without the furnishings that allow man to enjoy them?" he would demand, thumping his fist upon the table, rattling the coffee cups in their saucers. "Without its chairs and sofas and tables and beds a mansion or a palace is no more welcoming or inspiring than a tomb."

If anyone dared dispute this argument, he was vigorously tested. Eyes blazing beneath crow black brows, Chippendale would insist that his disputant "name then a single art so closely bound to the complexion of man." The silence allowed him to drive home his point. "A chair, you can only agree, embodies this fact. A stool underlines the humility of a servant, a throne the status of a king. And in between there is every permutation imaginable, all tailored to the size, shape, bearing of man. What other art can claim such significance?"

But his professional disgruntlement did not explain his heartless reaction to the news of Partridge's death, nor his inordinate concern for the drawings. Was a life so little to him? Particularly a life of such exceptional talent? Why did he value a handful of sketches so highly?

When he returned, he gave no sign of what was coming. His hair was tidied and tied smooth as a jet-black shell, his face the usual stony mask; the only indication of emotion was in the keenness with which his flinty eyes glinted in the firelight. He drew up his favorite chair—mahogany, with a back carved like a cathedral window. "Of course, like most troubles in life, this one centers on money," he volunteered somewhat unexpectedly. "I'm speaking of how it was that Montfort came to be in possession of the drawings from my *Director,* the book that established my reputation and has made my name known from Edinburgh to Truro."

Here I should explain that two years ago Chippendale took the greatest risk of his career. In the manner of a gentleman architect or a man of letters, he published a series of his own designs, *The Gentleman and Cabinet Maker's Director—Being a Large Collection of the Most Elegant and Useful Designs of Household Furniture in the Gothic, Chinese, and Modern Taste.* The pages of this mighty volume featured engravings of chairs, sofas, beds, commodes, desks, girandoles, screens, glasses, candlestands and bookcases, and much more besides. This was a volume intended to impress. No other London cabinetmaker had promoted themselves in such a manner. Several of his Slaughter's coffee-sipping acquaintances had snorted at the audacity of it. "Why, Chippendale the carpenter will have us bow to him as a man of taste. Pray tell us, Mr. Chippendale, what is your view on the gothic, and of the fashion for chinoiseries? Are they extravagant enough? Do you approve?"

He had answered their raillery defiantly, writing in the preface to his volume, "I am not afraid of the fate an author usually meets with on his first appearance, from a set of critics who are never wanting to show their wit and malice on the performance of others. I repay their censures with contempt."

What I did not until now comprehend was that to publish his book he had required financial assistance, which his usual backer, a Scottish merchant, having recently advanced a large sum for the setting up of the St. Martin's Lane premises, could not provide.

Chippendale gazed at the tongues of fire consuming the coals. He appeared to have almost forgotten my presence and was speaking candidly, confessionally even. "Soon after the opening of this new emporium, Henry Montfort presented himself—a discerning patron of the arts, in great need of a quantity of furnishings. As is my habit in such instances, I journeyed to Cambridge to take measurements and discuss his requirements in greater detail. The preliminary sketches I drew impressed him, and his flattery encouraged me to confide that I wished to publish a book of my drawings. He was interested in providing the necessary backing and offered the entire sum required. His terms were reasonable, the interest modest. The only security he demanded was the original drawings from which the engravings were made."

He paused and stared at me as if trying to gauge my reaction to what he was saying. I met his eye impassively, saying nothing.

"All this took place two years ago. Since then, as you know, the publication has been remarkably successful and the loan was repaid as agreed. *But the drawings were never returned.*" Here he paused and breathed deeply, as if he were battling inwardly with himself. "Each time I raised the matter Montfort stalled, citing some new commission that had yet to be completed, that bore no relation to the original agreement. I was anxious to give no offense, for Montfort was powerful enough to do inestimable damage to my reputation. Yet I also knew that unless I capitalized on the success of the first edition and published a second, my competitors would follow my lead and gain ground on me."

Against my better judgment I was drawn into Chippendale's dilemma. "But what did it matter if he had the drawings? You had the engraving plates. You could make a new edition from those, surely?"

"But the drawings Montfort had in his possession were virtually my entire collection of designs, *far more* than those that were eventually published in the *Director.* Many of these drawings were unique, for I'd made no copies of them; among them were some of my finest, most ingenious ideas, which I intended to use for the second edition. It would take years for me to repeat them all, by which time I'd have lost my advantage over my competitors."

"But why did Lord Montfort not keep to his agreement and return the drawings?"

"Montfort, as you have remarked, was an unpredictable and often unreasonable patron. He was also an avid collector who took great delight in amassing treasures for his house. He realized when the book made its mark that the original drawings for it would be of great value, a trophy in his collection. Perhaps he intended to try to buy them from me. As for the other drawings, the unpublished ones, I believe when he saw how urgently I wanted them he held on to them as a lever to get the library completed speedily and to his satisfaction. Doubtless, were it not for his death, he would now have returned them."

I thought this highly unlikely but didn't trouble myself to say so, for it was neither here nor there now. "Did anyone else know of this arrangement?"

"No one save Montfort and myself. There were letters of agreement between us, some of which I have here," he said, pointing to his bureau. "And so to the solution I have in mind—the reason I've confided in you, Nathaniel."

"What do you mean?"

"The death of Montfort is unfortunate as regards my payment for the library, but it puts a new—happier—complexion on the matter of the drawings. There is no reason now for them to be withheld. I have ample documentation to prove my case. I wish you to return immediately to Horseheath Hall with these documents and a letter from me, show them to the attorney Wallace, and recover my drawings. Then my unhappy predicament will be resolved."

I scratched my earlobe. "There is another matter that may hinder the immediate return of the drawings."

"What, pray, is that?"

"It concerns Partridge."

"Partridge has nothing to do with it."

"I am certain he does, sir. Have I not already told you I found him dead in the grounds of Horseheath Hall? In any event I have learned that a few days before his death Partridge called on Lord Montfort."

Chippendale's brows knitted together; his voice was biting. "Impossible. He wouldn't have dared."

"It seems he did. According to Miss Alleyn, Lord Montfort's sister, he came expressly to Horseheath to request a loan to establish himself in business. Her story is borne out by the fact that some of his drawings were mingled with yours in the library when Lord Montfort's body was found."

If my revelation unsettled Chippendale, it was only for an instant. "But what does this matter, since neither Partridge nor Montfort is here to plague us?"

I clenched my fists on the armrests of the chair so tightly that my knuckles bleached. Violence boiled within me. How I longed to take him by the collar and shake him till his brains rattled in his skull; instead I struggled to contain myself and put on an air of detachment. "Partridge's death confuses the issue. The justice, Sir James Westleigh, may wish to hold all the drawings until both deaths are resolved."

Chippendale snorted like an angry bull. "So Partridge thwarts me even in death. He deserves the end he met."

My head trembled. I lowered my gaze to examine my boots. I couldn't bear to meet his eyes, so intense was the loathing I felt for him at that moment. "Sir," I said, "why was it that Partridge believed Lord Montfort might assist him? Why did he need assistance? Particularly when you told me he was on his sickbed?"

There was a long pause, during which I scrutinized him intently. Unable to meet the gaze I leveled at him, Chippendale rose from his seat and walked to the window. It gave out onto the street, where a noisy vendor was waving his arms about, touting oranges to passersby. When he turned back his expression was bland and ingenuous. "I'm as ignorant as you on the matter."

I looked deeper into his eyes and thought I caught a flicker of something. What was it? Fear? Anger? Guilt? Whatever it was, I knew I didn't believe him. But before I could pose any further interrogation, a lady's voice was heard floating from the yard outside. Its tone was deep and melodious, with a faintly foreign timbre. She was arguing hotly with the apprentice boy, Craggs, who could be heard attempting—vainly—to halt her progress.

"Madam, I would beg you to wait in the showrooms while I call Mr. Chippendale to attend you. This is his private residence, he does not receive his patrons here," he stuttered, as her voice drew ever closer to the front door.

"Do you not know me, boy? I am Madame Trenti. Your master will be enchanted to receive me wherever I chance upon him."

"Nevertheless, madam, you would be more comfortable in the showroom. Mr. Chippendale will come directly to you."

She ignored him. Having rattled the door loudly, she swept past the unfortunate servant girl who answered it. Observing the parlor door ajar and Chippendale and me within, she announced herself with a rustle of petticoats and a twitch of the plume upon her hat. We stood respectfully. La Trenti, as she was billed in Drury Lane, was appareled in a wide hooped petticoat that filled the narrow doorway entirely. Craggs was hopping up and down in the hall, for he could not politely get past her to effect the correct introductions.

"Mr. Chippendale, sir, Madame Trenti demanded that I bring her to you. She would not wait in the shop," he blurted from behind her ballooning skirts.

Madame Trenti smiled alluringly, turned herself sideways, and edged through the door. In the center of the room she unfastened her cloak, like a flower opening its petals, to reveal a petticoat of buttercup yellow beneath a robe of purple tabinet. She smiled at Chippendale, revealing a row of faintly yellow teeth. "I trust you were expecting me."

He bowed low over the outstretched hand she proffered, his face a model of politeness. "Indeed, madam, I am, as always, honored to receive you. I trust you will forgive our modest surroundings, for there is something of great importance I have to show you."

"I am all impatience. Does it concern my furnishings?"

"Madam, I have concocted for you a design of such splendor as would make a monarch reel. Have you acquired a suitable residence?"

"There is a vacant mansion in Soho Square. . . . I am in discussion."

While the design was sent for, Madame Trenti, with my assistance, eased herself into the best chair the room could provide. Meanwhile Chippendale flattered her zealously.

"Your Cordelia I've heard was a triumph."

"The critics were kind. Did you attend?"

"I did not need to attend to hear the thunderous applause. It reverberated throughout the city."

"You are too generous. But yes, in truth, I believe my reputation does increase."

"No critic can do justice to the universal acclaim you so richly deserve for your radiance and your talent . . ."

A shaft of wintry sunlight flooded the room and fell on her face. Once she must have been a beauty, but now her skillful application of powder, rouge, and patches could not mask the shrinking flesh. I was reminded of a mannequin doll sént back and forth from Paris clad in miniature versions of the latest modes, whose paint had chipped with passing years.

When the designs were brought, Chippendale passed them to her one by one, explaining the significance of every pen stroke. "The drawings, madam, are for the king of all furniture: I speak, as I am sure you have guessed, of a writing cabinet . . . a cabinet of such curiosity and complexity as will cause everyone who sees it to marvel."

She rustled her skirts with impatient delight as he explained his vision. Every detail of the cabinet had been delineated; it was as real to him as the chairs on which they sat. "Picture yourself, madam, in the best room of your mansion, dressed in your finest silk, displaying this masterpiece to your callers, teasing them to discover the secrets held within. To an accomplished actress such as yourself I hardly need explain how such an extravagant prop will charm them, intrigue them . . ."

"Indeed, Mr. Chippendale, it sounds most enticing. Pray show me how it will operate."

"Perhaps a young gallant might press this catch, remove a section of the façade, and reveal a hidden arcade, which thanks to the judicious positioning of mirrors will seem to stretch to infinity. Next he will discover the hidden niche in which a figurine is concealed. Then the grand finale . . ."

"A grand finale?"

"You will step forward. You will turn this column, which will trigger a movable panel here, behind which some truly astonishing secret will be concealed."

She was quivering visibly, fluttering her hands with childlike expectation. "And what might that be?"

Chippendale held up a calming hand. "That, madam, is a matter for discussion and thought." He paused emphatically. "I believe it should be something precious yet personal. Perhaps a miniature in enamel, or a musical figurine in your form that dances . . ."

"Or a jewel of some description," said she, warming to his theme. "How magnificent it will be. I can hardly bear to wait. How long will it take to execute?"

"It is begun already, but still it will take a matter of some weeks, madam—for as you can see it is an object of great, indeed, I daresay, unparalleled complexity."

Her face fell a little. "And the price?"

"Such a unique and extravagant piece will of necessity require the best materials and craftsmen of the highest skill . . ."

She nodded her head briskly and handed the drawings back.

"Then let us talk of it later. I would not think of money in the face of such beauty. Let us consider instead the decoration. You have a talented craftsman," she said. "The young man to whom I spoke on my last visit. The foundling. He will surely be capable of this work. I am convinced from the last piece you supplied that his carving rivals the best in Europe, and is unmatched in this country."

"Madam, the craftsman of whom you speak, Partridge, is as you so rightly say an expert carver. But therein lies his greatest skill. You will see from these drawings there is little carving in this. The decoration is inlaid with marquetry and cast metal mounts. Pictures made from wood. Golden statues. An unfamiliar method of decoration these last decades, but one that will be intoxicating in its beauty."

Her face puckered with disapproval. "I would not wish anything that is outmoded."

"It is a style that already holds France, and will rapidly return to these shores. With this cabinet in your rooms you will be regarded as fashion's founding goddess rather than her slavish handmaiden."

She looked only slightly appeased. "Nevertheless I desire that Partridge work on it. If he can carve with such genius he can surely cut out shapes from wood with similar inspiration."

"Mr. Partridge is no longer with us."

There was a silence as she fixed him with her olive green eyes and raised a perfectly arched mouse-hair brow. "I am astonished to hear it. Where is he?"

Chippendale regarded her smoothly. "He has left London."

"What do you mean?"

"He means Partridge is dead," I interrupted coldly.

Madame Trenti turned to me, gasped in astonishment, and turned back to Chippendale. "Are you quite certain? Is there not some mistake?" She reached into her muff, withdrew her salts, and sniffed them loudly before leaning back in her chair and half closing her eyes.

Chippendale's eyes were blazing now, and his voice, when he addressed me, was chilling. "Nathaniel, do you not have duties to attend to? You are not required here and may leave us if you please."

I am not a man who delights in physical violence, yet I confess that at that moment my earlier desire to jump at him returned more forcefully, and it was all I could do to prevent myself from flooring him. In truth the reason I held back was mainly that I was afraid; I was fearful of my master, afraid of insulting him and incurring his further fury. And so I held on to what remained of my dignity. I drew myself up to my full six feet two inches and bowed briefly to Madame Trenti, who was still lying back in her chair wafting her bottle beneath her nose. "Good day, madam," I said and turned on my heels without saying a word more to my master.

For an hour after returning to the cabinetmakers' workshop, I sat at my desk and wrestled with a large-scale working drawing on which I was detailing the construction and dimensions of a circular table. I was still seething and spoke to none of the other craftsmen working in the same room. From time to time, however, I broke off my calculations to glance out of the window to the yard below. At midday I saw the rear door to Chippendale's residence open. Chippendale emerged, alone.

I put down my quill and rule and hurried out through the narrow passage from the yard to the street. By the time I arrived, Madame Trenti had already stepped into her sedan chair, the door was fastened, and her bearers were set to convey her hence. She caught sight of me careering towards her. "Mr. Hopson?" she said, leaning carefully out of the window so her plumage did not catch. "Is it I you seek?" She seemed to have recovered from her shock at the news of Partridge's death, for she gave me a glance that was practically flirtatious.

"There was something you said, madam. I wondered if I might presume upon you to explain it."

"What was it?"

"When you spoke of Partridge, you called him 'the foundling.' This was a matter of which he rarely spoke. I am intrigued to discover how you knew of it."

There was a long interval before she smiled beguilingly at me. "I too had intended to interrogate you more on the matter of Mr. Partridge. But first, pray tell me, why was it that Mr. Chippendale seemed so averse to our discussion?"

The suddenness of her question caught me by surprise. I didn't know how I should respond. But before I could stutter a reply, she waved her fan at me. "Have I baffled you, Mr. Hopson? Perhaps the matter is of no consequence. In any event what I wished to say was this—news of Partridge's death came as a profound shock. He was more to me than you know. Come to my lodgings tomorrow afternoon and we will satisfy each other's curiosity."

Chapter Seven

Sleet was falling from a pewter sky as later that same afternoon I made my way to the Strand to call on Alice. I need hardly mention that I went with my spirits in a lather of confusion. I had fretted about our postponed outing. I prayed she would have received the hastily written note explaining the reason for my absence. How would she greet my sudden reappearance? Would she chastise me for my failure to keep to our rendezvous? Would she feign indifference, and treat me with the businesslike detachment she had always employed until our last encounter? Each time I turned the matter over in my mind these wretched anxieties consumed me.

The warehouse, an imposing brick-built edifice four windows wide and three stories high, stood at the northern reaches of the Strand, beyond the Exeter Exchange, between a draper and a bookseller's. I entered through a cavernous hallway devoid of all furnishings but strewn with boards, planks, splinters, and shavings, in short, wood of every form. A narrow corridor led me into a small office, where I found Alice seated at an old oak table with a lighted lamp before her. From the number of handwritten sheets strewn around, it seemed she was in the midst of writing a letter.

I cleared my throat and gently, so as not to startle her, announced myself. "Miss Goodchild, how pleasant to see you again."

She looked up suddenly, then sprang to her feet. "Mr. Hopson! What an unexpected entrance. I didn't hear you knock."

My heart lightened unmistakably. "Perhaps that is because in my impatience to see you I forgot to do so."

"Are you well after your journey from Cambridge? Your note reached me—and Fetherby the driver tells me you encountered great sorrows there. I mean the death of your friend Partridge." I fancied I saw color flood her complexion, and there was understanding in her voice.

"I'm glad you knew where I was, even though I wish it had not been Fetherby who told you of what had transpired." Fetherby was employed by Chippendale to transport goods to and fro. I could not imagine anyone less suited to relay such delicate information.

"The loss must grieve you greatly. I too was shocked by the news of his death. Partridge visited here from time to time, when he had particular requirements."

I nodded, grateful for her sympathy. "The reason I've come so speedily to see you," I declared, remembering how I'd postponed even Molly Bullock's lusty embrace, "is that I'm anxious to find out what I can about this object." I removed the temple box from my pocket and passed it to her. "I wondered if you could identify the wood. It's unlike anything I've ever seen."

She placed the box close to the glass shade of her lantern before taking a magnifying glass and bending over it to examine the pattern of the wood, looking in turn at the flat-grained roof, the turned columns, the carved capitals and cornice. After some minutes she shook her head slightly, drew back from the light, and handed the box back. "The light is too poor to be certain, but it's unlike anything I've ever seen either—although I've no doubt if my father were here he'd know it."

I was disappointed, and my face must have showed it. "May I leave it with you and return tomorrow when you have viewed it in daylight? I don't wish to inconvenience you, but I fear there's no one better qualified to recognize it."

My crestfallen expression must have moved her, and I suppose she may have been a little flattered by my high opinion of her talents. She returned her attentions to the box, narrowing her eyes as if searching her memory for something. Suddenly her face cleared and she looked back at me. "Perhaps there is something I can do. . . . If you wait while I finish this letter, I've something to show you that may assist you."

For the next half hour, I sat in a chair while she continued with her letter. It was no hardship for me to wait. Her mind was obviously rapt in writing, and she ignored me so completely that I passed the time happily, studying her at my leisure. She was simply dressed in a well-cut cloth jacket and petticoat of deepest blue that served only to accentuate the fineness of her figure. Her hair was piled up in a white gauze cap with a single thick ringlet falling from one side onto her shoulder, where it shone like well-seasoned mahogany. She wrote fluently, forming her letters in generous loops, stopping only occasionally to dip her pen and gaze at the lamp as she searched for the right word or phrase, or referred to a page written in crabbed script beside her.

I should confess here that my interest in Alice had already led me to discover a little of her family circumstances from George Fetherby, the aged and garrulous carter. According to his information, Alice's father, John Goodchild, had left London to attend to his interests overseas, following the sudden death of his wife. Alice, though little prepared for trade, had been left in charge of the London side of the business.

"Do you write to your father?" I inquired, when she looked up after some time and caught my eye.

"Every week. There's much to master in this business."

"That's most commendable. And does he reply as regularly?"

She lowered her eyes to her script. "His letters are dependent on the whims of the weather and merchantmen returning from the colonies. He does his best."

Some minutes later she put down her pen, assembled her sheets in order—there were six in all—addressed them, and sealed the package.

"Come," she said, putting the letter she had written in her pocket, "I will send my brother to dispatch this and then you will have my full attention. Let's hope what I have to show you will be worth your patience."

She led the way through the warehouse proper, past hulking pyramids of boards, to the rear. A large oak double door, with a smaller entrance set in it, opened to the yard and her Dutch-gabled cottage beyond. Drawing back the bolts of the small aperture, she gathered her skirts in one hand and, without a backward glance, ran nimbly through the arrows of sleet to her front door. I lumbered behind, spattering my knitted stockings with globules of mud in my effort to keep pace.

Her brother was already returned from his school. He had the parlor fire roaring and was now seated beside it, busily constructing a ship's model. The hull had been carefully carved, and the masts had been stepped. He was fixing the cotton rigging.

"That's an impressive piece of work."

"A replica of the Indiaman *The Duke of Portland,* on which my father sailed," he declared proudly.

"I believe it was Mr. Partridge who gave him the idea," said his sister. "He came to the yard one day quite recently when Richard was at home and listless. Partridge distracted him with his suggestion of building the model and helped him begin it."

"It doesn't surprise me," I said. "He had a generous disposition, and no family of his own, and always profoundly regretted it."

"I didn't know it," said Alice. "How very tragic his short life was." She hesitated for a moment, looking at me as though she wished to ask more. Then, perhaps fearing her curiosity might be misconstrued, she turned to her brother and gave him the letter to post. There was an Indiaman due to leave as soon as the tides and winds were favorable, and she was anxious her letter should be on it.

No sooner had he left us than she took a key from the wooden box on the side table, handed me a lit candle, and led me back across the hallway to a small oak-paneled drawing room. The chill struck me as I entered. After the warmth of the blazing parlor fire, the air in here was cold and damp. No fire had been lit, the shutters were drawn, and the furniture veiled by dust sheets.

"My father sat here every evening to read while my mother did her needlework," she said, a shadow crossing her face. "These days my brother and I almost never come in here. That was why I nearly overlooked what I want to show you. It is this."

She pointed towards the far wall, where between a pair of tarnished brass sconces, a large looking glass hung by a rusty chain. She lighted the dusty candle stubs in the holders. The flames spluttered, grew tall, and were magnified in the silvered glass. Our reflections were likewise warped into elongated figures scarce recognizable as our own. The glass was mounted into a broad, flat frame intricately adorned with marquetry. I knew this form of decoration. Half a century and more ago it had been perfected by Dutch craftsmen who taught our native makers how to shade the wood like an artist's shadows using hot sand. But this was different. For a start, it was richer than any I had hitherto observed. Into a whorling background of walnut oyster veneers were inserted jewel-like marquetry panels of peonies, tulips, and scrolling foliage intertwined with exotically plumed birds. Unusually, it was unfaded by sunlight; the hues of the various woods encompassed every shade of yellow, red, green, and brown, creating images worthy of the Garden of Eden.

"Remarkable," I said. "It might be painted, and yet every petal has been formed with tiny morsels of wood, some cut narrower than a reed."

Alice looked gratified by my admiration. "The style is now obsolete, I know," she said, "but I'm fond of it, for it holds family associations. It occurred to me the multiplicity of timbers contained within this small area might assist you in your inquiry. The frame is almost a dictionary of woods; there must be a chance that the same wood is contained here as in your box."

"How will that help me to identify it?"

"That's not all I have to show you. Look here."

She walked to the adjacent wall, where she drew back a dust sheet covering a plain oak bureau. She unlocked the top drawer and extracted a yellowing paper, which she unfolded and held close to the flame. I could just make out a faint pencil drawing of flowers and birds identical to those adorning the mirror.

"The mirror frame was constructed by my aunt Charlotte, my father's sister. She was fascinated by the number of exotic timbers in the warehouse, and her greatest ambition was to become a marquetry cutter."

"And did she?"

"Her father was greatly averse to the idea. He was a prosperous merchant, and as all fathers do, he wished his daughter to marry well and thus advance the family fortune. Her story is a sad one, and I will not tire you with the details. Suffice it to say that for some time she did persist clandestinely, as this mirror testifies. After she died, this and the working drawing she made for it were handed to my father. If you examine it, you will find every morsel of wood she has used in the mirror is named."

With Alice's assistance I detached the mirror from the wall and carried it back to the parlor. We laid it on the table, spread the drawing beside it, and spent the next hour very agreeably, seated side by side, moving the box next to each sample of wood to see if we could discover a match. The woods were so minutely cut that this task necessitated the closest observation. Most in the jigsaw were familiar to me: holly, laburnum, box, ebony, tulipwood, amboyna. I scrutinized each one hard, searching vainly for a timber with the same distinctive streaked rays and straight grain as the box. Only occasionally did I tire of this search and allow myself to glance in the mirror glass, at our heads close together, her curls tumbling from the cap, so near that I could feel them brushing my cheek.

Eventually she pointed with the tip of a pencil to the vivid tail feathers of a bird. "Look here," she said softly. "I believe this is it."

I moved the box close. It was identical.

"It seems that this timber is employed in this one portion alone," said Alice, who was already busily referring to the drawing. "Its name she has written as *Caesalpinia granadillo,* underlined, as if there's some special significance to it."

"Grenadillo wood."

"Perhaps it was a great rarity and that was the reason for the underlining."

"Have you ever heard of it?"

She frowned and shook her head. "I am as ignorant as you, although I can consult the ledgers to discover where it originates."

"I wouldn't put you to so much inconvenience."

"It's no trouble," she said firmly.

At this instant her brother returned. Stamping his feet with cold, he threw off his greatcoat and made straight for the fire. For several minutes he stood there, clearly bewildered to find us leaning close together over the mirror. I stood up and went to stand with my back to the fire. I smiled at him amiably. I felt sorry to be the cause of his confusion, but more than that, I was reluctant to leave.

"I believe your brother deserves a meal after the errand he has just completed. And I can see he is perplexed at our activities. Will you allow me to take you both to supper and we can reveal to him what we are doing?"

She glanced intently at Richard's hungry face, smiled, and he smiled back. "Gladly," she replied.

We went out immediately. I paid a links boy to light our way, though I needn't have bothered. The weather had cleared, and a brilliant half-moon illuminated the street and turned everything in it to silver. Bathed in this ghostly light, the city was transformed to a magical place. It seemed the Strand resembled a luminous river over which we floated, while all around iridescent hawkers of chestnuts, oranges, and oysters wafted like sprites.

The air of enchantment vanished as soon as we reached Clifton's, a commendable chophouse in Butcher Row. An exhibition of amateur boxing was to be held that night at the tavern next door, and the crowd had overflowed here. The main rooms brimmed with the stench of mingled tobacco and ale, and the babble of spectators placing bets, cracking jokes, telling yarns, insulting one another. What Alice made of this city soup I couldn't guess, for to speak above the rowdiness was impossible. I thumped on the bar, shouting out for a table away from the throng. The obliging landlord showed us to a quiet room, where we sat in high-backed settles before a blazing fire, she and her brother on one side, I on the other, a rough trestle table and a candlestick between us. After an excellent meal of neat's tongue, boiled salad, liver pudding, and wine, Richard begged to be allowed to watch the entertainment and Alice laughingly agreed. He left us. Her eyes glittered and her complexion glowed with the wine, the nourishment, the friendliness. I felt emboldened to speak more freely.

"I trust the press and noise does not offend you," I ventured.

She laughed and shook her head. "Of course not. If I'm quieter, or less forward, than your usual companions it's because I so rarely enjoy company."

"My usual companions?"

She looked at me levelly. "Mr. Hopson, you must know your reputation for gallantry precedes you."

"Must I?"

"Fetherby remarks on it constantly."

I could happily have throttled the talkative carter. "It is ill-deserved, Miss Goodchild, I can assure you of that." I felt a small prick of conscience for this insincerity and hurried on to crush it. "Though I confess I enjoy company—that of both sexes—as much as any sociable young man. Yet you say you do not enjoy it?"

"I said no such thing. What I meant was that I rarely experience company, not that I don't enjoy it. I have no choice in the matter."

"Why is that?"

With evident reticence she began to tell me a little of her family circumstances. The Goodchild enterprise had been founded two generations earlier by Alice's grandfather, Jan Gudhuis. He was a Dutch sea captain turned merchant who'd retired from the sea and migrated to London along with sundry silk weavers, silversmiths, cabinetmakers, and moneylenders shadowing the Dutch King William of Orange. The decision proved shrewd. Within a few years providence and swelling profit allowed him to acquire the premises in the Strand and assume the life of a prosperous merchant. He concluded then that the more he forgot his native land and blended with his new surroundings, the easier the citizens of London would be in their dealings with him, and his commerce might further benefit. Thus had he changed his name to Goodchild and wedded a clockmaker's pretty daughter from Clerkenwell. They had two children: a daughter named Charlotte—the maker of the mirror—and a son, Alice's father, whom they named John. Charlotte died young, as I'd already learned. John took over the running of the business, married, and was blessed first with a daughter and then with a son—Alice and her brother, Richard.

"But that doesn't explain why you find yourself charged with such burdens when your father is still alive," I prompted, when her account trailed to silence.

For several minutes Alice regarded her glass. When at length she spoke, her eyes glistened, and I could see each word she uttered was painful.

"The family was thrown into disarray when my mother died suddenly in a smallpox epidemic. Without his wife to anchor him, my father felt he no longer belonged in this city. He yearned to distance himself from London. His head became filled with rambling thoughts; he was as careless of his enterprise as he was of his children, preferring to pore over travel journals, imagining the fertile hills and valleys and the strange trees and plants and creatures they described." She halted again.

"And where did his preoccupation lead him?"

"Nine months ago his passion for escape—for that is what it was—finally consumed him. He packed up his few possessions and, leaving me in charge of the warehouse and my young brother, set sail for Jamaica. He had heard talk of rich new sources of mahogany and other, rarer tropical timbers for which every cabinetmaker in London clamored. He would return, he vowed, when his thirst for travel was satisfied and when new supplies had been established."

"That's sad for you," I said. "For some would say he's neglectful of his responsibility to you and your brother."

She shifted on her bench and drummed her fingers softly on the table. Her russet hair tumbled softly from its bindings, glowing richer than the embers in the hearth, but her mouth and chin were set stern. "I don't view it in that manner. If he's found some solace then I'm glad for it. I trust he'll return when he's ready."

Now her account was complete her voice sounded pluckier, impatient even, with no hint of a tremor. She looked at me levelly, unblinking. I wondered if I'd imagined the earlier gleam of anguish in her eyes.

"And what of you and Richard meantime?"

"Richard's education continues uninterrupted. As for myself, why, I've opportunities few women enjoy: a business to run, little interference from anyone. I learn something new every day. There are many who would envy me."

"Are there no inconveniences in your situation? You are very young to take on responsibilities that properly belong to a man."

She waved an impatient hand as if my conventional view infuriated her. "There are those who disapprove of the manner in which I conduct my business, others who remark the negligence with which I run this house, the sea of papers and unwashed plates in my parlor. But the beauty of my situation is that I'm free of all obligation. I can disregard them."

"And you never yearn for the usual diversions a woman of your age and rank enjoys?"

She gave a half smile, her eyes shone, and for an instant I wondered if she were laughing at me. "Mr. Hopson, I would ask you to disregard my sex for a moment, if that is possible. Then you will begin to see why my primary concern must be to work hard to nurture the family enterprise and my brother. Other matters must take second place." She shot a knowing look in my direction and smiled more openly. "In any case I confess that, after nine months of business, a return to sewing and taking tea and promenading in the park doesn't seem so very diverting."

I laughed out loud at her wit and mettle. Her conviction that dogged-ness and energy were all she needed to surmount her tricky situation amused me. "I can't think of many who'd view the situation as you do, Miss Goodchild," I said, "though as to disregarding your sex, why, with such an abundance of charms as nature has bestowed on you, that would be utterly impossible."

She looked away. "You flatter me, Mr. Hopson. I've a reputation, as you must know, for being less ladylike than I should be, for speaking as plainly—even as rudely—as a man on occasion. But I'll tell you that I do so because I find the world of commerce is a man's world. I've been un-expectedly charged as the guardian of our family interest and have no al-ternative . . ." She was roused now, and her cheeks were flamed with feeling.

Instantly I cursed myself for my ill-timed compliment. "You needn't apologize to me for the strength of your resolve," I interjected soberly, anxious to smooth things as quickly as possible. "Only a fool would chas-tise you for it. In any case we have much in common, for I too have been charged with an unexpected duty. In my case the role is perhaps even more surprising."

Curiosity seemed to overcome her irritation. "What do you mean?"

"I've been assigned to discover the truth about Partridge."

She raised a quizzical eyebrow. "Searching for the truth preoccupies every one of us. But do we ever find the eternal verity of those we love? I think not. Most of us do not even know ourselves."

I furrowed my brow at this extraordinary response. What did she mean? I remembered suddenly my feelings of dismay when I'd discovered Partridge's secret involvement with Montfort. Was that what she meant? Had she too felt deceived by someone she believed she knew so profoundly? Her father perhaps? I wanted to pursue the matter further, but at that instant Richard reappeared, brimming with the excitement of the boxing he had witnessed.

"Tell me, Mr. Hopson," said he suddenly, "how did you come by the scar on your forehead? Were you ever a boxer?"

I laughed heartily at this and immediately forgot Alice's unsettling remark. "I've found myself in plenty of brawls but never in a professional capacity," I said. "As to the scar, that's another story. I'll tell you one day. For now I want to explain to you why I called on your sister today." I took out the temple box and showed it to him. "I came to find out what I could about this, for I believe it may shed light on the death of my friend Partridge. Your sister has discovered the name of the wood—grenadillo. We believe it is a great rarity, for neither of us knows it."

Richard took the box and, turning it in his hand, heard the contents shift.

"What's in it?" he demanded.

"That I do not yet know, for I have been unable to unlock it in the absence of the key."

He examined the box again. "I believe I might help you then," he said importantly.

"Indeed I should be grateful of any assistance, for I would prefer not to force it."

"I've a friend whose father is a master locksmith in Norfolk Street. If anyone can open it, it is he. And I've no doubt he'll do it gladly."

I smiled broadly at him and then at Alice. "That is mightily useful. Can I trust you to take this to him tomorrow and let me know when he has had time to look at it?"

He agreed to do as I asked, and with that we left the tavern. I walked with them the short distance to their cottage. At the door, without thinking, I bowed to Alice and kissed her hand. She accepted the gesture with a small curtsy and a smile. "Richard and I have enjoyed ourselves this evening, and we thank you heartily for it. I'll come in person or send word to you as soon as we discover anything more of your box, of that you may be assured."

The moon had vanished, but the sky remained clear and peppered with stars as I walked back to my lodgings, past the noble porticoes and walks of the Exeter Exchange. I knew the place was much vaunted as somewhere a man could find any mistress he required, and on occasion I'd sampled its diversions. Tonight, however, I'd no thought of them. I was more dizzy in spirit than if I'd drunk a flagon of wine, yet still strangely sober. I hunched my shoulders deeper into my coat and, without deflecting my gaze from the street ahead, walked briskly home.

Chapter Eight

Whitely Court   January 3, 1755

Sir

I arrive in London two days from hence and shall call on you directly to discover what progress you have made in the assignment we discussed. Meantime it might assist you to know the developments that have occurred here since your departure.

A search of the grounds has thus far yielded no sign of the severed fingers. This leads both Westleigh and myself to suppose they were either consumed by an animal or concealed—buried perhaps—by the perpetrator of this dreadful deed, so that finding them will prove impossible. A physician apothecary from Cambridge, Mr. Townes, a very astute man whose opinion I value highly, examined Mr. Partridge's body. He informs us that there was little water in Partridge's lungs. This and the manner in which he was embedded in the ice lead him to conclude that he lost consciousness due to the wounds to his hand and fell into the pond, dying soon afterwards. The blow to his head is too minor to have killed him but could, Mr. Townes says, have resulted when he fell. It is his opinion that the wounds to the hand were caused by a thick-bladed instrument, something like an ax. This would account, he says, for the bruising of the flesh and the manner in which the bone had splintered.

The groundsman verified what he told you regarding the removal of the ice to the icehouse. The men finished their work at four, when it grew dark. The man in question passed by the Italian Garden on his way to his cottage in the village at around seven and observed what he thought was the crouching figure of a man, although he cannot give any more detail than this. He fancies himself an expert in meteorological matters and estimated that the water would have been frozen too hard for a body to fall through by midnight. Therefore it is certain Partridge must have fallen into the pond in the early part of the evening, and it seems that the figure the groundsman saw may very well have been Partridge in the moments before his death.

Following his postmortem examination, the question arose of what to do with Mr. Partridge's remains. Since he had died within the estate, Miss Alleyn was charitable enough to order that, rather than being buried a pauper by the parish, Partridge should be given a decent burial in the grounds of the family chapel where servants are usually laid to rest. Robert Montfort attempted to dissuade her from this generosity, arguing that the family shouldn't pay to bury someone who was very possibly involved in his father's death. "What?" said Miss Alleyn. "Are you saying you no longer believe your father's death was suicide?" He fell silent then, seeing that if he admitted to believing his father was murdered he would have no means of preventing me from taking possession of a large portion of the estate. The burial will take place this afternoon.

Partridge's lodgings were traced to the Red Bull Inn in Cambridge. A search has revealed several pages of drawings and notes, which I will bring to show you. The drawings are, I confess, remarkably similar to several of those in the library, which you identified as being by his hand. I should add here that it is my intention to take all the drawings to Whitely and give them into the safekeeping of my librarian. My reason for this action is that no one at Horseheath regards them as having any worth; only today I found one sheet being used to line a damp drawer.

Lastly, I have also, since your departure, spent some time assisting Westleigh in searching through Montfort's papers. Among his correspondence I discovered the enclosed. We were unable to ascertain its author, but you may think, as I do, it has some bearing upon this matter. I have nothing more to add here but will discuss all this with you when we meet. You may expect me to call in the afternoon around four.

I trust that by now you have opened the box and will have its contents ready to reveal to me.

Foley

London   December 14, 1754

Sir

I write to inform you that, following your pitiless treatment of me twenty years ago, I have come to London to seek reparation. You do not need me to remind you how you took advantage of my youth and weakness in a most callous manner, abandoning me afterwards with promises that were nothing but falsehoods. You have ignored every letter I have sent, and I have consequently passed the intervening years mourning the loss of my child, biding my time until the opportunity arose to trace his whereabouts and make myself known to him.

That time is now arrived.

I am recently settled in London and have discovered (by what means I am not at liberty to discuss) the whereabouts of the child— who I now learn you also mercilessly abandoned many years ago. In the past days I have made contact with him, and I write to apprise you that at my behest he intends shortly to call on you.

Your behavior and your comfortable circumstances entitle both of us to expect restitution for the misery you have inflicted. Until now I have, with few exceptions, kept his unhappy history discreetly to myself. Should you fail to receive him or to compensate him fairly, I can assure you that the matter will be widely aired, as I have it in my means to ensure most effectively.

M. C.

Chapter Nine

I no longer recall how long I sat motionless. I no longer recall what I
felt—excitement, revelation, confusion—a little of all three? I remember only that question upon question spiraled through my skull. The
date on the second letter showed it was written three days before Partridge
disappeared. Could he be the lost child mentioned? Was that why he disappeared? This was evidently what Foley suspected, even if he had not said so
directly in his letter. Why would he bother to send it to me otherwise? As
quickly as this solution appeared I dismissed it. Foley did not appreciate the
closeness of the bond between Partridge and myself—could not know how
frequently Partridge had confided his desire to discover his past. Without his
history, he said, he lacked the very foundation of his future existence. Talent
and good prospects were no compensation for the void of not knowing who
you were or where you came from. I was confident that if Partridge had
learned something of his origins he would have told me of it. To keep such
a matter secret from someone who was closer than a brother to him, then
disappear without a word was surely inconceivable. Wasn't it?

With this thought the disquiet I'd felt at Horseheath when Miss Alleyn
had first disclosed Partridge's visit returned to trouble me. She had said
Partridge had fallen on hard times and had come in order to appeal to
her brother, Lord Montfort, for financial assistance. Was there more to his
petition than she mentioned? Did Partridge go to Montfort because he
believed him to be *his father*?

I felt heartily ashamed of myself, but I couldn't help my misgivings. There was no denying that Partridge *had* kept the reasons for his journey from me. Was it then possible that he had known more about his background and origins than he pretended? Was the tragic tale of his lost history no more than a fabrication to arouse sympathy? Yet the more I thought on it, the more it seemed to me improbably convenient that Partridge should be the child referred to in the letter.

I gazed at the floor, where a pile of corkscrew wood shavings, like perfect ringlets, had been swept into a mound. Who was the child? To discover this would be well nigh impossible. London seethed with countless wards, foster children, foundlings, and workhouse orphans, the dispossessed offspring of illicit or inopportune liaisons of every rank. The letter implied the child was sired by Montfort and raised by some convenient third party. Such arrangements were not unusual.

Yet how then to explain the appearance of Partridge at Montfort's estate? Whenever I asked myself this, a knot of anxiety, doubt, and suspicion gnawed away at me. The thought kept coming back that Partridge's appearance at Horseheath was clear proof I *didn't* know him as well as I believed, that he was not the transparent soul I'd taken him for. I recalled Alice's words to me the previous night. *Searching for the truth preoccupies every one of us. . . . Most of us do not even know ourselves.* The notion was alien to me. I was blessed with loving parents and a profession—a past and a future—that were the foundation of my self-belief. I knew precisely who I was. Furthermore, I'd believed (naïvely?) I knew Partridge better than anyone. His death had shown me otherwise.

I turned from this discomfiting realization. Far easier to concentrate on the author of the letter. Who was she? A lady who harbored great animosity towards Montfort, to judge from the tone of her writing. Someone who had recently come to London. The initials M. C. had a certain resonance, an echo of familiarity. I racked my brains to think why, but my memory was unyielding. From the table in front of me I grabbed a leather jug of ale, uncorked it, and held it to my lips. Bittersweet liquid gushed down my gullet. I waited for my agitation to be soothed by alcohol, for some inspiration to replace it. And when none came, I drank some more. I don't know how long I sat there, drinking, turning the questions over, intermittently rereading the letters, all the while growing more and more confused. At length, when my head began to whirl and I perceived myself no closer to resolving the dilemmas they raised, I folded the letters away in my coat pocket, placed my hat upon my head, and went out.

A wall of fog, gray as a gentleman's periwig, engulfed me as I left the workshop and turned right into St. Martin's Lane. The ale had fuddled rather than cleared my senses, and brought on a mood of melancholy. I walked slowly, with a mournful heart and pounding head, looking for answers with every step. I turned down Hemmings Row into Whitcomb Street, colliding with a milkmaid whose creamy load slopped over my shoes. What did that spillage signify? In the dinginess of Princes Street, I paused to listen to a street singer whose sorry air mirrored my mood. She held a baby to her breast and warbled "The Ladies Fall," to the accompaniment of a hautboy player. The lad was dressed in rags, miserable, skin paler than ashes stretched taut over his bones. He glared fiercely in my direction as he played, and I spun a silver six-pence towards his hat. The coin bounced on the rim and tinkled to the ground so that he had to scrabble desperately to get it before it rolled to the toe of a fish vendor's boot. I looked up at the red-faced man swearing at the child groping at his feet. There was a signboard above his head that caught my eye. It was in the shape of a shield, gaudily painted with fishes and oysters. Perhaps it was the sight of that creaking board which conjured a sudden image in my mind. I could picture Partridge carving those initials, M. C., carefully on a shield . . . but where? Where?

Half an hour later I emerged from a warren of narrow streets into Golden Square. This place, I should add for those not familiar with London in recent times, is no longer deserving of its gleaming name, lying pressed in on all sides by a maze of alleys and narrow, dingy passages. As the city has sprawled north and westwards, its grandest residents have moved on to the newer mansions of Hanover and Grosvenor Squares. These once-esteemed buildings are now home to temporary residents of modest means and dubious occupation, who will not rest long enough here to notice their gradual crumbling.

Through the mist I squinted at the shadowy forms of three small ruffians playing at chuck, shouting obscenities of incredible color and variety at one another. I wandered closer. I was heading, reluctantly, for my rendezvous with Madame Trenti, whose house was on the opposite side of the square. Although I confess I was in no mood for chitchat, I still felt honor bound to call on her and discover what she had to say on the subject of Partridge. And there was something else that drew me, a certain urgency, a compulsion to see her. I could feel it pulling me towards the house, although I couldn't tell you what exactly lay at its root.

So engrossed was I in worrying about Madame Trenti and watching the urchins at play, I didn't remark a black chaise emerging at breakneck speed from a side alley. It was only when the equipage careered dead towards me that I realized the danger and shouted loudly to alert the driver.

But still it continued to bear down on me, and now it was too late to escape. An instant later and I could feel the horses' steamy breath on my face and smell their sweat. I hurled myself flat against the railings, but the vehicle brushed so close that its wheel caught my kneecap. I fell tumbling to the ground, slamming my head on the railings as I went.

Looking back at that moment, I'm unsure where imagination and reality divide. I recall isolated details: my heart pounding as I rolled myself against the railings in an effort to escape what I believed was certain death; a vivid green stripe on the carriage door passing over me; the barreling silhouette of the horses' bellies; the jangle and shine of their harnesses; the clatter of polished hoofs on cobble, so close I feared they would penetrate my skull; then lying on my back in the filth of the street too winded and stunned to rouse myself. Undoubtedly the driver saw what he did, for I remember catching sight of a hunched figure swathed in a dark green caped coat looking down at me as the chaise thundered past. I looked up at him helplessly, and the chill finger of fear probed my heart as I recognized the look of malice in his eyes. I knew this man wanted me dead. Yet was it a figment of fancy that made me think there was something oddly familiar about the set of his figure? Was my mind merely addled by shock and terror?

I think I must have lost consciousness then, for I had the sensation of being bathed in dazzling white light before tumbling into blackness that made my skin creep with cold. Then I was in a gray fog of nothingness, oblivious to everything until I saw a shield like the one above the fishmonger's head, only this time made from gold that shone like the setting sun with the initials M. C. emblazoned upon it. The next thing I recall was the voices of the urchins close to my ear and the feel of their fingers nimbly rifling my pockets. I came rapidly to my senses, sat up, and swatted them away like pestilent flies. "Get away from me, damn you. Ruffians, rogues! How dare you take advantage of a man when he's down. Get off or I'll have you up before the justice for pickpocketing," I said, as firmly as I was able given my shaken state.

"We weren't doing no harm, sir. Just seeing if you was alive," said the largest, a pinch-faced urchin with a white scar down one cheek.

"I'm alive as you can see. Now be off."

"Been at the liquor, 'ave you, sir?" said one impudently. I made as if to cuff him, and he scampered a short distance off.

"Let us help you up first, sir," said another, holding out his hand. I let him haul me to my feet, for in truth my head was still reeling from the fall and my knee throbbed with pain. As I stood there, watching the square spin round, they turned on their heels and vanished in the mist. Only later did I discover they had relieved me of the ten shillings and the pouch of tobacco in my pocket.

I limped to the steps of La Trenti's house, where a footman in a striped Valencia coat and ribbon shoulder knot looked me up and down. I announced myself and my business, and it was in the midst of this conversation that I remarked a stench of dung rising like a foul mist around me. With a rush of shame I looked down. Every piece of clothing I wore, my skin, my wig, the very hair beneath it was saturated in filth from the tumble I had taken. I was a malodorous sponge. I smelled like a dung heap and resembled one too. Plainly the footman had judged me by my sartorial deficiencies and took me for a vagabond, for he stood with his nose in the air and refused to meet my eye.

"I've an appointment with your mistress," I stammered again. "I met with a misadventure just now, a carriage ran me down. I'm in no state to see her. Will you convey the message to her that I have not forgotten our appointment and will return . . ."

As my voice faded away a bell rang impatiently from within. The footman turned on his heels and mounted the steps to the entrance hall, closing the door behind him. I hovered irresolutely on the threshold. It was hopeless. I had turned to leave when the door opened again and a second footman appeared. Madame Trenti had somehow overheard my exchange with her servant. She deeply regretted my accident but was anxious nonetheless that we should not postpone our rendezvous. I was to be provided with facilities to put myself to rights, and we would then hold our discussions as previously arranged. I had little choice in this matter; Madame Trenti was quite adamant.

The first stony-faced sentinel now reappeared and became suddenly animated. I was herded up the stairs to the threshold, where the second footman took over, bustling me up another flight to a small closet set up as a gentleman's dressing room, with a copper bathtub, washstand with basin, jug, pomades, and shaving requisites. Without questioning why a single lady would have a room so well equipped for a gentleman, I allowed myself to be stripped of my foul apparel, only just managing to retrieve Foley's letters from my coat pocket before the garment was dispatched I know not where.

I'd soaked and scrubbed myself thoroughly and emerged from the bath when I realized the blow to my head must have been graver than I thought. I had a waking vision. I was toweling myself and standing naked at the window, waiting for clothing to be brought, when there came a sudden parting in the fog. I thought I saw Alice grasping the railings, squinting up at the house, directly at me. Did I imagine it, or was there fury in her eyes? I grabbed the drying cloth, closed my eyes tight, shook my head in disbelief, and opened them again. The fog was once more as thick as a wall. Alice did not exist.

Before I had time to dwell on this, the footman arrived to help me dress. Having donned a fine costume of purple broidered waistcoat, black breeches, white stockings, a dark blue frock coat, and a cut wig, I regarded myself in the looking glass. I don't know if it was the knock to my head or the newness of the clothes, but for once my lopsidedness seemed to have vanished. I was as fine as a Covent Garden beau. Feeling thus satisfied, I splashed myself with eau de cologne and descended the stairs, dapper, sweet-smelling, and self-satisfied.

Madame Trenti's saloon was the height of fashion: French-style furnishings, a gilded ottoman, an ingenious card table, a mahogany commode, walls swathed in sage green damask hung with a vast gilded looking glass and modish paintings—one of which portrayed a lascivious gentleman spying on a woman at her toilette, reminding me uncomfortably of my recent vision. But my eyes were chiefly drawn by the looking glass above the chimneypiece. A vague memory of this object had impressed itself in my mind as I'd watched the hautboy player in the street, and had even permeated my unconsciousness. Here was what had made me eager to keep my appointment with Madame Trenti.

More exactly it was the frame rather than the glass at which I gazed. It was elaborately carved with an almost life-sized image of Venus emerging from reeds. How well I remembered Partridge carving the figure. The beauty of the female form was matchless, but it was a further detail I'd recalled that interested me. Above the head of Venus fluttered two putti attendants. Between them they held a shield, like the one above the fishmonger's head, only this was gilded and embellished not with oysters and herrings but with their owner's monogram. I narrowed my eyes and deciphered the intricate interlaced characters. They were as I remembered them. The letters M. C.

Madame Trenti sat in a fauteuil upholstered in watered silk. She wore a gown of palest blue over an ivory embroidered petticoat. Her hair was arranged with a white-feathered pompon, and her face, as before, was meticulously painted and patched. She lowered her head to my bow and waved away my thanks for her assistance with her fan. "I am glad to see you are refreshed after your ordeal, Mr. Hopson. You look surprisingly well in that costume. Seat yourself, I beg you. Will you take tea?"

I should have known that it was unusual for a lady to receive an artisan thus, but I didn't ponder her motives. So mesmerized was I by the object suspended above her head and its possible connection with the letter in my pocket, I could think of nothing else. I settled in a chair opposite her, wondering as I did so how to raise the subject. She smiled enticingly, as if I were a gentleman of her own rank and she were trying to impress me, before launching immediately into her own inquiries. What had befallen Mr. Partridge? How did he die so tragically? Why was I the person to discover him? On and on the questions went, allowing me no opportunity to intervene without appearing rude, which I knew would be self-defeating. And so I followed the only course available, answering as candidly as I could, awaiting my moment to broach the subject of the looking glass. My description of Partridge's wounds seemed to unsettle her a little, but not so much as the mention of Montfort's name, which made her fan herself rapidly and ask me to shift the fire screen to shield her from the flames.

"Madam," I said during this short interval, "Partridge's death perplexes me greatly. But there is a further matter on which I would question you. I recall Partridge carved the looking glass frame hanging above you. Am I to presume the initials are your own?"

There was a short silence as she slowly stroked the carved arm of her chair.

"Mr. Hopson, I fail to see the relevance of this digression, but since you ask, Maria Trenti is my stage name, invented by my father. I was baptized Maria Carmina." The tone of her voice had grown suddenly haughty. I was no longer being addressed as a confidant but as an impertinent underling.

I felt in my pocket, thankful I'd had the presence of mind to salvage the letters, and handed her the page Foley had sent me.

"A minute more of your forbearance, madam, and all will be clear. This letter was written to Lord Montfort. You will see that it is signed with the same initials, M. C. Were you the author of it?"

She took the page and lowered her head. I was astonished to note her lip trembling as she read and that when she looked up her large green eyes shone with tears.

"You are correct," she admitted, suddenly returning to her former easy manner. "I don't know how this came into your possession, but it was indeed I who penned it. Before we speak further on the subject of Partridge and his unfortunate history—the subject which I know has brought you here—I should like to tell you something of my own past, for only then will you comprehend my involvement with your friend."

But at that moment a rattle of crockery was heard outside the door and she broke off. A servant entered with the tea she had ordered. She waited in silence as he placed the tray on a side table and brought her a silver caddy. Carefully she unlocked it, mixed leaves in a glass bowl, and placed them in the pot, clicking her fingers for the servant to pour water from the kettle over them. When this was done, without glancing in his direction, she flicked her handkerchief to indicate he should leave immediately. There was silence for a moment while she poured the tea and then she resumed.

"I own to you that I have come here from Italy, not simply to make my reputation in your English theater, but with a more pressing design in mind. Two decades ago I was a young girl in Rome with little to recommend me, apart from my talent for the dramatic arts. My mother, you see, died when I was very young. My father was a music teacher; he taught me from an early age, and encouraged me to perform at recitals, playing, dancing, singing for the English tourists. They lauded my talents, and so naturally I formed . . . alliances . . . among them." She paused, somewhat theatrically, to hand me a fragile tea bowl and saucer, leaning forward to allow me a glimpse of her powdered bosom.

"There was one, however, who was different. Who behaved dishonorably, who took the greatest advantage of me that a gentleman may take of the opposite sex. He procured a priest to perform a marriage ceremony, then abandoned me immediately after the union had been consummated. . . . I trust I need not say more . . ." Her chin quivered with emotion now, tears coursed her cheeks, tracing small furrows in her powder.

"I would not distress you further," I said. "This man, I take it from the letter, was Lord Montfort?"

She nodded, dabbing her eyes carefully with a lace handkerchief.

"And there was a child born from this liaison?"

"There was, as you say, a child born. My father discovered my condition and forced a confession from me." She dabbed her face again, before taking up the teapot and refilling my bowl. Her hands were tiny, with fragile wrists no stronger than a child's, yet her long slender fingers with

111

their immaculately manicured nails reminded me strangely of Chippendale. "He traced the priest, who pretended to have carried out the ceremony in good faith and said Montfort had taken the marriage certificate. My father pursued Lord Montfort to Venice, where he appeared the very embodiment of gentlemanly discretion. He said I wasn't abandoned, nor did he wish to ruin me, for had he not married me? He'd sent word to me that he was in Venice, but the letter must have gone astray. He was about to return to England but couldn't take me with him for the time being, until he had prepared his family for the arrival of an Italian bride. Now that my father had kindly apprised him of my delicate condition, as a gesture of goodwill he consented to leave a servant behind who would bring the child to England as soon as it was born. I should have regular news of the child's progress and join him in due course."

"And so you handed over your child?"

"What choice did I have? My father obliged me to submit to this plan. I trusted Montfort would send for me."

"But that did not happen?"

"It did not. The child—a boy—was taken from me within days of its birth. Montfort had given my father a small sum of money for my welfare and returned to England immediately after their meeting. Since then I've received no word from him. I wrote several times, imploring Montfort to respond. But my letters went unanswered. Some years later I learned he was already engaged to another woman when he met me. He married her within weeks of his return and had a child, a son, nine months later. If I didn't know it already, I realized then how terribly I'd been deceived. But still I could not rest without some definite news of what had happened to our child. Is it not every mother's right to have such information?"

I nodded sympathetically, although privately I wondered what mother could abandon her infant to a man she scarcely knew and wait so long to find out what had become of him. Behind the tears and trembling lips, I could have sworn her eyes were cold.

"Thus I determined to come to England, find Montfort, and confront him."

"And did you?"

She shook her head firmly; the feathers in her headdress shivered.

"Since my arrival he has proved more elusive than luck itself. Of course I already knew his whereabouts and wrote to him, but as before I received no response. The letters all remained unanswered. Until some weeks ago, when I received a curious letter from a person by the name of Miss Alleyn, who is, I gather, Montfort's sister." Here she rose, went to the commode, and took from it a paper. "Read and you will understand."

She handed me the page, which I unfolded, not knowing what to expect. It was written in a large and looped script, in unusual purplish black ink.

Horseheath Hall   December 18, 1754
Cambridge

Madam,

I have chanced upon a letter you recently addressed to my brother, for whom I keep house. As one who is childless but wishes she might have been otherwise, I am ashamed to learn of the cruel way you and your child have been treated. To make what amends I can, in the hope that it will go some way to easing your sorrow, I proffer you the following information. I will not trouble you with the details of how I discovered it. But suffice it to say that I've learned from a reputable source that nineteen years ago my brother returned from Italy with a child (a boy), which he placed in the care of a local wet nurse, a Mrs. Figgins. Four years later, hearing of a hospital that was shortly to open in London expressly to take in unwanted foundlings, my brother instructed that the infant was to be deposited there on the day it opened. As far as I can tell, these orders were carried out. What became of the child subsequently I have never discovered. I am, madam, yours obediently,

Miss Margaret Alleyn

I read the letter twice more, then handed it back to her. I did not allow my face to reveal what I thought, although I observed she was scrutinizing me intently. "Forgive me, Madame Trenti. I feel great sympathy for your predicament. But this still does not explain how you knew Partridge was a foundling, or your interest in him."

"Can you be so slow-witted? Have you not guessed?" she exclaimed, shaking her head at my doltishness. "Partridge was my son. It was I who directed him to speak to Montfort . . . his father."

Of course I knew this was what she had intended me to believe all along, but for some reason hearing her say the words "Partridge was my son" chilled me to the core. There was no warmth in her tone. She might as well have said, "That is my chair" or "This is my dress."

"Truly that's an astonishing claim. What proof have you?"

She pursed her lips. "Mr. Hopson, you are surprisingly skeptical for one so youthful."

"Age has nothing to do with it," I said coldly. "London is full of foundlings; I am merely curious to know how you settled upon Partridge as your child."

"Very well, let me tell you, since you insist upon it. I went to the Foundling Hospital and looked at the ledger—they call it the billet book. As you see, Miss Alleyn's letter is most specific about the date my child was left—the opening day. I consulted the records. The hospital opened on March twenty-fifth, 1741. I traced the child to one apprenticed to Mr. Chippendale on account of his unusual talent for carving."

Part of me of course wanted to believe her. Yet part of me did not. How was it, I wondered, that she had found Partridge so easily, while he himself had never succeeded in tracing his parents? Was my clever, gifted friend truly the offspring of this guileful creature and the odious Montfort? Nothing I could recall of my friend bore the remotest resemblance to either of them. However smooth her discourse sounded, however convincing her tears, I couldn't help feeling I was witnessing a consummate performance rather than an outpouring of heartfelt grief. She showed none of the emotions I associated with motherhood. There had been little distress when I'd told her of the violence of his death. On the contrary, her reaction, now I thought about it, had been one of shock, surprise—even, I fancied, annoyance.

"Why did you send Partridge to Lord Montfort? What purpose was there in it when you knew Montfort refused to meet you and had abandoned the child? Did you not suspect Montfort would reject him? As his mother, did you not feel it was a cruelty to send him?"

"I did not view it like that," she said, eyes widening at my criticism. "Partridge had a *right* to be recognized as Montfort's son. I am his wife, I too have rights. I wanted him to perceive that he could not shrug me off as some inconsequential courtesan. Both Partridge and I *deserved* justice."

"Justice or money?"

"Do not both go hand in hand? How else could Montfort make amends if not financially?"

"Had Lord Montfort paid you money in the past?"

"If he had, what of it?"

"Had the payments recently stopped? Was that why you came to find him?"

She fluttered her fan with annoyance. I knew I'd hit the mark. "That is really no concern of yours, Mr. Hopson. Indeed I fancy you forget yourself. Now perhaps, having cruelly accused me, you would be good enough to tell me what it is I need to know. What is the name of Montfort's executor and chief beneficiary?"

"Why do you wish to know it?"

"I wish to apprise them that I was the mother of his legitimate child. I wish to make clear *my* claim upon the estate."

"Do you have any proof of the ceremony?"

"The certificate must still be among Montfort's possessions. I have proof of the notes of credit sent to me for the past nineteen years."

I doubted very much that without evidence of her marriage she would have any claim. Indeed, knowing what I did of Montfort and his methods of seduction, there was no doubt in my mind that the ceremony had been a sham, engineered purely for his own gratification. Nonetheless I didn't care to voice my beliefs. I gave her Wallace's name and whereabouts and advised her to contact him. As I wrote the necessary information on a paper for her, the warmth of the room, the softness of my chair, and the scent she was wearing became suddenly overpowering. I longed to be away from this house, from this room, from her deception. There were probably more questions I should have asked, but after all I'd been through this day my mind was growing weary and I was becoming muddled once again and could not frame them.

With scant regard for propriety, I took my leave of her, promising to return as soon as I was able. I rejoiced to find myself stepping out of her door, gulping sour London air. Here there was no powder and perfume to hide the grime; you could see the dung heaps and the puddles and walk round them. It was as I was turning out of the square that I suddenly became aware of a carriage thundering up behind me. My heart began to race with fear that this was another mad driver bent on destroying me. I darted towards the nearest entrance, where I reckoned I would be protected, and watched as a hackney drew to an abrupt halt beside me. The occupant's gloved hand—female—emerged to press down the tin window.

Alice appeared in the aperture. She was holding my box towards me.

115

"Mr. Hopson, good afternoon," she said, returning my smile of relief with a worrying aloofness. "I came to inform you that the locksmith says he cannot help you with this box until you can show him the keyhole. He has never seen another mechanism like it." Almost without drawing breath she continued frostily, "How and with whom you pass your time is no concern of mine. But since I am here, perhaps I should make it clear that I do not wish you to call on me again for matters of a personal nature. Nor do my brother and I wish to attend the theater with you."

"I don't understand," said I, taking the box from her hand. "Have I done something to distress you?"

"I doubt very much you have it in your capacity to distress me. You know of my reputation for plain speaking—now since you provoke me you shall sample it. You have just passed the afternoon in the company of a woman whose services are well known to be easier to hire than a hackney carriage."

I was hurt to the quick by her assumption. Did she honestly believe I'd ever consider any intimacy with Madame Trenti? "That remark is utterly unfounded. Madame Trenti is a patroness of Chippendale. I called upon her to discover what she knew of Partridge."

"Was that why I observed you earlier standing naked at her window? Look at you now—dressed like her pet monkey. If this is your method of unraveling your unfortunate friend's fate, I will not be party to it."

"She offered me these clothes only because—"

Without hearing my response, she banged on the back of her compartment with her fist. The driver whipped up the horse, and the carriage sped off into the swirling mist, leaving me gazing after the disappearing lantern at its rear in utter bewilderment.

Chapter Ten

Foley arrived next morning. Before he could ask for me he was spied by Chippendale, who wouldn't allow such a finely dressed (if unknown) gentleman to call upon his premises without greeting him personally. I should say here that my master derived the greatest enjoyment from spying new customers as they entered his showroom. To reach his door they would have traveled half the length of St. Martin's Lane, traversing a stew of resident actors, architects, sculptors, quacks, wags, and wits, stepping over puddles and ordure, towards a deceivingly ordinary façade. What a contrast they beheld when the door of Chippendale's establishment was opened to them. In here the air was fragranced by porcelain pastille burners, and gilded looking glasses adorned the walls, magnifying and multiplying the furniture, carpets, bronzes, and chandeliers of every conceivable form.

Yet I noticed as I approached that Foley seemed all but oblivious to his surroundings. He displayed none of the usual amazement Chippendale delighted in observing, although the habitual nonchalance he affected had been replaced by a gleam of urgency. Was this because he'd discovered something momentous, I wondered. The instant he caught sight of me, Foley's expression altered and told me, as clear as any words, that he needed saving from Chippendale. The master was in the midst of an energetic performance.

"Permit me if you will, sir, to show you this small novelty: a set of transforming library steps that can double as a footstool, fitted as you see with a bookrest—as ingenious an invention as any devised—"

"Indeed, Mr. Chippendale," interrupted Foley, knitting his brows with impatience, "it is exceedingly fine and will suit my purpose admirably. But since Mr. Hopson is already known to me, I believe it may be prudent to show him my premises before placing an order."

Chippendale was plainly taken aback. "Hopson is known to you, sir?"

"Indeed. I am Lord Foley of Whitely Court, Cambridge, the estate neighboring Lord Montfort's. Hopson and I became acquainted during his recent sojourn there."

Chippendale's eyes flickered. Perhaps he recalled that I'd told him Foley might be the custodian of his precious drawings I'd found with Lord Montfort's corpse, drawings he believed were essential to his second edition, for he was now at even greater pains to humor him. "Of course Hopson shall accompany you, my lord. But permit me if you will to discuss some urgent business matters with him before he departs. If you would be so kind as to wait just a minute . . ."

Foley nodded curtly. He sat himself on a sofa, crossed his legs, and gazed at the ceiling, while Chippendale ushered me to his office.

His instructions were briskly given and came as no great surprise. I was handed the documents referring to the loan and a letter from Montfort corroborating the agreement over the drawings, and ordered to discover their exact whereabouts and advise Foley of the claim.

Moments later I was in Foley's carriage, heading not to his premises, which I knew to be in St. James's, but in the opposite direction, down Fleet Street, towards East Cheap. He spoke little in the carriage, except to declare that since the morning was dry and he had an urge to walk, he'd take me on a promenade and save his news till then. I was still somewhat drained from my adventures the previous afternoon, and my unfortunate encounter with Alice had left me in downcast spirits, yet I couldn't help pondering on the reason for his urgency. Compared with my last recollections of him at Horseheath, on the night I tumbled over Montfort's body and the following day after I'd discovered poor Partridge, when he had been gruff and arrogant, he appeared more animated, more approachable in his demeanor. I wondered what had effected this change. Had he mellowed because he wanted to nurture my trust in him? This seemed unlikely, and I returned to my earlier notion of some new discovery concerning the circumstances of Montfort's or Partridge's death as being the cause of his animation. What might this be? I considered the scene at Montfort's long-awaited dinner: Montfort irascible towards his guests and family and storming from the room, never to be seen alive again. Montfort dead in the unlit library, a pistol by one hand, a mysterious box in the other, leeches swarming over his neck, surrounded by bloody footprints and strewn papers. There was so much detail at the scene, so much to distract and confuse; I could conceive of nothing that Foley might have uncovered to unravel it.

Perhaps the answer lay not in the library but in the dining room. I racked my brains to remember the comings and goings I'd witnessed. Who had been present when the gunshot was heard? I recalled Bradfield emerging from behind the screen, two ladies, Foley's wife and Lady Bradfield, and Wallace the lawyer seated at the table. Where had everyone else been? Almost immediately a vision of shoes and hems came into my mind. I had been under the table when Foley reentered immediately after the gunshot; Robert Montfort and Elizabeth had followed. Margaret Alleyn had entered last. All this had taken place about the same time that the groundsman had reported seeing a figure close to the pond, where next morning I'd found Partridge frozen and mutilated.

Reviewing these events from a distance didn't really help me comprehend them, but it sparked further discomfiting thoughts. I had accomplished none of the tasks Foley had set me. The box was still unopened, its contents as yet undiscovered. I had found out no more about Partridge's movements prior to his journey to Horseheath. The discoveries I *had* made were scant and seemed to lead nowhere. I had learned the name of the wood from which the box was made; I had discovered that, according to Chippendale, Montfort had no right to the drawings in his possession. Madame Trenti had told me that Partridge had visited Horseheath because he believed Lord Montfort to be his father. These were not, I realized, impressive advances, nor did I expect lavish congratulations from Foley on account of them. More important by far was my discovery that, as I'd feared, my involvement in these matters had drawn down danger upon me. I shuddered to recall the way I'd been run down. There was no doubt this was an attempt on my life. How long would it be before another one was made?

Some quarter of an hour later we arrived at the Monument. Foley tapped on the window, the carriage rumbled obediently to a halt, and we descended. We strolled down Gracechurch Street to the top of London Bridge, from where, he promised, we should enjoy a spectacular view of the river from on high. We mounted the stairs to the top and gazed down from the parapet. Foley paced up and down, surveying various vessels and their comings and goings. For my part I was unmoved by the panorama before me. It seemed to me the bustling scene was no more than insubstantial shadows, bleached of color; gray buildings towering over dark quays, antlike people, crusted mudflats, and the smooth gray slick of river. The bitter cold of recent days had partly frozen the water, and fragments of ice, like jagged shards of stone blasted from a quarry, crashed into the hulls of vessels moored by the banks. It was only after staring at this desolate scene some considerable while that I became aware that Foley had stopped pacing about and now stood scrutinizing me intently.

"Something about you seems different, Hopson," he declared abruptly.

"I can't imagine what you mean, my lord."

"What is it precisely?" he persisted. "You have a purple bruise beneath your eye, and another on your forehead. You are walking with a limp. You look as if you have lately been involved in some alehouse brawl. Yet you have a lackluster, dispirited air about you that I do not recall observing even after the discovery of your friend's body in Cambridge. You look"—he paused—"older, like a man foundering under some burden beyond his capacity to support."

I was flabbergasted by the minuteness of his observations. Blood rushed to the roots of my hair, and my scar began to throb as it hadn't for several days. Was I so transparent?

"Lord Foley," I blurted, "I don't know how you read all this from my expression. I confess to being a little weary and am merely admiring the view until you deign to tell me why you have brought me here."

"Then without further ado let me tell you. I've brought you here partly to discover what you've unearthed these last days, and partly for my own satisfaction. I've loved this place ever since I was a boy, and it's some years since I saw it," he declared. "Now tell me, what have you discovered of the box?"

My cheeks reddened further with this reminder of my failure. "I've made little progress—save that the wood is a rarity known as grenadillo." This information didn't seem to interest Foley in the slightest.

"Haven't you opened it yet?"

I shook my head and fumbled in my pocket for the box, which I returned to him. "I gave it to a locksmith who was also confounded by it. But I was loath to force it without your instruction."

"Is that all you have to tell me?" he said, taking the box from me. Although he seemed dejected by the news, he didn't chastise me as I had half expected. Yet I knew I'd disappointed him, and for some unfathomable reason it irked me.

"No. There are other matters."

"Pray continue."

"The first surprises me greatly. It seems that Partridge believed himself to be the son of Lord Montfort and Madame Trenti, an Italian actress currently settled in London."

Foley's face blanched at the mention of Trenti's name.

"Do you know her, my lord?" I inquired.

"I knew her once, long ago. Now by reputation only. How has she embroiled herself in this?"

"It was she who directed Partridge to Lord Montfort. She led Partridge to believe Montfort was his father and she his mother."

"You say Partridge *believed* Montfort and Trenti to be his parents. Do I take it from this you are skeptical?"

"My mind is uncertain. I don't believe Madame Trenti was entirely open with me."

"That is in keeping with all I know of her. What was the second matter you wished to divulge?"

"It concerns Mr. Chippendale's drawings—those we found scattered in the library on the night of Lord Montfort's death."

"What of them?"

"Chippendale has told me they rightfully belong to him. It seems Montfort loaned him money for the publication of his book and kept the drawings as security. The loan was repaid but the drawings were not returned."

Foley gave a rueful smile. "How unfortunate for me if you are right," he said. "Of all Montfort's possessions owing to me, the contents of his library are what I covet most. Do you believe him?"

"Yes," I said firmly, "and he's given me the documents to prove it." Here I handed him the bundle Chippendale had earlier entrusted to me. He perused the first paper, then looked at the oily water beneath us.

"Curious, is it not, that I never heard mention of the matter? Before I concede to return the drawings I should like some confirmation. The Bradfields are come to town yesterday—George, their son, will accompany Robert Montfort on his voyage to Italy and is preparing himself for the journey. I had planned to call on Bradfield, who may know something of this."

To me there seemed little to debate, for I didn't doubt Chippendale's word. Nevertheless Foley was determined to visit Bradfield and investigate the matter further. He pressed me to join him, and since I was too dull to conjure a means to excuse myself, I fell in with him. On the way, in his carriage, he turned to me again. "You still have not explained to me the reason for your battered face, or your hangdog expression."

"I met with an accident yesterday. Outside Madame Trenti's house a coach ran me down and threw me in the gutter. As the driver passed over me I had the distinct impression that I knew him, that I'd been knocked over deliberately, perhaps with the intention of causing me greater harm than I suffered."

"Who was it?"

"The driver was cloaked and passed by very fast. There was no time to see."

Foley shrugged his shoulders as if my near scrape with death were a matter of little consequence. An instant later and the carriage drew up outside the stately stuccoed building in Leicester Fields that was the Bradfield town residence, and a footman stepped forward to open our door. Bradfield and his wife received us in a small parlor ornamented with portraits of ancestors and favorite dogs and horses. Their son, George, was away from the house, presently engaged, so Lady Bradfield informed us, in ordering his portmanteau and traveling garb for the tour of Europe he was to undertake with Robert Montfort.

"What news is there from Cambridge?" inquired Foley, as if he'd been in town for weeks.

"Robert arrived in London two days ago with Elizabeth and Miss Alleyn. They are lodging with us for the next few days. Last night at dinner Robert disclosed that he is uncertain when the matter of his father's death will be resolved and that his departure for Europe may be delayed. He had previously agreed with George to cross the Channel by the end of the month," replied Bradfield.

"Will he contest my claim?"

"He didn't say it in so many words, but I've no doubt he'll do all he can to prevent you walking off with a portion of his inheritance. He mentioned something about seeking out his father's apothecary."

"For what reason?"

"The fellow treated Montfort's melancholia, and Robert hopes he will support his theory that his father was in a frame of mind to do away with himself."

"And then Robert'll persuade Westleigh to declare his father of unsound mind and thus call into question the document in my favor," said Foley, nodding thoughtfully. "Exactly as I anticipated."

A shadow now crossed Bradfield's rotund face. "I confess, Foley, I have yet to tell him you have my support in this. I feel it would not be prudent yet to remind him that I was there when Montfort pledged you the sum and saw you win it fair and square."

"Why do you hold back?"

"Because it will assist your investigations to know what he is thinking and I can only discover that by feigning to concur with him. We do not know much of Robert, but do not forget, Foley, in all probability he is no more principled than his father. He will play a cunning game."

"Perhaps you have reason, Bradfield. I thank you for your discretion."

Bradfield flushed as he warmed to his theme. "You recall how Montfort cheated me of my prize hunter? I've never forgiven him for it. If you're not paid, it will be a grave iniquity . . ."

Foley raised his hand to halt the flow. "In that respect, Bradfield, you and I are trees grown from different soil. I never sought Montfort's money and hadn't planned to keep it. You will recall, however, that the document also makes over to me the contents of Montfort's library. This, unlike the money, I greatly desire. Which brings me to the reason for my call."

Bradfield was incredulous. "Upon my word, I can't comprehend your attitude, Foley—how you could value a set of books above a fortune. What is it you wish to know?"

"A curious matter has come to light concerning the cabinetmaker Chippendale. It seems he too has claims upon a portion of the library." Foley paused to brush a speck of dirt from his stocking. "You'll recall the drawings of tables and chairs discovered by Montfort's body?"

Bradfield nodded.

"Chippendale says they are rightfully his. That Montfort lent him money to publish a book, held the drawings as security, and when the loan was repaid refused to return them."

A gust of mirthless laughter burst from Bradfield's lips. "Why a set of carpentry scribbles should concern either Montfort or you is beyond me. Give them back if he's a civil fellow; burn them and damn him if not!" he cried.

Foley tightened his grip on his chair. "Bradfield, you must comprehend that I value those drawings as highly as you regarded your favorite hunter. I would keep them myself to add to my collection. But equally I adhere to certain scruples and won't stoop to Montfort's level. I wouldn't rob a man of what rightfully belongs to him, any more, I assume, than you would defraud another man of his horse. So what I wish to know is whether Montfort mentioned this matter of the loan and Chippendale to you."

Bradfield was chastened by the sharpness of Foley's tone. "I have heard him speak of Chippendale often enough, boasting of his commissions, complaining of the man's tardiness concerning the library. But drawings—no—I do not believe they came into it. Why, Foley, God's teeth, if you'd have 'em, keep 'em."

Foley smiled grimly. "On what grounds should I do so if he has a rightful claim?"

"On the grounds that your rank places your word above his," responded Bradfield, ripe with fervor. "I've heard Chippendale is a man of grandiose ambition who aspires to set himself up as a gentleman. In all probability he regrets selling Montfort the drawings and now wishes for them back at no cost so he can sell them again. I see no reason why you shouldn't hold on to them."

Forgetting my recent disaffection with my master, I began to seethe. How dare Bradfield cast such aspersions on his integrity? I longed to demand that Foley show Bradfield the documents supporting Chippendale's claim. But then it occurred to me that perhaps if he held back there was some reason for his reticence and I'd be wiser not to intervene. And so I sat there, biting my tongue, boiling with annoyance at Bradfield.

To distract myself from their conversation, I returned to my blunder with Alice. How would I resolve it? Why wouldn't she listen or believe me when I tried to explain? Most ladies of my acquaintance readily accepted my explanations (even when these were plainly sparing with the truth) so long as their dignity was preserved. But Alice was more impulsive, less pliant, and the injustice of her assumption that there was something improper in my rendezvous with Madame Trenti irked me even more than Bradfield's ramblings.

I cursed the wretched Madame Trenti. Of course Alice had reason to cast aspersions on her reputation. An actress such as she was bound to inhabit a seamy world of scandal and pandering and excess. But I had no desire to join this world. Madame Trenti held no allure for me. My only interest in her was in the light she could shed on Partridge. It occurred to me then that Madame Trenti was a curious figure. In Chippendale's dingy parlor, she'd appeared an exotic bloom in a wasteland, and he had accorded her as much homage as a duchess. Yet what was the reason for his deference? How could an actress such as she afford the lavish furnishings he supplied? Perhaps she had some secret wealthy benefactor of whom Chippendale was in awe. I could explain Trenti's insistence that Partridge should take charge of her cabinet on the grounds of her belief (or claim) that he was her son. But why had Chippendale appeared so troubled by her mention of Partridge? Because he was jealous of Partridge's talents? Unlikely—for Partridge was already dead by then. Because Partridge posed some threat to him? Impossible. It was then that a sudden realization dawned. There was some hidden intrigue between Trenti and Chippendale of which I was entirely ignorant.

As I was contemplating the nature of this intrigue, I became aware of a strange gurgling coming from a room nearby. I tried for the sake of politeness to ignore it, but the sound continued, growing in volume until it resembled a series of agonized shrieks. At length even Foley acknowledged it.

"What is that sound, Bradfield? Is someone taken ill?"

"As I told you, Robert and Elizabeth are staying with me."

Foley looked alarmed. "Are they indisposed? Is one of them making those dreadful sounds?"

Bradfield smiled benevolently and stood up. "I had quite neglected to inform you. It transpires Robert Montfort is something of an amateur surgeon."

"A surgeon?"

"I discovered it only this morning when one of the servants complained of a pain in his tooth. Robert heard him and charitably offered to operate for no charge when the man had completed his duties. He took up his scalpel some minutes before your arrival, and Elizabeth assists him. Judging from the noise, the operation is currently under way. Come. Perhaps it will divert you to see for yourselves."

He led us to the gloomy hall and then down the back stairs to the kitchens, where a small anteroom used for polishing silver was serving as an operating theater. The patient, a man in his middle years, lay stripped to the waist, stretched out on a table. Three leather straps were tied across his ankles, middle, and throat to secure him. There was an open bottle of brandy on the table and beside it a bowl of bloodstained liquor with a rotten tooth floating in its midst. At the moment of our entry, Robert Montfort, clad in a bloodstained leather apron, was pouring the brandy through a brass funnel into the man's mouth. Elizabeth was holding his mouth open with a wooden wedge. Whether or not she was a willing helper it was impossible to say, for although she was clearly engrossed by her role, her face was pale and entirely expressionless, as if she were in a waking sleep. No such serenity was visible in the patient; the poor man was wide-eyed, gnashing on the wood like some rabid beast, a mixture of blood, brandy, and foaming sputum streaming from the corners of his mouth and bubbling from his nostrils.

"How d'you progress, Robert?" said Bradfield. "I have brought some spectators. Is the offending tooth removed?"

"I have indeed succeeded," said Robert, eyes shining with triumph, "but the fool has at least half a dozen more that require extraction and refuses to lie still while I operate. Elizabeth is too feeble to hold him."

Suddenly his eye fell upon me.

"Ah, Hopson the carpenter, I see. You will surely have the brawn required to hold his head, and I'll finish the task in a few minutes."

I looked again at the man and the bowl and Robert Montfort. I felt the same chill creep over me as the day I'd discovered Montfort's corpse. The room began to spin, and my legs grew unsteady. I tried to retreat to the door, but it was no good; the entrance was blocked by the bulky form of Bradfield, who ordered me to follow Montfort's instruction.

Elizabeth gestured to me to stand in her place at the man's head. Robert Montfort leaned over the man's gaping jaw with his slender blade in one hand and a wrench in the other. I watched in horrified fascination as he incised the gum, grasped a tooth with his pliers, and twisted. The man writhed in agony. There was a ghastly crunch, and the tooth jerked free. Montfort waved it aloft, its pronged roots resembling pleading arms. My stomach heaved. The room, the man's head, the table, and the blood turned gray and merged to one. My legs crumpled beneath me just as from what seemed a long distance off I heard Foley's voice declare, "Great heavens, Bradfield! It seems Mr. Hopson now is indisposed."

The next thing I knew, Foley was slapping me hard on the face and wafting salts under my nostrils to revive me. As I coughed and spluttered my way back to consciousness, I was aware that he was still talking to me. "Come, Mr. Hopson, rouse yourself. My driver will take you to your premises. On the way there is something I have yet to give you. I've held it back till now for I knew it might disturb you."

My brain was still addled by my fainting, so that this announcement did not affect me as it should have. I staggered to my feet and allowed a footman to bundle me into the carriage while Foley took his leave of the Bradfields. When we were bowling through the park, he took out his gold snuffbox and opened it. A shaft of sun reflected off the shiny inner surface of the lid and shone directly in my eye as he addressed me. "Are you quite sensible, Hopson?"

I squinted into the splinter of light. "I am, my lord. Forgive me for fainting . . . it was the sight of the man's agony and the blood. I couldn't abide it."

"It's of no consequence now," he said carelessly. "I myself was quite disgusted by the spectacle, though I chose not to display my feelings as overtly as you. Now listen well. You may be surprised to learn that among Partridge's effects was an unsealed letter which he intended for you."

"A letter to me? What does it say? I take it you have read it?" I stuttered. I was still confused by the episode at Bradfield's.

"I will leave it to you to discover."

Foley placed a folded sheet in my lap. For several minutes I stared at it in bewilderment, unable to believe the evidence of my own eyes. The heavy, spiky script was indeed that of my dear friend. With a trembling hand I picked up the letter and unfolded it.

December 26, 1754

My dearest Nathaniel

Today I went to find you—for I have such prodigiously astonishing news to tell you that I scarcely know where to begin. Imagine my sorrow—not to say amusement—when I learned you had left London for Lord Montfort's Cambridge residence, the very place where I too am bound within the next hour. I am confident that we will soon meet, but since I have not spoken to you these last weeks, I can no longer contain myself. Thus I am setting down recent events, so that should chance intervene and prevent us from meeting tomorrow you will know immediately what has befallen me.

I do not doubt, my dear friend, that all this has the flavor of melodrama and an overwrought imagination. Nor am I unaware that my silence for the past days must have concerned you and you will have asked yourself why I did not contact you, where I was, and what I was about.

Can you believe me when I tell you that I have watched you daily since the day I departed? Or that the motive for my clandestine behavior was to protect your safety, not mine? The truth is that your lodgings adjacent to the workshops and Chippendale's house were too conspicuous. I did not dare call on you and feared that if I addressed a letter to you there it might fall into the wrong hands and you would not receive it. Thus I have bided my time until today, when the news I have recently received has caused me to throw all caution to the wind. But I run ahead of myself. I must go back many days and provide an explanation for my sudden disappearance.

I went not of my own volition but because I was forced to do so. You doubtless recall how during the past weeks my fondness for Dorothy Chippendale, our master's young sister, had grown. I had never felt so content because for perhaps the first time in my life I began to question the convictions that seem to have lodged themselves in my brain ever since my first consciousness. My preoccupation with my birth seemed suddenly ill-founded, idiotic. Why would my past matter if I had a companion such as Dorothy with whom to build a future?

What I did not perceive was the foolishness of my dreams. Never once did it occur to me that Chippendale might take great exception to our closeness, and that when he knew of it he would intervene in a most pitiless manner.

And so to the dreadful last evening at St. Martin's Lane. Chippendale called me to him. I presumed he wanted to inform me of some new commission and went without trepidation. You can imagine my astonishment therefore when I was greeted with a stream of invective. His sister had complained to him that I persisted in pursuing her. I should know that my advances were both unwelcome and odious to her. He wholeheartedly concurred with her opinion. The very prospect of a foundling marrying into his family, when he had worked so hard to better it, was contemptible and would never be countenanced. What right did I have to drag his family down into the mire from where he had retrieved them? Thus, for her own protection and at her own behest, he had sent his sister back whence she came.

Of course I was flabbergasted. I did what I could to defend myself. I replied that I had believed Dorothy *wanted* to marry me. That my suit had been welcome, not abhorrent. Moreover, I said, my origins were unknown but not necessarily discreditable, and I had done all I could to prove myself, having acquitted myself honorably in the seven years I had served him. "Well," says he, "that remark brings me neatly to my second grievance."

"What's that?" I asked him.

"That your uncommonly high opinion of your talent is unsettling my craftsmen, who should respect the skill of their master above all others. I have observed that you set yourself up as my equal in matters of taste—and I cannot support this."

I felt indignation to the depths of my soul at the injustice of this criticism. "What would you have me do?" I asked him. "Pretend that I cannot draw or carve as I do, or prohibit patrons from praise of my work? I do not vaunt my talents; if others laud me, there is little I can do to prevent it. And certainly I would never presume to place my opinion above yours."

He stared at me with loathing. "What I would have you do," he said quietly, "is leave these premises tonight and remove yourself from your lodging tomorrow morning without contacting anyone here. If you do this I will pay you your salary and a month in lieu. Otherwise you'll not receive a penny of it. Furthermore, should you incite Nathaniel against me, he will be out with you—and I dare predict his talents will earn him less than yours."

My dear friend, you may well imagine my bewilderment and dismay. That I did not deserve such treatment I was in no doubt. But my mind reeled with the sudden realization that my feelings of the past weeks had been nothing but a delusion. How could I have convinced myself that my birth didn't matter? Here was the clearest evidence that the past still blighted my future most profoundly.

In a state of confusion I started home, then praying what he'd said concerning Dorothy was all a fabrication, I retraced my steps. I hoped even then that there was a solution to this maze—that Dorothy might still be in the house, that if she knew what had passed between her brother and me she would agree to come with me. But this was another futile illusion, for the housemaid informed me that Dorothy had indeed returned earlier that day to her family in Yorkshire. No word had been left for me.

And so, dear friend, I returned home doubly wounded. I had lost the woman I loved, who I believed loved me. I'd received cruel ill-treatment at the hands of a master I had always respected. That Chippendale had seen fit not only to dismiss me but also to turn Dorothy against me made me comprehend the depth of his envy and hatred. And with this realization came the acknowledgment of a further dilemma. My friendship with you. He had already warned me to keep away from you. I had no doubt that he would treat you unjustly should he suspect I had contacted you, yet because you are my dearest companion, I yearned to confide in you. I thought on this all night, and by dawn resolved that I would not be responsible for your downfall as I had been for my own and Dorothy's. I would not contact you until I was sure it was safe.

But although that was indeed a most dismal hour, fortune had not entirely abandoned me. A kinder providence was about to intervene. After many days of lying low, I yesterday took a walk towards St. Martin's Lane. I admit, dear friend, that I half hoped to encounter you, for despite my resolve I have longed to speak with you. I was returning to my lodgings when a carriage drew up alongside me. I was halted by a lady with whom I was but vaguely acquainted. She bade me get in the vehicle with her, and when I did, she divulged the astonishing news that now takes me to Cambridge, news which prevailed upon me to seek you out today in spite of all my earlier scruples. I own I am not sure if what she told me is true; I must discover it myself.

I see that these ramblings have filled the past hour and that the coach is due to leave. I intend to complete this account tomorrow, when I trust the whole story will be clear and I can set it down for you. For now, my dear friend, I must set out for Cambridge, my heart with such hopeful fancies as you would not believe.

I am your loyal friend,

John Partridge

I reread this letter twice more while Foley sat beside me, staring out of the carriage window. "Well," he said brusquely, taking out his snuffbox again as I looked up from the last page, "is it not perplexing? What d'you make of it?"

His judgment that the letter would disturb me was exact. Indeed I longed to be away from him, to mull over the information contained here, and the implication of each phrase without being subjected to another of his interrogations. Yet certain sentiments struck me instantly. On the one hand I felt a strange relief to have Partridge's disappearance explained, to know that the reason he'd left me out of his plans was his concern for my well-being. Our friendship *was* all I had believed it to be. My suspicions and the vague misgivings I'd felt seemed spontaneously to dissolve. On the other hand I was struck with overwhelming revulsion at learning of Chippendale's duplicity. I'd always recognized his single-minded ambition. It was this that had spurred him to publish his book, to reach the pinnacle of success as one of London's most fashionable cabinetmakers. But to have treated Partridge thus revealed a callousness I had never suspected of him. I remembered his story of Partridge's illness; I'd always doubted its veracity, and now I knew I was right to do so. I wondered what he had told Dorothy to convince her to leave. I knew his story that Dorothy had complained about Partridge's proposal was fictitious because I'd seen with my own eyes that she cared for him. Above all, I thought, if only Partridge had braved the prohibition and contacted me, I might have helped him. I might have saved his life.

All this time Foley was fidgeting with his snuffbox while observing me closely. I knew I'd have to muster some response for him, however ill-conceived, or he'd never leave me be. I spoke as I felt, without really considering my words at all.

"It bears out what Madame Trenti said concerning Partridge. It suggests that she told him he was her son and sent him to Lord Montfort. And that would explain his presence at Horseheath."

Foley sneezed loudly, spraying snuff about the carriage. "But it does not explain his death in the pond, or why four of his fingers were brutally severed."

"Indeed," said I, flinching as I recalled the awful sight of Partridge's corpse. "Nor does it prove that Madame Trenti was telling the truth when she informed Partridge that he was her child. In fact, Partridge's doubts confirm my own suspicions."

"Why would she lie about it? What reason could she have for persuading Partridge he was her son if he was not?"

"Perhaps because she needed a convenient foundling to extract money from Lord Montfort? I believe the money he'd been paying her all these years to keep her silent had ceased. Perhaps that was why she came to

England. She needed to find her son to threaten Lord Montfort. If she couldn't find him, a substitute would serve equally well." I stared down at my boots as I gathered my thoughts. "Partridge would have been ideal for such a role. He was eager to trace something of his past, and after his mistreatment by Mr. Chippendale, he would be even more ready to believe her. She is, after all, an actress by profession." Again I halted, waiting for Foley to say something, but he remained stubbornly silent.

"But perhaps we are looking further into the matter than we need."

"What d'you mean?" said Foley.

"Let's for a moment assume that all was as Madame Trenti declared it: that Partridge *was* her child and Lord Montfort's, and that he presented himself at Horseheath as such. In those circumstances, who might wish him dead?"

"The beneficiaries of Montfort's estate?" suggested Foley.

"Precisely. For they might fear Lord Montfort would recognize a responsibility to his child, even though the child was in all probability illegitimate. And these beneficiaries, I presume, are Elizabeth Montfort, his wife, Robert, his son, and his sister, Miss Alleyn?"

"I am not apprised of all the details. Only that Robert is his heir, and there's provision for Elizabeth, including the right to reside at Horseheath for the duration of her life. Miss Alleyn, I believe, is expected to continue as housekeeper at the same stipend."

"So," I reiterated, as a shiver of anticipation ran through me, "Lord Montfort's heir is his son, Robert. His second beneficiary is his wife, Elizabeth. And as we have just seen, both are presently in London."

It was only as I spoke these words that my earlier fears returned. Whoever ran me down outside Madame Trenti's house was acting deliberately. And it was likely, then, that the same person had killed Montfort or Partridge, or both.

I thought back to the sense of menace I'd felt all around me at Horseheath Hall, and the pervasive fear that had remained with me on my return to London. I had not imagined it. The speeding carriage proved it. I *was* indubitably in the shadow of danger. Clearly, I saw, once this murderous driver discovered my escape, he would make another attempt on my life. I shivered with horror at this thought. What threat could I pose to this murderer? Why did someone want *me* dead, rather than Foley or Westleigh, who were leading the investigation? What was it about me that set me apart from them? A motive dawned on me that filled me with even greater dread. My life was in peril because the killer believed I *al-*

ready knew something that would lead me to him. It followed that now I had seen him he would be even more determined. And yet I did not know what the salient information was, or who the driver was. I had consciously neither observed nor learned anything that could help me. Here the full desperation of my predicament struck me. I had plummeted into an unfathomable mystery that seemed likely to destroy me, and I didn't comprehend why. But even as I sank to this nadir of weakness, a solitary course of action occurred to me. If I could discover who was driving the carriage that had tried to run me down, I would answer the mystery of both deaths. I must try to recall the face that had looked back at me.

I closed my eyes, filled with renewed determination. My ears once again echoed with the rattle of harnesses, I smelled again the horses' steamy scent. I felt the dread of certain death envelop my heart. I saw the carriage wheels advance towards me; I tried to picture the person who had looked down so menacingly. But all I saw was darkness.

Chapter Eleven

Partridge's letter shook me to the depths of my soul, but in one way it also helped me. There was consolation in the partial enlightenment it brought. I felt sorrow at the information I learned, yet it made me feel calmer, more certain of my friend, firmer than ever in my determination to uncover the circumstances surrounding his death.

After Foley left me at the workshop door, I returned to my desk and took out the letter again. It was as I was shuffling the pages that I remarked another small scrap of paper. Foley must have handed it to me, and I had previously overlooked it. The paper was dated December 20—a few days after Partridge was dismissed and six days before the letter to me was written. It was inscribed in Chippendale's hand.

St. Martin's Lane   December 20, 1754

John Partridge

For salary—four weeks	£4 4s 0d
Add workshop expenses	
linseed oil	2s 0d
turpentine	1s 6d
beeswax	3s 0d
1 lb. glue	9d

8 iron brackets	3s 0d
cove and beading	2s 5d
Turkey stone	6s 5d
Less	
Porterage of tool chest	1s 6d
Brought over	£5 1s 7d

I scoured the page, inconsequential though it seemed. Apparently Chippendale had paid Partridge a month's salary in lieu of notice. Clearly the frequent inquiries I had made as to Partridge's whereabouts convinced him the banishment of my friend had been effective. I scratched my head, reread the sheet, and this time found myself seized by an unexpected flash of hope. The expenses listed in the days prior to notice were unremarkable, apart from the porterage charge. Presumably this was the cost of moving Partridge's belongings from the workshop. I already knew from my visit to his lodgings that they hadn't been taken there. If Chippendale had used the usual carter—Fetherby—there was a fair possibility I might discover where Partridge had stayed in London after his disappearance, before he left for Horseheath.

It was early evening now; if Fetherby followed his usual routine, he'd be recovering from his daily toil in the tavern. The Coach and Horses was halfway down St. Martin's Lane, a small-windowed, low-ceilinged building that had stood on the same site for the past hundred years with scarcely a jot of difference in its outward appearance. Fetherby was indeed there, slumped by the fire over an empty tankard, watching a pair of rival carters compete at arm wrestling. He ignored my arrival, the only response to my greeting being a muttered "Set to it, boy—would you let Jameson get the better of you?" I deduced that Fetherby had (stupidly) wagered threepence on the younger and punier of the two contestants—a scrawny-looking youth with greasy hair and a poxy complexion. "You've backed the wrong 'un, Fetherby—and anyone here could've told you so," growled Jameson, an ox of a fellow with a head as smooth as a bell. These words had no sooner been uttered than the boy's arm collapsed on the table.

"So, Fetherby, how do you?" I said, replenishing his tankard from the quart jug I'd ordered.

He nodded curtly, grumbling that the competition was a fix if ever he saw one, and gulped his drink as if afraid I might think the better of my generosity. "Not too well, Mr. Hopson. There's too few who fill my mug. Too many like them willing to empty it from under my nose." He grimaced in the direction of the rival arm wrestlers, who now appeared the best of friends.

I nodded my head at the nearly drained mug. "There's more where that came from. And sixpence for your dinner if you can recall something for me."

Fetherby set down his mug and gave me his undivided attention.

"What then?" he hissed. "Something concerning Miss Goodchild?"

"Why no," I said sharply. "It's news of Partridge that troubles me."

"Who?"

"The journeyman. The one who's departed from Chippendale's."

"I know nothing of that matter."

"Perhaps you know more than you comprehend."

"What d'you mean?"

"Some days ago were you summoned by Mr. Chippendale to move a craftsman's tool chest?"

"Tool chest?" Fetherby poked at his wispy ear with his forefinger. "My memory's not all it used to be, Mr. Hopson."

"Then think harder, damn you. It would have been a large heavy chest, painted black. Can't be so difficult to recall."

"Rope handles?"

"Yes, I daresay—You *do* remember then?"

"Nearly cut my hand to the bone on account of 'em . . . 'ad to get a lad to help me on the cart with it, and that weren't easy. He insisted I came after eight . . ."

"He?"

Fetherby rolled his eyes at my stupidity. "Your master—Mr. Chippendale. Said I must come late when workshop was empty—so's to cause no obstruction."

"Anything else?"

"That the chest must be taken away 'cause the man 'ad gone. Tell no one where I took it." He grinned, revealing his gum, in which only three stained, broken teeth sprouted.

"Where did you transport it?"

"Didn't I just tell you? He said I mustn't speak on it."

I slid a sixpence over the table. "It will go no further if you do."

The temptation was too much. Fetherby bit the coin before secreting it in his pocket.

"That was the worst. Gave me the address of some lodgings at a court near the Fleet. Insisted I take it that night. That instant. Or I'd not be paid, nor get more work from 'im."

"Did he say why?"

"Didn't question him."

"And did you take it?"

"D'you reckon I might have turned him down after all 'is threats?" He shook his head again at my crassness. "Terrible place to get to. Obliged to carry it on my back the last part."

"Might you find your way there again?"

"Didn't you hear me? I'm forbidden. I'm not going there again, any rate. Place is crawling with those as'd cut your throat for the clothes off your back soon as say good day to you. I escaped with my life last time, I'll not put it to the test again."

"Fetherby, it is imperative I go there. I'll pay you a shilling to take me."

His face was mulish.

"Two shillings. My last offer."

Another long silence, before he sighed heavily and, grasping the handle of the now empty tankard, gazed thirstily into it. "Two shillings and a bite first?"

"Done. But I must speak to Miss Goodchild beforehand. Here's threepence for your food. Meet me at the yard within an hour." I left him gnawing on bread and a wedge of greasy mutton.

I don't know what sudden impulse had made me decide to call on Alice. She had made her dissatisfaction abundantly clear the previous afternoon, and I had no reason to suppose her feelings had changed. But her angry words continued to echo in my head. I felt an overwhelming urge to try to mend the rift between us, to explain myself, to apprise her of all that had happened since our last unhappy encounter. But what made me think she'd see me at all? Why, when she'd shown me how flighty and unreasonable she could be, did I value her opinion so highly? I thought of the warm and uncomplicated Molly Bullock, who last night had offered me a place in her bed. I'd refused, saying my head was sore from the fall I'd taken, not daring to tell her the reason my senses were in a spin was not the knock I'd received but a scolding from Alice Goodchild.

So it was that I strode briskly down the Strand and plunged into the narrow alley leading to her cottage. When I came to the door, I saw a stain of yellow candlelight flicker at the parlor window. I knocked boldly, trying to hold my gaze ahead—trying not to stare through the window at the shadowy forms that moved in response to my knock. Was she there? Would she answer? Through mottled panes I glimpsed what seemed a female form. I heard steps in the hall, a voice—her voice—call out.

"Who's there?"

"Nathaniel Hopson."

There was a long pause—an eternity, it seemed. The door opened a fraction, and I caught sight of a sliver of her face. She opened it a trifle wider. When she saw it was indeed I, she raised her chin and drew herself up, like a snake about to strike. "Did you not comprehend me yesterday when I said that I did not wish to see you on personal matters?" The tone of her voice was so disdainful it would have crushed bolder men than I, but I was determined to persist.

"I heard you, Miss Goodchild—but I feel honor bound to reason with you. I comprehend the reasons for your actions, nevertheless your judgment is unfounded. And since I regret this disagreement and wish most heartily to resolve our misunderstanding, I have come to implore you to give me leave to explain. Besides, I value your opinion and there's much to tell."

There was a long pause, during which I shuffled uncomfortably on the threshold, my fate in the balance, wondering which way she'd go.

"What makes you assume I wish to hear it?"

"Trust in your kindness . . . intelligence . . . curiosity . . ."

She blinked and bit the side of her cheek. Suddenly she seemed less sure of herself. "If I do consent to let you in, it will not be because I am less determined to keep my distance from you. On the contrary, it will be only because there's something I must tell you, that slipped my mind yesterday. And it will be on my terms."

"Name them."

"You will explain what you were about yesterday. Although it is no concern of mine, and I confess I don't know why I ask it. For, as I told you, I have determined to keep my distance."

A small hope grew in my breast that her anger might be an indication that she cared for me a little. Or was I deluding myself?

"Have I not said I intend to do so? All I ask is that you listen to me. I assure you when you hear the truth of the matter you will laugh wholeheartedly about it—as will I."

Warily, she opened the door and bade me enter. Now I could see her more clearly I thought she seemed paler and more nervous than usual, but whether this was due to our rift or some other cause I had no means of telling.

The parlor was once again in a state of complete disarray, with papers and dishes and mugs strewn across the table and floor. Her brother, Richard, was there. He nodded a brief greeting and, perhaps sensing our need for privacy, departed to the kitchen, where he started clattering pots and pans.

"Well?" she began abruptly, the minute the door closed behind him.

"Well," I said, trying to keep my voice steadier than I felt. "May I sit to explain myself?"

She furrowed her brow. "I suppose you may. But don't presume to make yourself comfortable until I've heard what you wish to say."

I outlined the gist of my visit to Madame Trenti, how I was run down by some madman in a carriage, how Trenti had told me Partridge was her child. Alice heard me out but remained skeptical. "Ruffians and a run-away coach . . . it all sounds even more far-fetched than a storybook," she said scornfully.

I felt rather foolish. "There's more to corroborate Madame Trenti's account," I persisted. "This morning Foley came to call and gave me a letter written by Partridge." I handed the paper to her and shifted awkwardly by the fire, watching while she read. When she came to the part where Partridge described his agonies and Chippendale's callousness, I heard her gasp and whisper, "This is indeed shocking."

At length she looked up. "And so Partridge died because Trenti wished to exact revenge on Montfort for a crime committed two decades ago—and sent her son in her stead?" Here, it seemed, was the calm after the tempest. Her fury with me had vanished as swiftly as it had been stirred. I now detected only straightforward curiosity in her voice.

I nodded. "So it appears."

"What will you do next?"

"I intend to go to Fleet."

"Why there? 'Tis a most foul and dangerous place, full of warrens and alleys and lanes where all manner of vagabonds and wretches conceal themselves."

"Fetherby took Partridge's belongings to a lodging house there in the days after he disappeared—or rather was banished by Chippendale. Perhaps he left something in his room to shed light on this matter."

"I'll go with you."

"You cannot. It's a menacing environ, as you said yourself. A young lady such as you would be in dire peril."

She tossed the papers towards me and rose abruptly. "If you do not wish to rile me again, Mr. Hopson, you will stop treating me as a half-wit. Two days ago you involved me in your intrigue because you needed my assistance. A moment ago you said you valued my opinion, yet now you no longer need my help, in case I would be placing myself in dire peril. Don't confuse the matter by citing my sex. I'm capable of running a business, and I'm certainly able to accompany you to Fleet."

The set of her mouth warned me to tread carefully. Nonetheless I might have braved her anger and protested more, but at that moment Fetherby's wagon creaked into the yard. She heard it as quickly as I, and before I could utter another word, she had fastened her cloak and clambered onto the wagon seat, from where she smiled defiantly down at me. "Are you coming, Mr. Hopson? D'you require assistance? Or shall I go with Fetherby alone?"

I got up beside her—what choice did I have? But I was damned if I'd let the matter go without a few words of warning. "I doubt you understand the danger you are putting yourself in, Miss Goodchild," I said solemnly. "If you must come, for God's sake stay close to me at all times."

She looked sideways at me. "If I believe your reputation, it is you I should fear, Mr. Hopson," she said slyly, "not the shadows of Fleet."

Observing this charade from his platform, Fetherby cackled. "She knows her own mind. There are few like her, Mr. Hopson, and she's saucy enough to be a match for you."

"Shall we leave before our blood freezes, Fetherby?" I said pointedly. "Or have you further wisdom to bestow?"

We rumbled ponderously along Fleet Street and across the bridge to Ludgate Hill. Here we left the main thoroughfare and wound our way past the butchers' stalls and slaughterhouses of Smithfield, into the labyrinthine alleys and courts within courts that mark the meanest London streets. Anyone familiar with our city will know the Fleet is famed in our time for its dreadful debtors' prison, and that the inhabitants of that place have become so numerous as to spill over into the surrounding streets. Thus the reek of poverty was all around us, a stench of dung and blood and entrails unwashed from the gutter. The unlit streets were lined with gin shops, bawdy houses, pawnbrokers, and stalls, within which I imagined all manner of harlots, thieves, and beggars to reside. Sometimes the mud through which we rolled was so deep it seemed we meandered through a sea of tar. Sometimes the lanes were so narrow the wheels brushed the sides of the hovels and shacks that lined them. Whenever we spied pedestrians in the gloom ahead, we called out for them to flatten themselves or be crushed by the wheels. Through all this Alice showed no obvious sign of fear. She sat upright, silent, although when the cart jolted her cloak apart I caught sight of her hands clenched so tight that the nails must have bitten into her skin. Taking this as a sign she might be more fearful than she showed, I endeavored to distract her.

"You never told me what it was you wanted to say."

"What?" She started, as if she'd almost forgotten I was there.

"When you let me in you said it was because there was something you wished to tell me."

"So I did," she replied. "It is curious, and I meant to tell you of it yesterday, only I believe my anger made it slip my mind."

But I never discovered what it was, for at that moment Fetherby drew the wagon to an abrupt halt. "I can take you no further. You'll have to go on by foot," he announced, spitting a large globule of phlegm to the ground.

"But which way is it now? You must give us directions," I said.

Fetherby swiveled round in his seat and sucked noisily on his gums. "Well now, let me consider. As I recall you take this lane till Foubert's Court. Go through to the far end. There's a yard, turn to your left. Across from the entrance to Mitre Court is an alehouse—Blue Boar, it's called. Go in. Ask for Grace Webb—landlord's wife, lets out rooms in her garret and cellar. That's where I took the chest."

Before I could hand Alice down she'd descended into the mire, lifting her skirts in one hand and holding the lantern aloft in the other to make it easier for me to avoid the potholes. I jumped down beside her, misjudged my step, and the mud oozed into the crevices of my shoes. I fancied I saw the corners of her mouth twitch, but she turned immediately to lead the way as Fetherby had directed.

We passed through a honeycomb of beggars' lodging houses, brothels, rookeries, garrets, and night cellars. Most resembled heaps of rubbish rather than dwelling places, with wood or paper substituted for broken panes of glass, and holes in the walls stuffed by rags.

"What could have possessed him to choose such a vile place?"

"The answer is surely that no one would reside here from choice," replied Alice. "He came, like everyone else here, because he had *no* choice."

"Not necessarily. He might have wished himself untraceable—to lose himself in this maze. Was that what Chippendale forced him to?"

"It wasn't essential to endure such squalor to lose himself. He could have left London, gone to the country."

"But London was all he knew."

By now we'd arrived at the threshold of the Blue Boar Alehouse, a miserable tumbledown mound of rotten beams and damp walls blackened by the surrounding filth. How Alice must have regretted her decision to accompany me as we turned the rusty handle in the door and entered. I thank God never to have entered such a hole of a place before or since and even now can barely dare to contemplate what she made of it all. The walls were as dark and putrid as those outside; in places great slabs of render had fallen from them, leaving the bricks and beams beneath leprously exposed. Spanning one wall was a crude counter hung with numerous tarnished tankards, bowls, jugs, cups, and flagons made of pewter, iron, and leather. Behind it a couple of harassed pot boys were busy filling these various receptacles from vast barrels and kegs, while an older man, a cutthroat rascal whom I presumed to be the landlord, leaned on the counter smoking a pipe. The whole room was in an uproar for, in the far corner, I now became aware, a couple of she-devils were engaged in combat. Their scratching and biting and hitting engagement had bloodied and bruised their faces and shredded their clothes so that their bare bosoms were exposed to view, much to the delight of the cheering crowd of men surrounding them.

At our inquiry the landlord crossly tore himself away from the spectacle and shouted at one of the pot boys to call his wife, who was presently occupied in the kitchens. Grace Webb, a small stout woman with a vast globular bosom suspended over a corpulent torso, appeared some minutes later. Her generous proportions did not reflect an amiable temperament. She emerged from her kitchen scowling furiously, sausage fingers braced upon fleshy hips.

"What the devil is this about? I'm up to my elbows in suet and tripe and you summon me?"

"I do beg your pardon, my dearest," said the landlord with mock gentility. "There's two fine people who wish to speak with you."

She snorted with disdain. "Why should I be interested in their questions, pray?"

"It's this lady and gentleman here." He winked and added in an undertone, "I've a feeling they'll be generous with those that help them. 'Tis the gentleman with the chest they're after. The one who's not paid his dues for two weeks."

She reconstructed her expression from fury to shifty curiosity.

"What is it then?" she demanded.

"Madam," I replied, bowing slightly and pressing a shilling in her hand, "I believe you recently gave lodgings to a man by the name of John Partridge, and that his work chest was delivered here a fortnight ago?"

She looked at the shiny coin and then back at me. "And what of it?"

"John Partridge was an acquaintance of mine. I would like to see his things—and make arrangements to remove them."

"Was?"

"He died recently, in tragic circumstances."

"Damnation if you will! How dare he die without paying my rent. I should've known better than to take him in the first place. There's four shillings due and you'll not touch anything till it's paid. I'll 'ave to sell his things to cover my costs."

"Madam, be assured I'll willingly pay the outstanding amount, and more for your trouble, for I entirely comprehend your inconvenience," I said. "Meantime here's another shilling if you'll let me just look at his room tonight." I could see from the glare she shot at me she thought I was an idiot to offer so much when a couple of pennies would have done as well, but she wasn't about to tell me so.

"Very well. Follow me," she snarled, snatching the second coin from my fingers.

She led the way through a maze of small rooms, each heaving with foul-smelling bodies. The sounds of the sparring women and the roistering audience followed us up a staircase leading four stories, to the garret. Mrs. Webb was grunting from her exertions by the time we reached the top landing. She took a key from her chain and unlocked the left-hand door. "This is it," she announced. "Everything there's like when he left. I'll give you ten minutes, no longer. You may look but take nothing with you. You'll come back with the monies owing before you take the stuff away."

She stood there blocking the doorway, waiting for us to respond. We stared mutely back. "I'm presuming the lantern's not enough?" She gestured towards Alice's lamp. "You'll be wanting a light or two more to see by," she said crossly, thrusting two tallow stubs at us. "In which case, that'll be sixpence." Money was incidental. I simply wanted to see Partridge's effects and be gone from this foul place. Without remonstrating at the exorbitant cost of this transaction, I produced another coin, which she stowed with the rest before mercifully clumping down the stairs.

The room was meagerly furnished: a bed and bolster—the covers little more than unwashed rags; two old cane-bottomed chairs; a cracked looking glass in a deal frame hanging from the wall; a small wainscot table, on which was an empty iron candlestick. There was only one object here I recognized as belonging to Partridge. Under the eaves beneath the window stood his work chest.

Alice placed her lantern on the table and holding her candle in one hand began rifling through the contents of the table drawer with the other. I meanwhile tried to open the chest but succeeded only in burning my hand with molten tallow. I set the stub on the floor and shook my hand about to cool it.

"Locked."

"Is this what you're looking for?" She held out an intricately wrought brass key.

I slotted it into the keyhole. Cautiously I turned the key in the lock and lifted back the lid. Partridge had spent many an idle hour adorning his chest with as much care as if he were decorating the richest commode. Within the unremarkable bitumened exterior were ranks of mahogany compartments, sliding tills and drawers in which chisels, gouges, files, planes, rules, and saws were neatly stored. In the center of the chest was a well divided into three sections: one holding the molding planes, another containing fretsaws, and a third covered with a panel. I retracted the panel and lowered my candle stub into the dark cavity. Here was something that might conceivably be of interest: a slender booklet in a card cover, Partridge's sketchbook. Before I'd time to examine its pages, Alice knelt beside me. I heard her gasp loudly. She was holding her candle close to the center of the lid, staring fixedly at it.

Last time I'd seen Partridge's chest, the lid had been lined with plain mahogany. Now an oval had been cut from the center of it and an intricate marquetry picture inset. "Partridge must have made this recently," I said, "for while I've often seen his chest, I never saw this before."

She was still gazing at the picture. "It's a curious subject. D'you recognize it?"

I studied it carefully. It was, as she said, most curious: a temple, a bird, and two figures clad in classical robes, one standing, the other prostrate before him.

"I don't believe I do," I replied. "But plainly it's taken from antiquity.

Partridge was fascinated by ancient legend. I daresay he took the design from a print." I squinted again, and then it was my turn to be thunderstruck. I shook my head, unable to believe the evidence before me.

"Why do you look so? What is it you are staring at?" demanded Alice.

"The wood. Look here." I pointed to the columns of the temple, the robes of the prostrate figure, and the wing feathers of the bird. "Is this not the very same grenadillo wood as the box taken from Montfort's hand?"

Alice leaned forward. Four stories below I heard a creak as Grace Webb began her ascent of the stairs. She was approaching with surprising stealth and rapidity. There was no time to lose. Without a thought for what I was doing, I stuffed the booklet of sketches in my pocket, slammed down the lid, locked it, and replaced the key in the drawer where we'd found it. Alice remained frozen in her crouched position. I offered my hand to help her, but she ignored me. "Miss Goodchild . . . Alice . . . stand up. She's coming, and I don't wish her to suspect we've taken anything from the chest."

Alice stood slowly, stiffly, head bowed, as if she'd scarcely heard me but was absorbed in some great problem.

"What's the matter? Do you not concede that it is the same timber? You have only to regard the figuring to see—"

Abruptly she raised her head and stared frankly into my eyes. "Of course I agree. It's that very matter I'm considering. It confirms more than you know."

Plainly my face must have shown astonishment and bewilderment, for she shook her head as if she was impatient with herself. "I owe you an apology, Nathaniel. I should have told you before now. You recall I said I had something to tell you?"

"Yes."

"It's all the more remarkable in the light of this. What I wanted to tell you was this: I looked for grenadillo wood in our ledgers yesterday. The timber came from South America; it was popular a century ago but has recently become scarce. And . . ."

"And?"

"I consulted another encyclopedia. It seems that when the timber was fashionable, it was termed something else."

I frowned at her, not following her drift at all.

"Nathaniel, grenadillo was also commonly known as partridge wood."

I stared back at her, feeling more dazed and giddy at this information than if I'd drunk a bottle of wine. "Are you certain?"

"There were many references."

"Can it be a coincidence that the wood used in the box found in Lord Montfort's hand and in this picture has the same name as our dead friend?"

"I think not," she said. "He must have seen it as his signature. Moreover, there's another question to address."

"What's that?"

"The timber grows only in Brazil, and as I said has been scarce for the past decades. We haven't sold any for twenty years, nor I'll vouch has any other wood merchant in London."

"And what of that?"

"How then did Partridge come by a wood that has disappeared from view these past twenty years?"

Alice and I gazed at each other and fell into puzzled silence. An instant later Grace Webb threw open the door and glared at us like a gorgon.

Chapter Twelve

L ondon's Foundling Hospital stands in the midst of the green expanse of Lamb's Conduit Fields, off the road that leads from the city of London to the outlying villages of Hampstead and Highgate. The edifice was newly built to a simple but imposing design: two broad wings flanking a central chapel, and a rectangular courtyard extending to lawns on either side. Pleasant surroundings, charming inmates, and an estimable collection of paintings by masters such as Reynolds, Hogarth, and Gainsborough exhibited on its walls had established the hospital as a fashionable visiting spot among London society. From my desk I gazed through long sash windows at ladies in fur-trimmed cloaks. They stood in a small cluster admiring a picturesque curiosity: a dozen or more uniformed children digging frosty earth, sweeping the courtyard, and working the pump.

What would it be like to be an inmate here? To be dressed in regulation brown, to sleep in a dormitory with a dozen other children who knew no more about their parentage than you? The place seemed clean and pleasant enough, the food adequate. I supposed it would be preferable to being abandoned on the street or consigned to the miseries of the workhouse. But how different it would have been from my own tranquil childhood, where no doubts about who would care for me had ever intruded on my consciousness.

I was presently seated in the grand courtroom, where I had come to sift through the hospital's records. I executed this task under the watchful eye of the warden, an elderly gentleman weighed down by a heavy braided coat and a flowing full-bottomed wig. Madame Trenti had told me that Miss Alleyn's letter had supplied her with the date—the very day the hospital opened, March 25, 1741—when her child was deposited here. From this information she had traced records relating to Partridge, records that made her certain Partridge was her child. Since hearing her account I'd felt uneasy; instinct told me her story was a deception. Yet my only evidence for these qualms was a vague prickling at the back of my neck and a feeling of emptiness in the pit of my belly—nebulous sensations that, I acknowledge, weren't a solid foundation on which to base my doubt. And so I'd resolved to come to the hospital to ascertain what exactly (if anything) she might have found to convince her that Partridge was her long-lost son.

I'd asked the warden about the events of that first evening. In answer to my inquiry he handed me the first committee book, in which the hospital's opening was thus described:

March 26, 1741

Having according to the resolution of the general committee with all possible diligence put this hospital into a condition proper for the reception of children, this committee met at seven o'clock in the evening. They found a great number of people crowding about the door, many with children and others for curiosity. The committee were informed that several persons had offered children but were refused admittance, the order of the general committee being that the house should not open till eight o'clock at night and this committee were resolved to give no preference to any persons whatsoever. The committee were attended by the peace officers of the parish and two watchmen of theirs, who were ordered to assist the watchmen of the hospital. They had orders to prevent any child's being laid down at our door and to give a signal to the parish watchman in case any child was refused to be admitted into the hospital, who thereupon was to take care that it was not dropped on the parish.

At eight o'clock the lights in the entry were extinguished. The outward door was opened by the porter, who was forced to attend that door all night to keep out the crowd. Immediately the bell rang and a woman brought in a child. The messenger let her into the room on the right hand, and carried the child into the stewards' room, where the proper officers together with Dr. Nesbitt and some other governors were constantly attending to inspect the child. According to the director's plan, the child being inspected was received, numbered, and the billet of its description entered by three different persons for certainty. The woman who brought the child was then dismissed without being seen by any of the governors or asked any questions, then another child was brought and so on constantly till thirty children were admitted, eighteen of whom were boys and twelve girls. . . . Two children were refused, one being too old and the other appearing to have the itch. . . . About twelve o'clock, the house being full, the porter was ordered to give notice of it to the crowd who were without, who thereupon being a little troublesome . . . and the governors observing seven or eight women with children at the door and more amongst the crowd desired them that they would not drop any of their children in the streets. On this occasion the expressions of grief of the women whose children could not be admitted were scarcely more observable than those of some of the women who parted with their children, so that a more moving scene can't well be imagined.

The account continued in similar vein, describing the agonies of these poor wretches, which seemed to me at once remote and indescribably poignant. And yet I found none of the details pertaining to each child that I wanted. I coughed gently. "Forgive me, sir."

The elderly warden stopped writing and peered at me between a frame of white-powdered curls.

"This ledger provides an admirable record of the hospital's first night, yet nothing specific relating to the children accepted. What records exist of them?"

"There are entries for each infant in the billet books."

I recalled Madame Trenti's mention of such books. Perhaps this was a sign she had come here after all and her account was not the fabrication I took it for. "Has a lady been here recently asking for the same thing? A small foreign lady, finely dressed?"

He gave a brusque laugh and shook his head, causing the lappets of his wig to flap noiselessly. "Every day there are callers wishing to trace an infant from some date or other. Do you really expect me to recall them all?"

"Of course not, sir. But this lady is a famous actress—Madame Trenti. Perhaps you recognized her."

He puffed himself up. "Do I look the type of man who is familiar with actresses?"

"No, sir," I said, chastened, "you misunderstood me. I merely thought you might recall her because she is very . . . flamboyant." He glared at me again. "May I see the first volume?" I added hurriedly.

He made a great show of putting down his quill, rising from his chair, and hobbling reluctantly to an inner office. Some minutes later he returned, carrying a slender leather-bound volume, which he placed on the table before me.

I opened it. Each child was described on a separate sheet, to which were pinned various poignant mementos and a record of any note left with them. On the back of each sheet was a number, the name of the nurse to whom the child had been sent, and one or two words which indicated the child's fate—*died* or *apprenticed*. I turned my attention to the first pages, which ran thus:

March 25, 1741

1. A female child about a fortnight old with the enclosed paper: "March 2, 1741. This child is baptized and her name is Dorritey Hanton."

2. A male child about 2 months old, gown flowered on white with a white dimity mantle with the enclosed note: "Robert Chancellor, born January the 29." Piece of fabric enclosed.

3. A male child 4 or 5 weeks old, a clout marked "FA" pinned on the breast, came in a brown cloak.

4. A male child about 3 weeks old, blue satin sleeves turned up with sarcenet.

5. A female child 6 or 7 weeks old, white dimity sleeves, laced ruffles, and white ribbon about the head.
"Elizabeth Ayers born Feb 14, 1741, christened at St. Clement Danes, I beg the favor that this paper may be kept with the child."

6. A female child about 3 weeks old, almost starved.

7. A male child, cleanly dressed, wrapped in a red cloak, with the

enclosed letter: "Whether this child live or die, be pleased to send account there of it to the Old Bell Inn, Holborn, in one month's time. Direct it to C.—it will be acknowledged a great favor."

8. A male child about 4 weeks old, with the enclosed letter pinned on its breast: "This child is not christened, the father has not been found, the mother has deserted it. The mother's name is Dorothy Smilk."

9. A male child about 1 month old very meanly dressed.

10. A female child about 1 day old with the enclosed letter: "I am daughter of Samuel Wilde, water gilder, who died February 24, I was born March 24, pray let my Christian name be Alice . . ."

So far as I could see, there was no mention here of any child who could conceivably have been Partridge. I looked up from the page, shaking my head in bewilderment. "These children were all extremely young, no more than infants?"

There was a great silence, during which my words seemed to hang in the air like a pall of smoke on a windless day. Eventually the warden looked up, flaring his nostrils as if infuriated by the crass stupidity of such a question. "It is a matter of record that the governing body stipulated only children under the age of two months should be admitted."

"And the infants accepted were all raised here?"

He put down his pen wearily, as if resigning himself to the fact he was dealing with a half-wit. "This building had not yet been constructed. The hospital was then quartered—as you would have read, had you paid proper attention to the committee book—in a building in Hatton Garden."

"And that is where they were raised?"

"No, Mr. Hopson. It is not. They were dispatched to nurses in the country, where it was felt the clean air would assist their chances of survival. Only at the age of five or six did they return to the hospital. Whereupon they were educated until about eleven or twelve years, then apprenticed to trade."

This was what I had suspected all along, and yet I was heavy with dismay. Far from confirming Madame Trenti's story that she had found a record of Partridge here, this information disproved it. The problem was one of date. If Partridge had been left in March 1741, as Miss Alleyn had claimed in her letter, he must have been about four or five years old. Far too old for the hospital directors' specification for children aged not more than two months. I pursued another track.

"If, for argument's sake, an older child had been presented, what would have happened to it?"

"Such a child would not be eligible to be granted a place—it would have been rejected. As you saw in the notes, there were guards and watchmen to ensure no child was abandoned." His tone was growing overtly snappish, and he gazed regretfully at the ledger from which I was still distracting him.

"Who was the warden that night?"

"My predecessor, James Barrow."

"Is he employed here still?"

"No longer. He retired some years ago."

From the way he glared at me I could see his patience was at breaking point. Still I was stubbornly determined to persist. "One last question if you please. . . . Where may I find James Barrow?"

"He lives in Hatton Garden, I believe. Nearby the old premises of the hospital. More I cannot tell you. Now I really must—"

"My heartfelt thanks, sir. What you've told me has been most enlightening."

I deflected my gaze to avoid antagonizing him further, and my eye came to rest on a painting in a massive gilt frame suspended above his head. A small plaque indicated the painting was by Hogarth and gave its title, *Moses Brought Before Pharaoh's Daughter.* Another foundling story. Hogarth depicted Moses as a small child, returned to the palace by his nurse. There was a touching humanity in the way the child clung to his nurse's dress, reluctant to greet the princess. The background was filled with a jumble of smoking buildings—not unlike a London landscape. Had Hogarth understood that the agonies of not knowing whether you belonged to a princess or a serving girl were as acute in modern London as in ancient Egypt?

I turned back to the description in the committee book of the first day that children were accepted. Certain lines now seemed to jump out at me: "They had orders to prevent any child's being laid down at our door and to give a signal to the parish watchman in case any child was refused to be admitted into the hospital, who thereupon was to take care that it was not dropped on the parish." Had some incident prompted the authorities to give this order to the watch? Could it be that earlier in the day—before the guards and watch were assembled—a child *had* been left who wasn't eligible? If not, why had such precautions been necessary?

I consulted the billet book once more. Halfway through the entries a thought struck me. One of the entries was different from the rest. I turned back and reread them. I hadn't imagined it. The discrepancy was there, as I thought. Child number seven had been entered without any mention of his age. I took out my pocketbook and transcribed the entry word for word.

Chapter Thirteen

I lay on the bed, wretched, half insensible, and chastised myself heartily for the weakness of my resolve. The room spun round my head faster than a whirligig, and with so much wine in my belly all I could do was pray and trust my penitence would keep me from retching. In vain I now regretted my chute from diligent research to drunkenness. How I wished I could undo my dissipation.

My transgressions had begun midafternoon, when I'd returned from the hospital flaming with good intent. I'd meant to show my face at the workshop and carry out my duties before retiring to my lodgings to think over all I'd unveiled. Instead, as I walked down St. Martin's Lane, fair Fanny Harling spied me from her window. She sped out like an enthusiastic puppy to halt me and, declaring I was just what she needed, implored me to come in with her. The reason for this fervent entreaty, so she said, was a tallboy. Its drawers were sticking and her linens impossible to arrange in an orderly fashion. Her husband, a silversmith who was well known to me, had presently gone to Deptford on business, leaving her alone, helpless, needful of my ministrations.

Of course I wasn't so green as not to recognize this invitation for the lure it undoubtedly was. I reviewed my difficulties with Alice and shuddered at the thought that my actions might cause a repetition of our troubles. Such a visit was impossible, I declared, I had important work to do. "Take a stub of tallow," I suggested, "and rub it several times over the base. You'll find it's the very thing to ease the runners." She chuckled naughtily, bubbles of laughter more infectious than any contagion, and begged me again. Now I found myself laughing back and my spirits becoming so violently exhilarated that to reject her seemed pointlessly cruel. Alice vanished like a phantom from my consciousness. I did what seemed right at the time, and the only thing I could think of. I succumbed.

We both had a terrible hunger and went first to the Shakespeare, where we regaled our bellies with oyster pie and doses of champagne, while our fingers kept busy with caresses under the table. When we had eaten and drunk and stroked our fill, she led me back to her dwelling. "This way for the 'tallboy,' " she said saucily, squeezing past the door to drag me upstairs, brushing the contours of my manhood beneath my breeches as she did so.

I had forgotten how lithe she was, how slender was her waist, how plumply her buttocks filled her petticoats. I could span her waist with my hands, and the champagne made her more ticklish than a salmon. She squirmed enticingly as I held her, placed a butterfly kiss on my mouth, and took my hand and placed it where I should toy with her. "Now tell me," she whispered as she leaned alluringly against her tallboy, "can you think of no other means to ease my problem?"

Neither of us was in a mood to wait. "Show me what you think might loosen it," I murmured as I clamped my mouth on hers, unbuttoned myself, and gathered her onto me. We thrust together, damp and desperate as storm-tossed travelers battling a gale, until we fell back on her bed to oblivion.

Some time later I was rudely awakened to find her shaking me by the shoulder. "I believe I hear Samuel's step downstairs," she said, suddenly matter-of-fact. "For God's sake go to the closet before he comes in."

Nothing is so sobering as the imminent arrival of a husband. Once before, on a memorable occasion I'd prefer to forget, I'd encountered Samuel Harling in a rage. It was not an experience I was ready to repeat. I leaped from her bed, grabbed my clothes and boots, and concealed myself while she descended the stairs to distract him. Five minutes later, having dressed inside the closet, I clambered through the window to the stable roof, from where it was a fortunately short drop to the street. But the effects of the champagne and burgundy and brandy I'd consumed made me maladroit. My ankle twisted beneath me, and I landed in a pool of mud. I yelped with pain, but mercifully the damage was slight and I recovered myself. With a prayer of thanks to a kindly Lord for allowing me to escape my transgression with such minor inconveniences as soiled breeches and a bruised foot, I limped home to my lodgings.

As soon as I lay on the bed, the effects of my debauch returned. The room swam, I fell into semioblivion, and my head pounded even more urgently than my loins a few hours earlier. Eventually, realizing there would be no possibility of sleep in such a state, I rose, took a drink, and vomited copiously into the chamber pot.

Now, somewhat clearer in the head, I lay down again and dozed. But my sleep was fitful and I was roused some hours later by the clatter of the night-soil wagon in the street outside. I opened my eyes and looked around me. Moonlight filled my bedchamber. My mouth was furry and foul-tasting, and my body was racked with cold. In my drunkenness I'd discarded my soiled clothing and lain on the counterpane without bothering to cover myself. I sat up, pulled on a nightgown, and crawled beneath the covers. Even with the weight of bedclothes upon me, I trembled so violently I couldn't close my eyes.

Thoughts of Partridge and Madame Trenti and Chippendale disturbed me, but I consoled myself that, prior to my lapse, I'd made some small advances. The letter I'd received from Partridge supported Trenti's claim that it was she who had sent him to Montfort. But, as I'd guessed, there had been nothing at the hospital to show that Partridge was Trenti and Montfort's child. Thus, although I still suspected Partridge was just a convenient substitute, I now comprehended the *reason* he had gone to Cambridge. He had gone at Trenti's behest, to petition Montfort for financial assistance. I also knew, thanks to Alice, that grenadillo wood was a rare timber sometimes known as partridge wood. This, together with the skill with which the box was made, was enough to convince me it was Partridge who had carved the grenadillo box and given it to Montfort as a signature piece, whose wood bore his own name. In this sense it was also an obscure calling card, identifiable only if you knew the name of the wood. Partridge loved conundrums, and this curious puzzle was entirely in his character.

But there was still much that perplexed me. First, the timber. I wondered where on earth Partridge could have laid hands on such rare material. And if I assumed Partridge was responsible for making the box and giving it to Montfort, did that mean he had entered the library on the night Montfort died to give it to him? I remembered the pool of blood on the windowsill, and the terrible mutilation of Partridge's hand. I suspected the blood was Partridge's rather than Montfort's, yet I couldn't begin to comprehend why anyone would injure him in such a way.

A shaft of silver light flooded the window, illuminating the top of my dressing table and on it Partridge's sketchbook, which I had recovered during my search of his lodgings with Alice. I had yet to examine the pages thoroughly, but a brief glance had shown me that they contained no more than designs and sketches for furniture.

The moment Alice's name returned to my consciousness, I was overcome with remorse for my antics with Fanny Harling. I tried valiantly to reassure myself. I was unattached, I'd made no commitment to Alice, such random connections were necessary for my equilibrium. To enjoy a woman hungry for the pleasures you offered could not be entirely wicked. One might even construe it as a form of generosity.

Yet deep down I felt uneasy. I suspected that Alice would not agree were she to discover the episode, and now I thought over it, I knew I'd been a fool. My coupling with Fanny had roused my body but not my spirit. I felt remorse rather than satisfaction. And this led me to a further disturbing point: *was* I unattached? Had Alice somehow inveigled her way into my consciousness and spirit without my recognizing or endorsing it? Was that why I now felt a disturbing rectitude, an amorous scrupulousness that was entirely foreign to my nature? Of course, in my heart I knew the answers to all these questions. I had done what I had never believed possible: I'd let myself become intoxicated with a woman who viewed me with suspicion. Alice had me ensnared.

With such perplexities tormenting my brain, it was little wonder sleep continued to elude me. At length, realizing that it was pointless to lie there thrashing and shivering and fretting, I rose. I wrapped myself in a blanket, took up the notebook, and in a pool of moonlight, began to peruse its pages.

I passed briskly over designs for cabinets, chests, moldings, and curlicues, marveling at Partridge's astonishing eye for detail and proportion as I viewed each page. Halfway through the book was a drawing for the inlaid panel we'd discovered in his tool-chest lid. It depicted the same two figures in classical costume, one old, one young, one standing, one lying before a Grecian temple, with a bird flying off in the distance. Underneath was a small inscription, *Daedalus and Talos, after Cipriani*. The title meant nothing to me, although Cipriani, an Italian artist lately arrived in London and enjoying success for his toga-clad maidens, was familiar enough.

I looked further. The next page was bare save for a more detailed study of the temple that formed the background for the vignette. I turned another page. This time a detailed drawing, which it took me several moments to decipher. I decided at length it depicted the same temple, in equal detail, but viewed from a strange perspective. My predilection for studying and dismantling structures made such an alternate view strangely fascinating. I turned back to the previous page to verify the accuracy of each study. It was as I was flitting between the two, scrutinizing the pen work, that the full significance of what I'd stumbled on came to me. This was not merely a sketch for the scene inlaid in the tool chest. It was also a design for a three-dimensional object. The design for the grenadillo box.

Anticipation clenching at my innards, I turned to the next page and found further drawings that explained the mechanism inside. There were details of every join and hinge. I could now see that the middle section of roof was a sliding panel, which would be released only by pressing on a tiny corner of veneer. When this was drawn back, another slide at right angles to the first was uncovered. Beneath was the cavity where the key was hidden. The lock was similarly concealed: by pushing down on the opposite wall, one of the columns could be retracted to reveal it, and thus the entire side of the temple hinged open to reveal the compartment—and contents—within. The mechanics of operation were straightforward but effective, an adaptation of methods used to conceal a compartment in a writing desk or cabinet. And, as I'd discovered, unless you knew precisely where to press, and in what order to proceed, the box was impossible to open.

I put down the book. The excitement of my findings had raised my pulse, and now that I'd unearthed the secrets I was in a fever of impatience to put them to the test. Alas! Where was the subject of this research, where was the mysterious box Foley had entrusted to me? I cursed myself roundly. I had returned it to him at our previous meeting on the bridge when I'd confessed myself incapable of discovering how it opened. It was two days since I'd heard from Foley, and I didn't know if he was returned to Cambridge. How fervently I prayed he remained in London. I'd half a mind to go immediately to his house and try to rouse him. But as soon as I'd thought of the idea I dismissed it. The chimes of the hall clock told me it was not yet four in the morning. If I woke Foley now he'd hardly be in a mood to receive me.

In this state of agitation I forced myself to close my eyes, even though I was convinced sleep would never come. Yet strangely my earlier restlessness no longer troubled me, and almost immediately I fell into a profound and dreamless slumber. When I awoke the clock was striking seven. Dawn was breaking, a clear cold morning that had deposited a veil of frost over my window.

I leaped from my bed, broke the ice in the washbowl, and washed Fanny's musky scent from my skin. The soreness of my head and ankle seemed to have vanished with the dark, and my mind was surprisingly clear. I splashed myself with rose water and dressed quickly—clean linens, brown breeches, and gray coat—scarcely noting my awkward reflection in the looking glass, relieved only that the anxieties that had troubled me last night had vanished along with the symptoms of my debauch.

The reason for my miraculous cure was obvious. I believed I held a key to the deaths of Partridge and Montfort here in my hand. For surely, I told myself, once the contents of the box were revealed, the fog shrouding these events would begin to melt away.

En route to Foley's, I made a detour to the workshop. I'd decided to explain this morning's absence—it would take an hour or two, no longer, of that I was convinced—by persuading Chippendale I must visit Foley on the pretext of checking a measurement for a drawing. To say the truth, while I felt slight qualms in this deception, these were snowflakes compared with the blizzard of my disillusionment at his deception. Partridge's letter had revealed how poorly Chippendale had used him and, as I saw it, had nullified the loyalty he was due. Ever since I'd read the letter I'd struggled to reconcile his guise of uprightness with what I now knew his true character to be. I recoiled from my master; my heart was irretrievably hardened, although I own even then a childish part of me still longed to believe in him as I once had done.

Chippendale's reaction to my petition was predictable. His overriding concern was that I should remain on good terms with Foley, and thus he drank up my excuses readily. So it was that by eight, having breakfasted on bread and cheese and a tankard of porter, I set out for St. James's with my master's blessing, and soon after I was knocking on Foley's door.

He was still in his nightgown, eating rolls and marmalade and seed cake on a porcelain plate, when his footman showed me to him.

"Mr. Hopson," said he, handing me a cup of coffee and lounging back in his chair. "You anticipate me uncannily with your visit. It was my intention to call upon you later today."

"Indeed, Lord Foley. Forgive my untimely intrusion, but I felt sure you would wish to be the first to hear what I have to say."

Foley sat up sharply, furrowing his mossy brows. "You have news, I take it. What is it, pray?"

"Let me ask you something first," I said, forcing myself to contain my excitement by speaking slowly. "Is the grenadillo box in this house still?"

"It is downstairs in the parlor. The servant will fetch it directly if you desire it. Why do you ask?"

"I believe, my lord, I've uncovered the means to open it."

Foley's knife clattered on his china plate. "Upon my life, Hopson, why did you not say so sooner?"

He clicked his fingers and briskly informed his servant that the box should be brought. Then he turned back to me and demanded that I explain myself. I was of course burning to show him what I'd found. I took out the notebook, laid it open in front of him, and briefly described the significance of the drawings. He flicked through them, scrutinizing each carefully, turning back and forth between the pages as I had done the night before. He was still examining these images when the footman returned with the box on a silver salver. Immediately Foley seized the box from the tray and thrust it towards me.

"Here you are, Hopson!" he cried. "Let's see what you can make of it."

With a trembling hand I placed the box on the table. It was as I remembered it: smaller than my fist, exquisitely carved and finished. Aided by frequent reference to the pages of the book, I pressed and slid and delved. I retrieved the key, removed the column that covered the keyhole, and just as the drawing delineated, the lock appeared before us. I put the key in and turned. A smooth click, the lock disengaged, the lid opened.

Foley had moved round the breakfast table and was standing beside me now. As if we'd stumbled into an unlit cavern, we both stared intently into shadows. Only here the cavity was so minute we had to squint to see its treasure. "What is it?" said Foley, craning over me in a lather of impatience. "Is anything there? I see nothing . . ."

"Yes," I replied as I frowned into the box. "There is indeed something, although I fear it won't answer as many questions as we hoped."

"God's teeth!" cried Foley, throwing back the chair in his agitation. "What on earth d'you mean? Show me!"

I picked up the contents of the box between my thumb and forefinger and dropped it delicately into his outstretched palm. "Here, see for yourself what you make of it."

As if it were quicksilver that might trickle through his fingers, Foley cradled the object in his hand. He bowed his head to examine it, then looking more perplexed than I'd ever seen him, he picked up a magnifying glass from his side table and held it to his hand.

"Not only does it fail to answer our questions, it is meaningless, is it not?"

"It cannot truly be meaningless," said I at length. "It must signify something or there would be no purpose in secreting it there. It's clearly a token of some sort."

"What makes you say that?" asked Foley, placing the object gingerly on a saucer and handing it to me with the magnifying glass so I too could look. "Confess it, Hopson. You are as flummoxed as I. And we are both as confounded now as before you opened the wretched box. What on earth is it?"

I held the magnifying glass up and focused on the center of the saucer. The object I scrutinized was a crescent of gold, engraved with the words "To C . . ."

That was all.

"I can see as well as you, my lord, that it is a ring that for one reason or another has been cut in half. Perhaps it was an engagement or marriage ring that was severed as a token, two people each taking a portion, possibly as a form of pledge," I said.

"Hopson, your 'perhaps' and 'possibly' are all very well. But what good does the ring do us? Has it actually helped in any way?"

"The fact we don't understand its significance doesn't mean it has no meaning. I believe it does represent an important advance, even if that advance is only to comprehend how little we know."

Foley glowered. "What the devil d'you mean?"

I met his scowl unflinchingly. "Imagine our inquiries into these deaths as if we were cutting a clearing in the midst of a forest. The larger the clearing, the greater the perimeter of dark trunks around us. The obscurity may seem impenetrable. But that is not to say we are not yards from the forest's limit."

Foley's testiness increased. "You are most poetic this morning, Hopson. Though I hazard there's little substance to your theory. To continue with your metaphor, who's to say we are not stumbling further into the undergrowth, widening the gap between the truth and speculation? And in any event, what d'you suggest we should *do* with this incomprehensibly significant advance?"

I confess this question took me aback, for I'd come here in such haste, certain all would become clear once we saw the contents of the box, that

I'd taken no thought of what I might do afterwards. I saw now I'd been foolish to think it would be so simple, but still Foley's glumness didn't flatten me entirely. However mystifying the ring was, however indecipherable Partridge's death seemed, I wasn't defeated. I only needed time in order to decipher it.

I looked again at the ring, and it struck me then how similar it was to the tokens I'd read of at the Foundling Hospital. This was just the sort of object a mother might leave with her child in order to identify him at a later date. But Foley permitted me no time to explore this notion. He was already rumbling on with further proposals.

"I think we should return to Horseheath," he declared. "I am confident that where the bodies were found more answers must lie."

A chill ran through my veins as I contemplated that fearful place. Foley seemed to consider the fact that my life had already been threatened as a matter of no consequence. I knew I was in peril enough in London, surrounded by the bustle of city life; Horseheath, desolate and hostile, where I'd barely a handful of acquaintances, was the last place I wished to go.

"I fear it will be impossible for me to obtain further leave from my master," I murmured, looking at my feet. "He is supremely pressed with commissions; if I don't assist him there's every possibility I'll be dismissed."

Foley considered for a moment. "Very well." He strode to his writing desk. "In that case *I* shall instruct Chippendale that I require you to assist me at Whitely Court. I want you to separate his drawings from those of Partridge. Since the return of his drawings is what he desires above all else, I don't anticipate he will disagree. Nor will he have any means of discovering that you are in fact at Horseheath rather than Whitely."

My heart sank as I contemplated my inescapable fate. My legs began to tremble. I'd no idea what I would do when I got to Horseheath, or how I'd avoid the menace lurking within it. And once again I was allowing myself to be separated from Alice, and the city most likely to hold the key to the cause of Partridge's death. "No, my lord," I replied, helpless as a twig carried off in a torrent. "I don't expect he will."

Chapter Fourteen

When I entered Chippendale's office, I found him seated on a high stool, staring at a carved and gilded goddess, while Craggs, the apprentice, hovered nervously by the door. The golden carving gleamed resplendently amid a bed of ruffled drapery. Fronds of hair tumbled about her breasts, and she held a garland of flowers invitingly towards him. Chippendale seemed entirely unaffected by these abundant charms. His lips were drawn into a thin line, his weathered complexion seemed uncharacteristically pallid, and his jaw twitched. He trailed a finger along the cool, smooth surface of her thigh, then as swiftly as if he'd been scalded he retracted his hand and turned away.

"Whose work is this?"

"Cowley's, I believe, sir," responded Craggs.

Catching sight of me on his threshold, Chippendale's eyes darkened.

"Hopson, is that you? I scarcely recognize you, so long is it since you graced these premises with your presence."

I'd come to break the news of my imminent departure for Cambridge, and was taken aback by the sharpness of his tone. That morning he had seemed willing enough for me to pursue his interests with Foley. Now, once he heard what I had to say and read Foley's letter, I'd expected he would drop any opposition and encourage me to go. However, when I sensed his anger, a small glimmer of hope began to smolder within me.

Perhaps he would object to the scheme and insist I stay in London. Perhaps I would escape another visit to Horseheath after all. "If you recall, sir, I have been with Lord Foley—"

He cut me off impatiently, gesturing towards the reclining Venus. "Look at this, will you! Her finish is rougher than the pockmarked cheek of a Covent Garden whore! Ground's uneven, patches of bole visible through the leaf. How can such shoddy craftsmanship adorn any pier table of mine? Would Cowley rather gild a king's throne or a close stool?"

"Indeed, sir," said I, anxious to appease him before embarking upon my own petition, "the carving, while excellent, appears wanting in finish. However, I'm certain it can be speedily improved."

He sighed deeply and fixed me with a pitiless eye. "Nothing is serious to you, Nathaniel, for this is not your enterprise. It is not your name and reputation that is marred by the lapses of such imbeciles. You have grown so accustomed to gilding and carving and drawing marquetry you believe, with the optimism of a simpleton, everything is likewise—shiny, exotic, rich, and polished. Had you been raised, as I was, to shave planks in a wind-blasted shed, or hammer nails in windows and doors while blinded with rain and snow, you might think otherwise!"

Although my master had a tempestuous nature, I was taken aback by the ferocity of this onslaught. I'd taken great pains to hide my disillusionment, and as I've said, only this morning we'd been on cordial enough terms. Was Foley's patronage causing him to grow jealous of me as he had done of Partridge? My instinct was to defend myself hotly and, while I was at it, to tell him precisely what I thought of his cruel treatment of Partridge. But of course I did no such thing. I feared any criticism I made might result in my dismissal and ruination, for having read Partridge's letter, I knew my master was eminently capable of such a cruel action.

"I confess I may have spoken carelessly. I am optimistic—it is in my nature and has always been so—but I trust I am not negligent. Far from it—the reputation and prosperity of your enterprise is my uppermost concern, as it always has been. It is to that end I have spent many hours advising Lord Foley to the best of my ability."

"You have been absent more than you have been present of late. Is this not negligence?"

"I repeat, master, I have been with Lord Foley. You will not have forgotten, sir, he came here wanting to commission furnishings for his London residence . . ."

"That was two days ago as I recall it. Can it take so long to visit a house not a mile from this door? An earthworm might have arrived there quicker."

"Master," said I with all the earnestness I could muster, "I've worked hard during this interval to win Lord Foley's favor—and with good reason. You spoke to me of your fervent desire to recover your drawings. During my conference with his lordship, I've discovered they are currently in his possession."

If I hoped that reminding him of the drawings he so desperately wanted would calm him, I was mistaken. His jaw convulsed as if it was all he could do to restrain himself from letting flow a stream of invective against Foley, me, and the evil fate that continued to withhold his precious drawings from him. When he spoke it was to spit out each phrase as if he was ejecting weevils from a biscuit. "If he has them, then you must get them back. I do not care what you have to do. . . . You know the entire prosperity of all I have here rests on those drawings, Nathaniel. . . . I must have them back for my new volume, otherwise you will see my rivals overtake me and my reputation founder. Perhaps I should accompany you."

My heart turned to lead. I could see plainly now that there was no avoiding a return to Cambridge, but his suggestion only alarmed me further. If he came with me, he would easily comprehend that the whole mission was a ploy and intervene between Foley and me, and then what chance would I have of ever discovering the truth behind Partridge's death? I didn't want to go to Cambridge, but if I had to go, let it be with Foley alone, not with Chippendale shadowing my every move.

"Calm yourself, sir," I said. "I come to you now to inform you Lord Foley has expressed his desire that I accompany him to Whitely Court, where the drawings are presently held. He is in urgent need of a new suite of furniture for his saloon, and has hinted that if I advise him well on this matter I may also look at the drawings and point out to him those by Partridge's hand, whereupon the remainder will be returned to you directly. It will be a straightforward task. There's no need for you to trouble yourself by accompanying me."

He turned away from me and paced the room, running his fingers through his lank, unwashed hair. "Is this true? Can I trust you?"

There was a note of desperation in the question, one I'd never heard before. Was this a sign of his perturbation regarding his drawings? Could a bundle of drawings truly mean so much? What else might have caused his distress?

"I have here Lord Foley's request to verify it." I took out the letter Foley had given me that morning and handed it to him. With a trembling hand, Chippendale broke the seal, unfolded the thick paper, and scanned its contents before tossing it to the ground.

"I see I have little choice in the matter," he said curtly. "When would you leave?"

"Tomorrow morning."

He rose and advanced slowly towards me until his face was only inches away from mine. For several minutes he stared silently into my eyes as if attempting to drink up the very core of my being. When at last he opened his mouth, his voice was little more than a whisper. "Let me warn you, Nathaniel, everything rests upon your journey. If you return empty-handed I shall not thank you for it."

I stared unblinkingly back for a moment before dropping my eyes. This quiet restraint seemed infinitely more fearsome than his earlier noisy rage. I was still livid with him for his treatment of Partridge, but faced with such menace I froze and was incapable of expressing it. "Nor should I expect it," I muttered.

This semblance of humility was enough to mollify him. He returned his fastidious attentions to the Venus. I was dismissed.

In the yard outside I made as if I were heading towards the workshop. I strode a few paces, then looked up surreptitiously at Chippendale's window. He was hunched over his desk. I could discern his slow, deliberate strokes from the shadow thrown by his quill. Satisfied he was engrossed, I deviated my course. There was an outhouse to my left; I dodged behind it and headed straight towards the path leading to the rear of Chippendale's house.

The back door to the pantry was ajar. I stood on the threshold and whistled loudly. After a few minutes a scullery maid carrying a bucket of slops appeared. She wasn't expecting to catch sight of a strange man lurking in a shadow by her sink and gave a startled shriek, jerking her bucket so the slops spilled over her skirt and the flagstones.

"Now look what you've made me do," she complained.

I reflected that, even without the garnish of vegetable peelings and whatever else her bucket contained, she made a singularly unsavory spectacle; small and squat with a greasy complexion and hair tightly pinned in a turnip bun. A rancid odor of stale sweat emanated from her, now worsened by the putrid stench of slops. I backed towards the door to gasp at the fresh air. "Forgive me, miss, I did not mean to startle you," I said, inhaling deeply. "I can help you clear the mess."

"You'll do nothing of the sort. Go away," she said, flapping her hands as if she was shooing poultry, "you've done enough harm already. You've no cause to be here in the first place."

"Forgive me," I reiterated, "I forget myself. I see you do not know me. I am Nathaniel Hopson, journeyman for Mr. Chippendale. I came here in search of an acquaintance."

"In search of an acquaintance?" she mimicked. "If it's only that, why go creeping about scaring the wits out of people? Why don't you knock on the door as any honest person would?"

"All I want," I said, evading this question with the most winning smile I could muster, "is to discover the whereabouts of Dorothy Chippendale. Since you belong to this household, perhaps you know where I might find that lady?"

A knowing gleam came into her bleary eyes, and she drew a breath. "Miss Chippendale, is it? And why would you be wanting her?"

"I've a message for her," I replied, lying through my teeth.

"Then give it to me."

"Is she here?"

"What makes you think she's not?"

"My friend—who gave me the message—believed she'd gone."

"Then why call here? You've no need of my assistance. You may ask your friend where she is." She picked up her skirts and squatted froglike to gather the slops in her hands.

"Look, miss," I said, "please help me, it's a matter of some urgency. I'll reward you as best I can for your assistance."

She stopped and squinted up at me a moment. "This much I do know. Miss Chippendale's not interested in the likes of you. Or any journeyman. And if your name is Nathaniel I've heard Molly Bullock's talk. You've more than enough female company to choose from, I'd say. Any rate, if it's intimacy you're after, I'll oblige, with a little incentive." Here she winked crudely and rubbed her forefinger and thumb together.

"It's not intimacy I'm after, it's something else," I said, crouching down some distance away from her. "I urgently need to know Miss Chippendale's whereabouts."

"Molly Bullock says there's not much else you're urgent about 'cept intimacy," she persisted, grinning wider to reveal her foul teeth. "And if Molly's too busy stuffing seats, you come to me and we'll find some other amusement . . ." As she spoke she sidled nearer to me.

I backed away but found myself wedged between the door, the sink cupboard, and a washboard. I was frightened half out of my senses. I might defeat Chippendale with guile, but not this malodorous monster. Abruptly I stood up, vaulted the washboard, and sprang away. "Is Molly a friend of yours?"

"What if she is? Don't mean I can't enjoy myself with you, does it?"

"Perhaps you might think on Dorothy's whereabouts, Miss . . . ?"

"Miss Ellen Robson."

"And if anything should come to mind, I'll be eternally grateful."

She wiped her nose on her sleeve before responding. "I'll be sure to tell Molly she's in competition."

Fearful that she was about to embrace me, I stepped hastily back into the yard, bidding her good day as politely as I was able before I made an excuse and scurried back to my workbench. It took some time and half a jug of ale before the terrifying spectacle of Miss Robson had retreated sufficiently from my consciousness to allow me to think sensibly again. Then I took up pen and paper and wrote the following letter.

January 7

Madam,

My name is Nathaniel Hopson. I trust you will remember me, for I was John Partridge's closest friend. It is on the subject of him that I write to you with tragic news, for I fear unless I do so you will remain oblivious of the sad fate that has befallen him.

Three weeks ago, around the same time you left London, Partridge went missing from the workshop. I tried to trace him, but the landlady of his lodgings could tell me only that he'd moved away leaving no note as to where he'd gone. Some days later I was in the vicinity of Cambridge installing a library for Lord Montfort of Horseheath. On the morning of my departure I discovered poor Partridge's corpse frozen in the pond.

You can imagine the shock and misery I felt on discovering my dear friend dead, and so far from London—which was his only home, as far as I knew. Since then I have tasked myself to find the truth behind this tragic death, for only then will I feel I have done our friendship justice. Indeed, it is in part for this reason that I write to you now. Partridge confided in me that you and he intended to marry. Yet after his death I received a letter in which he said your brother, Mr. Chippendale, had sent him away, partly on account of his affections for you, which you did not view favorably. These contradictions seem to me most curious, and thus, if you are willing to add to my knowledge of what took place during those last days, I would ask you to tell me what you can of them, for it may help me apprehend his killer. In particular I should like to know whether there was any grain of truth in what your brother told Partridge. Were Partridge's advances unwelcome? If not, what persuaded you to quit London without leaving him any word? Did you receive any communication from him afterwards? Did he mention to you his reason for visiting Lord Montfort? I cannot ask Lord Montfort the reason for his presence in Cambridge, since that gentleman also died a violent and sudden death on the same night as poor Partridge.

Be assured that anything you can tell me will be kept in strict confidence. I will divulge it to no one—especially not to your brother, should you not desire it.

I am, madam, your obedient servant,

Nathaniel Hopson

I lifted my pen and brushed the end of my nose with its downy tip. There were other questions I would have asked, more information I could have given her, but these matters were better left until I had ascertained I'd be able to contact her, and that she'd be willing to respond. I folded the page, took a wafer of wax, melted it on the candle, and watched the red liquid ooze like unctuous blood across the fold. I blew to harden it, then pressed it with my ring. On the front of my letter I wrote "Miss Dorothy Chippendale" in large, clear letters. Then, placing the letter in my pocket, I went in search of Molly Bullock.

She was squatting among the bales of hemp and cotton, nibbling a mince pie and warming her bottom against the stove. Quiet as a snake I stole up behind her, and with a swift gesture stooped and squeezed the succulent buttock beneath her petticoat. She squealed and spun round, chuckling with delight when she saw it was I.

"Nathaniel Hopson—you're a stranger. Come here this instant," she cried.

"I've a favor to beg of you first."

"As usual." She dropped her eyes and began to toy with the ribbons of her bodice.

My cheeks flamed. "Not that," I said, "something more pressing."

She pouted coquettishly and swiveled away. "Someone else, is there? A new attachment?"

"No, Molly. How could you think that? It's the whereabouts of Dorothy Chippendale I'm after."

"How should I know where she went?"

"An acquaintance of yours, the scullery maid Ellen Robson, knows it—I'm convinced of it."

At this Molly looked up. A great gash of a grin was stretched across her face. "That dung heap's no friend of mine. Why don't you ask her? She'd be enough to scare the wits out of you."

"I tried, Molly," I said, pushing her fingers away from my buttons.

"Why should she tell me?"

Molly continued to press herself on me, and I found myself growing hot with awkwardness on account of it. My hair stuck damply to my forehead, my spine prickled with sweat, and to my chagrin I felt my lust begin to stir. I backed away in an effort to restrain myself. "I hazard from the little I know of the female sex that if you offered her some morsel of tittle-tattle, she might . . . share her knowledge about Miss Chippendale."

Oblivious to my plea and reticence, Molly advanced towards me again. "I see your scar's healed well," she said, licking my temple indecorously. "Give her some intelligence on the subject of you. Is that what you mean?"

The discussion was becoming more awkward and intimate than I had intended. But I didn't want to vex Molly.

"I might have more intelligence to offer her if you would just refresh my memory . . ." She thrust herself against my leg.

"Not now, Molly, I have other matters to consider."

I stepped neatly back towards the door, opened it, and reversed, straight into a figure poised upon the threshold. I spun round to see who it was. A lady stood there, her hand frozen in midair as if she'd been about to knock.

It was Alice Goodchild.

I bowed to her, spreading my arms gallantly to hide the disheveled Molly from her view. Her arrival threw me into even greater confusion. I felt my face crimson and prayed she hadn't noticed Molly. "Miss Good-child! This is an unexpected visit."

Evidently she was as surprised as I, for she too flushed scarlet. "Indeed, Mr. Hopson, I trust it is not inconvenient. But I have come to inform you of a new discovery. A matter concerning your friend."

Molly had by now stepped up behind me. I could feel her suspicions branding the back of my neck. Before she could interpose I turned back to her. "Miss Bullock, I think my instructions are clear enough. I'd be grateful if you'd attend to them at once." With that, I pressed my letter into Molly's hand.

As the coolness of my tone registered, Molly's mouth opened and shut like that of a pike gasping its last. Any moment now she'd recover her senses, yell at me for my lofty airs, and Alice would comprehend we were intimate with each other. But if I moved speedily I might avoid it.

Turning my back on Molly, I held a protective arm behind Alice and shepherded her briskly towards the showroom, away from the upholstery shop. I glanced at her as we walked. She was as alluring as ever, in a dark blue velvet hat and fur-trimmed cloak. Perhaps it was the cold that made her eyes gleam like rare jewels in her face. Pleasure, warming as a draft of brandy, rushed through my veins. I dared to glance back over my shoulder. Molly was still standing thunderstruck by the door, her face a picture of unadulterated fury.

"It is a pleasure to see you, Alice. I'm due to leave for Cambridge in the morning and intended calling upon you later this afternoon. I've a favor to ask of you."

She seemed scarcely to hear me, for her mind was all on the scene she had just witnessed. "Who *was* that person?" she demanded in a low voice.

"An upholsteress by the name of Molly Bullock, whom I've asked to help me find out the whereabouts of Dorothy Chippendale," I said truthfully.

"Dorothy Chippendale?"

"Dorothy is Chippendale's youngest sister, whom Partridge hoped to marry."

"Has she too gone missing?"

"She disappeared at the same time as Partridge. You'll recall he mentioned her in the letter to me that Foley found. I thought it my duty to inform her of Partridge's death."

"That was indeed most kind of you."

"She was all but engaged to him, and in truth I wrote in the hope she may know something that can assist in unraveling the reason for his murder."

"And what does Molly Bullock know of Dorothy?"

"Nothing, but she has the means to find out. She's acquainted with the scullery maid in Chippendale's house, who could discover Dorothy's whereabouts if she'd a mind to." I paused. "Below-stairs gossip being what it is, someone in the household must have heard something of her sudden departure."

"She seemed very startled by your request."

"D'you think so? I didn't remark it. More likely it was your arrival that flummoxed her."

Before she could further interrogate me on the subject, I continued, "But enough of Molly and Dorothy. Tell me about yourself. What brings you here?"

"I have something to tell you that concerns the tool chest."

"Then let us go somewhere away from here so you can tell me properly."

She agreed to grant me the rest of the afternoon, and since the weather was pleasantly fine, we decided upon a promenade. In St. Martin's Lane I hailed a hackney carriage and directed the driver to take us to St. James's Park.

"Now tell me," she said gaily after I'd told her how I'd opened the box, "what's this favor you require of me?"

"The warden on duty the night the hospital opened was a man by the name of James Barrow. According to the intelligence I unearthed at the hospital, he lives in Hatton Garden. I would ask you to go and seek him out, find out what you can from him of that time, the first night the hospital opened. I would go myself but there is no time before I must leave."

"What should I say to him?"

"Ask him why, of all the children listed that first night, only one was entered without an age."

"It may have been a simple oversight."

"It may have been a deliberate omission. You see, if Partridge was accepted that night, he would have been aged four or five years. No longer an infant; no longer eligible by rights to be cared for at the hospital."

"You suspect this entry might be his?"

"Perhaps."

By the time we arrived at the park, the sun was sinking below the treetops, casting long black shadows interspersed with streaks of brilliant light. The skaters on Rosamond's Pond glided prettily by while we walked slowly, admiring the clusters of fallow deer gathering in the copses for the night. Alice took my arm, and I pressed my elbow into my side to draw her closer. To have her thus dispatched the downcast feelings and fears that had earlier troubled me and made me feel more content and hopeful than I had for some time. I led her to the far end of the park, where we found the cows just in for milking at their stalls. We joined the line, and I paid a penny for a cup of warm milk drawn fresh from the beasts' udders for her.

"And now," I said as she sipped it, "you must tell me your news, for I've told you all I am able and can bear the suspense no longer."

There was a small rim of cream on her upper lip, which she licked delicately away. "What I have to tell you concerns the picture we found on the lid of Partridge's tool chest. I don't quite understand the significance of it, but I think you should know."

"Go on."

She smiled gravely but wouldn't be rushed. "You already know a part of it, for you told me yourself you found the picture in Partridge's notebook, with a title."

"*Daedalus and Talos,* as I recall it. But it meant nothing to me."

"Indeed. As soon as I saw it I thought the image a striking one. You remember there were two figures, one standing, one lying prostrate on the ground before a temple. And a bird flying off in the distance. I am quite familiar with ancient legends, they have always enthralled me, but this was unusual and I couldn't identify it. So the next evening I searched my brother's schoolbooks."

"And what did you find?"

"The story that the picture illustrates is, as you discovered, Daedalus and Talos. I believe the scene Partridge has drawn is taken from the legend told in Ovid's *Metamorphoses.* What will interest you, I think, are the details of the story, for they seem to me extraordinarily apt in view of Partridge's own tragic tale."

She halted and seemed to search my face, though I knew not what for. "Go on," I said.

"Daedalus was a legendary inventor and craftsman in Athens. He had a talented apprentice by the name of Talos. By the age of twelve the apprentice surpassed his master—the legend says he picked up a fish bone and made a saw, that he invented the potter's wheel and a compass for marking circles . . ."

"And what became of him?"

"In time Daedalus grew unbearably jealous of the talented Talos. So much so that one day he led Talos to the roof of Athena's temple on the Acropolis and pushed him over the edge to his death. Afterwards, to avoid detection, he descended to the place where Talos's body lay and put it in a bag, intending to bury it. But the peculiar relevance of the subject is this. The soul of Talos the talented apprentice was said to have flown off from his body in the form of a partridge."

"What?" I was, I confess, incredulous.

"Yes," she reiterated. "There are various versions of the legend, but according to Ovid the soul of Talos was transformed into a partridge."

I was silent as the significance of her words registered. "It cannot, surely, be a coincidence? The sudden appearance of this picture in the tool chest. The sudden dismissal from the workshop. Above all the *name*."

"That's what struck me so forcefully."

"Then you believe he chose the subject of his picture specifically for that reason?"

"Perhaps," she said thoughtfully. "Though I would caution against reading too much into it."

But my mind was racing. I'd scarcely heard her. "Perhaps he intended it as a message? A way of communicating what was happening, when he was unable to contact anyone."

"I believe that's too fanciful," said Alice. "After all, he wrote you a letter, did he not, and told you plainly what had happened? More likely he saw in the legend some strange echo of his own condition, and he found it consoling. I mean the name, and the story of the jealous master and the talented apprentice. That doesn't mean he saw the legend as a presage of what was about to happen to him."

"But the parallel is so clear," I protested.

She shrugged her shoulders and looked at me, holding out her half-full mug of milk for me to finish. I was encouraged by the gesture, interpreting it as a signal of the growing easiness between us. I took the mug from her, listening while she reasoned with me.

"Think more carefully about it, Nathaniel, and you'll see the notion is plainly ludicrous. Partridge was killed in Cambridge, a day's journey from London, where Chippendale was. Partridge's death is bound up with Montfort's, which has nothing to do with this picture. Furthermore, if Partridge believed himself to be in jeopardy from Chippendale, why was there no mention of it in his letter?"

I refused to be discouraged. "I don't know. Perhaps because there was no time to write more?"

She shook her head vehemently. "Unlikely, I think."

"But then, as we've seen, unlikely events do sometimes occur."

I raised the mug to my lips and drained it in a single gulp. I thought back to my earlier altercation with my master. I remembered the cruel manner in which he'd treated Partridge, his jealousies, and the way he'd come between Partridge and Dorothy. I was heartily ashamed then that I'd failed to muster courage enough to confront him, and could excuse myself only on the grounds it was expedient to keep silent for the time being. I remembered the coldness in his eyes; the sudden change in his appearance and demeanor; his irrational outburst at my absence when but hours earlier he'd seemed content enough to let me pursue my quest; the menace in his whispered ultimatum to me. There was no doubt he was unpredictable and inconstant in his loyalties, no doubt he was capable of acting callously; but it was another thing to murder someone. And even if I could believe Chippendale *had* killed Partridge, there was Lord Montfort's death to consider. I could think of no good reason why Chippendale might assassinate such a prominent patron unless it was to recover his precious drawings, in which case they would not have been left scattered about the floor. Yet still I kept returning to the picture.

Alice seemed to read my thoughts. "You surely don't believe the subject of this picture proves Chippendale killed Partridge?"

Forgetting reason, I replied impulsively. "Don't I?"

Chapter Fifteen

So I came bowling back to Cambridge, seated this time in the plush comfort of Foley's coach. Before proceeding to his own residence nearby at Whitely Court, Foley was to deposit me at Horseheath among the Montforts, where, he declared, I'd be well placed to observe them. Of course my spirits plummeted when I heard this plan. Yet I knew Foley was a man who guarded his opinions zealously, and it crossed my mind that he might have cooked up his scheme of leaving me at Horseheath for some hidden reason of his own. Knowing how close I had come to death, he couldn't fail to be conscious I was still in jeopardy. Yet he was happy to deposit me in the jaws of the very danger that had already threatened my life once. I hadn't a notion what his motives might be, but I sensed something in his hooded gaze that made me uneasy. I tried to voice the terror I felt when I contemplated the house, yet Foley only laughed, as if fear was of no consequence, and said there was no way we could resolve the matter without entering it. And so, with misgiving in my heart, I fell in with him.

We arrived at the gates of Horseheath with dusk falling. It had rained softly but ceaselessly all day, and now the weather had worsened; black clouds were massed against an unpropitious sky, and large drops of rain lashed our window. We reached the final turn in the drive to see the house emerge before us, an expanse of dark, bleak stone and glass, with every window unlit and no sign of life. It was only after several minutes, when Foley (who refused adamantly to drive round to the rear) had gathered his flapping cloak about him and descended from the carriage to knock several times on the door with his silver-topped cane, that we glimpsed the flicker of a lantern approaching.

"Who's there?" called Mrs. Cummings. I had followed Foley to the porch and at once recognized the voice as hers.

"Lord Foley," returned the buffeted crowlike figure.

There was a loud scrape, the crunch of bolts unfastening, and the door swung open.

"Lord Foley! Forgive me for keeping you, my lord, I couldn't believe my ears. What brings your lordship here? No one's at home but me and Yarrow the butler, and he's retired to his chamber. The rest of the staff are away while the family are in London. I've had word not to expect them till tomorrow afternoon . . ."

Despite the rivulets running down his face, Foley flashed a gracious smile. "Fear not, good lady, I'm aware of the family's intentions," he said, "but I bring you Mr. Hopson, who's in need of accommodation for a night or two. I've no place for him at Whitely and feel sure your master will raise no objection. He's here at my bidding to examine the drawings in the library."

Mrs. Cummings complied readily with his request, though she muttered she'd been told nothing of me coming to look at any drawings. Foley left me with a meaningful glare and curt orders to begin sifting through the drawings as soon as I was able in the morning.

I knew that the drawings that concerned us were already at Whitely, so I deduced his real intention was that I should take advantage of the family's absence to ferret through any papers that might shed light on recent events. For all my trepidation, I recognized the necessity of this subterfuge. It might provide me with information regarding Partridge, and now that I'd braved my terrors and come here, I was determined to find whatever needed finding, to get to the bottom of Partridge's death and be gone. Nevertheless, I asked myself why Foley could not have discussed this on our journey, so that at least we might have concocted a proper strategy. Again I wondered if his reticence concealed some hidden purpose. Perhaps leaving me here unprotected and undirected was simply a ploy to disassociate himself from any blunders I made, while reaping the benefits of my advances. Or was he using me as bait, deliberately bringing me within the reach of the unknown person who wished me dead in order to draw him out?

Fortunately, perhaps, I'd no time to dwell on these worrisome thoughts. The moment Foley remounted his carriage and disappeared into the storm Mrs. Cummings took charge of me. She was touchingly hospitable; now she'd overcome the shock of seeing me, she was full of how pleased Connie would be when she knew of my return. She led me to the kitchens for a bit of supper, watching contentedly as I ate my fill of calf's-head brawn and seed cake, and while I supped I took the opportunity to probe her on the subject of my master.

Alice's account of the strange legend of Talos and Daedalus had convinced me the picture in Partridge's tool chest must represent some form of mystical clue as to what had happened to him. I'd already decided that Chippendale's strange manner at our last meeting might be construed as evidence of his guilty conscience, but I couldn't fathom how he could possibly have carried out a murder at Horseheath when, as far as anyone knew, he was in London. Thus I prised information from Mrs. Cummings: had she recently seen Chippendale about these parts?

"Mr. Chippendale? I believe he came once or twice several months ago, but I've never seen him since," she said, filling my cup with another ladle of hot ale.

"Could he have called on Lord Montfort unnoticed?"

She shook her head firmly. "I should doubt it. If I didn't hear of him someone else would, and then I should have heard anyway."

I was, I confess, a little disappointed in her reply, yet my conviction remained. The picture on the tool-chest lid could only be a sign. There was, I told myself, a fair chance that Chippendale had traveled here incognito. This was not so ludicrous a possibility as it might sound. If Chippendale were intent on murder, he would hardly go announcing himself wherever he went. But if he *had* followed Partridge to Cambridge, if he *was* responsible for his death, it would mean someone else entirely had murdered Montfort; the two deaths were not connected, and it was no more than a strange coincidence that they had occurred on the same night. But although I wanted to believe it, this theory sat uneasily with me. I was mindful of the connection I'd found between Montfort and Partridge, and couldn't convince myself their deaths had nothing to do with each other.

With a good supper in my belly, my eyes began to droop and my limbs grew heavy, and probing Mrs. Cummings further on the matter seemed suddenly less pressing than a good night's sleep. It was a relief therefore when she handed me a tallow light and bade me take my pick of the beds in the garret.

I mounted the stairs to the attic chamber, feeling a little strange to be all alone in a space more usually occupied by four or five servants. I paced around the trestle beds, testing each before at length choosing the one nearest the door. Here I thought I'd be best protected from the drafts of the tempest raging on outdoors.

Perhaps it was the richness of the food, or my underlying fears, or the fact I'd never before slept in such a lonely and uninhabited mansion, but I awoke after several hours to find myself gripped by a feeling of dread. The candle stub still flickered, and I strained my eyes in the half darkness, imagining unknown, indiscernible horrors all around me. It seemed to me the empty beds in the garret were spread out like corpses, that the shadows of branches outside reached out to grasp me. I struggled to suppress my terror, to divine what was real from what were figments of my fevered imagination. I squinted at the window, and the watery trails on the panes reminded me of the leeches I'd removed from Montfort's body; then in my mind I was back at the frozen lake with poor Partridge's mutilated body. An instant later, from the floor below, I imagined I could make out muffled, indeterminate sounds. I heard doors crashing and boards groaning, as if people paced around down there. Voices seemed to call shrilly to one another, though I couldn't understand a word of what they said. Yet hadn't Mrs. Cummings told me there was no one here but the two of us? I became more panicked with every passing minute. It seemed to me that these strange reverberating sounds of footsteps and shrieking voices were filled with menace, that they could only be the noises of the killer awaiting his opportunity to strike. Soon I was lying there bathed in perspiration, straining to separate each unfamiliar sound from the last, taut with horror that at any moment I would be pounced upon.

At length I could bear it no longer. Irritated by my own lack of courage, I resolved, despite my shivering jaw, to allay my terror by proving to myself how foolish I'd become. I would rise and patrol the corridor beneath me. Once I had satisfied myself there was no one there, I would surely sleep soundly.

I descended the back stairs in my nightshirt, holding my light in front of me, like some talisman of hope against the sinister darkness into which I plunged. As I descended the narrow stair, I paused every couple of steps to listen, telling myself I was an idiot to allow myself to fall prey to such feeble imaginings. I heard nothing. As cautiously as if I were about to cross a graveyard at midnight on Halloween, I rounded the corner where the stairs joined the landing. I paused again. Still nothing.

179

The corridor in which I now found myself was L-shaped, some thirty yards long, forming the backbone of the house, with windows overlooking parkland on the right side, and all the rooms opening to the left. The principal bedchambers lay at the far end of the landing, closest to the main staircase. Where I now stood were doorways leading to smaller bedchambers. At intervals along the walls were hung mounted trophies of the hunt. The heads of foxes, stags, bears, and wolves, their mouths torn back in frozen grimace, loomed over me. I began to edge my way towards the angle of the L, beyond which lay the main staircase. I trod slowly and cautiously, pressing my back to the wall, sheltering my wavering light with a trembling hand. Halfway along I heard a creaking sound. This was no figment of an overwrought imagination, but real enough. I blew out my light and shrank back into the shadow of a doorway.

At that moment a door further down the corridor from where I stood opened and closed again. Then a shuffle of approaching footsteps, a flicker of candlelight. The footsteps grew louder. A moment more and they would reach the corner. I had to escape or I'd certainly be discovered, but it was too far to risk retreating to the servants' stairs. I took the only route I could. I turned the handle of the door nearest to me, and finding it unlocked I went in.

I was in a bedchamber. The curtains were closed; a small fire, recently lit, burned in the grate; a single night-light flickered on the side table. I could make out the bed, a vast tester in the grandest of styles, festooned with draperies and surmounted with a plume of ostrich feathers emerging like some strange plant from the apex. The counterpane was thrown back and the pillows and bolsters in tumbled disarray as if someone had recently left it. Against one wall stood a dressing chest, its surface strewn with a snuffbox, a pocket watch, hair powder, pomade, eau de cologne, combs and brushes, and a periwig on a stand.

I was still standing in the middle of the room when I heard the unmistakable shuffle again and then the click of the door handle. There was no time to think. Instinctively I moved across the room, searching frantically for some means of concealment. By the time the door began to open, I was rustling at the curtains. Mercifully, behind them was a wide ledge. I leaped in and drew the damask screen back in front of me.

My heart was thumping so wildly I was sure it must be audible. I desperately wanted to see who the mysterious occupant of the room might be, yet I dared not look. I heard the person enter, stand for a moment motionless, then approach the bed and, to judge from the rustling of covers and creaking stays, enter it. After a minute or two curiosity over-whelmed me. I screwed up courage enough to open the curtain an inch and put my eye to the crack. It was as I was doing so that the door opened a second time and another person entered. Like a tormented snail I shrank back into my retreat and switched the crack closed. I listened as the second person padded to the bed, with a heavier step than the first, and got in without a word spoken.

Not long after, noises began to emanate from the bed. At first they were no more than gentle rustlings and stirrings, as if the occupants were restless and tossing and turning in an effort to make themselves comfort-able. Then the sounds gathered pace. They were cries that became louder, more insistent, interspersed with grunts and moans, which grew increas-ingly rhythmic as they moved towards a crescendo. There was no doubt: these were the sounds of a coupling of a most violent nature.

In one way, however, I saw their engagement as a blessing. It offered me an opportunity to escape from the room while they were noisily distracted. I wriggled down low, slid off the window ledge, and silently wormed across the floor on my elbows and belly. At the foot of the tester, curiosity over-came me. I raised my head slightly to identify the mysterious couple. Amid a turbulent sea of bedclothes all I could see was a pair of moon-white but-tocks heaving up and down between spread-eagled thighs. Impossible to identify to whom these portions of anatomy belonged. I continued hastily on my way, and by the time I was at the door the writhing bodies had be-gun to intersperse their grunting and groaning with speech.

"God's teeth," growled the man as he heaved into her, "you're hotter than a posset cup. I don't doubt that if my father hadn't dropped dead I would have perished from desire."

The woman gave a wail of ecstasy. "Dropped dead, what d'you mean?" she shrieked. "Did you not enjoy me often enough while he lived?"

It was an unmistakably shrill voice—the voice of Elizabeth Montfort. She was in the throes of passion with her stepson, Robert.

Without waiting to see what would happen next, I reached up for the handle and turned it. But the handle stayed fast. Alas, now I discovered that the last person to enter had locked the door and removed the key. I turned back to the bed. The key glinted on the nightstand. There was no means by which I could safely retrieve it unnoticed. I would have to re-turn to my hideout on the window ledge and wait for morning to make my escape. With mounting trepidation, for I knew I did not have much time left before their union reached its climax, I turned back.

I had half crossed the room, squirming on my belly, when I turned my head and remarked a second door I hadn't previously perceived. It was situated opposite the foot of the bed and doubtless connected to a drawing room or closet. I breathed a silent prayer of thanks. There was a fair chance that it might link back to the corridor from which I had come, or that there'd be a servants' entrance leading directly to it. I altered my course, and with a fervent entreaty to the merciful Lord that the hinges would not squeak, raised my hand and turned the handle.

The door opened, fortunately silent. I snaked through the narrowest aperture I could manage and inch by inch closed it behind me, cutting off the groans and moans that were still emanating from the bed. At last I was able to stand up. I rubbed my sore elbows, fumbled for a tinderbox, and lit a candle.

So relieved was I to be safe, or relatively safe, that I was entirely unprepared for the grim spectacle that now confronted me. The flame flared; a halo of light invaded the blinding darkness to reveal my surroundings. I looked around me and immediately felt the blood drain from my face.

The room I was standing in was furnished neither as a drawing room nor as a dressing closet but as a laboratory. Along one wall was a shelf on which were laid out an assortment of glass bowls and jars and bottles filled with shadowy forms. In the center stood a table, and it was as my eye flickered over its surface that my belly began to heave most disconcertingly. Stretched upon it, clearly visible in the tremulous amber light, I could make out the corpse of a dog. From its lolling head I thought I recognized Montfort's lurcher. What shocked me most was the present condition of the beast. It had been laid out on its back, legs stuck in the air with leather straps secured to each to hold them apart. An incision had been made from one end of the breastbone to the base of the abdomen, and the flesh was held open by pins to expose the entrails within. Some of these appeared to have been partially dissected and lay on the edge of the table.

Of course you will by now be familiar with my weakness when it comes to such gruesome spectacles. I'm an artisan without any scientific leanings. Blood and entrails of any description do not fill me with the same raptures of fascination as they do my enlightened counterparts, rather they sicken me and fill me with dread. One look at the open carcass and the bloody coiled mass beside it was enough. My head began to swim just as it had when I'd witnessed Robert Montfort's surgery at Bradfield's London residence. I knew I was in danger of falling in a dead faint to the ground. Yet even as the room began to whirl and I felt darkness closing over me like a murky ocean, I forced myself to climb back, to keep a grip on reality. I could not permit myself to lose consciousness here, for if I did there'd be every chance I'd be discovered, and this was a fear more terrifying even than the ghoulish specter on the table. Thus I cast wildly about for a means to escape, and my eye fell on a door leading out towards the corridor. Without a backwards glance I staggered towards it, clenching my teeth hard together to restrain my heaving belly. The door was locked but the key was in place. I threw it open with scarcely a thought for the couple who lay only a few yards away, and teetered back to the corridor.

Appalled and exhausted by my nocturnal adventures, I groped my way along the corridor and crept into my bed. And yet, as I pulled the covers about me, I found that while I'd been petrified throughout, a little of my terror had been dispelled. I now knew what had caused the sounds I'd heard. I swore never again would I give credence to phantoms or evil presences. How much more fearsome are vague, nameless threats than those we recognize. There is, I sleepily comprehended, some consolation in understanding the nature of our fears. A moment later and I fell into the welcome oblivion of sleep.

My sliver of newfound courage faded quickly next morning. I was overwhelmed by chilling thoughts of how close I'd come to being discovered, and the nauseating spectacle of the dog on the table had my stomach lurching and my heart thumping once more. I knew of Robert Montfort's fascination with science, but I'd never contemplated that his interest might manifest itself in such a macabre manner. Had Robert killed the dog after his father's death, I wondered, or had it died naturally? I remembered the dog coiled under Montfort's desk on the night of his death. It hadn't moved during all the commotion of discovering his body. Was it dead all along when I'd believed it to be sleeping? I cursed myself for my cowardice in not trying to rouse the beast. Perhaps Montfort's killer had destroyed his dog first, fearing the dog would attack if its master were threatened. This didn't rule out either a member of the family or an interloper.

I descended to the kitchens to be greeted by Connie, who had arrived early to assist Mrs. Cummings in making ready the house for the family's return later that day. I confess I rejoiced to see her, for she offered welcome diversion from my apprehensions. Over breakfast I told Mrs. Cummings about the noises I'd heard in the night and how I'd come across the laboratory and found the dog.

"That's Lord Robert's private room," said Mrs. Cummings. "Lord knows how you stumbled in there, for no one's allowed in without his permission and he usually keeps the door from the corridor locked."

I felt my face turn scarlet, but I didn't trouble to explain that I'd got in through the door from Robert Montfort's bedchamber. The thought struck me, however, that I'd left the door to the corridor unlocked. I'd no way of rectifying the matter now. Sooner or later Robert would surely discover his sanctum had been breached.

"The dog on the table. It resembled Montfort's lurcher?"

"It was. Died the same day as its master. Miss Alleyn told the gardener to bury it, but Robert said he'd dispose of it himself. I guessed he wanted it for his experiments. His room's filled with medical books, he'll dissect whatever he can lay his hands on. He intended to study at university, only his father wouldn't allow it. Said it wasn't a fitting occupation for a gentleman. Doubtless that'll change now."

"How did the dog die?"

"Dead in its sleep the same night Lord M. died. Curious, was it not?"

I remembered how the dog had remained immobile throughout the disturbance. "Was it old?"

"Not more than two years."

"Never mind the dog. The sounds you heard were doubtless caused by Lord Robert and Lady Elizabeth Montfort arriving earlier than expected," interrupted Connie, "which is why Mrs. C. sent for me to come back early as well."

As quickly as she said this, fear yielded to gallantry. "And delighted I am that you did," said I. "But why did just the two of them come? Where's Miss Alleyn?"

"Expected to return with Lord and Lady Bradfield and their son, George, later today. The Bradfields are to stay and assist Miss Alleyn in sorting through her brother's affairs. Though I believe the truth of it is that Lord Bradfield hopes to get his hands on the hunter Lord Montfort won from him a few months back."

"Is it not strange that Miss Alleyn didn't travel with her nephew and sister-in-law?"

Mrs. Cummings shrugged her ample shoulders. "I've too much to do to waste time thinking about the strangeness of who comes with who," she replied a trifle crossly.

"Perhaps Lord Robert and Lady Elizabeth were eager to have time alone together," said Connie, giggling and winking at me.

I raised an innocent eyebrow. "Is there something between them?"

Connie shot me a knowing look. "I'd say so judging by the linen I've changed."

"That's enough, Connie," snapped Mrs. Cummings.

But Connie had the bit between her teeth and refused to be daunted. "What she sees in him Lord only knows. She's soft in the head for sure."

"They are of similar age, perhaps she enjoys his company?" I hazarded.

She gave me a withering glare. "Whatever for, when she could have her pick of Cambridge and London now she's a woman of independent means? Wouldn't you think she'd have learned her lesson by now?"

"And what if Foley takes it all?"

She rolled her eyes and shook her head as if I'd confirmed my stupidity beyond a shadow of doubt. "Then Robert'll have naught either, so she'll still be best off without him."

By now Mrs. Cummings was fuming at the freedom of our exchange.

"Constance Lovatt," she bellowed, "there's enough mischief taken place in this house without you adding to it. Now take your box and be about your duties lest I warm your behind and send you packing before anyone else does. And as for you, Mr. Hopson, shame on you for encouraging her."

Thus censured, I began my investigation of the library. Confident that their tardy arrival and energetic nocturnal activities would make them sleep till noon, I presumed there was little chance I'd be interrupted by Robert and Elizabeth. The only hindrance in my investigations was Connie, who, directed by Mrs. Cummings to make ready the room, had accompanied me. She opened shutters, hauled all the movable furniture to the center of the room, and took up the hearth rug to shake it from the window. I meanwhile took a random folio from the bookcase, seated myself at the desk, and began leafing through it, feigning avid interest in its pages, as if this was what I'd come to do all along.

The folio contained a selection of amateur sketches of churches. I turned tedious page after tedious page of steeples and towers, belfries and shingle spires. I was scarcely looking at what was in front of me. My mind was all on what I wanted to know and what I had to do, and how to go about it without causing a rumpus. In the end my sham studying became so intolerable I resolved to brazen it out.

"Connie, can I ask you a question?"

"What's stopping you? Gone shy suddenly?"

"Has Mr. Chippendale, my master, ever been here?"

She stood up for a moment and stretched her back. "He came last year, when Lord Montfort was planning his library. Not since then."

"Certain?"

"Certain."

I sighed. She'd given the same negative response as Mrs. Cummings. And yet I was undeterred. I could not forget the strange tale Alice had told me, nor could I dispel my conviction that it must have some relevance in this matter, that my master *must* therefore somehow be bound up in all this. The fact that neither Connie nor Mrs. Cummings had seen Chippendale didn't make me waver. For, as I'd told myself before, it signified only that he must have come in secret. But I could not banish reason indefinitely. I couldn't help asking myself, Was such a thing possible? Could Chippendale have come to Horseheath and killed Partridge without being observed? Moreover, why did he choose to follow Partridge from London when it would have been so much easier to do away with him in London? And what bearing did Montfort have on all this? I could no more conceive an answer to these problems than when I'd wearily contemplated them the night before. Thus, while I couldn't shake my conviction that Chippendale must be to blame for Partridge's tragedy, small doubts began to intrude on my certitude.

Uneasily I returned to the matter in hand. I was curious to discover the letter book in which Foley had said he'd discovered the letter from Madame Trenti threatening Montfort. Perhaps there was more contained within it that might help my investigation. Dare I begin my search of the desk? I looked across at Connie; she was humming softly to herself, sprinkling moist tea leaves over the carpet to raise the dust, and sweeping them up again.

Surreptitiously I drew back my chair a little and looked down at the front of the desk. There were three drawers spanning its width, and underneath on each side two deeper drawers. One by one I opened the three in the top rank. They slid easily on their runners with so little sound that Connie heard nothing. But they contained nothing unusual: a few bills, pounce, quills, ink, sticks of wax, a couple of knives, a length of twine. I decided to work my way down the two remaining drawers on the left side. I opened the first, my eye flickering expectantly over the contents: small ledgers pertaining to expenses of the household, and several pamphlets. Then the lower drawer: it held only packets of writing paper and a rolled map of the estate tied with a red ribbon. I moved across to the right and slid open the first drawer: a bottle of ink and a plain rectangular wooden box. Could this hold the letter book for which I searched?

Filled with anticipation, I lifted the catch of the box and opened it. It contained a pair of dueling pistols far larger than the weapon we had found near Montfort at the time of his death. I knew already from Miss Alleyn's testimony that that gun belonged to Montfort, and that he kept it here for self-defense. Strange, I thought, as I snapped the box shut and closed the drawer, to keep a further set in the same room.

Only one lower drawer remained to be searched. With a sense of mounting anticipation I pulled it briskly. It didn't yield. I pulled again, this time more forcefully. Nothing. The drawer refused to budge. I lowered my head and looked closer. There was no visible keyhole. The drawer wasn't locked; something wedged it closed.

The obstruction didn't deter me. I knew how to release it easily enough, but I needed tools to do so. I coughed. Connie stopped humming and looked up. "Are you finished?"

"Almost but not quite. Tell me, where is the gentleman's toolbox I used to install the library?"

"How should I know—and why d'you need it? According to Mrs. Cummings, you aren't supposed to be *making* anything, only looking at some drawings. She gave strict instructions you were to disturb nothing else without the family's permission."

"Come, Connie, help me please. The drawer is stuck fast."

She had taken a goose wing from her housemaid's box and was flicking it briskly over the bookcase. "Ask Mrs. Cummings or one of the footmen, they might know."

"It's you I'm asking. They'll want to know why I need it."

"Why *do* you need it?"

"I'll tell you in confidence, but you're not to say a word. Because what's in here may shed light on Partridge's death."

She ceased what she was doing and regarded me. Perhaps my desperation showed and she felt sorry for me, for she seemed a little kinder. "Tried the toolshed?"

"Is there such a place?"

"Must be if I'm telling you there is."

"Will you show me?"

"And risk another telling off if she comes and finds me not at my work? No, I will not."

"Where is it then?"

"Beyond the dairy. Next door after the coal shed."

I was crossing the hall heading for the outhouses when I saw Bradfield's carriage approach and the spindly figure of Miss Alleyn, in mourning black, descend followed by the Bradfield family. Before any of them could apprehend me, I dived for the back corridor and scurried past the servants' hall and kitchens to the toolshed. Raising the latch, I went in.

Thin winter sunshine filtered through a screen of ancient cobwebs on the window. A bluebottle and sundry smaller insects had entangled themselves in the web and remained, now shrouded in dust, suspended upon the gossamer gibbet. Amid a confusion of boxes, garden implements, an old bellows, a rusty pail, I quickly discovered the toolbox. It stood at an untidy angle, as if someone had carelessly dropped it in the middle of the floor.

Certain that with no more than a turnscrew and a file I'd have the desk drawer loosened, I crouched down and threw back the lid. As soon as I'd opened it I saw that the tools were no longer in the carefully ordered state in which I'd left them. A small hatchet lay on top of a jumble of implements. I picked it up to see more clearly beneath and noticed that the blade was fouled with some dark brownish matter. It always irks me to see good implements treated with such shameful neglect, and I took a rag from my pocket to clean it. I was holding the hatchet in one hand and my cloth in the other, shaking my head at the jumble of tools, when my eye came to rest on something curious.

I considered it for a moment with detachment before the dreadful realization struck me. As if I'd been hit by a bolt of lightning, I jolted backwards, dropping the hatchet, which clattered noisily to the stone floor. Then chastising myself roundly for being as fearful and feeble as the night before, I inched forward to take a second look. There was no mistake. Wedged at the bottom of the box between the chisels and the molding plane, curled like a shriveled blood sausage in a butcher's tray, lay a human finger.

Even now as I write this my hand begins to tremble and it is all I can do to keep hold of the pen. I unloaded the tools pressing around it, then using the rag to protect myself—although from what I hadn't a notion—I gingerly picked up the finger and cradled it in my hand. The nail had turned purple and the flesh was withered and blotchy, like a rotten plum that has lain for some days in wet grass.

Suddenly I was back at that frozen pond, holding my poor friend's mutilated hand. Of course I knew without a doubt whose finger it was. Poor Partridge. I also understood now how his fingers had been severed—by this gruesome hatchet that lay beside me. I could scarcely bear to acknowledge that the debris I'd so unthinkingly wiped from the blade was my dear friend's flesh. And so I stayed there, cradling his finger, with tears welling in my eyes. But I was not simply distressed by the thought of the agony he'd suffered, I was angry too. Angry with Partridge for dying so strangely and plunging me into this muddle, when my life had hitherto been so straightforward. Angry at myself for my shameful doubts and my own stupidity in being unable to fathom the further questions now raised. How had this finger arrived here? Why was there only one when four had been severed? Where were the rest? And finally came the question to which inevitably I returned. What reason could there be to mutilate a body—a person—my friend—so horribly?

It took me some time to compose myself sufficiently to report my find to Mrs. Cummings. She said she'd tell the butler, Yarrow, who'd tell Miss Alleyn as soon as there was a spare moment. I didn't know when that might be, so I drifted aimlessly around the kitchens, not daring to go back to the library now that the Bradfields and Miss Alleyn had returned and quite probably Robert Montfort and Elizabeth were risen from their slumbers. In any case I found the clatter and bustle of the kitchens strangely soothing; it saved me from being alone and dwelling on my thoughts. It was a panacea for the horrific images that once again clamored in my brain.

It wasn't until later that afternoon that I spoke to any member of the Montfort family. I was with Connie, who was rubbing Elizabeth Montfort's kid gloves with a mixture of ammonia, turpentine, and pumice powder to clean them, when Miss Alleyn came in.

"Ah, Mr. Hopson, I've learned of your fearful discovery." She looked even paler than usual, and as shocked as anyone would be by the news. "There was only one . . . digit, I understand?"

"Indeed, ma'am," I said, rising to my feet and bowing to her.

She waited a moment, as if lost in thought, then kindly gestured me to sit.

"And what were you about in the toolshed? Mrs. Cummings was somewhat vague on the subject."

189

"It was Lord Foley, ma'am," I replied, blushing under this gentle scrutiny. "He directed me to sort through the papers in the library, the drawings found when your brother died . . ."

She looked puzzled. "But I understood he had taken them already?"

I felt a small prick of shame to be deceiving such a kindly lady, but since she'd cornered me I took no more than an instant to compose a suitable reply.

"Lord Foley believed several were missing, ma'am. That was the reason he asked me to come. There was a drawer jammed in the desk. I thought there might be other drawings in it."

Fortunately this lame explanation appeared to satisfy her; in any event she was distracted by Foley's name.

"Of course I've told Foley he may take as many drawings as he pleases from that room. Elizabeth and Robert have no interest in them."

"He would not wish to deprive you of anything that is rightfully yours."

"I think you mean rightfully belonging to the Montfort family, Mr. Hopson. I am merely a custodian here. Though, as you will find, I guard my domain assiduously."

"I understand, ma'am. And may I take the opportunity of offering you my heartfelt thanks for taking charge of poor Partridge's funeral. Lord Foley told me it was you that had him laid in the churchyard in the village, and I'm most grateful to you."

Miss Alleyn gave a slight smile in recognition of my thanks. "May I ask have you discovered anything more about your dead friend's circumstances?"

Doubtless it was the shock of my discovery that made me reply so unthinkingly, so rashly. "Indeed, ma'am, there is some progress. I've learned that Partridge believed himself to be your brother's son." I paused an instant, and against my better judgment forced myself on. "There is an Italian actress in London by the name of Madame Trenti who claims she is the mother. I think you are acquainted with her?"

As soon as I'd spoken these words I realized I'd overstepped the mark, and my cheeks flamed with shame.

Miss Alleyn was plainly astounded by my assumption, and it threw her into turmoil. "Partridge was my brother's son? By an Italian actress? I most certainly know nothing of the matter. I do not consort with *actresses,* Mr. Hopson." Her tone had abruptly changed to a more strident timbre.

Notwithstanding my discomfiture, I knew this was a lie. Had I not seen the letter penned by her own hand in Madame Trenti's salon? It dawned on me then that perhaps she was feigning ignorance because of Connie's presence. It would be entirely understandable for her to wish to hide the history of her brother's dalliances from the servants. How idiotic I'd been to raise the subject while Connie was in the room. Now I was in such a spot I'd have to leave the matter be. I had no wish to mention the letter, for it would only embarrass her and make her less willing to talk to me. I gave up probing and acted the remorseful fool.

"My apologies for my confusion, ma'am. And for being so bold as to suggest your brother might have fathered an illegitimate child. . . . Plainly the woman is a liar and I should not have given her credence."

But Miss Alleyn would not let the matter drop. "Did you say she 'claims' Partridge was her child? Do I take it that you doubt her?"

"As yet I have no proof she is telling the truth. Certainly Partridge did not know the identity of his parents until she told him."

"But what do you think, Mr. Hopson?" she pressed.

"I do not know what to think, ma'am. It is partly that matter I want to investigate, for I am convinced it has some bearing on all this."

She nodded silently, staring at the table where Connie sat still cleaning the gloves. Connie herself was pretending to be engrossed by her chores, though to judge by the slowness with which she rubbed the fingers she was riveted by the turn our conversation was taking.

"This is a delicate matter, Mr. Hopson. Not something I'd wish bandied about. And yet I agree with you it deserves our attention. Lovatt," said Miss Alleyn, suddenly wheeling round on Connie, "would you leave us alone?"

After Connie had curtsied and disappeared, Miss Alleyn paced about the room looking thoughtful. She picked up the gloves Connie had left behind, then switching them on the palm of her hand, chose her words with caution.

"There *is* something I learned recently that may be of interest to you, for it may relate to your friend. When I was sorting my brother's papers, I saw he had a ledger for household accounts in his desk." Her eyes rested on me for a moment. "But I daresay you are already aware of that?"

"Well . . . yes," I blustered, trying to stem the tide of guilt.

"And to save you the trouble of opening the stubborn drawer, I will tell you what it contains. There are no drawings inside. Merely journals that are no concern of yours. I'm sure you take my meaning." She put the gloves down on the table and turned to look sharply at me.

"It was Lord Foley who instructed me to undertake the investigation, ma'am. I wouldn't have presumed to look inside the desk unless he'd ordered me," I protested.

She airily waved away my explanation as if it was of no consequence. "Perhaps before I tell you of what I found pertaining to my brother, I should begin by telling you a little of my own history, Mr. Hopson. It may be helpful to your understanding of my knowledge of this household's workings.

"I have been a housekeeper to my brother for the past eighteen years. I came here after his first wife, Robert's mother, died when Robert was still an infant. Perhaps you wonder why I stayed so long," she continued quietly. "Having no means of my own, I had little choice in the matter. Offering me the position of housekeeper was my brother's way of taking care of me. Even after his marriage to Elizabeth, he allowed me to remain here because he knew I lacked the means to be independent. By then I'd become something of a mother to Robert, and Elizabeth was so young she had little inclination to take over the administering of this house."

I nodded, feeling rather sorry for her. If Montfort had been truly solicitous, he might have given her an allowance. I'd not forgotten the rude way in which he spoke to her on the evening of his dinner. But then, I reminded myself, he addressed everyone in a similar vein and she seemed happy enough with the arrangement. In any case, while it shed an interesting light on the Horseheath household, I was unsure of its relevance.

As if she anticipated my thoughts, Miss Alleyn continued. "The reason I tell you this is in order that you comprehend why I'm well acquainted with my brother's affairs over the last eighteen years, but less familiar with the history of his youthful dalliances. As I said, when I began sorting through my brother's papers, I glanced through the ledgers, happening to open the book relating to the period before I joined him."

"And you saw something in the ledgers?" I was anxious that she should return to Partridge. After all it was he that interested me, not her arrangement with Montfort or her fondness for Robert or Elizabeth's inexperience at housekeeping.

"There were payments."

"What manner of payments?"

"For a nurse."

"A nurse?"

"A person other than the one employed for Robert. The entries in the ledger read "For Figgins, Hindlesham, nurse." The woman employed to take care of Robert was May Bloxam; I know that because she was still here when I joined the household. I confess I didn't give the matter a great deal of thought at the time. But what you've just told me has caused me to recall it."

"Forgive me, madam, I don't follow your meaning."

She picked up the kid gloves again and wafted them against her palm, as if savoring their softness. "My meaning is quite simple, Mr. Hopson. Your probings have raised the possibility that my brother may have sired an illegitimate child, your friend Partridge, with an Italian actress. You expressed certain doubts about the veracity of that lady's testimony. In the light of your researches, the question we might justifiably ask ourselves is this: Why would my brother make payments to a nurse if the child she was caring for were not his own?"

Chapter Sixteen

I was still mulling over what Miss Alleyn had told me when Connie bustled in. "Letter's come for you with the carter. And Robert Montfort wants you to go to him directly in the library. From his black expression and hearty curses I'd venture he's vastly angered to learn of your presence here."

"Who's it from?"

"The letter? How'd I know? Letters and writing are mysteries to me, though John's tried more'n once to teach me."

"Where is it then?"

"Mrs. Cummings has it, and she reads well enough. I wager unless you hurry she'll have opened it and announced the contents to the entire kitchen." She chuckled at this thought as I scurried from the room.

Mrs. Cummings was flushed from the bread ovens when I found her. "It's safe enough for you here," she said, patting her capacious bosom in response to my inquiry, before stooping to remove three golden loaves from the oven with a long-handled spade. "It's from London. A delicate hand, a lady's I'd say, but I can tell you no more about it," she confided.

"Quite so. I'd be obliged if you'd hand it to me."

"Give me a moment to test these, would you." She rapped the loaves with her knuckles to see that they were done. "Have you not heard his lordship has sent for you? And if you'll listen to my prudent and sage advice, I'll tell you he's not one to keep waiting."

"I'll take the letter before I go, if you please."

"Course you will, Mr. Hopson. Here it is then, but you'd best read it quick or save it till later."

I took the letter, glanced at the hand, and realized with a shiver of joy that it was Alice's. But before I could open it Elizabeth Montfort appeared in the kitchen doorway. I started to see her thus in widow's weeds, her hair scraped back under a plain black bonnet with long lappets framing her face. She looked for all the world like a governess or shopkeeper rather than the mistress of a grand estate; it was hard to believe this was the same wanton creature I'd witnessed thrashing in ecstasy in Robert Montfort's bed.

"Hopson," she announced softly in her curiously childish voice, "I've been sent to bring you directly to Robert. The matter is most urgent." Her eyelids were lowered as she addressed me, but when she looked up for an instant it wasn't shyness I saw in her face, more a curious detachment. It was, I mused, the face of a woman in a trance, or preoccupied by some other far more pressing matter.

"Of course, my lady," I said. "You should not have troubled yourself to come. I was just on my way to him."

"He is most anxious that I escort you," she said. Again I felt myself fall under the scrutiny of her pale blue eyes.

I followed her down the corridor, but we did not progress directly to the library as I expected. Halfway along the passage she sidestepped into an anteroom and drew me after her. She closed the door, turned the key in the lock, then moved to the center of the room, where she stood facing the window with her back towards me. I stayed close to the door, shifting my weight from foot to foot, uncertain if I should speak and if so what I should say. The key was still in the lock.

"Hopson," she began, "there is something I should like to say before you speak with Robert." She wheeled round abruptly to face me, eyes flashing with intensity. "I came to find you because I wished to intercept you and converse with you in private before you spoke to him."

"I confess I am puzzled, my lady. What is it you wish to tell me so urgently?"

Her mouth was pursed, and I could see some private resolution burned in her eye. "First, I do not wish to tell you anything. I wish to show you something that I believe you will recognize."

I was astonished. What could she have that she wished me to see?

"Before I reveal to you what it is, let me forewarn you. Robert believes you were in his laboratory last night, that you entered from the corridor and that he must, inadvertently, have left the door unlocked."

"I do not know what gave him that idea," I lied, wishing I'd had the wit to lock the door behind me, though what I would have done with the key was another matter I couldn't begin to consider.

There was silence for a moment as she took something from her pocket. "Let me spare you from concocting any more untruths, Mr. Hopson. I have a different opinion as to the manner by which you gained access. I discovered this in Robert's bedchamber."

I looked at the article she held out in her hand. It was a brass chamber light, the one Mrs. Cummings had handed me, the one I had taken with me on my nocturnal adventure. I remembered only then I'd left it behind on the windowsill when I made my escape from the room. I felt myself redden to the roots of my hair. My jaw opened and closed, but no words came. Eventually I managed to stammer out with feigned innocence, "A chamber stick, how curious to find it on his sill. How do you think it came to be there?"

She grasped the back of a chair. Her slender white fingers were splayed across crimson damask silk like an open fan. "You knew where it was . . . without me telling you."

"No, my lady, I only presumed—"

"Hopson, don't try to deny you left it there. I have spoken with Mrs. Cummings, who told me this stick was given to you last night." I couldn't bring myself to meet her eye or to issue further denials; she already knew the truth.

"I will not ask you how it came to be where I discovered it, nor what you were about when you left it there, nor at what time you were in Robert's room. These are matters of little interest to me. Nor have I told Robert of my discovery. But if you breathe a word of *anything* you may have witnessed last night to Foley or Bradfield or Miss Alleyn, you may rest assured I *shall* tell Robert of my suspicions, and his temper in those circumstances will be most remarkable. I'm sure you have already observed that he has inherited his father's propensity for violent outbursts."

I nodded meekly, unable to think of any appropriate response save for a few stammered words of assurance that I would never speak of my foray into Robert's room, and that in any case nothing I had seen there was in the slightest way compromising. She waved me into silence. "There is no more time to lose if you are not to worsen Robert's temper. Let us go now."

As she ushered me towards the library, I wondered why she had chosen to keep this matter concealed from Robert. I knew it wasn't a question of saving me from his wrath, for she'd made her disdain for me eminently visible. Had she then some other plan for me? Could it be that *she* was the person responsible for Montfort's death? I remembered that she was absent from the room when the shot was fired. I'd presumed, however, that she was with Foley and Robert, and hadn't investigated the matter further. She had an obvious motive for wishing her unkind husband dead, but was she capable of killing him in such a horrific manner, and what possible reason could she have for murdering Partridge? I wondered too at the sudden transformation in her demeanor. Some new spirit had kindled in her. The girlishness and dazed expression had been replaced by a look of feverish animation. I could not be certain whether the cause of the sudden change was the supremacy she held over me or whether she had been feigning her weakness all along. In any case, she was far from the feeble puppet I had first thought.

The moment she stepped towards the door to lead me through to the library, the fire in her eyes faded. I turned and took a last look at her before entering the room. There was a smile on her face, but the expression in her eyes was once more that of a somnambulist in whom all emotions and senses are deadened. It occurred to me then that her sporadic remoteness was, in its way, far more frightening than the bellowing fury I expected Robert Montfort to bestow.

Robert Montfort stood before the blazing fire. Lost in some absorbing reverie, he gazed through the windows at the statue of a marble nymph in the Italian Garden. He was dressed in his boots and a heavy caped overcoat of dark green, as if he were about to go out, and he was holding something behind his back. As soon as he caught sight of me hovering on the threshold, he lost his vacant look. He gestured me to enter, stepped from the hearth, and advanced towards me. I could now see that concealed behind him had been a horsewhip. He drew closer, bringing the whip to the fore, flexing it and whisking it up and down on his thigh, as if testing its sting. I was oddly reminded of his aunt's gesture with the gloves earlier that morning.

"Hopson," he said, drawing his face so close I could clearly smell breakfast kedgeree on his breath, "finally you deign to answer my summons."

"I came as soon as I could, my lord. I was engaged with Miss Alleyn."

"Phaw," he spat, "you'd take me for a blockhead, would you? Don't lie to me, you impudent scoundrel!"

He thumped the crop down on the desk so violently the ink slurped over the rim of its cut-glass bottle and flooded the tray beneath. His bulbous eyes protruded like billiard balls. "Miss Alleyn passed by here ten minutes ago. I know where you've been."

The stench of his fishy breath repulsed me; I hung my head and tried to hide my disgust.

"I believe you've been prying and poking in places that don't concern you."

Cautiously I half raised my face. "Forgive me, my lord, I should have explained. I'm here because Lord Foley requested my assistance."

"And Foley gave you authority to skulk about in my laboratory, did he? Told you to nose about and see what you could find?"

"I'm sorry, my lord. I've been in the library this morning. I don't take your meaning."

"You'll take this well enough though, I presume!" he bellowed, flogging the chair closest to me so hard with his whip that he left a stripe in the velvet upholstery. "I am not quite the dolt you take me for. The door from the corridor to my laboratory is always locked from the inside. This morning, however, I discovered it unlocked."

There was a long uncomfortable silence while he glowered at me and I endeavored to muster my courage.

"Forgive me, my lord. What has this to do with me?"

"Let me explain. Since you and Yarrow and Mrs. Cummings were alone here last night, and since the other two know never to venture there, it follows that it must have been *you* prying before I arrived. I cannot conceive *why* you were in my private laboratory, nor what you thought you might find, but I'll tell you this. Lucky for you no damage was done, for if there was I'd thrash you within an inch of your miserable life."

"My lord," I said, "I beg you to give me leave to explain. I stumbled into the room yesterday afternoon by accident. I was looking for Mrs. Cummings. As soon as I realized she wasn't there I left. I was unaware of where I was . . ."

"Whatever your excuse, you won't alter my first opinion of you—I believe you to be no better than your dead friend, nothing but a detestable rogue, and I'll not have you under my roof a moment longer. Now leave this house and don't let me see you here again, or I give you my word at the very least I'll have you branded a thief and transported." He began once more advancing towards me while stroking his whip against his thigh. I knew if I did not move fast he would exact some awful revenge for my transgression. Without attempting to remonstrate further, I scurried straight for the garret, whispering grateful thanks to the good Lord (and Elizabeth) that he did not suspect the awful truth. Had he known I'd been in his rooms not *before* he arrived but *after;* had he suspected I'd witnessed the intimacy, there was no way I would have escaped his direst punishment.

I didn't linger to allow him time to reconsider. Five minutes later I'd bundled my few belongings together. I left a note on Connie's bed telling her I'd had to leave suddenly but I intended to stay in the neighboring village of Hindlesham. I had passed through this village several times on my travels to and from Horseheath. I would be in touch, I told Connie, and asked her to make my farewells to Mrs. C. Then I slipped out without a word to anyone.

The village of Hindlesham, some five miles distant on the Cambridge road, was a good hour's walk away. It was larger than Horseheath, almost a small town, for it boasted a neatly kept green, now silvered with frost, a steepled church, a small but apparently well-stocked grocer's shop, and a dozen or so well-tended houses built of honey-colored stone. Smaller, meaner ramshackle dwellings straggled along the road that led to and from the center. The inn stood opposite the church, a low ivy-clad building with a large stable yard behind. By the time I arrived, darkness had fallen and the church clock was striking six. The windows of the inn burned brightly with candles, seeming to draw me inside, where it was every bit as warm and welcoming as I could have hoped. The innkeeper, Samuel Morton, found me a chamber, and a maidservant placed a warming pan in the bed and lit a small fire in the grate. Morton meanwhile promised to prepare me a simple supper of broth, bread, and ham in an hour's time; until then I could rest myself.

I scarce need say that what with all I'd gone through with Miss Alleyn and Elizabeth and Robert Montfort, not to mention finding the finger, I was grateful to be left in solitude. I needed time to think. I sat down by the fire and closed my eyes for a moment; then, with leisure at last to peruse Alice's letter, I took it out. I turned the packet over in my hand, examining her elegant script, experiencing an enjoyable frisson of anticipation before I unfolded the pages.

January 8, 1755

Nathaniel

I write almost as soon as you have departed since I believe you will be as impatient to hear my news as am I to write it.

As soon as I left you I did as you asked and went to Hatton Garden to find James Barrow, the retired warden of the Foundling Hospital. It took me some time to trace his establishment, for no one by that name has lived there for many years. Eventually by chance I stumbled on the right street, and on an old laundress and a chandler who'd lived there for the last twenty years and remembered him. They both agreed on the tragedy that had befallen him. Apparently a bout of typhus carried off the entire family within a fortnight; that is, Mr. Barrow, his wife, and all his family living at the time in the house. The only survivor was a young daughter, who it seems was away visiting a relative. The chandler swore her name was Martha and remembered she'd married an ostler in Cambridge. With this information I've taken the liberty of sending a letter to the parish priest to discover her whereabouts. I trust he might remember (or have some record of) a girl who arrived from London some years ago, whose family had all died in an epidemic, and who'd married a local man. Thus we must pray no misfortune has befallen Martha, and that there is a speedy response to my inquiry. I'm confident I'll soon be able to tell you for certain, and since you are in the locality you may choose to call on her in person.

I learned also from my conversation that Mr. Barrow was famous as a most benevolent man. According to the laundress, he was "always doing more for others than he should, and it was that which killed him. He caught the contagion from one of his lame ducks and it did for him—where's the justice in that?" From this I'm sure you will agree the chances seem high that if Mr. Barrow did find a child on the doorstep of the hospital on the night in question, he would not have sent him to the workhouse. It seems to me entirely probable he'd have found some other home for him. The question is, where?

And now to another matter that has been troubling me. Last time we met you expressed your fear that Partridge's life and death were such a mystery that you'd never resolve them. When I told you the story of Daedalus, your tune changed. You took it as something of a revelation, a signal of the fate that might have befallen your friend.

Truthfully, Nathaniel, I believe you are mistaken to do so. Confusion often leads us to search for external messages to relieve our burdens. How easy it is to impose on history, legend, the stars, or random events some superior meaning, some manifestation of divine will, which in reality is no more than our misinterpretation of coincidence. Legends are for entertainment; we are mistaken when we take them as signposts for all we cannot explain. If legend has another purpose, it is only to console us with the thought that we are not alone in our adventures and experiences. I don't know what fate befell Partridge. I believe like you his history must play a part in it, but I am certain we'll uncover it more rapidly if we don't complicate events with a supernatural fog.

And now, my friend, I must broach a more delicate matter. On my return from Hatton Garden I chanced to pass down St. Martin's Lane. Whom should I see strolling up the road on the other side but two ladies, one of whom I recognized as your acquaintance the upholsteress Molly Bullock. She looked strangely at me so that I confess I felt most uncomfortable. I quickly comprehended, however, that she wanted to cross the road and have words with me, and so I waited.

She strode boldly up to me. "Are you writing to Nathaniel?" were her opening words.

"Yes," I returned, equally straight.

"Well then, I'd thank you to tell him I've found the thing he asked me, and sent his letter on as he desired."

No sooner had I answered, "I'll tell him," than she'd taken her companion by the arm and marched off as abruptly as she'd come, without a word of acknowledgment. This most curiously abrupt behavior made me suspect that there was some clandestine understanding between you and her, and that her rudeness was on account of jealousy at having seen me call on you. Am I correct in this suspicion? I beg of you to answer me frankly in this, Nathaniel. I wouldn't want her to believe I've any place in your affections and cause her needless distress. In any event, I've a mind to tell her I do not.

I will write again as soon as I've more to report.
I am, your obliged friend,

Alice Goodchild

I held the letter in my hand. The frankness in her tone heartened me, but the mention of Molly made me tremble. So far Alice only suspected what had passed between us. She'd certainly view me less kindly if she knew the truth, and from Cambridge all I could do was pray she'd thought better of speaking to Molly on the subject of our friendship. There was little doubt in my mind that if she did, Molly would tell her every detail.

I considered her comments concerning the legend. I was still reluctant to admit defeat, but I'd quizzed almost everyone I'd encountered over Chippendale. All had given me the same response: he had come to Horseheath months ago and not been seen here since. I was forced to admit to myself that if he'd gone missing from London at the same time as Partridge, I would have remarked it. Thus it now appeared that my theory of Chippendale's clandestine visit was impossibly insubstantial. I could twist it and turn it however I liked, but I couldn't explain how he might have played a direct hand in Partridge's death. Perhaps I'd given credence to the idea only because I'd felt so deceived by his treatment of Partridge.

Reluctantly I acknowledged that Alice was probably correct. The legend had distracted me. I would do better to confine my efforts to the here and now, not some story written centuries ago. If the legend served a purpose, it was simply to reveal that jealousy has ever existed between craftsmen. Chippendale had undoubtedly felt jealous of Partridge; his jealousy might indirectly have led to Partridge's death, by forcing him to call on Montfort. But our master had not been at the scene, and therefore had no direct role in my friend's tragic murder. Nevertheless, in my eyes both Chippendale and Madame Trenti were indirectly culpable. If Chippendale hadn't banished Partridge, he might not have listened to

Madame Trenti; he might never have felt compelled to approach Lord Montfort; he might not have died.

With this realization my thoughts swung pendulum-like back to Alice. Even now, after all that had passed, my sentiments for her were as confused as ever. How invaluable her assistance was proving. I held feelings for her I didn't believe I'd ever experienced in connection with a female. I felt profound gratitude for her assistance, and what else besides? Warmth, affection—and, I confess it, other more substantial emotions that were as yet unnamed and unacknowledged, even in my heart.

The church clock was beginning to chime seven as a scullery maid poked her head round my door and told me my supper awaited me downstairs. It was as I descended the creaking oak steps that I recalled that I had an important matter to pursue in this village. Miss Alleyn had mentioned the name of Hindlesham. It was here that Montfort had sent payments to a nurse.

Chapter Seventeen

Next morning I sent word to Foley that I was now in Hindle-sham and asked how he wished me to proceed. I waited in vain for a response, but just as my inertia became irksome, Connie appeared out of the blue to lift my spirits. It was her afternoon off, and she'd walked all the way from Horseheath. She had something she wished me to know, and since she couldn't write well enough to send me a letter she'd had no option but to come herself.

From her pink cheeks and the raw tip of her nose I could see she was chilled to the bone. I brought her to a settle close by the fire and ordered a jug of hot wine to warm her, which she sipped a little mournfully, I fancied. I sat down beside her.

"So, sweet Connie, tell me, what news do you bring me from Horse-heath?"

She sighed. "I'm glad enough to escape from that place for an hour or two."

"Why's that?"

"Some days there's nothing you can do without stumbling into trouble. This morning I had Mrs. C. scolding me on account of Lady Brad-field finding a saltcellar behind a book in the library. Turns out it's the one she accused me of breaking the night his lordship died. And I was to blame all over again for not finding it the other day when I made ready the room."

I pondered this information for a moment. "That was indeed most pro-voking. But is it not puzzling how it got there?" I said. "Why would any-one leave a salt on a bookshelf? 'Tis not something a gentleman might happen to carry about with him and put down absentmindedly, is it?"

"I neither know nor care," said Connie, sipping her wine. "All I desire is that the Bradfields leave Horseheath as speedily as possible. But there's small chance of that happening with one mooning over the horses and the other mooning over other things."

"Who are you speaking of? What other things?"

She tossed her head crossly. "George, you dolt. He's starved of female company and, since Robert is busying himself with Elizabeth, he thinks he may do as he likes with anyone he pleases."

"Anyone?"

"Me in particular, and without so much as a by-your-leave. This morning he approached me and . . . well I'd rather not say what he tried."

She looked outraged by whatever it was, and I couldn't help a chuckle escaping. "Ah, some forbidden intimacy, was it? Something you've never allowed me?" I looked sideways and winked as she drained her glass.

"There's nothing entertaining about it, Nathaniel. I gave him short shrift and I'll do it again. To you or him."

I replenished her glass. "Little wonder you miss me," I returned play-fully. She smiled and gave my arm an affectionate push.

"And why should I miss you, Nathaniel Hopson?"

"Am I not your friend? Do I mean so little to you?"

"What do you think you should mean? John the footman is more at-tentive, and he lives close by." She gazed at me over the rim of her glass, wide-eyed, innocent, earlier troubles apparently forgotten. I knew she was toying with me as much as I was with her. It was a harmless caper that delighted us both.

"Are you as fond of him as of me?" I queried in mock seriousness, tak-ing her hand in mine.

"Perhaps I'm fonder." The wine was now taking its effect. Her eyes shone crystal bright, and she was having to concentrate on every word she uttered. She withdrew her hand slowly and stroked my cheek. "Any rate I didn't come here to speak of John, for that's my business, not yours."

I made myself appear as miserable as I could. "You're all efficiency today. I fear I must have offended you."

She laughed merrily. "I'll prove I'm not." Impudently taking my face in

205

her two warm hands, she placed a clumsy but succulent kiss on my mouth, causing the wine in her glass to slop over her bodice. She began to giggle, whereupon I burst out laughing at her antics and dabbed at her wine-stained gown with my handkerchief. It was at that moment that I chanced to look round. Perhaps some small rustle distracted me in my mirth; perhaps some other presentiment troubled me. At any rate, I turned—and saw her watching me. By *her* I mean of course Alice Good-child. She was dressed in her outdoor clothes: a blue cloak, hood, and muff. Her skin was pale as alabaster, her eyes stormy.

The minute she knew I'd seen her, she raised her chin in defiance. "Why, Mr. Hopson. It is you? I thought it must be but I wasn't certain. It shouldn't surprise me, I suppose, to discover you thus entertained. How reassuring to find you are as well amused in the countryside as in town," she said before turning on her heels.

For a moment I sat there transfixed. I felt my face blanch with humiliation, then burn, then blanch once more. I leaped to my feet. "Alice," I burbled, pursuing her into the hallway. "Wait. What do you mean? This is not all it seems. Allow me to explain . . ."

Too late. I caught only a glimpse of her before she disappeared into a room upstairs.

I turned back to Connie, who was draining the final dregs from the claret jug. She waved her hand airily in the direction of the departed Alice, a somewhat glazed expression in her eye. "Don't distress yourself, Nathaniel. She'll come round, I'll wager. She's a good-looking woman." She replaced her glass on the table. "Proud too, I'd guess. Why did you never tell me you were sweet on someone?"

I fairly shouted back at her. "Sweet? I'm not sweet on her. She's a friend; an acquaintance; a wood merchant I happen to know. My only concern is that *she* seemed distraught."

Connie, God bless her, didn't take offense. She laughed at my rudeness and evident confusion and rose unsteadily to her feet. "You're more dis-traught than she, I'd say. And my head's spinning. I see I'll have to come back and speak to you another time. No matter. No matter at all. It was probably fancy anyway, probably no more than fancy . . ."

I'm ashamed to say, in view of what happened later, that I scarcely reg-istered her words. I never paused to question her meaning, or discover the subject that perturbed her. How could I listen when I was eager for her to be gone so I could repair the damage with Alice? Had I been less foolhardy, more perceptive, more prudent; had I stopped to ask her what she meant, then perhaps I might have come more quickly to my conclusion and thus prevented another tragedy.

But in my foolishness I did none of these things. I permitted Connie to walk back to Horseheath Hall without giving her a second thought. Then, like a scolded dog who yearns for pardon, I chased upstairs.

"Alice," I shouted through her closed door, "you are misled in your construction. That was Connie, the maidservant from Horseheath. She had just arrived to give me some news."

"News that required you to make adjustments to her corset? Then it was of a most curious, most intimate nature."

I stood humming and hawing outside the door, infuriated by her unwillingness to believe me. I tried the door. It was bolted. "Alice, this unreasonableness is most unwarranted. What on earth has happened? Don't lock the door against me. Are we not friends? Will you not hear me?"

"I believed you once before and much good has it done me. First there was Madame Trenti; then, I strongly suspect, Molly Bullock; now I arrive to find you fiddling with the bosom of yet another female. I must credit you in that, Nathaniel: you are constancy personified—in your inconstancy!"

"It is Madame Trenti and Molly Bullock that have misled you, not I. And as for Connie, she's naught but an acquaintance. You chanced upon us at an unfortunate juncture. She spilled her wine; we were laughing at the unexpected mishap."

"Then you may rest assured, Nathaniel, that unexpected occurrences will continue to befall you. I shall stay for the night, undertake what I've come to do, and depart directly afterwards . . ." Here her voice trailed off.

"Alice, tell me why you've come. I'll accompany you tomorrow if you wish."

"I do not," she yelled, opening the door so unexpectedly that I fell through it straight into her arms. She pushed me off as if I was a cockroach. "I am angry enough, Nathaniel, without the further insult of your pressing yourself upon me."

I blushed scarlet and stepped a circumspect distance from her, though it was not what I wanted to do. "I didn't intend to press myself on you, Alice. I wish only to relieve your anger and contempt for me. Can't we let the matter rest? I beg of you."

In the end, after much to-ing and fro-ing of this kind, she reluctantly agreed to let me sit down with her in her room while she explained why she had come, although she would not allow me to utter another word on the subject of Connie or Molly.

The gist of it was that Alice's letter to the priest of the Cambridge parish where James Barrow's surviving daughter Martha was last heard of had elicited a speedy and encouraging response. Martha Bunton, as she was now called, still resided in the vicinity. The priest had ascertained that she would be happy to answer questions regarding her father and help us in whatever way she could. Alice had impetuously (and, she now felt, foolishly) resolved not to miss out on what promised to be a crucial advance. Therefore she had come herself to find me so that we might travel together to interview Martha. Having called at Horseheath Hall, she had been told I'd had to leave unexpectedly and was staying at this inn, hence she had followed me here.

All this information was relayed to me in a decidedly distant, not to say angry tone. Despite her agreement to allow me in her room and to explain the reason for her arrival, I was left under no illusion. Her fury remained unabated. Her distrust of me was unwavering. Yet I was disconcerted to note that even under these strained circumstances I found her no less alluring. Her skin was luminous, her hair was coiled on the crown of her head with a ringlet falling to one side that shone like burnished copper. I felt myself stir with desire. I was utterly in her thrall, but then, catching the wintry glare once more, I came abruptly to my senses and determined to behave with irreproachable circumspection.

In what I hoped she'd see as a conciliatory tone, I related to her all that had happened during the time I was at Horseheath Hall. I told her of my nocturnal adventure and how I'd been bundled so unceremoniously away. I was glad to have a chance to confide in her face-to-face without other distraction, for I knew talking to her would help me make sense of all that had happened, and hoped it might distract her into forgetting her anger. But I might as well have whistled to a statue; she held firm against all my japes and pleas and anecdotes of midnight promenades. Not a flicker of a smile appeared to soften her stoniness. Nothing indicated that she viewed me with anything but profound distaste. And when at length my conversation ran dry, Alice refused adamantly to dine with me. Instead she bade me send word to the kitchen: she would eat a light collation on a tray in her room and retire early to bed.

Next morning after breakfast she seemed subdued rather than cross. I wondered if this was a sign her mood had lifted; perhaps after all she did feel a flicker of remorse for the harsh way she'd treated me? It wasn't long, however, before I realized the futility of this hope. When we went to mount the gig I'd ordered, she refused my suggestion that she should sit up beside me, climbing instead behind the driver's seat. I was left to sit in front by myself like a common coachman.

So we traveled in uncomfortable silence until we reached a neat cottage on the outskirts of Cambridge. I uncoupled the horse and tethered it, wondering when her mood would lift, or if we were destined to be ever thus estranged. Alice meanwhile strode ahead and knocked on the heavy oak door.

A stout young woman with black hair and skin as dark as that of a gypsy appeared at the door. She held a round-faced baby in her arms, and another dark, curly-haired child peeped out from behind her skirts.

"Mrs. Bunton?" enquired Alice.

"Aye."

"I'm Alice Goodchild. The lady from London who's been making inquiries regarding your father, James Barrow, and the Foundling Hospital. This is a friend"—she termed me thus without a tinge of irony—"who is also involved in the research, Nathaniel Hopson."

Mrs. Bunton's face broke into a broad smile. "Of course. The reverend told me you might call. Come in to the fire and ask all you like."

She led us into her kitchen, sat us on Windsor chairs, and deposited her baby in a crib, setting herself close enough to allow her to rock him to sleep. The older child kneeled at her feet and began rhythmically to run a wooden horse up and down across the flagstones.

"What was it you wished to know about my father?"

Alice glanced curtly in my direction, indicating she'd leave the questions to me.

"It concerns something that took place at the time the hospital opened. I believe a friend of mine, who may have some connection with Lord Montfort of Horseheath Hall, was deposited there on the night of the hospital's opening . . . ," I began.

"He may well have been. I was only a young girl then, I have no recollection of all the unfortunate babies who were taken in."

"Of course not, I would not expect it. But this particular child was somewhat unusual. First his age set him apart. He was about four, too old according to the regulations to be taken in by the hospital. Yet I believe that for some reason the institution did accept him. Perhaps he wasn't left at the same time as the others? Perhaps your father simply found him? Do you have any recollection of such an event?"

She was silent for a while, but when she replied there was no vestige of hesitation in her tone. "My father was the very essence of kindheartedness to all children. I've no doubt that if he'd found a child he'd have done something for it. He'd never the heart to send them to the workhouse. He always said he deplored those places, that they were no more than death sentences for any child consigned there." She halted, looked at the child playing by her side, and patted his head. "However, as to remembering this particular child, I do not. You must understand that there were many occasions when he brought home street children and tried to find homes for them."

"Did you ever hear word of Lord Montfort sending a child to the hospital?"

She shook her head. "This cottage is some ten miles from Horseheath. I have no connection with the estate, nor any knowledge at all of the comings and goings there."

"Did your father keep any record of his time at the hospital that might shed light on the matter?"

Here she broke out laughing. "He was as fond of writing as he was of children. There's a large box of his papers here. I brought them with me from London though I've never sorted through them and am no wiser than you as to what they might contain. You may see them if you wish."

She showed us to a parlor where she took out a strongbox from a coffer and handed it to me. Alice had remained mute all this while, but when Mrs. Bunton asked if she would care to sit by the fire in the kitchen and keep her company, she thanked her kindly and said we would make speedier progress if two of us looked through the papers.

I've long believed that every young man, lacking the wisdom to know better, believes himself more or less immortal. To a youth such as I, what remains after I'm gone to mark my thoughts, ideas, beliefs, all that is the nub of my character, is of supremely little consequence. I hazard it's only when years pass, and experience reveals how tenuous is our grip on this world, that our desire to leave reminders of our existence is sparked. Perhaps that is what drives us to beget children, build monuments, write journals, or create whatever else we fancy might outlive us.

I pass this observation only because I quickly judged from his box of papers that James Barrow was as bountiful in death as in life. He had left much to remind those who cared to look of his profound good nature. There were letters to relatives and his children and his wife. Letters to and from Captain Coram, the doughty founder of the hospital. There were notebooks in which he'd commented upon and commended or criticized prevailing trends—for philanthropy, the latest style in hat, a new design of barouche, some court gossip concerning His Majesty King George II. There were in addition journals in which he noted the birthdays of each of his children, with observations on the stages of their development from birth to the first letter they formed, the first plate they broke.

Above all there were endless records of his administration at the hospital. Details were given of the balloting system used to decide as fairly as possible which children would be granted places when there was a surfeit of applicants. (The women were asked to take a colored ball from a bag. Those who drew white balls were sent with their children to the inspecting room, where their children were examined for signs of disease; those who drew black balls were immediately turned out of the house with their infants.) There were records of the hospital staff: two wet nurses, two dry nurses, a messenger, a receiving matron, a watchman, a porter. All this paper was bundled together in no particular order, and we passed several hours rummaging through it, searching in vain for anything of relevance to our inquiry. Meantime Alice maintained a neutral expression, carefully avoiding my eyes, replying with the utmost brevity to all my attempts at conversation.

After what seemed hours of pointless, silent scanning, the box was empty but for a few stray sheets that must have come loose from one of the journals. Our efforts had yielded nothing, and moreover, I recognized with a stab of dismay, the atmosphere between us was no less strained. Despondently I picked up a crumpled sheet wedged at the side. It was dated February 1751, ten years after the opening of the hospital, the same year that James Barrow died. The shakiness of the hand made it almost impossible to decipher, and I nearly discarded it without further examination. It was only by good fortune that my eye lighted on a single word: *Partridge.*

It was addressed, c/o The Old Bell Inn, Holborn, To C.—or whomsoever else it may concern:

I write this now fearing that if I do not and my fever worsens, as it seems sure to do, a confidence will die with me that is not mine to keep, and that this might cause needless misery. The matter concerns a child taken in by the Foundling Hospital unbeknownst to anyone but me and a handful of others whose names I am not at liberty to disclose.

I am speaking of a night ten years ago when I came upon a young boy abandoned on the hospital steps. There were about him two things that made him particular from all the other children taken in. First, he had come a day early; the hospital wasn't due to open till the following evening. Second, he was too old. Anyone who knows anything of the Foundling Hospital will understand that the institution accepts only children under the age of two months, whereas this child could already walk and talk, and I judged him to be aged four years or thereabouts.

On those two counts I should by rights have rejected him. And yet I did not. If you could have seen the night you might understand why I acted as I did. Rain lashed and wind stormed—to leave him outdoors was to condemn him to certain death. So I did what I believe any Christian should have done: I deliberately flouted the regulations by which I was bound and took him in.

I questioned him closely as to his circumstances. At first he said nothing, traumatized, as any child would be, by his abandonment. After some time he relented a little. I ascertained that his name was John, that he'd been left because his mother was dying of consumption and had no one to care for him. I examined his person and found he was not badly nourished, and that she'd left him with two tokens. One was a severed portion of a ring inscribed "To C." The other was a package containing as curious a token as ever I saw—of which I will write more in due course. The package was wrapped with a note that read:

Whether this child live or die, be pleased to send account thereof it to the Old Bell Inn, Holborn, in one month's time.—C.

(The child could not tell me why she had selected this particular establishment.)

What was I to do? As I have writ already, I knew the child would not survive defenseless and alone in the streets of London; if I were to send him to the workhouse he would also surely die. And yet he was not eligible for the hospital.

I took him home with me, pondered the matter over the next two nights, and at length, resolved what to me seemed a satisfactory course of action. I made an entry in the billet book. I placed him among the other listings of infants as if he had been accepted by the committee. I followed every detail, only I neglected to mention his age. I felt no scruple in this deception, for I reasoned it was not such a heinous crime as leaving a child to die, and in the eyes of God the end surely justified the means.

A week later, I handed him to the care of one of the hospital's nurses in the country and bade her say nothing of his age. Here for four years he was kindly raised, surrounded by clean air and nourished by good food, all paid for by the hospital's benefactors. All this time, however, I still feared that if his existence were discovered by the committee he might be cast out. Thus I took pains to keep his identity concealed. As part of this subterfuge I ignored the letter from his mother, in which she pleaded for regular word of his progress to be sent to the Old Bell. I convinced myself his mother would surely be dead and that it was in his own best interests to keep his whereabouts and progress a secret.

When he was eight and the first foundlings were returned from their nurses to complete their education at the hospital, I had the child brought back to London with them. For the next few years he acted as an older brother to the younger children, assisting with their classes and other simple duties. By then the committee accepted him and, assuming he was a child I had employed rather than a true foundling, never thought to question his age. Eventually, when the time came for his apprenticeship, I confided a little of his circumstances to Mr. Hogarth (who probably assumed the child was mine). He had noted that the boy showed exceptional talent in drawing, and thought he should be employed in a trade which made use of his dexterity. And so we apprenticed him to a young cabinetmaker of his acquaintance, a Mr. Chippendale.

The last I saw of this child was a few years ago, when he left the hospital to begin his new occupation and I waved him good-bye, feeling I had done the best I could for him. It is only in recent weeks, since I caught this contagion, that my opinion of my own actions has altered. The child now haunts me—or is it simply that his mother's letter lingers on in my memory? For whatever reason, I have it on my conscience that I did not follow her instructions, that I never sent news to the inn as she stipulated, and that this action was wrong. Suppose she had survived and wished to trace him? Suppose some other relative discovered his existence after her death and desired to offer him a home? My actions would have impeded any such possibility. In saving him I had obliterated his true identity entirely.

And so, to redress these misgivings, I pen this letter and direct it to the inn as I was asked to do. Anyone who wishes to discover the whereabouts of a male child abandoned ten years ago at the steps of the Foundling Hospital a day before it opened may look for him at the premises of Thomas Chippendale.

He goes there by the name John Partridge. I christened him thus on account of the parcel he carried when I found him. As I said, it was a singular memento. It contained a piece of wood labeled by the name of partridge wood.

May God forgive me for disregarding the hospital rules as I did.

I am with respect your obedient servant,

James Barrow

I handed the letter to Alice.

"It seems the letter was never sent to the Old Bell," I said as she finished reading it.

"To judge from the handwriting, he was already ill when he wrote this," she said. "He must have died soon after, and it was probably lost in the aftermath of his death."

I frowned as I pondered the contents of the letter. "There is nothing here to connect John Partridge to Montfort. On the contrary, the story of a mother dying from consumption is entirely unconnected with all we've learned. I doubt Mrs. Figgins, the nurse Montfort employed, would have traveled to London had *she* been dying."

Alice's mind was on the tokens the letter mentioned. "We can be certain Partridge made the temple box from the block of wood left to him. Montfort had it when he died. It contained the ring mentioned here. Is that not evidence of their connection?"

I shook my head resolutely. "No, it proves only that Partridge had been to see Montfort and gave the box to him because he *believed* Montfort to be his father and that the box would therefore have some significance. It doesn't prove Montfort *was* his father, or that he understood the significance of the box or the ring."

Alice stared at me. "You believe the box was of no significance to Montfort?"

"Indeed."

"Yet he held it in his hand at the moment of death?"

I paused. I had to admit the presence of the box at the scene of death was baffling. "Perhaps Montfort chanced to pick up the box at the moment he was shot?" I suggested lamely.

Alice put her head to one side. "That seems most unlikely. Are you sure your reason for denying a connection between Montfort and Partridge is not simply that you can't acknowledge that such an odious character could have fathered your friend?"

Her comment was disquieting; I was reluctant to admit it, but the same thought had crossed my mind. "I've looked at this as dispassionately as I am able."

She gave a small smile, one I knew meant she was unconvinced.

"Don't forget that the box could have been intended to cast suspicion on Partridge. The killer might have known it was made by him; perhaps he placed it there to incriminate Partridge," I said.

Alice frowned dubiously but said nothing apart from suggesting it was time we left Mrs. Bunton in peace. My pulse was racing at her obstinate refusal to comprehend my sentiments. Yet I knew it was pointless to pursue the matter at this juncture, with so little to bolster my case. Thus, in chilly dissension, we took our leave and made our way back to Hindlesham.

We journeyed in uneasy silence, distance widening between us. I wondered why she constantly questioned my judgments, why she had insisted on accompanying me when plainly she detested me still. I longed to reach out and touch her cheek, or squeeze her hand. Yet some instinct held me in check. I knew full well that now was not the time, that she was different from Connie and Molly and all the rest, and that if I dared to ignore this fact and touch her she would scourge me mercilessly with her fury.

With this thought I acknowledged the real root of my anxiety. I felt as if my very existence were spiraling beyond my control and I was no longer master of my being. The deaths of Montfort and Partridge had forced me to face a plethora of unwelcome truths. I'd found that my friend's history wasn't quite the void I'd believed it; that my master was more treacherous than I had suspected. Robert Montfort had revealed himself to be duplicitous rather than devoted towards his father; he was involved in a passionate liaison with his stepmother, who was certainly not the demure, put-upon wife I'd taken her for. Moreover, Alice was as changeable as a weather vane, and I'd developed sentiments for her that made me feel both feeble and stupid. In short, my ordered world seemed to be melting like an icicle, transforming itself to murky mayhem where nothing was as it seemed. I wanted the people around me to conform to my trusting perceptions of them. If Partridge turned out to be someone other than I thought, would the same be true of everyone else I knew? Were Foley and Miss Alleyn and Connie and Mrs. Cummings as devious as the rest? Would the same prove true of Alice?

Chapter Eighteen

We returned to the inn to dine—a hearty repast of pigeon pie and ale, which our landlord, Samuel Morton, didn't stint in supplying. Since Alice was still angry and awkward, I fell into conversation with him. Having exchanged routine pleasantries regarding the inclement weather and the monuments of interest in the area, I asked him if he knew anyone by the name of Figgins living in these parts. A cloud seemed to sweep across his jovial face when he registered the name, and his eyes became oddly guarded.

"She's no friend of yours?"

"What makes you say so?"

"The little I've learned of her. I've often heard her name—though I thank God I don't know her. She's not one to tangle with, of that much I can be sure. You'd be advised to stay clear."

"What can you tell me of her?"

He scratched his chin thoughtfully. "Not a great deal, though she's lived in these parts ever since I can remember. People are wary of her, always have been. She's odd, they say, and by some accounts grows odder as the years pass."

"What do they find so strange about her?"

"I can't rightly say. For a time she worked up at the hall at Horseheath. She left under some sort of a cloud. I've no doubt it had to do with thieving or drink—her family are no strangers to either."

"Did you ever hear of her caring for children, as a nurse?"

"Don't recall it, but that don't mean that she didn't. Though I'd pity any infant left in her care."

"Does she live alone?"

"Husband died some years back. There's a son—a man now—aged nineteen or twenty, works in the woods as a bodger by summer. During winter months he stays with her and makes a living from poaching. He's no better than she. Most round here keep away from them both."

He had little more to say on the subject, except to give me directions to her dwelling—a hut somewhat out of the village on the road back to Horseheath Hall.

Alice retired to her room immediately after dinner, leaving me alone, dejected, and with little else to do but call on Mrs. Figgins.

The weather had turned cold again, overcast and bleak with a keen wind that chilled the tip of my nose and threatened snow at any moment. My path took me beyond the shop and church and genteel houses I'd observed last night, towards the outskirts of the village. Samuel Morton had instructed me to take a turn that doubled back parallel to the village green. The course brought me to a stagnant corner of the village, as different from the rest as the front of a fine piece of furniture differs from its unpolished back.

The dwellings here were tumbledown constructions of wattle and daub, with holes in their walls and crooked chimneys from which wisps of smoke melted in the January air. Beyond the cottages, the terrain rose again to an area of common ground on which some scrawny beasts were forlornly tethered among clumps of reeds and a few sparse bushes. Between the houses the land was swampy and had claimed occasional casualties among the livestock. On the far borders, two great dark slimy carcasses protruded from the pools of brown frozen mud, like shipwrecks revealed by an ebbing tide.

I circled the marsh and headed towards the last hovel in the row, as Samuel Morton had directed me. I could now see that of all these dismal dwellings this was the most vile. A putrid smell assailed me as I approached—a combination of dampness, dung, and decomposition. The windows were crudely boarded; nothing but a few small apertures allowed light to filter inside. Mold invaded the walls, spreading upwards from the foundations, where it doubtless flourished due to the dankness of the surroundings. Here and there the moisture had dissolved the fabric of the walls, which had melted away, leaving scars through which the wooden structure was visible.

I made my way towards the door, called out, and when that raised no answer, thumped upon it. After some minutes, when still no reply had come, I lifted the latch and went in.

I entered a small, low-ceilinged room. Everything in it was encrusted with the grime of ages and in the same advanced stages of decay as the building outside. The walls were brown with filth, the scant furnishings broken and poorly mended, the floor strewn with damp rushes that had clearly not been changed for months. At the far end of the room an old crone sat staring at the dead ashes of the fire. So hunched and wizened and small was she that at first I took her for a bundle of rags.

"Excuse me, ma'am," I said, "I am searching for a Mrs. Figgins. Would you be that lady?"

From the glare she darted at me I could see there was no fear in her. Far from it. She muttered to herself, held up a gnarled finger, and boldly beckoned me closer, as if she wanted to confide in me.

"Do you wish to tell me something, mother?" I said. Remembering Samuel's warnings, I approached her cautiously, although I couldn't believe this decrepit hag could pose me any threat.

She muttered an unintelligible reply and urged me closer still. I stepped towards her. "What's that you say?"

Another indecipherable whisper. I thought I could make out the words "Give it mouth, wind . . . come here." But I couldn't be certain. I placed my hand on the armrest of her chair and leaned down. An instant later, from the ragged folds of her skirt she whisked out a long, narrow bladed knife of the sort butchers use for filleting meat. She drew it across the back of my hand, so swiftly I felt only the faintest sear of pain. Then she brandished the point towards my eye. "One move and I'll have you. And it'll be quicker than you know!" she cried, suddenly lucid. "God damn you! What devilish wind has brought you here? Come to steal from an old woman, have you?" She grinned, as if the irony of this remark amused her.

I drew back in shock, tucking my wounded hand into my armpit, where I could feel it begin to smart. "I can assure you, madam, I've no intention of stealing from you. On the contrary, I've something for you, if you are Mrs. Figgins."

"Something for me?" she said, growing suddenly confused. "Something for me?" The knife was now waving dangerously about.

"Put down the knife and I'll show you."

"A secret to take, and I'll put it down . . . a secret, that's it, a secret." She kept repeating this meaningless ditty to herself, still clutching the knife.

I could see she'd never put it down unless I distracted her. With my good hand I felt in my pocket, took out the bottle of gin I'd procured from Samuel Morton, and handed it to her. As soon as she saw it she dropped the knife and grabbed the bottle from me. She gazed lovingly at it for a long moment before tearing her rheumy eyes away and looking up sharply. "Who are you to bring me gifts?"

"A friend."

"You want something."

"I merely wish to talk to you."

"Do I know you?"

"I've come to ask about your days of nursing. You did work as nurse to Lord Montfort, I understand?"

"Montfort." She spat out the name as if it were a piece of rotten meat. "May he rot in hell with the devil for his wife."

"He's gone, ma'am, though whether to hell or heaven I cannot judge. That's why I've come."

"Gone, gone? Heaven, hell?" She grew vacant again and turned towards the ashes.

"I mean he's dead." I faltered, wondering if she was as demented as she seemed, or what mischief she might be concocting. "I have come because I should like to know what you can tell me of the child you looked after for Lord Montfort. What became of him?"

As suddenly as it had appeared, the vacant look vanished and I thought I saw a sly flash in her eye. But either I'd imagined it or she was deliberately ignoring me, for there was a long pause. I pressed her again.

"I am most anxious to find this child. I can offer you money if you can recall anything at all. He was newborn, I believe, when he came to you."

"If you know, why ask?" she sneered.

"I should like to know what else you recall."

"Have you more of this?" She gestured to the bottle.

"If you wish it."

It was while she was still pondering what she would divulge to me that a shadow fell over the room. I looked up and saw the hulking figure of a man framed in the rotten doorway. He wore a torn piece of dirty blanket lashed up with twine in place of a coat. Where his hat should have been, a grimy rag was wound turbanlike round his head. He carried a dead rabbit in one hand, and in the other a club matted with fur and blood.

"What the devil's this, Ma?" he cried, flinging the rabbit down on the table and pointing his bloodstained club in my direction. "More vermin, is it? Shall I deal with him?"

"Jack, is that you? It's no vermin, son. 'Tis a visitor, come with questions and bringing us liquor," replied his mother, signaling to the bottle in her lap.

I shivered as I felt his eyes fall upon me. His skin was bristly and encrusted with dirt, and one side of his mouth was yanked down by a long scar running from his cheekbone to his lip. He must have sensed my repulsion, for he leered close to me. "Not as fair as you, am I, sir? What d'you want coming here?"

I swayed a little and stepped back from him. "I did not wish to disturb you or your mother. I came only to ask about the child she looked after for Lord Montfort."

"Montfort? Why's that? He's dead, I heard."

"The child?"

He spat on the floor disdainfully. "What of the child?"

"That child may be a friend of mine. I am trying to discover the truth. What became of the child? He must have been about the same age as you. Do you recall him? Does your mother never speak of him?"

"Don't need to. We were reared together, she nursed the two of us. . . . He got the milk, I got the pap. It's 'cause of him I got this." He pointed a grimy finger towards the scar.

"How's that?"

"We fought."

"I'm sorry to hear it."

He shrugged indifferently and spat again, this time aiming at the fire. A ball of spittle hissed as it hit the embers.

I pressed on. "For how long did he live with you?"

"Not so fast. If you want to know so much, it don't come for naught. You pay for it."

I delved in my pocket and handed him a florin, which he took as eagerly as his mother grasped the bottle.

"Four years, maybe five."

"Then what happened?"

"She was told by his lordship to take the child to London. To a hospital that would care for him."

His mother seemed suddenly to catch on to our conversation. "Hospital, aye, hospital," she echoed. "That was it, of course he told me to take him there."

"Do you remember?" I said, addressing myself now to her directly.

I saw a furtive exchange of glances. The woman's eye clouded over and she fell silent.

"Do you recall taking the child to London?" I repeated more insistently.

Still she said nothing. I looked helplessly at her son. "I have another florin," I said, chinking the coins in my pocket.

"Tell him, Ma," he urged her. "Montfort's dead, there's no harm can come to us now."

But the old woman had turned deaf as well as dumb and gave no sign of responding.

"Do you know what happened?" I said, looking now at her son. I was still turning the money over in my hand so he could hear it.

There was a long pause while he thumped the club gently on the table. I watched his face, mesmerized, waiting for him to speak, willing him to relent, to tell me what he knew. And yet, even though my attention was all on him, I was entirely unprepared for what happened next. Without warning he let his weapon fall, then he reached out with his other hand, seized me by my collar, and held me close to his grimy face.

"The child is *dead*. She never took him to London. Is that the truth you wanted? Now we've naught further to say. I'll have the coins before you leave . . . unless you wish me to make your face a little more like mine, or end up cold and stiff as this rabbit?"

With a violent thrust he ripped my hand from my pocket, grabbed the coins, then hurled me backwards. I fell sprawling in the mud as the door slammed in my face.

Chapter Nineteen

I picked myself up from the mire and hastened back to the inn to tell Alice what I'd found. I mounted the stairs to her room three steps at a time and thumped on her door. My earlier trepidation had been replaced with an acute sense of urgency; I was impatient to tell her that my hypothesis had now been proved beyond doubt. I was not the fool she believed me. My instinct was correct: Partridge was not Montfort's child.

In a sense my discovery resurrected my confidence in my friendship with Partridge. I remembered the raucous sound of his laugh, the fun of our trips together on the river. I remembered the firmness of his handshake, how his brow furrowed when something angered him, and how swiftly he gulped his ale. I had restored him to what I'd believed him to be. There had been no hidden side to his character, no family secret, no concealment. Partridge was an anonymous foundling still. He was the child taken in by James Barrow, tended at the hospital until he was of an age to be apprenticed.

Nevertheless, when I considered Partridge I found my sentiments towards him had shifted perceptibly. A distance had grown between us, like a boat untied from the quay drifting on the ebbing tide. At the same time I felt older and more purposeful, less daunted by the task that confronted me, as if the divide liberated me from burdensome emotion, allowing me to view his death with a clearer, more judicious eye.

"There must have been two children intended for the hospital," I explained to Alice after telling her of all that had passed with Mrs. Figgins. "They chanced to be about the same age. One was my friend, John Partridge, who was left by his ailing mother on the steps of the hospital with the morsel of wood and the portion of ring. This was the child James Barrow discovered, took in, and later apprenticed to Chippendale."

"And the other child?" With relief I noted that Alice was captivated by my information, her earlier aloofness apparently forgotten.

"The other child was Montfort and Trenti's, the child tended by Mrs. Figgins. This child died while still in Figgins's care, before he ever reached the hospital."

"Why then did Miss Alleyn tell Madame Trenti the child had been taken to the hospital? Why did she not tell her the child was dead?"

"Because she *believed* she was telling the truth. Neither she nor her brother knew the child was dead. That was Mrs. Figgins's secret."

"What reason did she have to conceal the child's death?"

"Put simply, money. She was being paid by Montfort to nurture his child. The child perished in his infancy, perhaps from neglect, for I can't believe she was ever a diligent guardian. But Mrs. Figgins knew that once Montfort learned his child was dead the payments she received for tending him would cease. And so she claimed her allowance for as long as possible, until she was told to leave the child in London. Doubtless she pretended to Montfort she had done as he ordered, and neither he nor his sister ever learned the child was dead."

"And Madame Trenti mistakenly believed Partridge was the child taken to the hospital?"

"No. There is nothing to connect Partridge in all this. Partridge merely served Madame Trenti as a convenient stand-in when she could not trace her own child. She must have discovered that he was a foundling from something Chippendale said and then used the information for her own selfish purpose."

Alice nodded thoughtfully. As yet she had given me no inkling of whether she'd forgiven me. Nevertheless, the fact that she was freely discussing the implications of my findings with me, and that I had been allowed to sit in her chamber for half an hour, led me to presume our altercation was at least fading from her memory, and before long our intimacy would advance once more. So it was that, after we'd discussed the matter at some length, I felt confident enough to propose descending to take a glass of wine and continue our discussion over supper.

We came down to the parlor to find Lord Foley seated in an armchair waiting for us. He stood and raised a somewhat quizzical brow as I escorted Alice towards him. "Charming, quite charming," he murmured so loudly it was perfectly audible to us both. Then he took her hand, bowed chivalrously low, and expressed his profound gratitude for her invaluable assistance in this mysterious quest. She took this homage in her stride, although from the gleam in her eye I'd say she was flattered that a gentleman clad in a coat of such impeccable cut should treat her so gallantly.

I don't know why but the exchange of pleasantries between them unnerved me, and it was some relief when it were over. Afterwards we wandered to the parlor to order supper; while I began to recount all we'd discovered, Alice excused herself to attend to matters in her chamber. She would see us presently. It was half an hour later, when the waiting woman appeared to tell us our collops of veal awaited us, that I saw the table was set for two rather than three and inquired as to the whereabouts of Miss Goodchild.

"Why, sir," returned the bemused serving woman, "didn't you know that the young lady altered her plans? She left some half hour ago, in Mr. Morton's gig, saying that an unforeseen occurrence compelled her to return immediately to London, and she would not sup after all. She arranged for the stable groom to drive her directly to Cambridge, from where she'll take the stage to London."

I was, I own, flabbergasted at this information. "Did she receive any communication that made her alter her plans?"

"None that I know of, sir."

I joined Foley at the table feeling utterly downcast. What conclusion could I draw from her actions but an inauspicious one? In hurrying away without so much as a cursory good-bye she left me in no doubt that, far from forgiving me, she had decided I was an unsuitable companion, not worthy of even the smallest courtesy. Not worthy of bidding farewell.

The realization threw me into first a fit of despondency and then an impulsive urge to relieve it. I longed to follow her to Cambridge, to demand an explanation for her sudden disappearance. Nonetheless I doubted such a course was prudent. I told myself sternly I'd be better to act as if her precipitate departure was the most normal thing in the world. Rather than confront her in person, it would be preferable to write a long letter in which I stated my case. By the time she read it, distanced from me, her irritation would be more likely to have subsided, in which case she might take my words to heart. This thought no sooner occurred to me than I dismissed it. Far better to go myself in person. To reiterate my mistakes, declare my sentiments. For the frustrations and misunderstandings in our friendship had done nothing to deter me. Quite the contrary. My desire was inflamed by every obstacle she raised. My feelings towards her were more profound than any I had previously experienced towards a member of the female sex, and come what may she should know it.

This hurricane of emotions served to curb my usual appetite. I toyed with my meal, swallowing only the merest morsel of meat and pudding. An excellent shrub wine offered the only salve for my jangling nerves, although its calming effect didn't prevent me mulling over my dilemma as I drank and drank, uttering scarcely a word to Foley. Conversation was beyond me. In any case Foley was the last person with whom I wished to converse. His arrival had precipitated Alice's departure. If he hadn't come she might still be here. So I kept my troubles to myself and replied only with brusque grunts to Foley's attempts to rouse me. He seemed to accept my ill-humor, and it was only when two courses of his dinner were done, and he was dabbing at his mouth with his napkin before the final assault on a fruit compote, that he barged his way into my thoughts.

"I passed by Horseheath Hall on my journey here. You will be relieved to learn that Robert Montfort was leaving for a two-day sojourn in town. Elizabeth has remained at Horseheath with Miss Alleyn."

I shrugged indifferently. "I too should return to London and continue the quest from there. There seems little purpose in remaining here when I'm barred from the house."

"On the contrary, Hopson, I would urge you rather to return to Horseheath Hall now the coast is clear, for I am convinced we have barely begun to uncover the secrets concealed within that house."

I pushed my half-finished plate to one side, took another gulp of wine, and tried to banish Alice from my thoughts. Her disappearance and the wine I'd consumed had demolished my earlier optimism and purposefulness. "Perhaps so," I mumbled. "But I've been barred from going there by Robert Montfort, and threatened with all kinds of castigation if I ignore the warning. And in any event, I confess that each new discovery makes me more rather than less confused as to what befell Montfort and Partridge. I feel as if I am wandering deeper into a maze, becoming more hopelessly entwined with each step."

Foley curled his lip in a patronizing semblance of a smile, as if my consternation were a source of amusement. "Rest assured, my dear fellow, that this is merely the dark before the dawn," he returned with mock conviviality. "I've every faith in your ability to discover the source of all this intrigue. Look at the progress you've made today. If you lack anything, it is not intellect or insight but tenacity. Surely what counts now is not *whether* or not Partridge was related to Montfort (for we know now he was not) but who *believed* him to be."

I emptied my glass and filled it again. He was confusing me, and his composure irked me. He must have observed my dismal expression, yet he paid no heed to it, as if I, a mere hireling of his, were somehow not entitled to the luxury of sentiment. I considered the generous allowance he'd paid me for my assistance so far, but it did nothing to appease my annoyance. Why should sentiment be the prerogative of privilege along with fine carriages, fancy clothes, and large houses? I gulped my wine again, struggling to keep hold of my temper. "What d'you mean?" I said sharply.

"If Partridge presented himself to Montfort as his long-lost son, who else knew of it?"

"Any member of the family, anyone in the house."

"Precisely."

"And perhaps any one of them who stood to benefit from Lord Montfort's death, or who depended on him in some way, might have felt sufficiently threatened by Partridge's claim to want to dispose of him."

"That," said Foley, as if I'd only reiterated a conclusion he'd arrived at aeons earlier, "is what I now believe."

The wine was adding self-assurance to my irritation. I could see no reason for deference to him. On the contrary, it occurred to me that if I annoyed him sufficiently he might send me packing back to London sooner rather than later, which would suit my purpose admirably. My tone became more overtly caustic and audacious. "What do you make of them all? I take it you have detected a . . . fondness . . . between Robert and his stepmother?"

Foley's eyebrows knitted in concentration. "It should not surprise us, I think. After all, Elizabeth is closer in age to her stepson than to her erstwhile husband."

I finished the wine and called for a tankard of ale. Drinking coupled with my addled frame of mind was making it increasingly difficult for me to articulate my thoughts. "Elizabeth Montfort . . . always keeps herself private . . . but I've a feeling that she's a woman of considerable force and passion. She was held in check by her husband, who, I'd say, she plainly detested and feared." I sighed deeply, gathering further ill-considered thoughts. "Now Robert Montfort . . . He seems to me a frustrated young man. Frustrated by his passion for his stepmother, and moreover by his father's objections to his interest in science."

"And Miss Alleyn?"

"Protective of them all. Frustrated mother? No less complicated than the rest."

"What d'you mean, no less complicated?" The muscles in Foley's jaw had frozen; he was staring intently at me.

"On the first occasion that I broached the subject with her, she was anxious to conceal her brother's relations with Madame Trenti. She pretended she'd never heard of the woman, even though Trenti herself showed me a letter from Miss Alleyn dated not two months earlier. Later, when I told her Partridge might be her brother's child, she became more forthcoming. She informed me of her brother's payments to Mrs. Figgins and hinted that he *had* most probably made them on account of an illegitimate child. That is most curious, is it not? Why should she deny knowledge of Madame Trenti, yet be unafraid to tell me of Lord Montfort's child?"

I paused to slake my thirst, not troubling to explain to Foley what I had already concluded, that Connie's presence during the first part of our conversation was the reason for Miss Alleyn's earlier denials. I noted with some satisfaction that Foley seemed discomfited by my ponderings. I wanted to unsettle him further, to show him I did not think him quite as high and mighty as he believed. "Of course there were others in the household who might equally be involved."

"Such as?"

"Lord Bradfield . . . Lady Bradfield, their son, George, Lady Foley . . . yourself."

At this Lord Foley's usually sallow complexion whitened alarmingly. "Hopson, you forget yourself. Are you suggesting that my wife and I might somehow be involved in Montfort's death? I trust it is the wine you have consumed that makes you utter such a ludicrous impertinence."

I drained the tankard. My head was beginning to swim, and I had to concentrate hard on what I would say.

"Surely, my lord, the purpose of this investigation is to discover the truth. Is that not what you told me on the very first day you asked me to become involved? Is that not why you persisted in demanding that I assist you? There is no guarantee that the truth will be pleasant or what you want it to be. You cannot deny an interest in Lord Montfort's affairs. After all, *you* are the chief beneficiary of the changes to his will."

Foley shot me a murderous look, then gazed at the ceiling as if to underline the superiority of his motives. "I did not need Montfort's money. Nor did I encourage him in any way to become indebted to me. Rather the reverse: I attempted to prevent him. He lost his fortune by his own folly. He had only himself to blame for his despair. As for Lord Bradfield and his son and our wives . . . why"—here he gave a mocking laugh—"the suggestion is too far-fetched to warrant a reply." He scowled at me again. Two livid stains the size of half crowns had appeared on his cheeks.

"One thing I will say, Hopson. Before you make any further wild accusations of this kind, you might consider two things. First, that although I might discuss matters with you as an equal, the conventions of society continue to exist, and I expect circumspection from you. Second, you might do well to remind yourself that I am paying your expenses in order that you will help me get to the bottom of these deaths. Would I do so if I were responsible for them? Now, if you have finished your ridiculous postulations, I shall leave you at Horseheath, where I trust you will continue your research more soberly."

I was chastened by what he said, but a certain pigheadedness remained. "Have I not already told you, my lord, Robert Montfort has refused to allow me to go there? He says he'll have me branded and imprisoned as a thief."

"And have I not already told you Robert Montfort is gone to London? He will not know of your presence until after you are gone. I'll give you a note for Elizabeth or Miss Alleyn to ensure they raise no objections."

I was sorely tempted to tell him to go to the devil, but despite my drunken confusion I dared not, and besides, the logic of his argument was clear to me. This might be my last chance to gain entry at Horseheath, a final opportunity to unearth material pertaining to Partridge. And so without further demur I allowed him to settle the bill and scribble a note for me. We walked outside. I was still fuming; gloom at Alice's departure gripped me like a nagging ague.

Foley ignored me entirely in the carriage. Depositing me at the gates of Horseheath Hall, he left me to stagger up the drive, saying the walk would bring me to my senses and he would call on the morrow to see how I was progressing. I swaddled myself in my coat, my head pounding as though pressed in a vise. I longed to lie down and close my eyes and dream of Alice. I toyed with the idea of turning on my heels and pursuing her to Cambridge, then dismissed this scheme as foolish. I had no way of getting there apart from walking the ten-mile distance, and by the time I got there she would certainly be in bed asleep. I turned the corner, and the gloomy expanse of the hall came suddenly into view; against the flat, lowering sky it seemed heavy and shadowless, like a prospect drawn by an architect rather than a three-dimensional building in which people lived and wept and died.

I consoled myself with the thought that at least I would find solace in the company of Connie. I dimly recalled she had something to discuss with me, and I longed to confide in her about Alice. Now at least there would be plenty of time to talk without interruption.

But when I skulked round to the rear (a prudent measure in case Foley had misled me and Robert hadn't gone), further disappointments greeted me. Connie had left earlier that afternoon with Elizabeth to stay overnight with friends in Cambridge. Mrs. Cummings took one look at my swaying figure and wild eyes, and said she was up to her elbows in salting hams, too busy to talk. If I wanted anything, John the footman would take me to see Miss Alleyn.

The imminent audience with that lady had a sobering effect. For all my drunkenness, I knew if I bungled the conversation I'd ruin my chances of making further discoveries concerning Partridge. As if I'd doused myself in a water trough, my head grew instantly clearer.

Miss Alleyn was in the morning room, stitching at a crewelwork counterpane. When John led me in, she greeted me cordially. She pushed away her embroidery frame, glancing regretfully down her long nose at the intricately embroidered fruit and flowers. What was it I required? she asked quietly.

I bowed, breathed deeply, and concentrated on my every word. "You will recall, madam, that the last time we spoke you mentioned that the drawer of your brother's desk, the one that was stuck fast, contained his journals."

"Indeed."

I blinked at her, thanking God for her placidity, praying she hadn't remarked the slight slurring of my words. "I wondered if I might glance at the one relating to the days immediately prior to his death? It occurs to me it may contain something that could shed light on the matter . . ."

She was toying with her box of yarns, twisting a sky blue skein between her long fingers. "You still pursue that matter, I see. Are you no closer to discovering why your friend died? Have you found nothing pertaining to my brother?"

I swallowed uncomfortably. "A little perhaps. I now know for certain that Partridge was *not* Madame Trenti and your brother's child. I think I mentioned that lady to you and voiced my doubts concerning her truthfulness."

Miss Alleyn looked down at the tangled mass of vivid yarns in her box. Even though I was having difficulty in focusing, her expression of bewilderment didn't escape me.

"Not their child?"

My reactions were becoming quicker now. "I believe pretending Partridge was your brother's child was a deliberate deception dreamed up by Madame Trenti for venal motives. The child she bore your brother, the child raised by Mrs. Figgins, did not survive early childhood, and was certainly not my friend Partridge."

"How can you be sure?"

I hesitated. I saw no reason not to tell her. "I traced Mrs. Figgins. She—or rather her son—confessed that the child she raised for your brother died. He was never taken to London to the hospital. Madame Trenti simply employed Partridge—who was reared at the hospital—as a convenient substitute to apply pressure to your brother."

"Was Partridge involved in the subterfuge?"

"No. He was entirely innocent. Madame Trenti duped him, knowing he knew nothing of his origins and would believe the tale she spun him."

She shook her head slowly. "Then your friend was most unfortunate. Such villainy as Madame Trenti has displayed is hard to comprehend . . . and all the worse in a female."

I felt more confident now to divulge my theory. "Madame Trenti is an adventuress, a stranger to moral probity. Now that her looks are fading, her concern is to secure her future. She believed your brother might be coerced into helping her achieve that aim. And in order to do so she sent Partridge here to his death."

Miss Alleyn tutted disapprovingly, clearly most put out by what I was telling her. I think she would have pursued the matter more, only I cut her off. "To return to the journal—I wonder if I might see it?"

Although distracted by what I'd told her, she willingly escorted me to the library and indicated that I might open the drawer in question. My head was still pulsating, but not so badly that I didn't notice a striking change in the appearance of the desk. Where before the drawer had been tightly jammed, now I noticed it jutted proud of the carcass, as if it had been recently opened and could not be pushed back in. I tugged at the drawer. Unlike the others, it moved stiffly on its runners. There was a dark stain covering half the drawer lining. Some liquid had recently spilled inside, causing the wood to swell so that the drawer would not close. It had a faintly cheesy smell. I blinked when I saw inside, as if my eyes might be deceiving me. The drawer was empty.

"The journals are no longer here. Have you removed them to save them from the damp?" I queried.

"What can you mean?" replied Miss Alleyn, her thin cheeks coloring with confusion. "The journals were there. I saw them myself."

"It would seem then, madam, that some other person has removed them. Perhaps on account of the spillage. Is it milk? Could you hazard a guess as to who might have removed them?"

"Why," she replied swiftly, "I haven't a notion whether it's milk, though I agree there is a smell of something noxious. As for the journals, I don't believe Elizabeth would have meddled with them, for how could she have opened a drawer that you were unable to shift? Lord and Lady Bradfield rarely come here alone. I can only presume therefore that Robert must have taken them. He has recently displayed a fascination for his dead father's papers that I never saw when he was alive. I fancy he hopes to find some trace of his father's affection for him. Poor boy. My brother never displayed much fondness towards any member of his family. Robert's mother died when he was an infant. That is why he has always displayed a tender disposition towards me; I believe that's also why he has grown close to Elizabeth."

Even in my somewhat addled state the thought crossed my mind that Robert Montfort was the last person I would describe as having a tender disposition, and that he had other, less pure reasons for his interest in Elizabeth. But I held my tongue.

"I'm sorry to hear it. Might he have taken the journals with him to London?"

"It is possible but unlikely, I think. Most probably he has left them in his room. You may look there if you wish."

I recalled his fury at my previous visit to his laboratory and shivered apprehensively. "Will he not object?"

"Why should he?" she replied patiently, as if she were addressing a child.

"Because he barred me from this house . . ."

She regarded me in thoughtful silence. "I have few secrets from my dear nephew, Robert, and would do nothing willingly to disturb him, but in this instance, in order to aid you in the search for the truth, I feel justified in giving you my word—I will not divulge your visit to this house."

I offered her my profound thanks, although I felt cold all over at the thought of entering Robert Montfort's room. I held back an instant, whereupon she urged me on, reassuring me once more that Robert was nowhere in the vicinity and that she would willingly accompany me. Thus, reluctantly, did I acquiesce.

We mounted the fine carved staircase to the main landing and proceeded, beneath the beady-eyed animal heads, to the door I had so fatefully opened a few evenings before. With Robert gone the room seemed oddly impersonal. The silver boxes and bottles and brushes which had previously littered his dressing chest were either stowed in the inner compartments or had been taken with him. Only the wig stand remained, a bald wooden orb gleaming in the dwindling light of a solitary candlestick.

Miss Alleyn unlocked the door leading to the laboratory with one of the keys from a large bunch attached to her chain. She handed me a pair of lights and suggested I begin by searching the shelves while she glanced through his dressing chest. I nodded, listening carefully for an instant, though I knew it was unnecessary to do so, for there was no one in the house to threaten me. Then in silence, for my heart thumped too wildly to allow me to speak, I walked into the room.

Mercifully there was no longer any sign of the eviscerated dog. The table was scrubbed bare, a few brownish patches the only indication of its gruesome purpose. I positioned one of my lights on the table and, holding the other aloft, looked about me. Behind the table, lining one wall, were two shelves. The upper was filled with what I can only describe as large scientific curiosities: fossils and shells and jars of liquid in which floated various unsavory specimens—a large pinkish beetle, a lamb's head, a heart and other unidentifiable, ragged organs. I glanced along the shelf below. This was less fearsome, ranged with various boxes and papers and books. With Miss Alleyn urging me to search as thoroughly as I pleased, I began by standing on a chair to scour the upper shelves, pulling out each jar to see that nothing lay behind it. Nothing did.

It felt most strange to be trespassing through Robert's private rooms under the approving eye of Miss Alleyn. Yet now I'd overcome my initial trepidation, my wine-fueled bravado seemed to return. Having fruitlessly combed the upper stage, I turned to the lower one. At one end lay a folio containing engravings of the human anatomy and various past editions published by the Royal Society. Again no sign of the journals. Next was a pile of shagreen-bound notebooks. I opened the pages of the first, wondering if these were the volumes I sought—only to find it contained accounts and annotated drawings of various experiments, presumably those conducted in this very chamber. One was a detailed anatomical section of a dog, another of a human jawbone. Tucked in beside the notebooks was a small wooden casket bound with brass.

I lifted out the casket for closer examination. It was a simple receptacle, probably intended to store letters or surgical implements, or even, I thought eagerly, the journals I was looking for. The clasp was unfastened. I opened it.

At first sight the cavity I looked into appeared to be stuffed with nothing but a jumble of torn cotton rags. Were they bandages for Robert Montfort's surgical operations? It occurred to me they could not have been there long because as soon as I released them from the pressure of the lid they sprang up and cascaded over the side. With the expectant curiosity of a child who unwraps a gift, I lifted them away. The lower rags were not clean and white and springy like those on top but stiff and stained dirty brown. Even as I removed them my stomach began to clench in anticipation of some as yet unknown fright.

A moment later and I'd recognized the horror with the wretched familiarity of a recurring nightmare. Wedged along the base of the box, as neatly as spoons in a cutlery tray, was a cluster of severed fingers, three in all—though I scarcely needed to count them to know it. With the sight of those poor dismembered fingers, my wine-soaked pluckiness vanished. Yet my responses were distanced, as if I were merely viewing an unpleasant picture, or witnessing a harrowing scene on a stage; what I'd seen was nasty, yet also fantastic. My feelings of numbness were not, however, impregnable. My eyes blurred, my head grew dizzy with panic. I gripped the top of the table for support and closed my eyes, hoping that I was in some kind of foggy dream, and that when I opened them again I'd be somewhere else, or gazing on some entirely innocuous object, rather than at these shriveled portions of my friend.

At some point I must have gasped out loud, for I heard Miss Alleyn say, "Are you not well, Mr. Hopson? Why have you grown so pale?" Seeing the dread upon my face, and that I was apparently transfixed and unable to respond, she must have moved closer. I heard her give a small cry of shock when she looked inside the casket herself. I opened my eyes to find the receptacle closed and Miss Alleyn laying a light, sympathetic hand on mine.

"Come," she said softly. "There is nothing for us here, and no need for you to distress yourself further with this. I will send for Justice Westleigh and let him take whatever steps he deems necessary."

It was several hours before Westleigh arrived to collect the foul casket, by which time the numbing effect of the wine had long vanished and the full import of what I'd found had struck home. Miss Alleyn had left me alone to wait in the library and listen to the oppressive quiet of the room, and the inexplicable creaks and shudders of the passages outside. Soon my nerves were jarred and my terror returned. I couldn't think how or why I'd allowed myself to be inveigled back to this house. Had not my life been threatened? Had not Robert warned me what he would do if he ever caught sight of me here? However well meaning Miss Alleyn's assurances that she would keep my visit to Horseheath and my exploration of his room secret, I could not rely on her entirely. If Robert returned unexpectedly, there would be no hiding of the truth. Panic surged within me each time I contemplated my helpless situation, the horrid contents of the casket, and Robert's warning to me. Upon reflection I saw that this discovery changed everything. Miss Alleyn could not possibly keep my visit a secret; I was foolish to think she could. She would be obliged to disclose that I had come, and for what reason. For how else could she explain the discovery of the casket?

Before long Robert would know I had ignored his warning and returned. He would learn I had been in his rooms, among his possessions, and he would vent his violence upon me. Whether this was in London or here would make little difference. Terror overwhelmed me. I knew I was in danger of losing my faculties altogether. I tried to muster my powers of reason, and tell myself that he would not come here now, and that when I was in London I would be surrounded by friendly faces and thus protected from his malice. But my dreadful thoughts persisted, and the wait for Westleigh seemed interminable.

It transpired, however, that providence smiled upon my craving to be gone. No sooner had Sir James arrived than he declared that the contents of the box should be delivered forthwith to Cambridge, to the apothecary physician who'd earlier examined Partridge's corpse. He would be happy therefore to give me a ride to town in his carriage. It would be late evening by the time we arrived, too late for any transportation to London, but I could pass the night at the Hoop Inn and take the first stage south in the morning.

In making this arrangement, I ignored the fact that Foley was coming to see me next day and deliberately neglected to send word to him of my sudden change of plan.

I'm not certain if Miss Alleyn knew of the appointment, but in any case she seemed to view my distress with true compassion. Instead of trying to place obstacles in my way, she bade me farewell with a gentle solicitude that reminded me uncannily of my mother.

Chapter Twenty

As it turned out, it was a whole week before I finally returned to London. A sudden Siberian blizzard howled across the flat lands of Cambridge, leaving in its wake snowdrifts so deep a man or a horse might easily perish in them. The coachmen understood that if they ventured out in such conditions they would end up helplessly marooned in a drift or a frozen ditch, and refused to budge. I had no choice but to pace my chamber in the Hoop Inn and watch the snow fall. A week may not seem a long time, yet to me the hours seemed like days, and the days an eternity. What could I do but return to the events that so dominated my life? And over the long days spent before a paltry fire, it dawned upon me that I'd become ensnared in the jumble of recent weeks. I'd behaved no more cannily than a kitchen dog on a treadwheel, trotting endlessly round, rotating the spit, and larding myself in the process.

I thought about the grenadillo box I'd taken from Montfort's hand, surely one of the most exquisite objects Partridge had ever made, and of the half ring I'd discovered inside. Thanks to James Barrow's testimony, I now knew the ring and the wood from which the box was made were left with Partridge when he was deposited at the Foundling Hospital, but I was still no closer to comprehending where they had come from before that.

At the heart of the deceit surrounding Partridge's death lay Madame Trenti. I now understood it was she who had precipitated that tragedy. It was she who had fabricated the story that Montfort was his father and dispatched Partridge to Horseheath Hall, in order to wreak revenge for the injustice Montfort had wrought upon her two decades earlier. Granted Montfort *had* wronged her when he deprived her of the child and promised he would bring him up as his own, but my concerns and sympathies lay with Partridge. By raising Partridge's hopes of his parentage, Trenti had driven him to his death. Moreover, her actions and falsehoods insinuated that *birth,* not *talent,* offered Partridge his deliverance. This was her supreme treachery. That Partridge had no history was bad enough; to have a fabrication foisted upon him annihilated the little he knew himself to be.

I knew Trenti would offer no help over the matter of the ring, but I was nonetheless determined to confront her. While I was incarcerated in Cambridge, my hatred towards her grew until I was overcome by rage and a determination to face her with the evidence of her unscrupulousness.

No sooner had I decided upon this course of action than thoughts of Alice intruded. My ruminations about our last meeting disturbed me profoundly; I'd rouse myself, determine that she attracted me only by her elusiveness, and thus banish her from my consciousness. Yet later my resolve would vanish; she'd return to haunt my thoughts and leave me worrying how I'd ever appease her. This pendulum of uncertainty swung constantly, so that when I left Cambridge after a week of musing I was no closer to unraveling my sentiments towards her than when I arrived.

And so I returned to the granite skies and grime of London. I was mud-spattered and wearied by my journey and went first to Nerot's Baths in King Street, where the heat of the water went some way to soothing my aches and chills. Returning to my lodgings, I donned fresh linen and a clean suit before penning an impetuous note to Alice.

In it I said I trusted she had managed to escape the inclemencies of weather by leaving when she did, although I was disappointed that her departure had been without a word to me. Now that I was returned, there was a matter of a private nature I had to discuss. I begged her therefore to accompany me next afternoon to the Theatre Royal, where I'd heard a musical spectacle was due to be held. Unless I received a message to the contrary I'd assume she was agreeable. I thought about mentioning the discovery of the fingers but decided I'd save her distress and tell her this gently when we met. Then I tipped a post boy twopence to deliver this message and, feeling slightly relieved for having sent it, repaired to the Black Lion for a hearty meal of kidney pudding.

I sat in solitude in a corner stall amid laughter and jostling and a never-ending flow of tankards. I began to fret about Alice's reaction to my note, and I shunned the attentions of several ladies who presumed me an easy target for their charms. My detachment seemed not in the least perturbing to them. They caught my eye, raising their glasses with knowing glances. It struck me suddenly how long I'd been without company. In Cambridge I'd scarcely spoken to a soul for several days. Fretting that I might be turning into a recluse, quite unlike my true character, on impulse I beckoned to the two fairest to join me. They sashayed over and squeezed themselves on either side of my stall. It was their company rather than the private pleasures they had to offer that drew me, and I quickly regretted my decision. Close up, their faces were nothing but paint and pockmarks. The reek of sour clothes, cheesy breath, and chalk powder turned my stomach, and when they began to finger the collar of my clean coat and stroke my face, I could take no more. I pushed them away with a shilling and in solitude tramped home to my bed.

All that night strange dreams troubled me. I thought Partridge was alive, and I could hear him calling me beneath a window of ice. Then I saw Alice at the window of a building that oddly resembled Chippendale's cabinet. She too called me to come to her, but each time I turned a corner new compartments and rooms opened before me. Every wall concealed a hidden door, every cupboard led me to another compartment. All this time Alice's voice directed me until I reached the very heart of the building, at which point her voice disappeared and I knew I would never find my way out again.

Next morning I woke to find a filigree of ice intricate as Brussels lace screening my window. The sky had cleared, and as if some celestial artist had daubed the world with white, a thick frost had bloomed. Within this bright tableau the alchemy of city life brewed. A confusion of chaises, carts, and coaches crunched and rumbled over icy streets; smoke belched from soup-kitchen caldrons and chophouse fires; youths shouldered baskets of stiff baked bread and steaming hot pies amid a throng of laborers, gentlemen, beggars, urchins, and whores. I breathed air thick with the stench of cooking meat and rotting vegetables, soot and dung, perfume and coffee, and my spirits soared to be returned from the loneliness of Cambridge into the midst of it.

I took a chair to Trenti's house in Golden Square, snapping off icicles from the window and throwing them like daggers to the ground. I shuddered as the bearers turned into the square and passed by the railings where I'd been run down. At Madame Trenti's door I knocked and waited for some time before a maidservant appeared.

"I have come to see your mistress," I declared, my breath turning to clouds of steam in her face.

"I'm not certain if she's at home. If you would care to wait . . ."

At that moment I fancied I heard footsteps above my head, muffled voices, then a brief but high-pitched cry and the echo of further footsteps retreating.

"Someone is at home if not she," I persisted.

"I believe she may be engaged, sir. I'll inform her you wish to see her."

"Don't trouble yourself, I'll tell her in person," I replied rudely, barging past her and bounding for the stairs. "I'm more than happy to offer her an additional breakfast surprise."

My churlishness was not only due to my anger towards Madame Trenti. I presumed a lady of her habits and reputation was still abed, and that the "engagement" mentioned by the maidservant was no more than a beau enjoying her favors. Had not I observed the facilities she had installed to accommodate her masculine visitors on my previous visit? The footsteps and sounds I'd just heard only confirmed my supposition that she was in the throes of entertaining someone.

"But sir, sir," called the poor servant girl helplessly towards my retreating back, "it may not be convenient . . ."

I headed straight for the landing, where I intended to open every door until I found her. Imagine my surprise, therefore, when just as I turned the last twist in the staircase I almost collided with a person coming in the opposite direction.

I recognized him instantly. As usual he was smartly dressed, although just now he seemed singularly red in the face and flustered, as if he'd recently exerted himself. Evidently he was as surprised to see me as I to meet him. For some moments we both stopped dead in our tracks, neither of us saying a word, both gripping the banister as if it offered our only hold on reality.

It was Chippendale who spoke first. "Why, Hopson, I believed you to be in Cambridge." His voice was soft and quiet and showed no sign of the anger I might have expected, having been thus apprehended.

"So I was, sir. I returned only yesterday night. It was my intention, once I'd made this early visit, to present myself at the workshop directly." I paused to gauge his reaction to my faltering excuse. I was curious to know what had brought him here, yet dared not inquire and risk riling him. In any event I expected he would speedily recover himself and chastise me for my unsanctioned presence here. But on the contrary, he looked somewhat bemused and responded with unusual candor. "I myself had called on Madame Trenti to discuss the installation of her cabinet. It is to stand in her bedchamber, and I presumed I would find her waiting for me there. However, it appears she is sleeping, for I've knocked several times and cannot rouse her."

It occurred to me that it was an unusual call for the proprietor of a large workshop to make at this early hour, especially to a woman of Madame Trenti's reputation. But, as I said before, I did not wish to inflame his temper, and so I said none of this, merely remarking that it seemed strange he had not found her, for I was quite certain I'd heard footsteps, a cry, and a voice not a minute or two earlier.

"Perhaps the steps and the voice were mine, or those of a servant on the back stairs. As to a cry, I too fancied I heard something but presumed it to have come from down below," he returned.

"Where were you standing, sir, when you heard the sounds?"

He pointed to the first door on the landing behind him. "That is the door to her chamber. I knocked and waited there."

I lifted my eyes towards the landing and strained my ears. The house was as silent now as the square outside. In front of me were four large oak doors. All were closed. Thus, I reasoned, any noise I'd heard was more likely to have come from this landing than from inside Madame Trenti's chamber.

"Perhaps I might try," I suggested.

Chippendale moved to let me pass. I went to the door and turned the handle. It rotated in my hand, but the catch held fast. I pressed my ear to the panel and listened. Not a sound came from within. I knocked and listened again. Still no clear sound, although some way off I fancied I heard a patter of footsteps descending a stair.

A footman accompanied by the maidservant I'd treated so rudely now joined us.

"Is this your mistress's door?" I asked. "I fear she may be unwell, and the door is locked."

They nodded. "That is most strange," said the girl. "There was naught wrong with her an hour ago when I brought up her breakfast tray."

"Did she expect any callers?"

"None that I know of, save Mr. Chippendale."

"And you didn't show him up?"

"He said there was no need, he knew his way."

I marveled at the intimacy this comment implied. Never had I once suspected that a woman such as Madame Trenti would have appealed to someone of Chippendale's fastidious taste. I'd always assumed him to be immune to the desires of the flesh. I turned to the maid again.

"And when you brought in the breakfast, did you enter by this door?"

"No, sir, I came up by the back stairs."

"Show me."

She led us to the door next to Madame Trenti's, a chamber furnished as a lady's boudoir. Opposite the entrance was a second, smaller door. It was almost invisible since it was flush to the wall and hung with the same pink watered silk as the walls. The footman opened the latch and ushered us through to a small landing from which a narrow staircase led directly down, presumably to the kitchens. A few feet along was a second door, presently standing ajar.

"The servants' door to Madam's bedchamber," signaled the footman, pressing himself back against the wall to allow us to enter.

Madame Trenti's bedchamber was luxury incarnate. The walls were hung with Chinese paper on which strangely plumed birds fluttered through a forest of wispy bamboo and gnarled trees and monstrous gaudy blooms. In one corner stood a vast dressing table, its looking glass festooned with billowing silk draperies, its surface strewn with more silver-lidded bottles and enamel boxes, porcelain trays of cosmetics, more puffs and perfumes than I'd ever beheld.

The bedstead opposite was equally ornate: japanned fire-breathing dragons perched over a pagoda headboard; the tester hung with yet more swags of pale blue damask. Usually these draperies would have been artfully arranged, but now they had been violently ripped from their supports and hung limply across the bed, like laundry hung out to dry.

I strode across the room and whipped back the drapery screen. A sea of rumpled bed linen confronted me. It took some moments before I realized that the contorted object in the midst of this derangement was Madame Trenti. She was without her wig, and her thin, mousy hair was spread in seaweed strands against the pillow. A strip of white lace that might have trimmed the flounces of her finest gown had been wound deadly tight about her neck. Her face had turned livid and waxy, and her eyes and tongue protruded unnaturally from her head.

I pulled away the ligature and put my hand to her neck. She was still warm, but I could detect no vestige of a pulse. As I touched her, the loathing I'd lately felt towards her was transformed. I can't pretend what I felt was straightforward pity, even if her frailty seemed more accentuated in death. Nor did I immediately experience the same panic or flood of emotion as I had on confronting Montfort's or poor Partridge's corpse. Perhaps I had become hardened to these dreadful discoveries, for fear came later. No, my only sensation was profound frustration, for Trenti had died before I managed to speak to her.

Why had someone wished her dead? The obvious answer was that she'd discovered a foundling (Partridge) and pretended he was the child she had conceived with Montfort. Foley had already suggested that someone who stood to profit from Montfort's estate felt threatened by Partridge. Could this be the reason both men and Madame Trenti were killed? But once both Partridge and Montfort were dead, the killer's aim had been achieved. Why then was it necessary to kill Trenti? Moreover, why kill her in broad daylight, when there was a high risk of detection? The only conclusion I could draw was a frightening one: having killed twice already, the killer was becoming more audacious and more self-assured. Murder, no matter how unfavorable the circumstances, was becoming increasingly easy.

My eye fell upon Chippendale standing frozen at the bedside, whereupon another train of thought took over. At Horseheath my fruitless questioning had convinced me he could not have been directly involved. But now I'd discovered him outside the door of the woman who'd unwittingly sent Partridge to his death, my doubts about him returned. I recalled my earlier suspicion that there was some conspiracy between Madame Trenti and him. I searched for signs of what this might be, of what he was feeling, but apart from noting that his fists were tightly clenched, and his face looked more strained than usual, I could detect no glimmer of emotion. He was impassive, impenetrable as ever.

It struck me again that there was much that was curious in his relationship with Madame Trenti. In the shop his behavior had been deferential and obsequious. The sumptuous cabinet he was making for her was an expensive item, and her luxuriously appointed saloon had been furnished with several other costly pieces supplied by him. Yet the letter she'd written to Montfort intimated that she was financially pressed and not above using extortion if necessary. I returned to the possibility that blackmail might have been Madame Trenti's regular occupation. As I'd already observed, an actress could not afford to live in such luxury without some other means of support. It almost seemed as if *Chippendale* was supporting her, if only by providing her with furnishings that must be far beyond her means. Why? Was this because she had a wealthy benefactor who paid Chippendale for all her furnishings? It seemed likely that if this were so, the gentleman's name would be common knowledge. Did Chippendale believe Trenti's house was a suitable showcase for his furnishings, by which new patrons might be drawn in? But why then was the cabinet intended for her bedchamber?

The other possibility was that Chippendale was under some obligation to Trenti, that she had some hold over him that forced him to oblige her. But what could this be? I knew he couldn't have fathered a child on her, for she had resided in Italy until recently. Perhaps she had uncovered some other transgression or weakness that permitted her to milk him for favors. Chippendale's most obvious weakness was his concern for his reputation. He would allow nothing to threaten it. I shivered, remembering his ruthlessness towards Partridge. Perhaps Trenti had coerced furnishings from Chippendale, threatening to besmirch his name if he didn't oblige. He would have viewed such a threat as a powerful one. But would he have retaliated by murdering her?

Another alternative came to mind, which did not necessarily preclude Chippendale. Suppose Madame Trenti knew, or thought she knew, who the murderer of Montfort and Partridge was; suppose, having failed to extort money from Montfort, she had tried the same with the killer, threatening him with exposure if he did not comply? The killer might have come here at her request to make a payment, and then committed his dreadful crime.

This thought, which seemed most credible of all to me, brought my own fears to the fore. I cast my mind back to the morning I'd been run down. It occurred to me that the attempt on my life might have been spurred by the murderer's assumption that I knew, or was close to knowing, his identity. Now he had killed again, would he return his attention to me? As I went about my solitary investigations, was I in greater peril than ever?

It was my affection for Partridge that had driven me into this mire. I returned to the manner in which he and Montfort died, and asked myself what the methods of killing, viewed alongside Madame Trenti's strange death, indicated about the killer's character. The means of killing were different in each instance. This suggested either that the killer *enjoyed* experimenting, *enjoyed* death, or that he had improvised with the weapons available. Montfort's death seemed to me distinct. It had been by gun-shot—a conventional means. In contrast, the other deaths were both un-usual in that the weapons employed were opportunistic. The toolbox containing the hatchet used to sever Partridge's fingers happened to be in the library because I had left it there; Madame Trenti had been strangled with her own lace trimming, which presumably the murderer had chanced upon. If I added my own misadventure to the equation, I could surmise that the attempt on my life had taken place because I chanced to be out walking as the killer passed by.

The thought struck me then that, as well as being more conventional, Montfort's killing was also more deliberate, more considered. The other deaths seemed haphazard, less organized by comparison. And so I asked myself the final question. If the killer was now striking so impulsively, did this mean that he was insane?

The unexpected clatter of carriage wheels and horses' hoofs outside in-terrupted my musings. I rushed to the window and looked down to the square below. It had been devoid of life when I arrived, but now a car-riage drawn by a handsome pair of chestnuts tore past. I caught sight of a streak of green on the chassis and had a fleeting glimpse of the driver's hooded head and a flash of his arm as it whipped up the horses. I knew then with dreadful certainty that this was the same vehicle that had al-most run me down.

"Whose carriage is that?" I cried.

Chippendale was behind me and spied the vehicle. "It closely resem-bles an equipage used by Lord Montfort when he called on me. I re-marked its fineness when he visited my premises last autumn," he replied.

"How peculiar," I murmured under my breath, before turning back to the room and the two trembling servants. "The one person who cannot possibly be driving the carriage is Lord Montfort."

In due course the formalities that the discovery of Madame Trenti's body necessitated were neatly resolved. Chippendale summoned a justice with whom he was well acquainted, stating it was common knowledge that in this modern city the detection of crime relies upon fortuitous ac-quaintance. I remembered Westleigh's rapport with the Montfort family and nodded. No sooner had the justice arrived and surveyed the scene than my master preempted his questions by offering a detailed statement. In it he declared that Madame Trenti was a well-known actress with a large coterie of admirers, one of whom had almost certainly become disaffected and perpetrated this wicked deed. He had arrived here with me on a business matter shortly before ten (here he introduced me as his journeyman). We had failed to raise Madame Trenti and, when we found her door locked, the servants had shown us the back stairs entrance.

When we entered we'd found her dead but still warm. The maidservant had stated that Madame Trenti was alive and well when she took in her breakfast, at nine, though she was uncertain whether or not the main door was locked. Thus whoever committed this crime had done so within the last hour, in all probability as we approached her door, since a shriek had been heard that might well have been her death cry. The killer must have crept in by the rear entrance adjacent to the kitchens (whose door the footman told us was always left open), ascended to her room unnoticed via the back stairs, strangled the unfortunate Madame Trenti, and left by the same way he had come in.

All the while he made this statement I scrutinized Chippendale to see if I could detect some chink in his carapace. And yet, as before, he seemed to draw upon his remarkable capacity (which I don't believe I shall ever master) to put all his feelings aside. Not once did his voice waver or his composure lapse, not even when he described the moment we entered Trenti's room and found her sprawled upon her bed.

I suppose this coolness shouldn't have surprised me, for he had displayed the same detachment when I'd told him of Partridge's demise. And yet I own that, having often seen him in a frenzy over some matter pertaining to business, in my heart of hearts I expected something more.

In any event, his version of events satisfied the justice and, after a quiet exchange in which I believe I heard Chippendale offer him a purse "to cover his inconvenience," he was content to summon his deputy to interrogate the servants in greater detail and permit Chippendale and myself to leave.

So relieved was I to be free to keep my rendezvous with Alice that it was only some time later, as I made my way along the Strand, that it occurred to me Chippendale's behavior was unusual in several respects. As soon as the justice had released us, he had scurried off in the direction of St. Martin's Lane, without a word to me. The account he had given to the justice was far from honest. Why pretend we'd arrived together when we both knew he'd been descending the stairs as I arrived? The offer of the purse was a further troubling detail. Was it usual to compensate officers of the law for inconvenience when they were merely carrying out their duties?

I returned to my earlier notion of some intrigue between Madame Trenti and Chippendale, and wondered again if he'd had a hand in her demise. I added up possible signals of his involvement. His flustered demeanor when I met him might well have had a sinister cause. The extraordinary lengths to which he'd gone to satisfy Madame Trenti were possible proof of her hold over him. Taken together, they seemed impossible to read as anything other than ominous pointers of guilt.

But like scratches on a polished surface, the flaws in this theory emerged. I had seen the carriage and had heard descending footsteps as we approached Madame Trenti's chamber. The steps were those of the murderer. The carriage was the means by which the murderer had made his escape. Chippendale might know more than he'd disclosed, he might have some involvement with Madame Trenti that he wished to remain hidden, but he could not be the person I sought.

I arrived at the Goodchild warehouse to be told Alice had already departed and had left word she'd meet me at the Theatre Royal. As I bade my driver make haste up Drury Lane, the sun sagged behind the buildings, staining the sky with a sulfurous halo.

As we drew closer, the crowd became dense and then all but impassable; at length I had no choice but to descend and make my way on foot. I pushed ahead urgently towards the doors, fretting that I'd never find her. Would she be among the hundreds clustered outside the entrance, or amid the finely dressed throng within? Finding no sign of her, I paid half a crown for a ticket at a turnstile and allowed myself to be swept through the barriers by the tide of people pressing from behind.

Lit by hundreds of tallow candles in ring chandeliers, the auditorium already seethed with people gossiping and drinking and sitting on the benches in the pit and gallery. An orchestra was playing on the stage, and a sizable crowd had gathered to watch. I had combed the entire arena several times before I finally caught sight of her.

Instead of waiting for me in the pit or the gallery as I expected, she had somehow found her way into a gentleman's box and was now sitting in comfort, searching the throng clustered around an orange seller for my arrival. I began to push my way through the crowd towards her, waving to attract her attention, for I was eager to extract her from the box without causing her embarrassment.

But even when I came closer and waved madly she looked straight through me and seemed to be gesturing at some other person behind. I turned to see what drew her. A tall, velvet-cloaked gentleman in an immaculate powdered wig emerged from the crowd. He was holding a plump orange. Entering the box, he greeted her with an easy bow and a kiss on the hand. I could see him smilingly incline his head towards her lips, as if to hear what she said above the hubbub. I could see the bloom of her cheeks, the dazzle of her hair, her eyes shining brighter than the myriad chandeliers. If I had been too warm from the heat of the crowd, my blood was now turned to ice. The gentleman with whom Alice was conversing in such companionable intimacy was none other than Lord Foley.

They were so engrossed with each other that I was thumping on the balustrade in front of them before they acknowledged my presence.

"Why, Hopson," said Foley as coolly as if we'd dined together that very day, "Miss Goodchild promised we should find you here."

Fuming with frustration, I nodded curtly at him and turned to Alice. "Miss Goodchild," I said, "how pleasant to see you again. May I take it you received my message?"

I was rewarded with a flicker of a smile. "I received it, but since you neglected to mention a time or a place for the rendezvous, and since Lord Foley was most anxious to find you, I asked him to accompany me here, and he kindly accepted."

"I hadn't realized you were such friends."

"Lord Foley and I are barely acquainted, as you well know. He called on me yesterday only to discover your whereabouts. He had tried at Chippendale's, but you weren't there. I could tell him nothing apart from suggesting that he might meet you here."

I stood there lost for words, furious within, grinning like an imbecile without, then frowning at my boots. There was much I wanted to discuss with her, many questions I wanted to ask of her; but with Foley present, not only was I unable to speak freely as I desired but it was also impossible to gauge whether her feelings towards me had warmed a little since her abrupt departure from the inn at Hindlesham.

It was Foley who broke the silence. "Well, Mr. Hopson," he said, "am I to be honored with an explanation as to why you left Horseheath Hall so prematurely, without keeping our appointment, or must I divine it?"

Irritation at his intrusion made me retort more bluntly than I intended. "I left after I discovered Partridge's mangled fingers stuffed in a casket in Robert Montfort's chamber. After that grisly find, I had no more stomach for searching, and in any case I wanted to confront Madame Trenti with her deception."

Alice's eyes widened at this shocking statement, and I cursed myself for speaking thus. Foley, however, seemed scarcely moved. "And have you done so?" he barked.

"I went to see her this morning but found her dead. Strangled in her bed."

Alice turned paler than a winding sheet, and even Foley was thunderstruck. "Good God!" he said. "Who else knows of this?"

I explained that Chippendale was also present when the body was discovered, that we'd seen Montfort's carriage pass by the window, and that I was convinced the vehicle contained the murderer.

"Montfort didn't keep a carriage in town," said Foley. "He lost it at cards some time ago, and ever since was in the habit of borrowing Bradfield's or mine."

"This was a fine equipage, drawn by a handsome pair of chestnuts, with a green stripe on the side."

"Then I'll wager it was Bradfield's," said Foley, taking a circular gold snuffbox adorned with a star of diamonds from his pocket. "He's fonder of horses and vehicles than almost anything." He paused while he flicked open the sparkling lid, then turned to me. "Are you implying that Bradfield is involved with Trenti's death?"

"Possibly but not necessarily. If Lord Bradfield loaned the vehicle to Lord Montfort, is it not likely he also loaned it to others? Some other person might have used his coach this morning. By the by, I believe it was this very coach that tried to run me down on my previous visit to Madame Trenti."

"In that case we can rejoice in the fact that it will be an easy matter to ascertain the identity of the murderer, for whoever it was will doubtless be staying with Bradfield. I shall call on him after this afternoon's entertainment and discover it. Hopson, I think you should accompany me. And perhaps Miss Goodchild would be interested to come with us?"

By way of reply Alice gave Foley a brief nod of acquiescence. Without another word she flashed me an inscrutable smile, then turned her gaze in the direction of the brilliantly lit stage.

Chapter Twenty-one

At ten o'clock that night lights blazed from every window of Lord Bradfield's mansion in Leicester Fields.

Foley had scarcely reached the door when a footman, assuming we were latecomers to the card and supper party, ushered us indoors. Foley, Alice, and I entered the saloon, a vast room with a ceiling stuccoed so heavily with nymph musicians it seemed they might swoop down at any moment. Bradfield, pink and plump as a wood pigeon, was holding court amid a group of gentlemen all dressed in embroidered finery. He greeted Foley jovially as if his unexpected arrival were the greatest good fortune.

"Foley, sir, I had no idea you were in town," he said, vigorously shaking his hand. "My profound apologies, I should naturally have sent you a card had I known it."

"On the contrary, dear fellow, think nothing of it. This is an entirely impromptu visit, and it is extremely good of you to receive us at such short notice," answered Foley, bowing low as he did so. "The Cambridge weather, I'm sure you know, has been treacherous of late. I was uncertain whether or not to come to town. But in the end I found I had business to attend to, and here I am."

Alice and I had hovered behind Foley during this exchange, but we had not escaped Bradfield's notice. His brow furrowed in puzzlement as he glanced in my direction.

"I see you have Mr. Hopson in attendance. He is becoming quite a favorite of yours, I think."

"His assistance has been invaluable in the matter of Montfort's death. He continues to help me all he can."

Bradfield now addressed me directly. "You are quite recovered from your tumble, I trust, Hopson? No more thoughts of a profession in surgery, I take it?" He guffawed at this jesting reference to my fainting.

I was in the midst of a halting apology for my indisposition when Foley saved me by interrupting again.

"Bradfield, I must tear you from Hopson and present to you Miss Goodchild, an acquaintance of ours who is accompanying us this evening. Miss Goodchild, I should add, is a most formidable woman. She runs the finest wood merchant's in London, I'm told."

I expected Alice to find such an introduction awkward, for she had told me she was not much used to company. But she handled herself with remarkable aplomb. Blushing only enough to enhance her complexion, she curtsied low and murmured a dignified "Good evening, my lord."

Bradfield was dazzled, or at the very least intrigued, by what he saw. "A woman of business, how enchanting. You must meet my other guests. I'm sure they would be amused to know of your enterprise."

I watched this exchange, helpless and impatient. I was conscious that Alice's presence here offered what I'd been craving the past week—the opportunity to speak to her alone. Yet these meaningless pleasantries created still more obstacles between us, and I had to admit, her vexingly ambivalent manner left me utterly confused. Surely she could see from my desperate glances that I yearned to speak to her. How easily I could whisk her away to some quiet corner if only she'd look at me straight. But her eyes flitted over me and glanced about the room, apparently drinking in every detail of the decor and the assembled guests. I harbored a niggling suspicion she was cold-shouldering me, and the thought irked me like a splinter under the skin. I edged my way closer to her, intending to wait for a break in conversation to make a direct attempt to speak to her. But before I had opened my mouth, Bradfield stepped in and whisked her away. Now I saw he was introducing her to a cluster of ladies, including Miss Alleyn and Elizabeth Montfort, who were sitting together by the fire.

It was at this point that the throng parted and I caught sight of Robert Montfort. He was dressed more stylishly than I'd ever seen him, in a black brocade suit; he was looking with rapt interest at Alice. As he watched Bradfield usher her away, I fancied he shot a black look at Foley and then caught sight of me. His brow furrowed as if for a moment he was unsure who I was, then his expression clouded. I looked away, trembling at the thought of what his reaction would be to my presence. Surely by now he must have heard of my discovery in his laboratory. Would he dare to carry out his threats in the midst of this assembly? Was I about to be called a thief and branded and thrown into prison? When I mustered sufficient courage to look back, to my extreme astonishment I saw he was paying no attention to me whatsoever. Instead, he proceeded to present himself to Alice. Having kissed her hand, with what I judged unnecessary slowness, he began to converse with her. I couldn't hear what he said, but whatever it was it seemed to charm her, because from then on her eyes never wandered from his face.

The very thought of Robert becoming friendly with Alice filled me with revulsion and dread. That he would single her out for some hidden purpose of his own I did not doubt. But what that intention was, and whether Alice was aware of the nature of the man who was making her laugh so gaily, I was less certain. Should she chance to speak of my discovery of Trenti's body, should she happen to mention the carriage I'd glimpsed, she would place me in greater jeopardy than she knew.

Alice needed my protection. I was poised to advance towards Robert and interrupt his conversation when Foley obstructed me. He was in the company of another young gentleman.

"Mr. Hopson, I don't believe you have met Lord Bradfield's son, George. He intends to accompany Robert Montfort to Italy. Is that not so?"

"Indeed," answered his companion, a well-made, rather baby-faced young gentleman in a gold and crimson coat. "Although I believe I should be cross with you, Foley. The death of Lord Montfort is spoiling all our plans, and I hear you have something to do with it."

Foley was unruffled by this accusation. He took a leisurely pinch of snuff from his box before responding. "Only insofar as Robert's father was indebted to me. I wouldn't say I'm hindering—in many ways I'm assisting. I've been appointed to investigate the matter. Hopson here is my assistant. It's a devilishly complex affair, d'you see."

George tossed his head somewhat effeminately. "How very tedious for us all."

"I trust it will be soon resolved," soothed Foley. "For I make fine progress, thanks to Mr. Hopson. But tell me your news, George. How long have you been in town? I gather you were in Cambridge last week, though I never saw you."

"I spent a few days at Horseheath with Robert, but we found it dreary, the weather being what it was. So we all came back here yesterday."

"I trust city life has proved more amusing?"

"The usual pursuits have occupied us. This morning Robert and I took a turn in the park. Pleasant enough. We dined. We passed the afternoon drinking coffee at the Smyrna."

"And the ladies?"

"A little shopping, I fancy."

I shuffled about, growing increasingly uncomfortable. I wanted to break away and intervene between Robert and Alice, yet I knew convention (and Foley) demanded that I concentrate on this meaningless exchange. Although I account myself no less civil than any gentleman, every minute I stood there was torment. My desire to shield Alice from goodness knows what perils and to speak to her in private was being hampered by this petulant stranger.

But I soon realized that Foley was making a discreet attempt to find out who might have taken the coach to Golden Square this morning. Of course he was approaching the matter by a typically roundabout route, and one that had yielded nothing precise enough to be of any use. I looked helplessly over towards Alice and saw that she had now left Robert Montfort and stood in a group by the piano where another lady was in the midst of a recital. It was impossible for the moment to approach her. Thus to calm my impatience I applied myself to the identity of the driver of Bradfield's carriage.

We were in need of information about the movements of the household and its guests. The easiest way to uncover these would be to quiz a member of the staff. Leaving George and Foley, I drifted out of the room. I sat down on a hall seat opposite a window, the curtain of which was undrawn. I shivered as I caught sight of my uneasy, diffident self reflected in the glass panes. Did this face really belong to me? What had become of my former carefree rashness? I had sat there staring at myself no longer than two minutes before, as I'd hoped, I was spotted by the elderly footman standing vigil at the door. Seeing me gazing into space, he probably assumed I'd taken too much wine and came to attend to me.

"Carriage, sir?"

"Not yet. The room is uncommonly stuffy with tobacco smoke; I'm merely taking some air until my companions are ready to leave."

I hesitated. "Have you come with the Bradfield family from Cambridge?" I inquired as nonchalantly as if I'd asked him to fetch me a glass of brandy.

"No, sir."

"You live here?"

"Yes, sir."

"Have you worked here many years?"

"Ten, sir."

"Then you must be well acquainted with the family and their friends?"

He blinked uncomfortably, as if he were uncertain how to respond. "I do my duty, sir. No one's said otherwise."

"The Montforts, for instance?"

Silence. His face turned to wood.

"I ask these questions only because I'm assisting Lord Foley to find the truth about the death of Lord Montfort."

Still he said nothing. I remembered the purse Foley had given me to cover my expenses. It was still half full. "I've half a crown to pay you for your trouble."

He blinked, and looked at me. "Very well. But I don't promise what I can tell you will help."

"Let me be the judge," I said sharply, for I had his measure now. "Just answer the questions as best you can. The Montforts visit frequently, I believe?"

"They do. Though it's none of my concern."

"And they sometimes borrow Lord Bradfield's equipage?"

"He's proud of the carriages and likes them to be shown off."

"And today?"

"The carriages have been at their disposal."

"Did you say carriages? There are more than one?"

"Three in all, sir. A gentleman's traveling coach, a four-seater town coach, and a smaller chariot."

"Can you describe them?"

He looked at me as if I was soft in the head. "They are handsome enough vehicles, two lined with green leather inside, the larger town vehicle with matching green silk curtains. The smaller is a light modern chariot such as a gentleman might drive, with a single passenger."

"And the paint?"

"Little worse than new."

"The color, man."

"The larger is black, as are both the smaller, although they have dark green stripes on the side. They all bear the Bradfield crest upon the door."

"And today who took them out?"

"The traveling coach wasn't used. The town coach was taken by the ladies, who went shopping. The chariot was taken this morning, as it usually is, by Lord Bradfield's son and his friend Robert Montfort. They are partial to racing round the park, I believe." My heart sank at these words. How right I'd been to fear Robert Montfort.

"At what time did they depart for their promenade?"

"Their usual hour. Around ten-thirty."

I was exasperated at this reply. It was too late; half an hour *after* the carriage I'd seen. "And before that, did anyone use the chariot? Perhaps Robert took it out alone?"

"If he did, I'm unaware of it, for I only see the carriages that come to the door. If someone goes directly to the mews, I wouldn't know it."

"And the mews is where exactly?"

"Behind the square. But I don't advise you to visit now. There's no one there but the horses. The grooms'll all be abed. You'll have to wait till morning if you want to know more."

I was now certain that the vehicle that had run me down, and that I'd seen from the window of Trenti's bedchamber, must have been the smallest of the three, the chariot, for it needed no coachman to drive it. But I was no closer to discovering the identity of the hunched driver, unless someone at the stables could help me.

"Excellent," I said, slipping him the half crown I'd promised. "That's all I need to know. You've been most useful."

I walked slowly back to the saloon and took a glass of wine. I glanced in Foley's direction in a vain attempt to communicate my wish to leave. But it was impossible to catch his attention since he, like most of the company, had joined the congregation at the far end of the room. Several people, among them Robert Montfort, sat around a circular table playing piquet; the rest had gathered round a spinet to listen to Elizabeth Montfort play. I could not see Alice, but I presumed, since she was not playing cards, she must be where I last saw her, at the front of the musical group.

"Are you always so unfriendly, Mr. Hopson, as to turn your back on your acquaintances?"

I spun round, astonished. Alice had somehow crept up behind me.

"What do you mean?"

"Merely that I've been looking for you these last ten minutes. What have you been doing?"

Her eyes danced and her voice sounded different from earlier that evening. In place of distance there was a note of mirth, as if her anger had suddenly dissolved and she was laughing at me instead.

"I've been outside in the corridor. It was too warm for me in here."

"And hence you've returned to the fireside," she replied archly.

"Very well. I've been questioning the footman about the Bradfield coaches."

"And did your questions bear fruit?"

"I found there are three carriages, two of which have been used today. But who took one out early this morning I have not yet discovered, though I'm confident that tomorrow morning I shall have the answer."

"I see."

I wondered if I should tell her that I suspected the culprit might be Robert Montfort and warn her to be guarded in what she told him, but the color in her cheeks and the energy in her manner made me suspect her nonchalance wasn't all it seemed. Rather than risk riling her, I decided to hold my tongue. She was safely away from him now; I would speak to her on the matter when her mood was more settled. There was a pause while we looked at each other, uncertain how to proceed.

"Alice," I said suddenly, "I'm wretchedly sorry if I upset you in Cambridge. If I could have avoided it I would gladly have done so."

I realized as soon as I said it that this was not what she wished to hear. She drew herself up.

"What gives you the impression I'm upset, Mr. Hopson? Do I not seem full enough of merriment?"

"Yes, but . . ."

"But what?"

"The manner of your leaving Cambridge . . . it was so hasty and unexpected, and since then I think you have been somewhat standoffish. You did not wait for me this evening—I presumed it was because you were still angry about Connie."

She gave a little laugh which I knew she did not mean.

"I grant you I am a woman who acts on impulse from time to time. But you flatter yourself if you believe you have aroused such passions in me. I left Cambridge because I feared the weather might deteriorate and because I'd completed what I set out to do. If I did not disturb you it was out of consideration rather than pique, for if you recall, you were deep in conference with Foley. Since then you have had nothing to complain of. Why, I have been as cordial to you as to any acquaintance. I left word I would meet you at the playhouse, and so I did."

"But your manner is somewhat . . . guarded," I stuttered.

"Are you certain you do not imagine it? After all, it is I who have come to speak to you now. And you who hid yourself in the corridor."

Whatever she said she didn't convince me. I knew she was still annoyed and that this parrying was just another way to irk me. She would not have left Cambridge without a word or have spoken so coldly to me in the playhouse otherwise. Both of us knew it, only she would not admit as much. A rush of exasperation at her stubbornness filled my veins. I had no reason to fear her; rather I should fear my own weakness for not confronting her properly.

"Good God, don't you comprehend my meaning, Alice?" I said. "I have been trying to tell you if only you'd listen. I thought, and hoped, that we had become something more to each other than acquaintances."

Her eyes opened very wide, and she drew breath as if she was about to say something. But for some reason she held back. Before I could press her further, I felt Foley's hand on my arm. "Well," he said, "I believe the moment has come to leave. I trust, Mr. Hopson, the time you spent in the corridor with the footman was useful?"

His intuition on top of Alice's obstinacy infuriated me. Was I so transparent I could do nothing without him second-guessing it?

"Indeed, Lord Foley," I replied icily, "I went there for air, and I found it most refreshing."

"You shall tell me all in the carriage," he replied, oblivious to my coolness. Then he turned to Alice. "Come, Miss Goodchild. I must congratulate you also. You were something of a success with Robert Montfort, I see. Did you discover anything of interest?"

She gave Foley her sweetest smile. "I found him most charming," she replied. "We discussed his family's favorite pastimes. I have discovered nothing of great note so far, yet I do not despair."

"What do you mean?" I snapped.

"I mean," she said, threading her arm in mine as we descended the steps, "that he told me he wishes to continue his father's redecoration scheme at Horseheath. He plans a new staircase to replace the old oak one. It will be made from the finest Cuban mahogany, which he wants me to supply. I've promised him a tour of my premises tomorrow morning. I am invited to visit Horseheath Hall and survey it next day."

Chapter Twenty-two

W hen I showed my face at the workshop the following day, two letters were waiting. The first had been sent a week earlier from Yorkshire. It was from Dorothy Chippendale.

Otley, Yorks   January 14, 1755

Dear Mr. Hopson,

The last time we met I little thought that our next communication could be under such tragic circumstances. You may remember the occasion, late last November, when you accompanied John Partridge and myself to Richmond and we all larked about on the river. Now, after all that has taken place, the day seems so distant, it might have happened years ago. I can scarcely believe none of us had any presentiment of the terrible events waiting to overwhelm us.

I won't burden you with the grief that engulfed me when I read your letter and learned of John's death. The tragedy that grieves me grieves you too, and I see no reason to add to your suffering by worrying you with mine. I will say only that while the violent nature of John's death shocked me most profoundly, in a sense I mourned for him even before I learned of it—the reason being I've

known since leaving London that we'd never be wed, and it made
me as miserable as if he'd died.

Don't think me unfeeling when I say I'm deeply thankful to you
for troubling to write and tell me of these events. How much more
painful would it have been to be left wondering for the rest of my
days what had become of him. For all that, it's impossible for me not
to think on his death and not to share your sense of outrage, and
obligation to bring whoever's responsible to justice. Thus, since you
ask me, of course I shall do all I can to help you. To this end I've
recorded as fully as I can the details of my last days in London.

It was soon after noon on December 17—the same day, I presume, that Partridge went missing—that my brother Thomas Chippendale called me to him.

I'm not sure if you are aware of it, but at that time I had lived
with my brother's family for some four months, having been
brought from Yorkshire to help my sister-in-law Catherine with her
three young children. Until then all my life had been spent in Otley,
a quiet market town ten miles from Leeds, the same region where
my brother Thomas was born and raised. I was the youngest of our
father's fifteen children, Thomas being the eldest; his mother had
died soon after he was born, and our father remarried and sired
fourteen more children. You will understand, however, that since I
was born almost twenty years after him, until my arrival in London
we were scarcely acquainted.

The little I knew of my brother was gleaned from my father, a
country joiner, who'd naturally intended his eldest son to follow in
his business, as generations of Chippendale sons had done before
him. He told me how, ever since Thomas was a child, he'd harbored a burning desire to better himself. He was just beginning his
apprenticeship in my father's workshop when a London architect,
working on the mansion of a local landowner, commissioned him
to make a model of the same mansion. So impressed was the architect by Thomas's work, he offered to sponsor him to go to York
and then to London to learn the cabinetmaking trade. Thomas,
acting as if he'd been expecting something like this to happen all
along, took it as his due and departed without a backward glance,
five years before my birth. Our father meanwhile continued as
he'd always done in his country enterprise, fabricating furniture
and wainscoting and staircases and whatever else was needed, with

only the occasional letter from his son to inform him of his progress.

But after my brother married and his third child, Mary, was born, he wrote to our father asking if I would care to join his household to assist his wife with the children. We all knew by then that he had made something of a name for himself, so when this request arrived from his illustrious son, my father could hardly refuse. He accepted on my behalf, only mentioning it to me one day after dinner when I was due to leave next morning. Thus at the age of eighteen I was dispatched two hundred miles to London, a city I'd never expected to set eyes on, to live with my brother whom I'd met only three times before in my life.

I first encountered John Partridge one day last summer. He'd been sent to the house by my brother to repair a wall sconce in the hallway. My sister-in-law was occupied in the nursery and told me to watch over Partridge and be sure he did the job properly. He was aged nineteen, a tall, gangling youth with a mischievous smile, yet a look of sadness in his eyes. Perhaps it was his poignant expression that made me forget my gaucheness. At any rate he made flippant conversation with me, to which I made some clumsy replies, which only encouraged him to joke and chatter more. In any event, when the sconce was fixed and he was about to leave, he turned abruptly and asked me to accompany him on a promenade to Vauxhall next Saturday. I was so startled I accepted.

Reading this you may think that we had little common ground on which to build our friendship. I'd come from a modest yet well-established family; he was haunted by having none. He'd lived almost all the life he remembered in London; I was a stranger in the city. Yet despite our differences, our friendship ripened. By autumn he spoke of marriage and, as Christmas approached, we decided to make our intentions known to my family.

So that nothing would mar our future happiness, he was anxious all should be done correctly. But we were unsure how to proceed. Should he first approach my brother, since he was my guardian and employer, or should he apply directly to my father for my hand? By now I'd grown close to my sister-in-law Catherine and decided to seek her advice.

I mentioned the matter to her the day before my sudden departure. She gave me no cause for alarm, congratulating me warmly on our mutual affection while hoping I wouldn't leave her household immediately. As for the etiquette of asking for my hand, she promised that as soon as an opportunity arose, she would raise the matter with my brother, and discover from him what we should do. Thus I'd no sense of foreboding the next day when my brother summoned me to him. It was only when I entered his study that I saw something was terribly amiss. His face was contorted with rage. His mind was quite made up.

I must leave the household that very afternoon, without a word to Partridge or anyone else.

I was, needless to say, dumbfounded, especially since having made this astonishing proclamation he seemed unwilling to provide an explanation for it. Eventually I overcame my shock and pressed him. The least I deserved was to know how I'd displeased him, since I had thought until then that he was satisfied with all I'd done. But my brother refused to respond, saying only that I'd performed my duties well enough but that I'd grown too close to Partridge for his liking.

"Evidently, for we wish to marry," I replied boldly.

"It is not a union I think in the least desirable, nor one to which I will ever give my consent," he thundered.

I dared to persist further, whereupon he fell into an even more violent rage, shouting repeatedly that we were too close, that Partridge was a common bastard of no known background, that his mother was without doubt some form of strumpet, and such a marriage would do nothing for his reputation or mine, indeed, would bring disgrace on the entire Chippendale family.

Overwhelmed with grief, I sobbed and wailed as loudly as I was able, but far from rousing his compassion and altering his resolve, my distress left him utterly unmoved. By now it was nearly two o'clock. Still ignoring my anguish, and with evident distaste, he wrapped me in my cloak and bundled me into a hackney carriage, into which he climbed beside me. I was thus summarily escorted to the White Hart at Holborn, where the stage for York stood ready to depart in half an hour. Without any consultation, my brother paid the fare and put me on the coach, watching from the yard—presumably in case I should dare to try to escape. Just before it pulled away, he approached the window and gave me this final warning: I should know by now how great was the sphere of his influence. I should not under any circumstance attempt to write to John Partridge. If I disobeyed him he'd easily discover it, in which case he'd accuse John of theft or some other trumped-up crime, instantly dismiss him, and do whatever was necessary to ensure he never again found work in London.

Thus was I silenced. Of course I longed to write to John, to explain my sudden disappearance, but knowing that he had no family to protect him and that without his profession he would have nothing, I dared not defy my brother's wishes. Naturally I assumed that my brother would likewise keep his part of the bargain and leave John to continue quietly in his employment. It was only thanks to your letter that I learned how cruelly he had deceived me.

I am, sir, your grateful and obedient servant,

Dorothy Chippendale

The second letter was from Constance in Horseheath. It was written in a childish, scarcely decipherable hand, dated two days ago.

Nat

I've been wantin to tell you since I saw you last. 'Tis too tricky to write it, tho' John's helped a bit, it has to do with Lord M's dying. 'Tis stupid but you mightn't think it. Anyway now Lady E's sent for me in London so I *will* tell you. Meet me Wed by the church in Covent Garden, six o'clock. How's Alice, still lovesick are you?

Connie

I read both these letters again more slowly, pondering the significance of each. Connie's letter was tantalizingly cryptic and confused. Dorothy's letter, by contrast, completed my understanding of the events leading to Partridge's departure for Horseheath. I now realized how stupid I'd been not to have guessed much of it. From what I knew of their devotion to each other, I should have known that Dorothy would have abandoned Partridge only if he was threatened in some way. I'd already surmised that the story of Partridge pestering her was a mere fabrication.

I was well aware of Chippendale's ruthlessness, but the treatment he had meted out in this instance startled me. What had made him send his own sister away so abruptly and dismiss Partridge? Why did he refuse to discuss the matter candidly with her? Neither had committed any wrong—unless affection had become criminal in his eyes. Was it merely a matter of Partridge's doubtful birth, or did jealousy lie at the root of it? I suspected Chippendale had grown irritated, threatened even, by Partridge's effortless talent at drawing and cabinetmaking. Perhaps the prospect of marriage into his family made him see how easily Partridge might usurp his position. So he had banished his sister and dismissed Partridge, assuming that he would simply disappear and take up some other life where their paths would never cross.

Of course it had been a grave misjudgment. With so little bedrock in his life, Partridge would inevitably cling to whatever he had, grasp whatever opportunity presented itself. His craft was all he knew; thus when Madame Trenti happened at this vulnerable moment to confront him, naturally he'd readily embraced her story that Montfort was his father and gone to Horseheath praying for acknowledgment and financial backing to begin his own enterprise. Yet tragically not only had Montfort denied him but something else had taken place that had left him dead and frozen in the icy waters of the pond.

I now understood what had driven Partridge to Horseheath, yet I was still no closer to fathoming *why* he'd been killed. I considered Foley's theory that his death might have been the result of someone *believing* him to be Montfort's son and discounted it. There was no proof of Madame Trenti's assertion that Montfort and she had ever been married. This was doubtless another of her manipulations to gain sympathy. And in the eyes of the law, what right did a bastard have even if he knew his father? None.

I thought about the injuries Partridge suffered. Were they more significant than I realized? To mutilate a craftsman's hand would effectively condemn him to penury, even if the wounds themselves were not fatal. He could never have worked again. Was there therefore some symbolic import in the manner of his death? If Chippendale could have devised a punishment for his talented, threatening employee, this surely would have been it. Yet why did I still consider Chippendale? My inquiries at Horseheath, coupled with the circumstances of Madame Trenti's death, had forced me to discount such a convenient solution.

I tucked the letters in my pocket and headed towards the back streets of Leicester Fields. With luck, by now Bradfield's grooms would be at work in the mews preparing the horses and carriages. One of them must be persuaded to divulge who had used the smaller carriage on the previous day. Thus would I discover the identity of the driver of the chariot I'd seen outside Madame Trenti's house. Thus would I identify the person who had run me down and murdered Montfort and Partridge and Madame Trenti.

The carriage, with its distinctive black and dark green paintwork, stood in the alley outside the coach house. A small boy polished its brass lanterns and moldings, while a groom harnessed up a pair of chestnut mares. Were they the same horses that had nearly trampled me to death? The same horses that had flashed beneath Madame Trenti's window?

The whole place reeked of straw dust and horse dung. I strode closer, trying my best to avoid the pools of slurry, and addressed myself casually to the groom.

"That's a fine chariot."

He turned slightly to eye me, gave a noncommittal grunt, and continued securing his buckles.

"I myself intend to purchase a similar equipage. Does it ride well?"

The groom turned warily and looked me up and down. I was wearing a newish blue coat and clean linens, and even though I'd spattered my stockings, I knew I might pass for a middle-ranking merchant.

"Well enough, sir."

"I believe it is identical to Lord Bradfield's?"

"That is because it is his. Are you acquainted with Lord Bradfield?"

"Slightly. I was at his entertainment last evening. I've met him in Cambridge once or twice, at Lord Foley's."

This explanation reassured him further. His face relaxed. Time to broach the subject for which I'd come.

"Does Lord Bradfield take it out frequently for airings?"

"Not so often. He prefers the comfort of the town coach. 'Tis more usually his son, George, that likes to take turns in the park in it."

"Does he drive alone?"

"Sometimes. Sometimes with his friends. And 'e says it gives the ladies a thrill to race round the trees and nearly crash into them."

"What of gentleman acquaintances?"

"Robert Montfort takes his turn. You might be acquainted with him?"

I nodded to show that I was. "I believe I saw the two of them out yesterday morning."

"Aye, I'd guess 'tis for the two of them we're preparing it now."

"D'you not know who takes it then?"

"Not always. We drive the carriage round to the house. Sometimes they might come immediately, other times they might not, and if we have orders to get ready another vehicle, we leave it with the footman."

I felt a slight twinge of disappointment. "And yesterday?"

The wariness returned. "What's all this for, sir? Nothing to do with buying a carriage, I'm thinking."

"I'm interested, that's all," I said, with an affable smile. I took a shilling from Foley's purse and slipped it in his pocket.

He shook his head as if I was taking a terrible liberty but answered me nonetheless. "Yesterday I saw the two gentlemen go in the carriage at their usual hour."

"At what time was that?"

He answered without hesitation. "Ten, ten-thirty." This was as I expected.

"There was nothing out of the ordinary?"

"What d'you mean, 'out of the ordinary'?"

"Had the carriage been used earlier?"

He cast another curious glance in my direction. "I don't know how you've become so well acquainted with their comings and goings, or what it is to you, but yes, as I recall, it was taken out early, before the two gentlemen drove it."

"By whom?"

"By a lady. Miss Alleyn."

"Miss Alleyn?"

The reply left me speechless as a baby.

"Was she alone?" I persisted.

"She was alone in the mews, but I fancy there was someone waiting nearby to drive her."

I breathed again; this was more probable. "Did you see this other person?"

"No, but she mentioned her nephew's name. And one of the grooms arriving late that morning said he saw the carriage cross the square driven by a gentleman in a dark green coat."

"Did Miss Alleyn return with the carriage later?"

"No, she said she'd take it straight to the house for her nephew and George."

Finally I comprehended the extent of the murderer's guile. Hadn't I seen Robert wearing a gentleman's green coat? Until this moment I'd mistakenly thought it was merely the painted stripe I remembered, but now I knew that the hunched figure within had been wearing a coat of the same hue. The figure had been Robert Montfort. Miss Alleyn's complicity was easily explained. When she told me of her history, she had disclosed that she lavished affection on Robert. She had become a surrogate mother to him. Had I not observed how she protected him from anything that might cause him disturbance, how she forever ascribed to him the noblest of sentiments?

And so I unscrambled the orchestration of Madame Trenti's murder. With such a devoted aunt at his beck and call, it would have been easy for Robert to persuade her to order the carriage and then hand it over to him. Thus Robert had completed his gruesome scheme safe in the knowledge that if the carriage were seen and questions asked it would be she who was identified, not him. He could be certain Miss Alleyn would never betray him; certain that her loyalty would blind her to his deviousness.

The very unexpectedness of the groom's information made me skeptical, made me question it, and spurred me to reach my judgment. And so, as if a beam of light had suddenly illuminated a dark room I'd always wanted to see, I looked in through the open door and observed what I wanted to be there, what until then I had only imagined.

All along I had correctly divined that the evil that had sparked this vicious sequence of events emanated from Horseheath Hall. Now I saw I'd have to make one final visit there if I was to curtail it, for it was only within those desolate, unhappy walls that I would be able to reconsider and comprehend all the perplexing details we'd found at the deaths of Montfort and Partridge—the grenadillo box, the pistol, the leeches, the footprints. There would be logical explanations for all of them, of this I was in no doubt. Furthermore, although I knew how Madame Trenti was killed, I had yet to comprehend *why*.

Despite my resolution, certain of my anxieties remained unaltered. I hadn't forgotten Robert Montfort's malice towards me, nor that he was due to return to Horseheath the next day. Alice herself was due to accompany him and stay there at his invitation. Although I was more tremulous than ever when I thought of Robert, a new purpose infused me. I would slip into the house unseen; Robert Montfort wouldn't discover my presence until I was ready to reveal it and have him apprehended.

I pondered Robert's strange invitation to Alice. Why had she, rather than I, become a focus for his intentions? For what reason other than an evil one would a vicious murderer invite a lady he scarcely knew to his home? Something she had let slip in her conversation with him must have made him suspect she was closer than I to discovering the truth. What could this be? The answer came with dreadful certainty. Doubtless she had viewed her conversation with Robert as an opportunity to gather more information. Possibly she had tried to discover the driver of the carriage. It was, after all, the reason we had gone together to Bradfield's party. Perhaps (and this thought filled me with dread) she had innocently asked him if he had been out driving that morning. In any event, once he had divined how much she knew, it could be no coincidence that Robert had asked her to Horseheath. The invitation had been tendered not because he wished to hear her opinion of his projected works *but because he wished to silence her.* Afterwards, presumably, it would be my turn, and then perhaps Foley's, for I was convinced that Robert Montfort was the demented maniac behind all these deaths, and that he would kill and kill again to avoid detection.

I recalled the hideous images of Montfort's blasted head, Madame Trenti's broken body; of the dog laid out on the table and Partridge's fingers crammed in the box. It was clear as a looking glass that if Alice went to Horseheath she would be placing herself in the clutches of Robert, and the shadow of inconceivable danger would fall upon her.

And so, having reached this great conclusion, I realized that it was paramount to protect Alice, to prevent her from leaving for Cambridge. She had mentioned that Robert planned to call on her that morning. If I happened to appear at her home at the same time, she might accuse me of overprotective jealousy and go off with him in a fit of pique. Thus I returned directly to the workshop and scrawled this hasty note.

St. Martin's Lane   January 20

Alice,

Forgive me for writing to you so directly and not coming to see you in person. I have to leave London again, but before I go I want to caution you most strongly against journeying to Horseheath as you propose. The reason for my heavy-handed warning is this. I have just returned from a visit to Bradfield's stables. The groom there told me something quite astounding, which I scarcely believe, though he was honest enough in saying it. Miss Alleyn took the carriage that morning, procuring it for another gentleman—who from details of his dress I have now identified.

As I wrote this line I heard footsteps ascending the stair. I knew I'd have to finish quickly.

I told you the figure driving the carriage was familiar but I could not recognize it. Now I know why. It was Robert Montfort that I saw—

The door opened and I broke off.

Chapter Twenty-three

Chippendale burst through the workshop door, sending wood shavings flying like autumn leaves in a gale. "Hopson," he bellowed, without any preamble whatsoever, "you're nowt but a trifler. And I don't take kindly to your waywardness. I'll tell you plain, I've had my fill of you."

I tried not to feel flustered, but my heart began to pound. Here was the anger I'd anticipated at Madame Trenti's establishment, only he'd unaccountably decided to unleash it now, a day late. And I hadn't time for it.

"I am sorry for your displeasure, master. If you'll allow me leave to explain—"

I might as well have said nothing, for the torrent surged on with barely an interval. "When I encountered you yesterday morning, I presumed two things. First, you'd returned from Cambridge having accomplished the task I set you—to retrieve my drawings; second, you'd come back to your duties directly. On both counts you've deceived me. This greatly displeases me, and I conclude you no longer value your position here."

"Master," I protested, "there can be no question of that. I am dedicated as ever to your enterprise. Why, I—"

Again he brusquely cut me off. "Enough. I won't listen to your babble a moment longer. There are just two things I want to know from you, Hopson, and then you may leave. Where were you yesterday afternoon? And what has become of my drawings?"

"It is that I intended to explain. Events in Cambridge took an unexpected turn—"

His face ripened to an even deeper shade of purple. "Do you dare to ignore my questions, Hopson? *Where are my drawings?*"

I hesitated just long enough to concoct a response to suit my purpose. "Still at Horseheath as far as I know."

Chippendale shook his head. "As far as you know," he echoed incredulously. "Of what use is such a lukewarm assurance?"

I looked sheepishly back, saying nothing, which only annoyed him further.

"There is little influences an employer more in favor of his workman, when he wants something awkward, than if the workman is able to deliver it. You, however, have done the very opposite. Knowing what I wanted, you have repeatedly *failed* to deliver it. Ask yourself, Hopson, were I a patron employing you to furnish my house, would I continue to use you?"

I forced a penitent sigh and looked at my feet, hoping the meeker I appeared, the quicker the storm would blow itself out, and he'd leave me to get on with my pressing business.

"You know the terms upon which you entered my service?"

"Yes, sir."

"Yet you deliberately flout them?"

"Not deliberately, sir. If I could ask you again, permit me to explain—"

"Damn you, Hopson! Who are *you* to make such demands of *me*? Nothing but a slip-slopping dawdler without an ounce of spirit. When I was your age I'd sooner have hanged myself than carried on in such a manner."

I looked about the room, and my eye came to rest on Chippendale's vast cabinet standing in the corner. The inner compartments and complex interior were complete, and the veneers had been applied. But although I could appreciate it as a masterpiece of craftsmanship, it struck me suddenly that it was utterly frivolous. What was the point of the hours lavished over the creation of something whose purpose was merely to amuse for a few minutes, before its novelty paled and some other entertainment beckoned? It was then that my temporarily suppressed temper got the better of me. Why should I endure such insults from a man who revered such frippery, who had treated Partridge so cruelly, whose ramblings were preventing me from assuring Alice's safety?

I stood up and faced him defiantly. "Sir," said I, "I've listened to your complaints and cannot disagree that you have it in your power to dismiss me. But if you do so without first hearing my explanation, I guarantee you'll stand *no chance at all* of retrieving your precious drawings."

The shaft hit home. Thunderstruck by the sudden change in my demeanor—my expression now bordered on contemptuous—he viewed me in incredulous silence. Sensing my advantage, I continued in the same belligerent tone. "I sorted your drawings as I agreed when I was last at Horseheath, and had secured Miss Alleyn and Lord Foley's permission to remove them." (This was untrue, but I'd abandoned all scruples in my quest to be rid of him.) "When Robert Montfort returned unexpectedly to the house, he took against me, and I found myself evicted before I could take them. After I saw you yesterday, at Madame Trenti's house, I went in search of Lord Foley, in order to suggest that he should accompany me to the house to claim them, whereupon they will be immediately returned. I would have told you this yesterday, only you vanished after speaking to the justice and I didn't wish to compromise the account you gave him of our arriving at her house together."

My fabrication did not hold him at bay for long. He was unabashed by my reference to his untruthful record of the circumstances surrounding Madame Trenti's death. "So the nub of what you propose is that I must continue to endure your disobedience; for if I don't I'll never retrieve my drawings?"

I nodded gravely. I could see he was still smoldering and that everything hung in the balance.

"I swear if you do not bring them to me you shall certainly starve. This is your final chance to acquit yourself of the task set you. If you fail, have no doubt I'll have you carried to the watch house and tried by the justice for fraud."

Knowing the threats were far from idle, I made no reply. Was not this similar to the way he had dealt with Partridge? Fortunately, however, he read my silence as meekness and it seemed to satisfy him. He stalked away without a further word.

As soon as he'd gone I finished the letter to Alice, stuffed it in my pocket, and grabbed my surtout, ready to dispatch the letter before any further hindrances presented themselves. Alas, I was too late. An apprentice darted in, saying Lord Foley had arrived in the shop and was asking for me. I sighed but went directly, knowing the sooner I spoke to him the sooner I'd be free to leave.

Foley was dressed in his usual finery—a pale blue velvet coat with curious silver buttons in the form of frogs. "Hopson. Good day to you, sir," he drawled as ceremoniously as if I were a duke.

His civilities infuriated me. "Forgive me, my lord, there is a matter of some urgency. I am obliged to leave immediately. Perhaps we may postpone this conversation for some other time?"

But Foley obtusely refused to comprehend my desperation. Rather he seemed intent on detaining me. The minute I had entered the room where he was waiting, he had closed the door and stood in front of it.

"Very well," he said after a maddening pause, "let us be brief then. I came to discover what you learned from Bradfield's grooms at the mews. I had hoped to meet you there, but you had already departed by the time I arrived, and I confess the stench and the puddles were enough to deter me from questioning the men myself."

"It is for that reason I must leave you," I blurted. "I must send this letter at once to Miss Goodchild, or I fear her life will be in danger. And then I must return forthwith to Cambridge."

Foley smiled and fingered the door handle. "In which case, my dear fellow, it is fortuitous that we are having this conversation. I have saved you time as far as Miss Goodchild is concerned. I passed Bradfield's chaise galloping along the Western Road some half hour ago. In it were Robert Montfort and your Miss Goodchild."

I started with alarm. "What the devil was she doing going today, when she told me it was tomorrow she was leaving? Are you quite certain, my lord?"

"Unquestionably. But gently, gently, Hopson, what's the reason for your urgency? Is it a young man's whimsy or something graver?"

I shot him a withering look. "Then it's even more urgent that I travel to Cambridge this instant. For I am convinced that Miss Goodchild has inadvertently put her life in great peril, and that Robert Montfort murdered not only Partridge and Madame Trenti but his own father as well."

I fancied a flicker of anxiety crossed his face, although his voice remained unruffled as ever. "In which case we shall travel together, in my carriage. On the way you will tell me all you know, for it seems there have been considerable advances since yesterday evening."

And so for the second time in a month I found myself coaching in comfort to Cambridge with Foley. Once we'd passed the Hatton turnpike I'd told him all I'd gleaned and what I'd made of it. He gave no sign whether he concurred with my opinions, gazing out of the window, lost in silent contemplation, turning back only occasionally to take a large pinch of snuff. After several hours' traveling, as we thundered through Royston, he seemed to recall my presence.

"I think it best, Hopson, if for tonight at least you stay with me at Whitely Court. Bearing in mind your suspicions, and Robert Montfort's threats, it would be unwise of you to present yourself there unexpectedly, even in my company."

"But what of Alice? It is her safety that concerns me, not my own," I blustered, incensed that he still refused to acknowledge the danger she was in.

"If Robert Montfort apprehends you, your presence will only excite his suspicions that the net is closing round him, and might spur him to take drastic action. In any event, Bradfield's coach is a lumbering vehicle. Miss Goodchild will not have reached Horseheath until late this evening. I wager, however demented our quarry may be, she won't be in any immediate danger."

"What makes you believe so?"

"Another sudden death with no one else in the house would point the finger of suspicion in his direction. However crazed, I hazard our bird is also a wily one."

I was exasperated by his casualness. "Lord Foley, it's her safety you are gambling with, not a hand of cards. By what right do you treat her life so lightly?"

His eyebrows shot up, but it was in half mockery; I hadn't riled him, for his face remained as tranquil as it always appeared. "For one so young you have an audacious line in argument, Hopson. Perhaps that is why you so often fall foul of those above you."

"I speak as I see fit, my lord, and make no apologies for that. You have always bade me address you frankly."

The corner of his mouth twitched. "Very well, if you persist in your concern, I give you my word I'll visit Horseheath myself this evening on some pretext. I'll have a word with her, give her your letter, warn her of the danger she's in, and insist she'll be safer if she comes and stays at Whitely."

"I urge you not to press too forcefully," said I. "All I have learned of Miss Goodchild in recent days has taught me she is not a lady to be ridden roughshod over."

He smiled at this and concurred. He too had observed a certain rebelliousness in her character and concluded she required gentle handling.

"May I make one other request, my lord?"

"Name it."

"Would you let the maidservant, Connie, know that I'm here? There's some matter she wishes to discuss with me. She sent me a letter, and mentioned it once before when I was at Hindlesham, so it must have preyed on her mind. Tell her I'll speak with her tomorrow."

It was already past seven o'clock by the time we reached Whitely Court and I caught my first glimpse of Foley's mansion, a gracious two-story Queen Anne house with none of the pedimented pretensions of Horseheath. Lady Foley, a tall woman with a serene expression, greeted her husband with a brisk but affectionate peck on the cheek and professed herself ashamed. She hadn't expected him till the morrow and had nothing to offer but a bit of cold mutton for supper. Foley waved away her concerns with an airy assurance that we'd eaten already on the road. My spirits sank to hear him, for I'd taken nothing since breakfast and had been craving a good meal for the past hour. Lady Foley must have suspected something of the kind, for she amiably reproached him. Even if he were not hungry I must be, she said, for young men were always in need of nourishment, and she would hear no objections to her offer of a plate of something cold and a glass of wine.

Foley was now impatient to pay his call to Horseheath. While his wife sent instructions to the kitchens, he escorted me to his library, directing me to entertain myself as I wished until his return, which he expected to be within an hour or two.

I ate my supper by the fireside, staring at the walls around me as I munched, trying halfheartedly to distract myself from my fears for Alice. It occurred to me then that there was more to Foley than frog buttons and velvet finery. This was the room of a true connoisseur of wide-ranging taste. Ranks of leather-lined volumes filled the shelves, some broken and cracked, others newly bound with gold tooling on their spines; a large library table overflowed with papers, pamphlets, and correspondence, and a microscope with various slides in a box sat among them. Above the fire hung a canvas depicting antlike gentlemen surveying a vast building I recognized as the Pantheon in Rome. In a collector's cabinet various antiquities were ranged—a piece of mosaic, a few ancient coins, cameos, and an old silver buckle. Many of the objects were chipped and cracked, but each had an idiosyncratic appeal, as if flaws were irrelevant; each item had been chosen from a true understanding and appreciation rather than a desire to impress.

But all the while I'd gazed about the room my anxieties had not diminished. Far from it: I kept thinking of Foley, wondering if I'd been wise to agree to let him go to Horseheath Hall alone to speak to Alice. Should I have braved Robert's wrath and gone with him? Sitting here I felt a sense of inexpressible helplessness. What would I do if Foley arrived too late? Suppose, horror of horrors, Alice was already dead?

Suddenly I had no appetite for supper. I pushed away the tray, turning disconsolately to the table, where in order to distract myself from my rambling fears, I picked up the first volume that came to hand, an album of engravings after Italian old masters. The cover inside was beautifully dedicated in copperplate script, "To Jane from your loving friend Margaret on the occasion of your birthday, November 1754." I was halfway through the pages when I heard a soft step behind me. Lady Foley had entered the room to ensure I had all I required. She saw the book in my hand and smiled.

"You have discovered something of interest, Mr. Hopson?" she said, locking her eyes on mine.

"Forgive . . . forgive me, my lady," said I, stumbling over the words in my confusion. "I didn't mean to pry among your belongings. His lordship bade me read what I chose and I happened upon this book to distract me from my concerns."

"Don't trouble yourself, Mr. Hopson, you are welcome to look at it. And as for your concerns, I take it they are regarding Horseheath. I don't know all that goes on in that house, but the little I have heard is enough to unsettle me too. Miss Alleyn, you see from the inscription in that book, is an old friend of mine, thus I am apprised of some of it."

"What has she told you?"

"Nothing of late. Since her brother Montfort's death that night I have not seen or heard from her. She has passed some time in London, Foley tells me. I pray, however, that she is happier now than she was before her brother's death." She halted for a minute and looked attentively at my face. "I did what I could to help her, though sadly I must own it was not a great deal, for Foley opposed me. You see, I asked him several times to help Miss Alleyn, but he always refused. Her position in that house was dreadfully precarious."

My face must have shown my puzzlement. "I had understood her brother was most solicitous of her, that he stipulated particularly that her future in the household should always be secure."

Jane Foley shook her head. "Then I fear you have been misinformed. Montfort blighted her life."

"In what way?"

"She was engaged to be married once. It was a short-lived engagement, for Montfort's first wife, Robert's mother, died soon after she became betrothed. Her brother, finding himself in need of a housekeeper and someone to raise his infant son, demanded that she leave the small cottage where she lived happily as a companion to a distant elderly relative and come and run his household. She didn't conceive, when she agreed, that her brother would take every opportunity to involve himself with her husband-to-be and ultimately to dissuade him from marrying her. I do not know precisely what passed between them, only that at some stage Montfort encouraged her betrothed to join his gaming activities and cheated him in some way. Within a month of coming here she found herself no longer betrothed, without a chance of rearing a family of her own. Instead she became what she has been ever since: a spinster housekeeper."

I felt sympathy now for Miss Alleyn's plight, for the selfish way her brother had treated her. I now comprehended her unusual nervousness; but it didn't alter my conviction. She had been duped by Robert to abet him in the murder of Madame Trenti. Robert lay at the root of all this. "Did not her affection for her nephew, Robert, compensate for her brother's unpleasantness?"

"If you believe that then you deceive yourself, Mr. Hopson. Miss Alleyn was fond of her nephew, it is true. But that did not outweigh the fact that her brother was a notorious bully who delighted in making her feel her dependence on him. I wanted Foley to help her, but whenever I raised the matter he said the Montfort family was no better than a nest of adders, no more deserving of sympathy, no more susceptible to guidance . . ."

I nodded sympathetically. I could almost hear Foley saying it, although I was surprised to learn that he had always been so unfeeling towards the Montforts. Hitherto I'd assumed it was only the gambling debt that had cooled the relationship, and that prior to that he and Lord Montfort had been the closest of friends.

"Miss Alleyn explained a little of her predicament to me quite recently, though she gave me no inkling she was so unhappy in her position."

"She's a woman of extraordinary resolve, Mr. Hopson. Imagine the two decades she has spent living under Montfort's roof. Imagine the daily humiliations, the frustrations of realizing that if she had only refused his demand to live with him, she might have enjoyed the happiness of wedlock and a family of her own. In return for her unselfishness, how has she been repaid? The only outlet she has had for her maternal warmth is Robert, whom she regards as her own son. Furthermore, when Lord Montfort married Elizabeth, she was kindness personified towards her. That is why I hold her in high esteem and wish to assist her."

"And have you done so?"

"Not yet. But perhaps now that Montfort is dead everything may change. If, as I trust he will, Robert repays his aunt with but a fraction of the kindness she has shown him, her security will be assured and her old age will be a happy one."

"Do you think he will?"

She gave me a level look. Her face betrayed nothing. "I wish I knew, Mr. Hopson, for it would ease me greatly to know she was well cared for. My fear is that Robert resembles his father in many respects, not least in the ingratitude he shows towards his aunt. Now, if you'll excuse me, I'll send the maidservant for the tray."

Left to my own devices, I speedily forgot Miss Alleyn as my impatience grew for Foley's return. What was detaining him at Horseheath? Had he handled Alice discreetly as I'd bade him, or had he stirred up her rebelliousness? I paced the room, then finding this exercise only made my blood race more, took a seat at his table to calm myself.

Looking back, I cannot now be sure whether it was the conversation regarding Miss Alleyn's tribulations that focused my mind on Montfort's warped character, or whether instead the breadth of Foley's collection— artifacts of antiquity and science mingled together—made me concentrate on the conundrum of Montfort's death in a new manner. In any event, it crossed my mind that all my actions to date had centered on my desire to discover the reason for *Partridge's* murder. I had begun in an entirely ridiculous manner, by searching the distant past for his lost history, ignoring recent details, making matters more complex than necessary. Once I'd realized this error, I'd pursued more recent events pertaining to my friend. I'd discovered the reason for his journey to Horseheath, the connection between Partridge, Montfort, and Madame Trenti, whose death had led me to the discovery that Robert Montfort was to blame.

Yet all this time I'd regarded the problem from a single vantage point, that of Partridge. I had yet to consider in any depth the other death that had taken place the night Partridge died—the death of Montfort. And yet the scene at Montfort's death brimmed with evidence. And all of it, with the exception of the grenadillo box, I had neglected to pursue.

Robert Montfort had a clear enough motive to wish his father dead. With Montfort out of the way, he would inherit his estate; he would be free to pursue his interest in science and his passion for Elizabeth. He had two equally strong motives for wanting to murder Partridge. He believed Partridge had a claim on his father—and Partridge dead provided a useful culprit for his father's murder. But although this theory satisfied me, there was a fundamental matter I had yet to fathom. *How* had the murders of Montfort and Partridge been achieved, when as far as I recalled Robert was present at the dinner table, apart from the briefest absence before the gun blast?

In the center of Foley's table was a small pile of blank writing paper and a silver inkstand: all I needed to occupy myself. I took up the quill, charging it with ink. I confined my attentions to the night Lord Montfort and John Partridge died and began to compose a list of the main points I might usefully address.

> Leeches—apothecary
> Pistol
> Footprints
> Montfort's estate
> Grenadillo box
> Drawings

Beneath these I drew a line, before adding:

> Connie
> Desk drawer
> Salt

I was scratching my head, wondering what else I might add to it, when Foley appeared. He was alone. There was no sign of Alice. He smiled wryly when he saw me seated at his desk, writing with his pen.

"Good evening, Hopson. I see you have forgotten your worries and made yourself at home as I bade you."

"I am no less concerned than I was. Where is Miss Goodchild? She will arrive directly by carriage, I take it?"

He lowered himself into an armchair and stretched towards the fire. "The visit did not go entirely as we expected or hoped. I was unable to speak to Connie. She left for London two days ago and has yet to return. Robert Montfort was in the foulest of humors when he saw me."

"And Alice?"

"As for our dear Miss Goodchild, yes, I saw her. Yes, I endeavored to pass on your concerns. Only I regret to say she was far from amenable to them."

I glared at him. "What d'you mean?"

"Merely that the moment I handed her your letter and mentioned you were staying with me, and were worried for her safety, she scoffed. She said she was convinced any danger was a convenient exaggeration dreamed up by you to prevent her involvement. I replied that she had only to read your note to see that your fears for her safety were well founded. You had found out that Robert had driven the carriage you had seen on the morning of Madame Trenti's death. He was to blame for the deaths of his father, Partridge, and Madame Trenti, and for the attempt on your life. Thus you were sick with worry that the reason he had invited her to Horseheath was because he intended, for his own demented purposes, to kill her."

"And what was her response to hearing all this? Didn't she read my letter? Surely she must have felt some glimmer of apprehension?"

"Far from it. She replied merely that your postulations were all very well, but that she regarded herself to be as able as you in reading a character. Robert Montfort didn't strike her as a maniac, and it wasn't he who'd invited her to Horseheath. It was Miss Alleyn. Did that make Miss Alleyn a maniac?"

I sensed the ridicule Alice intended even as Foley repeated her words. Speechless at such folly, I shook my head.

"The only concession she'd make was to say she'd bolt the door and stay where she was, for she was quite well able to take care of herself." Foley hesitated.

"Was there something else?"

"She said she was eager to help resolve the matter, and would certainly not be so easily deviated from that task as you have shown yourself to be."

I put down my pen and looked at my hands. My heart was thumping steadily. This was the realization of my worst fears. The fact that Miss Alleyn had tendered the invitation made not one jot of difference. Had not the stable boy told me she had procured the carriage that Robert had driven? The likelihood was therefore that she had been coerced into aiding her nephew again.

Foley noticed the effect of his reply and felt perhaps a glimmer of chagrin, for he tried his best to distract me. "Now tell me, Hopson," he said in a brisker tone, "what were you writing about?"

"I was preparing a plan of action for tomorrow. I expected that Alice would be safely here and believed, with a little effort and your cooperation, we might then resolve the matter speedily," I said.

"Hopson, I am growing mightily weary, but before I retire to bed let me put your mind at rest once and for all. I may have failed to persuade Miss Goodchild to come here, but that is partly because I allowed her to refuse my offer. Had I *really* been convinced she was in danger, I would have *insisted* upon it. Do not think me unfeeling. I do not disregard your concerns, but the reason I am without qualms is that I have seen Alice and witnessed the arrangements in the house. Mrs. Cummings is present, as are several other servants. Alice has promised to bolt her door. Tomorrow morning Miss Alleyn, Elizabeth, the Bradfields, and Connie will return. If Robert wishes to dispose of Miss Goodchild, he won't do it tonight, and tomorrow morning there will be others around to protect her. No, he will wait for the right moment, by which time we will have returned to Horseheath and resolved the matter."

His words did little to console me; on the contrary, I felt myself falling further into the grip of such fear as I hadn't felt since the night when I'd wandered into Robert Montfort's room. Only now my dread was not vague imaginings about my own safety but frustrated terror for Alice. How was I ever to persuade her of the peril she was in if she refused to hear me? How could I save her when she would not allow herself to be saved?

Chapter Twenty-four

Next morning I descended from Foley's carriage in Bridge Street, Cambridge, amid slanting motes of winter sun and a sewery stench that reminded me of London. The sense of helplessness that had descended upon me last night lingered on. I had passed a wakeful night, and this morning felt barely master of my faculties. By contrast Foley at breakfast appeared calm and irrefutably in control. He refused to countenance my appeal to go immediately to Horseheath Hall. He had pondered the matter all night, and upon reflection declared he was unconvinced that Robert Montfort was to blame for the murders. Granted, he could see strong motives for Robert to wish both his father and Partridge dead; granted, Robert stood to gain most from his father's demise; granted, if he accepted Partridge as his illegitimate half brother he also had a motive to wish Madame Trenti dead, for he may have feared his father would make over part of his inheritance to her as well as to the new interloper. That said, he could see no way to explain *how* the Horseheath murders were accomplished. The night of Montfort's death Robert had followed Foley out of the room. Foley was as sure as he could be that Robert had been in his sight all the time he was not at the dining table.

"But, my lord," I declared helplessly, "it would be an easy matter for a man such as Robert Montfort to procure an agent to kill both his father and Partridge."

"An agent whom not a soul in the house saw or heard? That is most implausible, I think, Hopson."

"But I have proved beyond doubt that Robert drove the coach I saw on the morning of Madame Trenti's death. And that it was he who ran me down."

"Hopson, there is a difference between proof and assumption. What you have discovered is interesting; it places suspicion on Robert, *but it does not prove anything.* Recap a moment. What you discovered was that Miss Alleyn took the coach and that soon afterwards the groom saw a gentleman driving it. There is no proof at all the gentleman was Robert Montfort." Putting down his toast, he then waved the list I'd made under my nose like an accusation, and insisted we investigate systematically the matters I'd raised. Only then would we stand a chance of proving once and for all the question of Robert Montfort's guilt and resolving our quest.

"But what if you are mistaken?" I cried frantically. "Suppose he did slip away and you didn't remark it, suppose even now he is plotting Alice's death . . ."

He shook his head firmly and said we'd been over all this the night before. The only concession he made was to send Lady Foley to Horseheath to watch over Miss Goodchild till our arrival. If she discovered anything untoward, she would send word to Cambridge that we should come immediately. In the meantime I was to question Townes, the apothecary physician who had regularly treated Lord Montfort. I should recall, said Foley, that Robert Montfort had also intended to call upon Townes to garner support for his theory of suicide. Thus, as well as inquiring about Montfort's condition, it would be interesting to discover what questions Robert had asked.

The shop crouched in a dark alley between a printer's and the Rose Inn. The building was heavily gabled, with oak beams and lattice windows, and a peeling signboard that had once been emblazoned with a rhinoceros and a figure of Apollo vanquishing the dragon of disease. Inside, the acrid stench of chemicals mingled with perfumed unguents and dust. Dust veiled every surface, from a stuffed crocodile clutching a medicine bottle propped in the window to rows of jars filled with mysterious substances—oil of absinthe, syrup of violets, syrup of meconium, oil of earthworms—and a chest of minute drawers in which remedies such as

King Agrippa's ointment, Vandour's pills, gum tragac, and James's fever powder were stored.

In a back room a hunched, gray-haired figure ground powders in a mortar. He noticed me watching him and shuffled into the shop, carrying his stone mortar before him as reverentially as a chalice. He was a man of broad stature, with yellowish skin hanging loosely about a tortoiselike head and heavy-lidded eyes. Ignoring my presence, he took out a fragile balance and set to decanting the powder into one side, loading and unloading small brass weights on the other to counter it. Only when this delicate process was complete did he turn his eyes on me.

"Fine morning, is it not?"

"Indeed, sir."

"And what can I do for you, sir?"

Despite my preoccupations I marveled at his directness. How different from the endless obsequious pleasantries with which Chippendale greeted his customers.

"It is knowledge rather than medicine I seek, sir."

His eyes rested on me. I fancied I saw a crafty expression in his wide, wrinkled face. "Knowledge? In the case of ignorance that too may be a curative of sorts. What variety of knowledge do you seek?"

I informed him I'd come on the authority of Lord Foley and Sir James Westleigh to investigate the events surrounding the recent demise of Lord Montfort. There were doubts concerning the manner of his death; we desired that he might tell us something of Montfort's medical condition prior to his death, for this might have some bearing on the matter.

"What is it you wish to know?"

"When did you last see Lord Montfort?"

"The day before he died."

"He sent for you?"

"Not that day, no. He'd been unwell for some weeks, and I'd attended him regularly."

"What precisely was the nature of his ailment?"

"Aching of the head, sleeplessness, fatigue, restlessness."

"Your diagnosis?"

"Melancholy, despair, call it what you will."

"Was the condition a chronic one?"

"His recent, unfortunate gambling losses I believe sparked this bout, although the disposition has always been there. It is a common enough affliction among those in his comfortable circumstances."

"Do I divine you were not entirely sympathetic towards the complainant?"

Townes paused, turned back to the scales, and began scooping the powder from the tray into papers, which he folded into careful symmetrical squares. "If you or I suffered from the same we'd be chastised for idleness and set to work harder," he said neutrally. "It is a disease, true enough, but one that I've remarked breeds strongest amid luxury, dissipation, and indolence."

"And the treatment?"

"The usual for the complaint. Bleeding, an amulet of peony root, and a potent sleeping draft."

"And you bled him with leeches the day before he died?"

"No. When I bled him it was by cupping, a speedier method. Lately he'd grown more demanding, insisting on some treatment he could administer himself the days I didn't come. To satisfy him I supplied a jar of leeches."

"Who was to administer them?"

"His sister or his wife, I believe."

"And the leeches remained with him?"

"He paid five shillings for twenty of the finest beasts, the very same as these." He gestured to a gallon jar of greenish water alive with the same writhing black creatures as I'd removed from Montfort's neck.

"And what directions did you supply with them?"

"I demonstrated how to place the leeches on the temple or neck when the ache was bad. I explained how when they'd done their work they fell off and then the bites should be bathed with water to stop them bleeding further. The leeches could be returned to the jar, or placed in a dish of salt to vomit the blood."

"How often?"

"I suggested a wait of at least two days after my visit. I'd taken two pints, sufficient to last some time; to take more would weaken him and worsen his symptoms. In the meantime, if the headaches troubled him I recommended he retire to bed with a dose of his sleeping draft to alleviate the pain."

"In other words, had he followed your instruction he would not have administered the leeches the next evening?"

"There was no reason for him to do so. Furthermore, I'd warned him clearly against it."

I considered this information, perplexed as to why Montfort had so deliberately flouted his instructions. Failing to muster a solution, I pursued another avenue. "In which room did the bleeding usually take place?"

"In Lord Montfort's upstairs closet."

Here too I was baffled. Why then had Montfort bled himself in the library?

"And the sleeping draft consisted of what?"

"A liquor containing laudanum mixed with sage leaves, seeds of anise, powder of orris, and powder of pearls. One dram would be sufficient to deaden any pain and make him sleep soundly for several hours."

"And more?"

"I cautioned against it. To drink more would be dangerous, for it contained grains of poppy."

"How quickly would a fatal dose take effect?"

"Two hours—less if alcohol had been taken . . ."

"Tell me," I broke in, "do you believe Montfort shot himself?"

He looked up from his powders and pursed his mouth thoughtfully. "I can tell you only what I know. His mind was turbulent enough for self-murder to be possible, probable even. However, I know nothing of the circumstances of the event."

"Has anyone else inquired after Montfort's death?"

"Only his son."

"What did he want to know?"

"The same as you. His father's state of mind, and if I thought it likely he killed himself."

"Did he ask after the other person who died—John Partridge?"

"Not him, no. It was Westleigh who summoned me to attend that body, and I believe Lord Foley was there as well."

"And what did you find?"

"They wanted my opinion of the wounds. I told them the amputation of the fingers was crudely done. Not enough to kill him outright, had he stanched the flow of blood, but since he did not—I believe it was loss of blood caused him to lose consciousness, whereupon he fell in the water and died either from loss of blood, being frozen alive, or drowning."

I shivered to hear him pick over Partridge's fate with such detachment. "What do you mean, the amputation was crudely done?"

"I mean it was not the work of a surgeon or a butcher. A blade of some description had been used, but something else as well."

"You are very detailed in your analysis."

He glanced sharply at me with a slight shake of his head. "My opinion was confirmed by what I saw of the fingers in the casket. The bones were hacked through, not cut cleanly as someone with strength or knowledge would have done. They weren't severed at the joints, d'you see, simply hacked. Moreover, there were livid bruises on the backs and palms of both hands, as if something blunt but heavy had struck them with great force."

"Could you hazard what that might have been?"

He shook his head firmly.

"Come, Mr. Townes, try and think. Could it have been a riding crop perchance?" I said.

"I doubt it was a riding crop, nor any weapon I know. I told you I don't know what it was. I've never seen wounds like them, and hope never to again."

As chance would have it, just then a young woman with a wailing infant entered. I left the apothecary mixing an ointment of hare's brine and capon grease to ease the child's teething pains.

I crossed the street and strode off towards the Turk's Head, a coffeehouse in Trinity Street. Foley had agreed that, while I interrogated Mr. Townes, he would call on Lord Montfort's attorney, Wallace, and persuade him to join us here. Once we'd questioned him on the delicate matter of Montfort's estate, we would proceed immediately to Horseheath.

With every moment that passed, the gravity and precariousness of Alice's situation loomed larger in my mind. It was insupportable to leave her in such jeopardy. The moment I saw Foley I'd tell him I couldn't continue here; I'd insist we abandon our plan and proceed straight to Horseheath. I would naturally prefer him to accompany me and endeavor to protect me from Robert Montfort's wrath, but if he refused he could stay with Wallace. I'd find my own means of transport and take my chances with Robert.

But when I stepped inside the dark, pungently scented room, I detected no trace of either man. A handful of youths, university students perhaps, sat round a table poring over a newspaper, laughing at an electioneering cartoon and its gross depiction of the king, bare-bottomed and seated upon a commode while sundry ministers looked on. There was no one else. I took up another journal and began to turn its pages. But so engrossed was I by other thoughts the words before me were gibberish.

What had made Montfort storm from the table and apply the leeches in his *library*? The only reason I could conceive was that he'd been maddened with pain, forgotten the instruction, and applied them. But even this seemed unlikely. The leech jar was probably kept in his upstairs closet, where he was usually bled. There was no plausible reason for him to go upstairs, bring the leeches down to a unlit library, and employ them there. In any case, if the ache to his head had returned, why not take the sleeping draft as Townes had directed and retire to bed?

But what if someone else—his killer—had placed the leeches on him? Why would he do so? Leeches were never fatal; what reason could there be to put them on a man you were about to shoot? Because you were pretending to help him? Because you wanted to see his blood seeping from him the instant before he died?

I sighed. My mind was once again fogged with confusion. Townes's statement raised yet more perplexing questions. Like layers of varnish on a tabletop, the more I discovered, the more truth seemed to disguise rather than reveal itself.

I thought of Partridge lying frozen, mutilated, and dead in the pond and asked myself for the hundredth time what possible reason there could be to do such a thing. Partridge was no one. He didn't know who he was and couldn't possibly pose a threat to Montfort, despite Madame Trenti's assurances. Montfort would have laughed when Partridge announced himself as his son. Realizing this made my resolve wane further and my sense of inadequacy return.

My foreboding grew, and a dread beyond all others possessed me. A fog of evil seemed to surround Horseheath. And at its heart was Alice. What was I doing sitting here waiting for Foley and Wallace when she was in mortal jeopardy? Cursing my negligence, I drained my coffee and stood up.

I'd scarcely begun to step towards the door when Foley arrived, suave and unhurried as ever in his velvet-collared cape. Lagging a little behind was Wallace, looking as miserable as if he'd just sat on a wasp. I knew exactly how he must feel, for I was experiencing similar sentiments.

"Here he is, as I said he'd be," said Foley to Wallace. "You see, it's no trouble at all for you to come and take a coffee with us. A welcome break from the tedium of your documents rather."

Wallace said nothing, but I judged he was far from easy to be with us in so public a place. He scurried to the furthest corner of the booth, lurking in the shadows until more coffee was ordered. His voice, when he spoke, was no more than a rasping whisper. "I really do not know why you wish me to come and speak with you. Should Robert Montfort catch sight of me, my business with him might be jeopardized. He's an important client, one I can't risk losing," he hissed.

"Don't concern yourself," boomed Foley in a far more resonant tone than usual. "Montfort is firmly ensconced in Horseheath, I saw him there myself yesterday evening. The substance of this conversation will never reach him. And in any case, bear in mind, my good fellow, that our desire to speak to you isn't born of idle curiosity. You might recall I'm authorized to make inquiries by our justice, Sir James Westleigh. Hopson here is assisting as my deputy."

In desperation I broke in. "Forgive me, my lord," said I, sitting down and standing up again. "I really think, since Mr. Wallace is uneasy, we should postpone our discussion. I believe we should lose no more time. We must proceed directly to Horseheath."

"What?" said Foley, a little sharply. "That was not our intention. Sit down, Hopson. Horseheath and its occupants will wait."

I sat down unthinkingly and then immediately stood again and thumped my fist on the table. "Suppose something terrible happens before we return? Suppose Miss Goodchild is murdered and mutilated as was Partridge? Even as we sit here discussing the matter, might the murderer not have her in his vicious sights? Might she not be falling prey to his foul appetite?"

Foley shrugged his shoulders in exasperation. "Quiet, Hopson, you are growing tiresome," he said.

I would not be rebuffed. "Why did Robert Montfort engineer to have her alone with him at Horseheath last night? The story of the staircase is nothing but a fabrication, and we both know it. Upon my word, Lord Foley, listen to me. We can consult Mr. Wallace any time. Once Miss Goodchild's life is lost, we cannot bring her back."

He was utterly unmoved by my passion. "I say again, sit down, Hopson. Why, you are up and down more rapidly than a whore's petticoats. And once again you are working yourself into a frenzy. Ask Wallace what it is you wish to know, it will take no more than five minutes. Then I give you my word I'll drive you to Horseheath faster than the devil and all the horses of hell."

Drawn by his booming tone, the students stopped their chatter and gaped at us. I had the distinct impression that Foley relished Wallace's shiny-faced discomfiture and my anxiety, that he was toying with us both by making such a noisy spectacle of himself.

Wallace turned in my direction. "What is it you wish to know?" he mumbled.

"The details of Lord Montfort's estate," I replied, perching myself on the edge of the bench, unable to stop my foot tapping with impatience. "Money usually has a bearing on such sudden deaths."

He nodded without enthusiasm. "You will understand I cannot speak specifically on such a confidential matter, but the details broadly are these: on the day of his death, Lord Montfort drew up a legal document making over a large portion of his estate, lands, and revenues thereof to Lord Foley in settlement of his gambling debts. His death does not invalidate that document, which indeed takes precedence over his previous will."

"Did anyone apart from Lord Montfort and you know of this new document?"

"There was a witness who was unaware of its contents."

"Who was this person?"

"Elizabeth Montfort, Lord Montfort's wife."

"Tell me, Mr. Wallace, whom do you believe would be most directly affected by the changes to Lord Montfort's estate?"

"His heirs, evidently, were adversely affected. His wife, Elizabeth, was to have received a generous allowance for the remainder of her life, and as such would have been a woman of independent means for as long as she remained unmarried. The bulk of the remainder was left to Robert. Both would have received considerably less as a result of this document. And self-evidently Lord Foley was to profit."

"What do you mean by 'the bulk of the remainder'?"

"There were a handful of other bequests, to Lord Bradfield and his wife and various acquaintances. Nothing of note."

"And what of his sister, Margaret Alleyn?" interrupted Foley.

"A small sum. Nothing of significance. But a stipulation she was to stay on at Horseheath as housekeeper."

I pressed on, shooting a warning glance at Foley to prevent him interrupting with irrelevancies and delaying matters further. "At what time did you arrive at Horseheath to draw up the document?"

"Around ten."

"And do you remember anything out of the ordinary when you did so?"

"What do you mean?"

"How did Lord Montfort seem to you? Did he expect any other visitors that day? Did anything unusual take place while you were there?"

He considered a moment. "Lord Montfort seemed less agitated than he often did. As if he knew what he desired and simply wanted to get it accomplished." He gazed nervously at the youths, as if to reassure himself they weren't listening. "Lord Montfort saw no visitors that I recall, but I do fancy Miss Alleyn might have entertained someone. I remember the maidservant mentioned it when she was sent to fetch her to sign the document. That was why it was Elizabeth Montfort who witnessed it."

"Did Elizabeth say who Miss Alleyn entertained?"

"She did not."

"And was there anything unusual in Elizabeth's demeanor?"

"Nothing I recall. She was a little subdued, but that was her habitual appearance."

"Anything else?"

He blinked rapidly and scratched his ear. "Yes, now I think of it. I recall Miss Alleyn came in flustered after the signing was complete. She was embarrassed to have been occupied, and I remarked that she was holding something in her hand."

"Do you recall what it was?"

"The box that was in Lord Montfort's hand when he died."

I stared at him wildly, my mind seething. Bearing in mind I was certain Partridge had made the box, did this mean Miss Alleyn had been in communication with Partridge earlier that day? If so, why had she concealed this information from me?

I knew this was an important point, yet I was incapable of fixing on it. Reason was crowded out by thoughts of Alice, of how badly I wanted to see her, of how much I needed to assure myself she was safe. Nothing else mattered. I stood up abruptly. "Thank you, sir, you've told me everything and more than I needed to hear. That is all."

Then I turned and made a final desperate address to Foley. "My lord, as I implored you before, I believe there is now but one thing we must do, and it should be done immediately. If you do not agree to assist me, I must do it alone."

Foley leaned forward. "And what is that, Hopson?"

"You know as well as I, my lord. We must return directly to Horseheath and pray Miss Goodchild is safe, and that there is still time to protect her. Otherwise I fear a tragedy of the greatest magnitude will occur and we will be to blame."

Chapter Twenty-five

The presentiment of doom that had troubled me all morning became overwhelming in Foley's coach. I felt that I was infected by some terrible contagion, that a fever within me had yet to break, and that there was no knowing how I'd survive it. I wanted to shout, to explode, to bellow at Foley to make him understand why Wallace's testimony had done little to shake my conviction. Robert Montfort was the murderer. Why did Foley not comprehend it, when it seemed to me as plain as the mole on his cheek? Most of all I wanted to make him understand my fear for Alice's safety. And yet as we raced towards Horseheath with Alice uppermost in my mind, I found myself incapable of communicating these frustrations to Foley. My tongue was fettered by fear.

Now we were on our way, Foley seemed to sense something too, for his cheeks were tinged with pink and in place of his habitual languid self-possession he seemed unusually animated. We were rattling past the London milestone and had nearly reached the junction in Trumpington village where the ancient millhouse straddles the river Cam when he suddenly took a large pinch of snuff from his box and began to interrogate me.

"May I ask, Hopson, what you made of our morning's interviews?"

I confess I was somewhat taken aback by the abruptness of this question. I turned towards him and answered spontaneously. "If I hadn't seen Lord Montfort's corpse with my own eyes, I think I would truly believe he'd taken his life. The state of his health, as testified by the apothecary, and the sudden alteration to his circumstances, as testified by Mr. Wallace, both point that way."

"If he *had* killed himself, would you hold me culpable?"

"In what respect? He plainly didn't kill himself. And in any case, why should *you* feel any blame? I understood from her ladyship that you viewed him with abhorrence."

"Forget my relations with him; forget the details of his death. I'm speaking hypothetically. D'you believe what the apothecary told you? That it was his gambling debt to me that pitched him into melancholy, and that I should not have held him to it?"

"Do you believe that yourself?"

He lowered his eyes for a minute, then, raising his chin, turned to the window just as the lofty arches of Trumpington church flashed past. "A man may be straight in his outward appearance but warped in his spirit. I feel little pity for Montfort. The responsibility for his misfortunes lies in his own foolish actions, not mine. Besides, do not for one moment believe I would have held on to his tainted money."

"What would you have done with it?"

His lips curled in an enigmatic smile. "Something to rectify the havoc he'd wrought," he muttered, more to himself than to me.

"And yet he considered you his friend?"

Foley gave a snort of scornful laughter. "Montfort had no notion of friendship, only rivalry. He surrounded himself with neighbors of similar rank out of self-conceit, not sociability. Engendering envy of his wealth, his young wife, his library, his collections, was the greatest source of delight to him. Other than that he took little pleasure in either family or friends or possessions."

I felt as if a firm hand had grasped me by the collar and forced me to stare at something I'd previously ignored. Until this juncture I'd mostly believed Foley to be the very embodiment of detachment and composure. Granted, he was not afraid to resort to ruthless manipulation where required. I hadn't forgotten the threats with which he had forced me to embroil myself in this tangle, or how he'd deliberately withheld Partridge's letter, or the time he'd encouraged me to witness Robert Montfort's surgical operations. But in general his humor had always seemed smooth as windless water. Hence the sudden glimpse of emotion took me by surprise. What was it precisely he felt towards Montfort? Envy? A desire for revenge, signaling some hidden bitterness between Montfort and himself? I remembered how he'd scoffed when I was bold enough to suggest he had a powerful motive for wishing Montfort dead. Had I been foolish to allow myself to be deflected by ridicule from following this track? Had I made a grave misjudgment in ignoring the history of their association?

"When did you first become acquainted with Lord Montfort, my lord?"

"I have known him since my youth. Did I never tell you that when Bradfield, Montfort, and I were all young men we traveled together to Italy? Madame Trenti, the unfortunate wretch, was discovered by me, and for a time I believed myself in love with her. Our liaison lasted until Montfort intervened. He seduced her, not very kindly, I believe, and then, as you have seen, abandoned her and deprived her of her child. That was the character of the man."

I shrugged my shoulders. "Madame Trenti scarcely led a blameless life. She was not above extortion when it suited her. She treated Partridge abominably and brought about his death."

"Does that exonerate Montfort from blame for what he did? Perhaps his depravity helped to taint her; perhaps he made her what she was."

I half smiled as if I didn't disagree entirely, then pursued another course. "If you held him in such low regard, is it not an indictment of your own character that you continued to accept his invitations?"

There was a lengthy silence, and his voice when he responded was somber. "Have you not considered, Hopson, that I may have had other motives for so doing?"

"Are you telling me you courted his hospitality because you intended to take revenge on him? That you see his death as your salvation? That you *were* responsible for it?"

He smiled superciliously, rubbing his nose with an extravagant flourish of his silk handkerchief. "Calm yourself, Hopson. We've covered this ground before, have we not? You know as well as I Montfort couldn't have died by my hand."

"I know no such thing. As I recall, you were absent from the table when the shot was fired. I have only *your* word that Robert Montfort was with you all the time you were outside the room. Perhaps the reason for your insistence is to provide you rather than him with an alibi. You may rest assured I intend to quiz him on the matter at the earliest opportunity."

"But I wasn't in the carriage that ran you down, or that you saw from the window of Madame Trenti's bedchamber. Of that you *can* be sure, can you not?"

"Not necessarily. I told you I couldn't see the person who ran me down. All I saw was a coat. On the morning Trenti died, Miss Alleyn might have procured the carriage for *you*. It might as well have been *you* wearing the coat I saw."

"What conceivable motive could I have?"

I stared back wordlessly, unable to think of a reason, yet unconvinced by his argument. He waited a while and when I remained silent, shook his head, as if exasperated by my obtuseness. "In any case you are missing the point entirely," he said, meeting my accusing glare. "What I mean you to understand is that we are all guilty of duplicity in some form or other. Servants and gentlefolk are made of the same flesh and blood. Even you, Hopson, cannot claim immunity from the sin."

"I would not feign friendship with a man I despise," I retorted.

"You say not. Yet is it any better to continue in the employ of the man you believe has indirectly brought about the death of your dearest friend? You address Chippendale with as much deference as ever. I'll wager you have never even raised the manner of Partridge's departure with him. Is that not a greater hypocrisy—treachery even—than if I enjoyed dinner with Montfort after I'd beaten him at cards? Depriving Montfort of his money was all the revenge I needed for the wrong he did Madame Trenti and myself all those years ago, because money was what mattered most to him. The proof of this is that, as you have seen, the loss of his fortune propelled him into melancholy. You, in contrast, have done *nothing* to right the wrong Thomas Chippendale did your friend. I have given you the chance to aid me in bringing the perpetrator of Partridge's death to justice, and yet, at every opportunity, you concede defeat and scurry back to London. Are *your* actions so entirely commendable?"

I knew he was goading me, but like a chained bear I couldn't restrain myself from lashing back. "Have you never considered, Lord Foley, that plain speaking is a luxury someone of your standing affords more easily than I? Chippendale is my employer; I have no other means of earning my livelihood."

"You could seek employ elsewhere. There are other cabinetmakers in London, I believe," he said softly.

"If I am so wanting in forthrightness, why have you insisted on my help?" I was fairly snarling at him now, but he seemed not in the least put out. On the contrary, he broke out laughing, then seeing by my scowl he was only making matters worse, patted my shoulder and fell into silence.

I turned my back to him to stare at the muddy plains of Cambridge flashing by the window. I had no heart to pursue the matter, neither could I escape the shaming truth in what he said. I had acted weakly and foolishly. I'd known it in my heart for some time, but it was only Foley's question that forced me to admit it. There was just one way I could see to make atonement for my lapses. I had to bring the murderer to justice; I had to save Alice.

The next thing I knew was a heavy weight pressing upon me and small grunts and snorts coming from my side. I turned to see Foley asleep, his head lolling on my shoulder, his hot, moist breath wafting on my neck. The remainder of the journey I spent fretting over Alice, leaning back uncomfortably with an arm around him to stop him falling when the carriage jolted over ruts. In my heart I suppose I knew my doubts regarding Foley were spurious. I knew he was innocent of any crime, and even though his presence irked me, I didn't push him away.

"What are *you* doing here?" shrieked Mrs. Cummings, setting aside the scalded pig she was shredding for brawn to accost me as I burst like a firecracker through the kitchen door. "Are you foolhardy or demented? Have you forgotten his lordship declared you are never to set foot anywhere in this house? If he finds you here there's no knowing what he'll do. . . . More than a sound beating, I shouldn't wonder."

"I've no time to spare for that," I said brusquely. "Tell me quickly where Miss Goodchild is."

Connie was working at the table, scrubbing flatirons with a mixture of beeswax, salt, and powdered brick. She looked me hard in the face. "Still sweet on her, are you?"

"This is no time for jest. Just tell me where she is," I fairly shouted at her.

"Calm yourself, Nathaniel. Don't worry yourself over your precious Miss Goodchild, rest assured she's stayed safe. I'll tell you the same as I told Lady Foley two hours since. I saw her go out this morning early in her walking clothes."

"And where's Robert Montfort?"

"It's him not her that should be your worry," said Mrs. Cummings, nodding sagely. "His lordship's temper's no better than his father's. He meant it when he told you never to set foot here."

"Where is he?"

"He has passed the morning quietly in the library, at his papers. I took coffee in to him not half an hour ago," interrupted Connie. "But Mrs. C. has reason, you'd be foolish not to take heed . . ."

I waved away her worries impatiently. "Don't trouble yourself on that account. I've come with Lord Foley, and he's gone to smooth things with him. In any case I believe Robert was responsible for his father's and Partridge's deaths, and that he suspects Alice knows as much and will kill her for it."

"Oh my good lord, pray tell me it isn't true," said Mrs. Cummings, growing pinker by the minute.

"I wish I could assure you, ma'am, but I cannot. I fear he is capable of perpetrating the most vicious evil."

"And how exactly does Lord Foley propose to smooth things for you?" said Mrs. Cummings.

"He will say I am here to ask some questions of Connie concerning Lord Montfort's death."

Mrs. Cummings was now caught up in the urgency of my quest. "And you think that will keep him quiet, do you?" She shook her head as if astonished at my stupidity. "In that case, for heaven's sake, man, ask the questions you came to ask. You haven't time to sit about and chatter."

I nodded and turned to Connie. "The pistol in Montfort's hand—it was his own, I believe?"

"If it was I'd never set eyes on it before. He kept a pair in a drawer, in case of robbers and vagabonds, but this was a different weapon," she replied.

Her reply surprised me. I was certain that on the night of Montfort's death Miss Alleyn had identified the gun as her brother's. "Are you sure? Whose was it then?"

"I just told you I don't know. If you're not going to believe what I tell you, why bother asking?" she said.

"Never mind the pistol then. What do you know of leeches?"

She gave me a pert wink. "More than you, I'd be bound. I've applied the creatures to all parts."

"There's enough sauce already in the jug, Connie," said Mrs. Cummings. "Any more and it'll be spilling on the table."

Connie scowled back and scrubbed harder.

"Did you tend to Montfort's leeches?"

"Tend to them? No more than I tend to you."

"I mean did you look after them? Answer me plain, Connie. This is important."

Her eyes rested on my face. "I did more often than not. Though Miss Alleyn or Elizabeth more usually applied them."

"Where were they kept?"

"In a stone jar in his closet. The jar was filled with water. When he called for them, we'd fish them out half an hour early, to make them bite better. Then we'd take them to him in a glass with a dish of milk."

"And then?"

"Usually Miss Alleyn or Elizabeth would wipe the part the leeches were to bite—neck or head in the main—and smear that part with milk to encourage them. Then the leeches, two or three of them, were put in a glass and turned over on the spot. Afterwards we'd return them to the jar or, if he wanted, put them on a dish of salt so he could see the blood they'd taken."

During this exchange Mrs. Cummings was still busy with her brawn, listening with half an ear to all we said. Knowing this made it difficult for me to ask Connie what it was she'd tried to tell me when I was staying in Hindlesham, and again in London when she wrote to arrange a meeting. I sensed she'd say nothing in front of Mrs. Cummings. Just then, however, the cook finished pressing the meat into muslin cloths and bustled towards the larder, muttering something about bay leaves, mace, and vinegar. Connie was still engrossed in her description of the habits of leeches, but seeing Mrs. Cummings would not be gone long, I dared interrupt her.

"Connie, tell me quick. What was the article of news you had for me when you came to the inn, and when you wrote to me?"

"Oh, that." She shrugged. "I thought you'd taken no notice, for you never came to meet me."

"I couldn't come to Covent Garden when I was with Foley at Whitely. Course I took notice, I've come here quick as I could, haven't I?"

She tossed her head as if my lack of interest didn't bother her. "It was the valet that remarked it first. And afterwards when I thought on it I wanted you to know."

"Know what?"

But Connie said no more except that she'd rather show me, so I could decide for myself, than tell me and put thoughts in my head. She turned her gaze in the direction of the larder, where Mrs. Cummings was still conveniently occupied. Abandoning her half-finished work, Connie placed a finger to her lips and beckoned me to follow. She led me up the narrow back stairs, through the first-floor servants' passage to Henry Montfort's bedchamber.

It was a vast, splendidly furnished room of pea green walls and heavy damask curtains. Two walls were adorned with extravagantly framed family portraits, the largest of which was a full-length likeness of Henry Montfort in hunting dress with an array of dead game spread at his feet. Another wall sported a dozen or more swords, pistols, and lances mounted to form an intricate design. Opposite, a large bay window overlooked the park, through which streamed motes of winter sun. Despite the light, the room seemed somehow dulled by the heavy pictures and draperies. Looking around, I felt this was a room in which one would never be warm or comfortable. I fancied I could still see the indentation of Montfort's heavy body on the counterpane where they'd laid him out. I felt myself observed by his portrait. I could hear his rasping voice, smell his tobacco and sour brandy breath.

I gazed disconsolately out of the window. Clumps of woodland led to the reed-fringed lake and the island with its tower folly set like an accusing finger against the sky. I wondered where Alice had chosen to take her stroll, then feeling irritable and impatient for her return, turned back to the room and Connie. She was standing on the far side of the window, where a gentleman's embroidered jacket, waistcoat, and breeches were hanging on a coat stand before a cheval mirror, as if waiting to be donned. Ranged beneath was a pair of colored slippers.

I recognized the costume as the one Montfort had worn the night he'd died. The rusty bloodstains were still visible on the collar and sleeve of the coat. Connie came directly to the point. "Do you remember remarking anything about Lord Montfort's feet on the night he died?"

"His feet? I remember that his shoes had no blood on them, and from that deducing it could not have been he who made the footprints."

"Anything else? Did you observe his feet earlier that same evening?" she persisted.

I thought back to that night. Dimly I recalled crawling on the ground among the seated diners to retrieve the oranges I'd spilled. I'd seen the diamond buckles on Foley's and Robert Montfort's shoes from beneath the table. But that was *after* Lord Montfort had left.

"No. The last thing I remember of Lord Montfort alive is hearing his footsteps retreating. Where's the significance in that?" I said.

Ignoring my question, she stooped to pick up the slippers by the mirror and handed them to me. They were made from soft blue morocco with a small heel and a black riband, such as fashionable gentlemen often wear indoors.

"Are these the same shoes that were on his feet in the library?"

"I believe so, yes."

"You are correct. I assisted the valet Forbes to lay him out. You may be quite sure there is no mistake; they are the same pair."

I put the slippers down gently where she'd found them. I was on the point of saying "What of them?" when suddenly I stopped and picked them up again. I flexed the shoes in my palm, feeling the softness of the soles. Such soft leather as I had never worn, such softness as would make it impossible, were I wearing them, to make my footsteps audible. *And yet I'd heard Montfort's angry footsteps retreating down the hall.*

Connie saw my dark expression and must have suspected the line of my thoughts. "Forbes too was most perplexed when he saw them. He swore Lord Montfort wasn't wearing these shoes when he dressed. He'd have said nothing of it, only the shoes he *was* wearing that night were new, and Robert Montfort asked for them, and now they've disappeared. Forbes says something else has gone missing too. A flask from Lord Montfort's closet. It contained a sleeping draft prescribed by the apothecary."

I turned back to gaze from the window, still muddled by this information. During some part of the evening Montfort had been wearing different shoes. Why would he change them? Because there was something about them he disliked; they were uncomfortable perhaps? It seemed unlikely that a man with Montfort's preoccupations would worry about his feet, and it didn't explain why the first pair had vanished. Had someone else changed them? The murderer perhaps? I remembered the bloody footprints in the library—the fashionable square toe of a gentleman's shoe. Were Montfort's shoes responsible for those prints? Was that why his shoes had been changed? Then I considered the medicine bottle. Why would that go missing? Had Montfort taken a sleeping draft that night after all? In which case, why employ the leeches as well? I looked back at the garments hanging on the stand, and at the rusty stains of blood spattering both sleeves. It was the blood on both sleeves that had made me sure Montfort had been murdered. But I hadn't comprehended then, nor did I comprehend now, the reason for the leeches.

I returned to the matter of the gun. Connie said it wasn't Henry Montfort's. Guns raised another disturbing thought in my mind. Alice had said she had discussed pastimes with Robert Montfort and he had declared himself a keen shot. Was this the reason for the invitation to Horseheath? Had he inadvertently let slip to *her* that the murder weapon belonged to him, then realizing his error decided to plan her death? In this confused state I cast about the room to see if anything else here might afford any prospect of a clue. I looked at the weapons on the wall to see if any of the pistols were missing. None was. The arrangement was perfectly symmetrical. Connie waited attentively by the bed, observing my face for signs of my thoughts. My gaze swept past and came to rest in the alcove behind her. In it stood a plain mahogany writing bureau. I had never considered that such a piece of furniture might be in Lord Montfort's bedchamber, assuming that since he possessed such a finely appointed library, all his private correspondence would be contained within it. But of course this was a foolish assumption; the library was only recently completed. While I was installing it Montfort must have kept his private correspondence here.

I strode towards the alcove, even as I opened my mouth to speak. "What you say is all most interesting, Connie, and I believe it to be mightily significant. And now, since you have brought me here, it occurs to me there may be more to find in this room, perhaps inside this bureau."

Without waiting for her reply, I turned the key and tried the flap. Lying inside was a slender monogrammed leather-bound volume. It contained sheets of paper, several of which protruded from the binding. Clearly this was Montfort's letter book. I had searched for it in the library, wondering who might have removed it, never drawing the obvious conclusion that he might have kept it elsewhere.

The first page was a note scrawled in a hand I identified as Montfort's.

What reason have I to continue? Foley, you may bear this much upon your conscience for the remainder of your days. I pray to God it may send you more demented than I. Thanks entirely to your actions I am deprived of a great portion of my estate. You have pitched me into a melancholy from which I can discover no release, you have transformed my days to perpetual night. . . . I cannot continue in the knowledge that you have triumphed over me.

Montfort

The second was written in the elegant, careful hand that I recognized as Partridge's.

Cambridge   Dec. 31

Madam,

How can I thank you for your kind offer to intervene with his lord-ship on my behalf? I would urge you to explain to him that while I have been told he is my father I have no proof of this, and even if I did I wouldn't wish to make any claim upon his estate or his fi-nances. Despite being raised as a foundling, I have been provided with a trade and a talent, and thus, I always believed, the where-withal to support myself in the future. Only in recent weeks have a chain of unhappy events altered my circumstances and cast my fu-ture into doubt.

Thus to my petition. I humbly request that his lordship will grant me a modest *loan* with which to start my own enterprise, on the solemn understanding that the money *will be repaid* as soon as I am able. The security for the sum will be my stock. I send herewith a box as a sample of my skills together with several drawings. If the box and its contents make no impression on him, I pray it will nonetheless prove to him that I am no adventurer or fortune hunter but an honest craftsman.

I will, as you suggest, arrive at Horseheath this evening after dark and wait until he is willing to speak to me. I'll come to the library window as soon as I see your signal.

Until that moment I am, madam, your most grateful servant,

John Partridge

I lowered myself heavily onto the bed and dropped my head in my hands. For some time I sat there, dazed by my discovery, dazzled by the startling thoughts it provoked. All that I had groped so long to compre-hend was now becoming clear. Understanding emerged from confusion like a landscape becoming slowly visible as dawn breaks. I saw now how my logic had taken a wrong turn, how I'd run upon false premises. I understood how my consuming preoccupations had deceived me. I felt as though I were on the deck of a ship that has come into port after a long voyage, watching antlike figures moving on the quayside. I knew the people were familiar to me, I knew that they were preparing themselves for my arrival, yet for the time being I could not make out who was who, and I had absolutely no connection with them. Connie seemed to sense my distance and to know she couldn't reach the place where I had gone. She looked on wordlessly, waiting for me to speak.

I walked over to the window, still holding the letters in my hand, wondering how to begin, how to frame a coherent explanation of the path my thoughts now traced. I had yet to open my mouth when my attention was abruptly diverted.

In the parkland below, some short distance from the house, two ladies emerged from a copse of trees and began to traverse the grassland in the direction of a Palladian bridge leading to the island. They walked leisurely, cloaks billowing softly as occasional gusts of wind caught them. Even from this distance, by the way she raised her hands to speak, inclining her head towards the other, I could see that one of them was Alice.

The other, standing slightly behind her, was no less distinctive. She was wearing a tall black hat, veiled to mask her face, and a cloak of oxblood red. Who was she? I looked down at the letters which I still held in my hand. Dreadful conviction gripped me. The person with Alice was the person to whom Partridge had addressed this letter. The person who had promised to help him. I knew her identity with as much certainty as if she had been standing barefaced not two feet distant from me.

"Dear God, I thought you said the other ladies would not return till this afternoon?" I cried out. "I thought you told me Miss Goodchild had gone out alone?"

Connie looked askance at the sudden change of my tone. "I said nothing of the sort. Miss Alleyn and Elizabeth Montfort altered their plans. They arrived early this morning, just in time to see Miss Goodchild going out for her walk. One of them must have taken it upon herself to accompany her. I can't tell from this distance which of them it is. Why do you look so pale, Nathaniel? You told me it was Robert you feared, not one of them."

By now Alice and her companion had followed a narrow winding path that bordered the reed beds on the edge of the lake and arrived at the bridge leading to the island and the tower in its midst. At the center of the bridge I saw them halt and lean over the balustrade to gaze at a pair of swans gliding beneath them. I saw the veiled figure gesture to draw Alice closer towards the edge. I saw Alice lean further over to see more clearly what her companion pointed out. Then, horror of horrors, I watched the scene unfold as in a dream. I saw her companion move behind her, hunching her shoulders purposefully, raising her hands as if she would thrust Alice over the rail. Instinctively I opened my mouth to shriek out a warning: *Alice, come away! Beware of your treacherous companion!* But the window was closed fast, and even if it had been open the distance was too great for me to make myself heard.

I was quite unable to help her.

But perhaps the strength of my feeling reached her on some mystical level, or perhaps some kind angel watched, for just at that moment Alice's attention was drawn by a bird taking flight. She raised herself, looking upwards, stepping away from the edge, colliding with the figure behind her. I could see Alice's jolt of surprise, her bow of apology, and the other figure nodding and patting her arm, as if to reassure her she'd taken no offense. But even as I sighed with relief, another dreadful threat became manifest.

Instead of returning the way they'd come, the two women turned in the opposite direction. The veiled figure signaled towards the wooden mound on the island and the tower that rose from it. Alice nodded her acquiescence. The next thing I saw was the two of them strolling off arm in arm over the bridge, towards the tower, out of sight.

I knew then with absolute certainty two things. First, Alice remained utterly oblivious to the danger she was in. Second, what was about to happen. Alice had stumbled upon information that would identify the killer, but she didn't yet know it. Once Alice reflected on what she knew, or discussed it with me, her identity would become clear. For that reason she intended to kill Alice as a matter of urgency.

"Dear God!" I shouted. "I know who it is. And Connie, I must stop her! Did you not see her try to push Miss Goodchild over the parapet? Go immediately to find Foley. Tell him I know the answers now, and to send someone for Westleigh. Do it quickly, for pity's sake!"

Even while I was gabbling these instructions, I'd grasped the late Henry Montfort's sword from its mounting on the wall, buckled the belt round my waist, and gone out of the door, down the stairs, bounding through the corridors, almost running John the footman through with the sword before I heard her screeched assent. I hollered back and charged off again through the kitchen. With the clumsiness of haste I stumbled into the table, sending a bowl of goose fat flying across the flag-stones. But I ignored Mrs. Cummings's cry of "Where has Connie got to, and what in heaven's name are you about?" For by then I was already in the yard, racing towards the tower.

Chapter Twenty-six

The lake lay in a saucer of ground, surrounded by thickets of firs and deciduous trees, towards the southern boundary of the estate. In its center was a steep, densely wooded island with a gothic tower rearing from its summit. The only access to the island was via the Palladian bridge, which spanned two small promontories where the gulf between island and shore was narrowest.

When I began to sprint across the grass, I caught occasional glimpses of the tops of the ladies' heads bobbing through the trees. But soon, as I descended lower and they progressed deeper into the woods on the island, neither woman was visible.

I gulped great breaths of air, all the while praying to God to protect Alice by aiding me on my way. But my prayers went unanswered. The deeper I descended towards the bridge, the more hostile the landscape became. The grass was meager; the path meandered among bare willow trees and tufts of reeds taller than I. The ground here was soft and marshy; oozing mud gripped my soles in heavy clods, making every step feel as if the soil itself were intent to hinder my progress.

After what seemed an eternity, at last I came to the bridge and crossed to the island. Once on land again I followed a leaf-strewn path that ascended through the undergrowth towards the lonely tower. Now the ground rose steeply and grew firmer. Surely, I told myself, I must be gaining ground on Alice and her companion; but if I was I had little sense of it. All around me the trees formed a dense wall. Dwarfed by proximity to one another and molded by exposure to the wind, they were strangely misshapen, bowing over the path with intertwined branches, allowing no glimpse of the route ahead or the tower, and only the slenderest of openings to the sky. Thus it seemed I had traced the dark meandering tunnel for an interminable distance when the woods abruptly ceased. I emerged into a grassy clearing suffused with brilliant winter sun. The tower stood a few yards away, a slender construction with narrow pointed windows punctuating smooth walls and a battlemented platform at the top. An arched door had been flung open to reveal a shadowy staircase leading to the top.

I could see no sign of Alice or her companion, but I could hear their voices echoing from within, and halfway up I thought I glimpsed a shadowy figure flash past the tracery. Without pausing to recover my breath, I clambered to the door and began to scale the spiral staircase three steps at a time, holding my sword tight against me so it didn't clank against the stone wall and alert them to my presence.

All the while I ascended I could plainly hear the voices of the women above me growing closer. Snatches of their conversation were audible. I caught Alice, oblivious to the danger she was in, saying, "So kind of you to take the trouble . . . the greatest gratitude . . ." To which her companion answered, "The panorama . . . so splendid . . . you will be enchanted."

There was no mistake. I could not avoid the chilling intention in the voice of Miss Alleyn.

I acknowledged then how foolish I'd been, how dangerous an emotion compassion can be, how Miss Alleyn had beguiled me. Her financial dependence on her relatives had reminded me more than a little of my own situation with Chippendale, and I'd sympathized with her predicament. By treating me with kindness, by making concerned inquiries, by seemingly helping me in my quest, she'd nurtured my solicitude, and I'd never considered the possibility that she alone might be responsible for these dreadful crimes.

I scaled the corkscrew steps, and little by little the dark became less profound. By the time I drew near to the top, dizzy with turning, shafts of light speckled with motes of dust streamed down on my head. I staggered molelike out of the stairwell and stood for a minute watching. Neither Miss Alleyn nor Alice had suspected my approach. They stood with their backs to me. Miss Alleyn had Alice by the elbow and had led her to the very edge, to a place where the battlement dipped no higher than her knee. She pointed down at something beneath, as I'd seen her do on the bridge. Beyond their heads, in the far distance, the silhouette of Horse-heath Hall stood black and dismal against a bright blue sky.

Horror overwhelmed me, but I dared not shout. To do so might pre-cipitate Miss Alleyn into acting too swiftly for me to intervene. "Do you see the hall?" she was saying. "Is it not a spectacular prospect?"

Those words caused my hands to tremble and blood to pound as if dri-ven by a piston through my skull. I unsheathed Montfort's sword and rushed headlong towards them.

"Good day to you, ladies," I cried out.

Both women spun round. Alice looked first at me and then at the sword with openmouthed astonishment. Beneath the dense black veil Miss Alleyn's face was invisible, but I believed I could sense her hatred.

"You? Why do you come here? What does this mean?" she spat.

"What it means," I said, lowering my sword and stepping neatly be-tween Alice and the parapet, "is that I have discovered your evil secret."

"I've no notion to what evil secret you refer," said Miss Alleyn. Abruptly, she released Alice and strode some distance off. She surveyed the silent landscape, the glittering lake, the skeletal trees, the sullen mass of Horseheath Hall beyond. "I didn't kill my brother, if that's what you're implying. What reason could I have to wish him dead? I do not profit from his demise, as I'm sure you're aware."

"I know you did not kill him," I replied softly. "But I also know what malevolent deeds you *did* perpetrate. And what evil is in your mind now."

"What is in her mind?" interposed Alice, who was clearly still baffled by my presence. "Tell me instantly, Nathaniel. I believed her to be a gentle soul. Does she mean *me* ill?"

"Alice," I replied, "before I explain any of this, there is one thing I have yet to prove and I would ask you to answer me plainly. When you discussed pastimes with Robert Montfort, did he chance to mention his aunt?"

"What?" said Alice in puzzlement.

I repeated myself more slowly. "The conversation between you and Robert Montfort—it took place at Bradfield's reception. I believe it was crucial, and that something said then was the reason Miss Alleyn intended to kill you. I recall you discussed pastimes with Robert. Was mention made of Miss Alleyn during that conversation?"

"Why yes," she replied, "I believe he did mention her. He said he en-joyed shooting, then he laughed and I asked him why. He commented then that the entire family partook of the same sport, including his aunt, Miss Alleyn. He said that it was a most curious hobby for a woman of her demure and timid appearance. No one would suspect her of squashing an ant, let alone brandishing a pistol."

I nodded heavily. "And where was Miss Alleyn during this conversation?"

"I don't rightly recall, but I suppose she must have been nearby, for it was not long after that she invited me to Horseheath."

Here was confirmation, though by now I scarcely needed it. The flaws in many of her explanations were now all too obvious: she had concealed Partridge's visit on the day of his death from me; she had told me the gun that shot Montfort was his own; she had pretended to know nothing of Madame Trenti. The gun that shot Montfort must have belonged to her.

Alice opened her eyes wide. "Do you truly believe Miss Alleyn brought me here *to kill me*?"

"Yes, for ever since this business first began she has become increasingly fearful of apprehension. It was that fear which propelled her most brutal actions."

Until now Miss Alleyn had stood rooted to the spot. My mention of her viciousness seemed unaccountably to agitate her. She began to circle Alice and me. "Hopson, didn't I tell you already *I didn't kill my brother?*" she screamed.

"Hush, Miss Alleyn," said I to her. "Did I not tell you I believed you? I know you were not responsible for his death, but what of the other two? What of poor Partridge, whom you murdered so brutally? What of Madame Trenti, whom you told me you didn't know, yet strangled in her bed?"

Alice gave a short gasp. "Nathaniel, can you be sure of this? Only yesterday you declared it was Robert Montfort who was responsible for Trenti's death."

"And you were right to disbelieve me, Alice. As to Miss Alleyn's intentions—there is no doubt in my mind. I saw her try to kill you on the bridge. If I hadn't arrived, I believe you would already be lying dead at the foot of this tower."

At this Alice's face became so pale I feared she was about to faint. Seeing her predicament, Miss Alleyn gave a short burst of laughter and moved towards us both, until she was standing no more than two feet away.

I addressed her directly. "Madam, you should understand the time for subterfuge is over now. Come with me back to the hall. We will call for Westleigh and Foley, and you can explain your actions honestly to them."

Still Miss Alleyn said nothing, but her head was now bowed, as if she were considering her position. An instant later and her emaciated shoulders began to shudder, her bony fingers twisted at her veil. Then with a swift gesture she threw back her veil and revealed herself. The expression on her face was such as I had never seen before, and hope fervently never again to witness. Her eyes were wild, the nostrils of her long nose flared, her lips no more than a line. "My actions were the only solution," she hissed. "What fate decrees I should endure being treated as a servant? Why should I be denied my right? Why should I not reclaim it?"

With this she fixed her eye directly on Alice. Before I realized what brutality was in her mind she swooped towards her, grabbed her by both elbows, and hauled her backwards to the edge of the tower. She was a tall woman, far stronger than she had previously appeared. Alice struggled, wrenching her arms in frantic efforts to pull free. She surveyed the dizzy drop beneath and stared back at me in bewilderment. I began to inch forward, but as I did so Miss Alleyn moved a step closer to the edge. "Stay away!" she howled. "Any nearer and we'll both fall."

"What do you want?" I said quietly.

"What Foley promised me. What is mine by right!"

Alice tugged at her captor's grip, her face contorted with effort.

"Release Miss Goodchild and I will do what I can to assist you."

Miss Alleyn gave a hysterical laugh, tears now coursing down her cheeks. "Never."

"You must know that what you ask is impossible to provide in an instant."

Alice was still writhing and twisting vainly.

"Then this is all the choice I have!" Miss Alleyn screamed.

I was already raising my sword. Alice was so preoccupied by her struggle to be free she was taken by surprise to find herself suddenly released. She lost her balance at the very moment Miss Alleyn gave her a firm push.

I thrust Miss Alleyn out of my path and ran to Alice. I recall the cunning in Miss Alleyn's eyes at the instant she eluded me, seized Alice again, and hurled her in the path of my sword. I dropped my weapon; it clattered to the ground and Alice tumbled alongside it, shrieking in pain at a wrench to her ankle. I recall then the triumphant gleam in Miss Alleyn's eyes, swiftly followed by a very different expression. She lost her footing and tumbled backwards over the parapet. Sheer terror was writ upon her face as she fell, openmouthed, howling. Until her body hit the ground with a final thump, and the landscape was once more silent.

Chapter Twenty-seven

Beyond the library windows the last rays of afternoon sun streaked the park with gold as a carriage set out for the apothecary's shop in Cambridge, bearing the injured Alice. Inside, a somber group—Foley, Bradfield, Elizabeth, Wallace, and I—waited for the arrival of Westleigh and Robert. In a turmoil I strode the length of the room, at once anxious to avoid the attentions of others and yearning to unburden myself. Up and down, back and forth I went, head bowed, pondering, shaking my head as I reflected on each strange feature of these events, marveling at how each piece that had once so confounded me now fitted so easily into place.

My ruminations were still under way when we heard footsteps in the hall and Robert Montfort entered, accompanied by Westleigh. They had been cursorily apprised of recent events, and their faces revealed candid astonishment and a hunger to know the details of all that had passed. Robert, still dressed in his caped surtout and outdoor boots, glanced at me with what seemed a conciliatory air. I wondered briefly if Foley had pacified him as he'd promised, or whether I'd misread his mood and was about to fall prey to a violent assault.

"So, Mr. Hopson, I gather you have finally concluded this matter in the most dramatic manner and desire to explain it to us," he said, addressing me with customary hauteur but no obvious menace. "My aunt is dead. I understand she was the murderess you sought." He began unbuttoning his coat as he spoke. "I confess her duplicity still astounds me. How inconceivable to think she killed her own brother! My aunt was evidently lunatic. Would you not agree?"

I shook my head grimly. "Your aunt was a murderess, sir. She murdered my friend Partridge and she murdered Madame Trenti. But I do not believe she was lunatic—indeed there is a warped logic to all her actions—nor did she kill your father."

Bemusement flitted over Robert's face. "I don't take your meaning, Hopson."

"He did it himself. I mean, my lord, that your father took his own life in a fit of melancholy brought on by his gambling losses. Miss Alleyn found his body and tampered with it to make it *appear* he had been murdered."

Robert Montfort regarded me distrustfully. "And why should she kill two people entirely unconnected with her?"

"May I suggest, my lord, that before we consider the murders we begin with the death of your father, Lord Montfort. For therein lies the key to this entire tragedy."

There was no mistaking his readiness to protest. "I see you still insist upon ignoring the directions of those of superior rank, and give yourself the airs of a gentleman," he said.

"That was far from my intention, my lord."

Robert's expression darkened. Observing the rapidly deteriorating situation, Westleigh held up his right hand. "One moment please, gentlemen. Robert, I pray that you give Hopson leave to explain these events as he thinks fit. For like it or no, it is he who's apparently unraveled them."

Robert scowled and sat down in a chair by the fire. Westleigh nodded curtly towards me. I needed no more encouragement to begin my address.

"On New Year's Day, Lord Montfort was filled with despair. He had lost a considerable sum to Lord Foley and spent the morning with Mr. Wallace, his lawyer, arranging the settlement of the debt. To him, life without such a substantial portion of his estate seemed worthless. In recent weeks he had often considered taking his own life, but he resolved to do it not simply as a means of relieving his misery but also as an act of vengeance. The final gamble was that if he killed himself he stood to cheat Lord Foley of his winnings. I think if we question Mr. Wallace he will verify that Lord Montfort was much preoccupied by how the *manner* of his death might affect the validity of the documents he had drawn up immediately prior to it. At the dinner table that night, I overheard a snatch of conversation suggesting they had recently discussed the matter at some length."

Wallace nodded his affirmation. "Indeed, you are correct, Mr. Hopson. Lord Montfort asked me repeatedly what might happen if he died that night."

"But what was the purpose of meddling with the corpse? Why did my aunt act as she did?" interrupted Robert harshly.

"Her motive was simple enough, bearing in mind her predicament. Remember, since becoming a housekeeper here, Miss Alleyn had found herself in an embarrassing position. Her brother treated her little better than a servant, delighting in tormenting her with threats of casting her out." I turned to where Elizabeth Montfort was seated. "You, my lady, battling under your own preoccupations, offered her little support." I looked at Robert. "You, whom she'd treated as a son, were no more solicitous. Consider then how this impotence, this apparent ingratitude, must have eaten away at her. Consider how she must have yearned to alter her circumstances, to have what she believed she justly deserved."

"Do you accuse Elizabeth and myself of being unkind to her and turning her demented?" said Robert sharply.

I replied unfalteringly, for no longer did he hold any fear for me. "No, my lord, I am merely explaining what took place. I am trying to make you comprehend the logic in her actions. To continue: your aunt spoke of her tribulations to Lady Foley, who in turn discussed the matter with her husband. Lord Foley pondered the situation and when, soon after that, he beat Lord Montfort at cards, he promised Miss Alleyn that the winnings should be hers. This was his revenge for a slight committed by Montfort some twenty years earlier."

"Then *Foley* was to blame . . . ," interposed Robert Montfort.

At this Westleigh stamped a boot upon the floor. "Silence, sir, I beg of you! Allow Mr. Hopson to speak without further intrusion. The time for apportioning blame will come later, when we have heard *all* he has to say."

I hurried on, avoiding Robert Montfort's eye. "Once Lord Foley's offer was made, Miss Alleyn saw the independence she craved come within her reach. Then, some time before the settlement date arrived, she made a calamitous discovery. Perhaps she overheard a conversation between her brother and Wallace, or perhaps she was present at a consultation between her brother and the apothecary Townes. In any event, by whatever means, she fathomed beyond any doubt that her brother intended to kill himself."

I hesitated and surveyed my audience one by one. Their gazes were on me; they were engrossed by my discourse. "Suicides, as all of you are doubtless aware, are generally declared *non compos mentis* in order to prevent their estates being claimed by the crown. Miss Alleyn certainly realized this. She also comprehended that if her brother were declared insane, his agreement of debt with Lord Foley could be called into question and she might never receive the money she had been promised. Thus it was desperation that prompted her to act as she did."

"But if Montfort shot himself, how did Miss Alleyn have time to meddle with the body? She appeared in the dining room a minute or two after the shot was fired, did she not?" said Westleigh.

"Lord Montfort did not shoot himself. He killed himself with a dose of laudanum, having ascertained a lethal dose by first killing his dog. The valet Forbes observed that the medicine bottle disappeared from Lord Montfort's closet early in the evening of the night he died. In all probability he took a draft before dinner, dosing his dog at the same time. And a second after he left the room. The alcohol he had consumed would have speeded the effects of the dose." I paused, waiting for a reaction, but Westleigh merely waved his hand as if urging me to continue.

"This I believe is what happened: Miss Alleyn found her brother dead or dying in his library. As I said before, she had anticipated such an eventuality, having overheard his threats of suicide. Thus she had formulated a plan and was ready to implement it when the need arose. The necessary equipment had been secreted in the library—I'm speaking here of the leeches, a table salt, some milk in a saucer (necessary, I understand, to make the creatures bite), and a small pistol, which doubtless belonged to Miss Alleyn, and which she was adept at firing."

"How did she know he would kill himself in that particular room, on that particular night?" quizzed Westleigh.

"Naturally she could not be entirely certain. But the equipment was easily portable; once she'd assembled it she could have moved it anywhere she chose. In any case, the library was the most likely choice, given the inordinate significance he attached to the new furnishings. And furthermore, on the very day when he was expected to display the room to his guests, he ordered Miss Alleyn to tell the servants that the room was to be left dark and the fire unlit. What more obvious sign could he give that this was when and where he intended to kill himself?"

"Very well," said Westleigh, a trifle begrudgingly, "continue. What happened when she found Montfort dead?"

"First, she locked the doors to the servants' corridor and the hall to avoid interruption, then she attended to the corpse. Blood was necessary to confuse the scene, thus her next action was to administer the leeches, using milk to encourage them to bite more readily. After some minutes she poured salt on the leeches and thus garnered enough blood to spill some of it on the body and use the rest to form the faint footprints leading to the window. Then she hid the empty salt in the bookcase, where Constance Lovatt later discovered it, and secreted the milk in a drawer of the desk, where it spilled and caused the wood to swell. I noticed the stiffness of the drawer and a strange cheesy smell when I examined the desk recently."

"And the gunshot?" said Westleigh.

"Only when all the arrangements were in place did she shoot Lord Montfort with her own gun."

"But would not the wound from the gun provide all the blood she needed? Why trouble herself with the leeches?" he persisted.

"Because the gunshot would instantly alert the household. It was imperative that immediately afterwards she return to the dining room. There would be no time to make any adjustments to the body, she had to have everything prepared beforehand. She had to leave her brother's body arranged in such a manner that there would be no doubt he had been murdered, and make it appear that the murderer was an intruder, someone outside the household, thus averting suspicion from herself."

Until now Foley had been remarkably subdued. Since my return from the tower he'd sat morosely by the fire, eyes closed as if lost in thought. Hearing Westleigh's last inquiry, he seemed to rouse himself a little and join in. "But she didn't entirely succeed, did she, Hopson? For there *has* been doubt all along as to whether Montfort killed himself. Why did she leave the gun so close to his hand? For it was that which made us doubt the manner of his death."

"Therein lies the irony of the whole episode," I said. "She left the gun some distance away. It was I, in my clumsiness, who stepped on it in the dark and skidded forward, moving the gun within Lord Montfort's reach. I tried to say as much on the evening of the dinner, but Robert Montfort wouldn't hear me. Of course, when Miss Alleyn entered and saw the body, this confused her. She couldn't comprehend how the scene she'd created had been so crucially altered."

Foley was still perplexed. "Whose were the shoes that made the footprints, and why were they different from those outside?" he demanded.

"The footprints inside were made by Miss Alleyn, using her brother's shoes. She took them off his feet, smeared them with blood from the leeches, and then I believe put them on her own feet to walk across the floor. Again this was a detail designed to make us believe an intruder had entered, murdered her brother, and escaped."

Foley scratched his beaklike nose pensively. "But, as I recall, Montfort's shoes were pristine."

"Indeed," I said, "but the valet Forbes remarked that the shoes Lord Montfort was wearing when he dressed for the evening were not the same blue slippers he was wearing when we found his body. The first pair have disappeared, along with the medicine flask. Thus I surmised that after she'd used his shoes to make the prints leading to the window, Miss Alleyn must have disposed of them and put slippers on Lord Montfort's feet in their place."

"And the flask was similarly discarded?"

"Yes," I said. "I own, Lord Foley, I have been as blind as a baby in all this, but it was these trifling details that finally provided the key to my understanding. I thought back to my conversation with the apothecary. He was adamant Lord Montfort was in low spirits and preoccupied with the idea of taking his own life. I remembered Lord Montfort's conversation with Wallace during dinner, when he'd asked if the document would stand even if he killed himself, and how interested Miss Alleyn had been in their exchange. And yet never once did I suspect Lord Montfort actually had taken his own life, until earlier today when I went to his room."

"And what did you find there?" demanded Robert, unable to contain himself an instant longer.

I put my hand to my breast pocket, pulled out the two papers I'd discovered, and handed him the one his father had written in his last moments. "I found this, my lord. I believe it to be your father's suicide note. I took it from his letter book. It is fortunate for us that Miss Alleyn did not realize he kept some of his private correspondence in his bedchamber while his library was being installed, for undoubtedly, had she found it, she would have destroyed it."

While he read his father's last words, I stood up and walked to the window, from where the tower was just visible between two clumps of trees. In my mind's eye I relived the terrible events of that morning. I imagined the figures of Miss Alleyn and Alice poised on the parapet. I saw myself

315

lumbering towards them, sword aloft, the awful shrillness of Miss Alleyn's voice at the moment of confrontation. I saw Alice's terrified face as she comprehended Miss Alleyn's intention; Alice falling; and then the final haunting cry as Miss Alleyn tumbled from the parapet. . . .

"And what is the other letter you hold?" demanded Robert. "Did you also remove that from my father's room?"

"Yes," I said slowly. "It was in his same letter book. It is a letter from my friend Partridge addressed to Miss Alleyn. It was this letter along with your father's that gave me the key to unravel the whole matter, for it showed me that your aunt had arranged for Partridge to be present the night of Lord Montfort's dinner."

Robert held out his arm, clicking his fingers impatiently to indicate I should hand it to him. He read it quickly, then with a shrug of annoyance handed it to Foley, who having perused it, passed it on to Westleigh.

I couldn't tell them how my heart wrenched every time I looked at the paper bearing Partridge's hand. Or how I could picture him sitting in his room writing that letter so innocently to the treacherous woman who would bring about his death.

"Why did Miss Alleyn hand this letter to her brother?" demanded Westleigh.

"I would like to think it was because she wanted to help poor Partridge, but I think it more probable she simply intended it to add to Lord Montfort's distress. He had tormented her for years; she felt justified in tormenting him with evidence of another claimant for his wealth."

"What then was her reason for killing Partridge? He posed no threat to her."

"The killing of Partridge happened inadvertently. Remember, in all this the character of Miss Alleyn is central. She was a deeply troubled woman, consumed by a need to secure her future. She was not prone to sudden outbursts of rage or despair as Lord Montfort was, rather she was cunning and manipulative; a woman of warped moral rectitude, but rectitude nonetheless. She had a great capacity for kindness—I will never forget that she insisted Partridge have a proper burial at Horseheath (perhaps remorse prompted her action), yet she was also capable of acting with rash brutality when threatened. Her unhappy history, you are all familiar with. The loss of her fiancé, her humiliation at her brother's hands, and her desperation to be free of him propelled her actions. She did not *intend* to kill when she embarked on her scheme, though it was always her intention to incriminate an innocent man. She must have known that

Partridge might end at the gallows, for no other reason than that it suited her purpose."

"But why did she pick on Partridge?" said Westleigh.

"Partly because of his link with Lord Montfort. At the time he appeared here unexpectedly she honestly believed he was her brother's son. Had *he* not become enmeshed in her scheme, doubtless a member of staff would have sufficed; perhaps she would even have attempted to lay the shadow of suspicion upon me. At any rate, the unfortunate Partridge was an ideal culprit, with an all-too-convincing motive for murder after his confrontation with Lord Montfort. Thus she lured him back to the house, on a false pretext of helping him—the arrangement is mentioned in this letter. Her real intention, however, was to make Partridge appear responsible for Lord Montfort's "murder." For this reason, she placed the grenadillo box in Lord Montfort's hand and scattered his drawings on the floor, alongside designs by Mr. Chippendale, thus ensuring that the story of Partridge's earlier visit and Lord Montfort's rudeness to him emerged. Remember, Miss Alleyn was very quick to tell us of that disagreement once Partridge's body had been found."

"Why then did she kill Partridge so gruesomely?" asked Foley dubiously.

"Because her plan didn't run as smoothly as she intended. She expected that Partridge would appear *after* the gunshot was fired. But I believe that while Partridge stood waiting in the Italian Garden, he saw lights flickering in the dark windows of the library. He approached the house in the belief that this was the signal he awaited, and that Lord Montfort was now amenable to his petition. Instead, when he scrambled up to the windowsill and looked in, he witnessed Miss Alleyn tampering with her brother's corpse. Perhaps she was poised with the gun at the very moment Partridge caught sight of her, only he couldn't know Lord Montfort was already dead. Imagine then how frantic he must have been to see her holding a gun at the head of the man whom he believed might be his father. Naturally he attempted to intervene. He tried to enter by the window, which I'd left open. At that point Miss Alleyn must have heard him. Realizing that Partridge had witnessed her actions and was on the point of entering the room, she briskly altered her plan. Partridge would still serve as a scapegoat, but she would silence him first."

I broke off then and went to stand by the window where the pool of blood had been. Night had fallen swiftly; there was now no parkland prospect, no Italian Garden, only dark nothingness beyond my own haggard reflection mirrored in the glass.

"I hold myself partly culpable for what happened next. Foolishly I'd left the toolbox by the window. Had I not done so, perhaps Partridge would be with us still. Picture him trying to clamber in from the ground that is some six feet below this room; he must have scrabbled at the wooden frame of the sash here." I pointed to the frame in front of me. "And held on to it like so." Here I made a clawed grip onto the back of a chair. "Seeing him suspended thus, poised to enter and destroy her carefully laid plans, Miss Alleyn was driven by instinct rather than reason." I brought my other hand down in a chopping motion. "She slammed down the sash ferociously on his hands, thus pinioning him to the sill by his palms, and causing the bruising on the backs and palms of his hands that Townes later observed. Then she cast about for a weapon; for some means of getting rid of him. Her eye fell upon the tools left lying there since I had used them, and she picked up a small hatchet."

I faltered again and closed my eyes, trying to banish the hideous image from my mind. "After several brutal blows, she severed the fingers of his right hand. Then she raised the sash again and watched Partridge fall back to the ground, knowing that he might bleed to death, and that even if he survived no one would believe his story. Next she gathered up the severed fingers and hid them in the bottom of the toolbox. The pool of blood on the sill was now the only marker of her butchery, and she hoped it would be read as further confusing evidence that her brother had been murdered after a struggle in which his assailant was wounded."

"Then the bloody mess on the windowsill was made by Partridge, not by Montfort at all?" said Westleigh sharply.

"Yes."

"And the footprints outside were Partridge's?"

I explained slowly. "After he had been attacked, Partridge stumbled away. There was no trail of blood because he'd thrust the wounded hand in his pocket in an attempt to stanch the flow—his coat was heavily blood-stained when we recovered him. But the trauma of his wounds coupled with the cold was too much for him to survive. He walked only a few yards before he became faint. He staggered to the pond, intending perhaps to use the parapet surrounding it as support while he recovered his strength. One of the undergardeners remarked seeing a man leaning over the pond in the early evening. But poor Partridge did not recover his strength. Instead, dizzy from loss of blood, he fell into the pond, where if he was not dead already, he drowned or froze to death. A miserable end for a man who asked no more from life than to know his origins, wouldn't you say?"

Foley looked down at his feet. His brows were knitted in thought, and by the dismal downturn of his mouth I could see he too was moved.

"And the gunshot?" said Westleigh impassively.

"Once she had disposed of Partridge, Miss Alleyn returned her attention to Lord Montfort. She took out the gun, fired it. Then, unlocking the servants' door to the hall, she hurried along the corridor back to the dining room, where she behaved as if she were as astonished as anyone."

"The three fingers discovered in my room," interrupted Robert Montfort. "How did they arrive there?"

I turned to him slowly. "Miss Alleyn placed them there to incriminate you in both deaths when she realized that Partridge was not seriously suspected of the killing of your father."

His face lengthened. "But my aunt was devoted to me," he protested. "She often said I was the son she never had."

"Perhaps, but she had grown disaffected with you of late. Did I not tell you just now that she felt you neglected her predicament? I suppose she was careless when she gathered up the fingers, and that was how I came to find one of them at the bottom of the toolbox."

"And Madame Trenti? What were Miss Alleyn's reasons for killing her?" asked Westleigh, taking command of the proceedings once more.

"Vengeance for her duplicity. You will recall I described Miss Alleyn as a woman of a curious moral rectitude—it is partly this episode that caused me to describe her thus. Miss Alleyn learned of Madame Trenti's pretense from me. Until then she believed Partridge *was* Lord Montfort's child who had been sent to London to the Foundling Hospital. She didn't know that the child died before it ever left for London.

"Hearing that this was nothing but a fabrication, she became outraged. By then, after she had successfully killed Partridge and meddled with her brother's corpse, death no longer seemed fearsome to her. I hazard, moreover, it afforded her an inward satisfaction, because it countered the feeling of weakness she so detested."

"Tell me precisely then, how was Madame Trenti's murder accomplished?" demanded Westleigh.

I answered as plainly as I could. "On Miss Alleyn's next visit to London she was staying with the Bradfields as usual. She was well acquainted with the habits of that household, having stayed there many times before. She rose early, before the household was about, and ordered the groom to prepare a coach, which she drove to Golden Square. Leaving the vehicle hidden in a convenient alley, she found her way into the house through a rear entrance that leads directly to the servants' stairs and to Madame Trenti's chamber. This, by the way, was not a difficult matter since none of the other rooms on that floor were occupied, and most of the servants were busy downstairs in the kitchens.

"Thus, with minimal effort but immense daring, did Miss Alleyn come upon her quarry, who we may imagine was dozing in bed after her breakfast. She tiptoed in through the servants' door, locked the door to the main corridor, then brutally strangled her with a length of lace trimming that was conveniently to hand. Madame Trenti must have awoken as the ligature tightened about her neck, for she gave a single cry just as I stood downstairs, and while Mr. Chippendale approached the door and knocked on it. Soon afterwards he and I met upon the stairs, and returned to try the door again. Miss Alleyn at this time was probably already making her escape. She descended the servants' stairs the way she had come in and hurried back to the waiting carriage." I paused very briefly to draw breath, then continued on, directing my speech now towards Robert Montfort.

"While I was outside the room, I fancied I heard the sound of light footsteps descending the back stairs. They should have told me the killer was a woman, but Miss Alleyn, continuing in her efforts to cast suspicion on you, my lord, had donned your traveling coat. That is why, when I saw her passing beneath the window after I'd found Trenti's body, I believed she must be a man, and suspected you of the murder. Even after I learned your aunt had procured the carriage early that morning, I remembered that coat and her fondness for you, and assumed she had taken the carriage for you."

Robert Montfort was goggle-eyed. "I think it quite preposterous that you should even consider me capable of such a thing," he blustered. "I have warned you before now, Hopson, that I will not tolerate your effrontery."

"Truth is no respecter of rank, my lord. I have been asked to explain it. That is all I am attempting to do."

Robert half rose from his chair, as if he would attack me. I did not drop my gaze.

"Gentlemen, gentlemen, pray calm yourselves!" said Westleigh, swiftly stepping between us. "Mr. Hopson, I would be grateful if you would complete your narrative as briefly as you can. Robert, I have implored you several times already—give him leave to speak."

I waited while Robert sat back in his chair and turned away from me to scowl at the fire. "The only matter I have yet to describe is what I believe to have been an attempt on my life that took place on my return to London after my first visit to Horseheath. My memories of the incident are hazy, but I remember two things quite distinctly. The carriage, banded in green, was the same as the one that I saw flash beneath the window when Madame Trenti died, and the driver wore an identical garb."

I walked nearer to Robert Montfort, fixing him with an accusing stare. "As I have said already, there is no doubt in my mind that the person I saw from the window was your aunt, Miss Alleyn. The previous occasion, however, is altogether different. I cannot be certain whether the driver was the *owner* of the coat, in other words you, my lord, or whether Miss Alleyn had borrowed it."

Silence fell upon the room; Robert Montfort scowled more darkly than ever but refused to meet my eye. Eventually Westleigh intervened. "Whatever makes you doubt it was Miss Alleyn, Hopson?"

"Miss Alleyn had no obvious motive at that juncture to wish me dead. Quite the contrary, I was aiding her cause by trying to discover the killer of her brother."

Westleigh now turned to address Robert directly. "My lord," he said, "a challenge has been made. You are honor bound to answer it honestly. Was it you who ran down Hopson and left him for dead in the gutter?"

Robert Montfort lifted his head but still refused to answer.

"I order you to respond, my lord. What have you to say?" repeated Westleigh more forcefully now.

"What difference does it make, damn it?" cried Robert at last. "If Hopson happened in my way, he has only himself to blame for any accident that befell him. Why, he's nothing but a meddlesome upstart. He was never in peril of dying—and he deserves no better than to find himself in the gutter."

I came towards him, halting squarely in front of his chair. He was seated before the fireplace, beneath the picture of the fall of Icarus against which his father had been sprawled in death. I looked up at the winged figure tumbling helplessly from the sky into the azure sea beneath and the figure of Daedalus flying off to Naples or Sicily, oblivious to the fate of his unfortunate child.

"It was far from being an accident, my lord. You intended to damage me, if not kill me. Your violent action was entirely deliberate, a way of scaring me into submission because you feared my inquiries might diminish your inheritance."

Puce with fury, Robert Montfort stood up and faced me, muttering numerous indecipherable insults. I turned away in disgust, but this only seemed to annoy him more intensely. How dare I have the effrontery to address him thus? How he wished I'd go to the devil. How he wished he had beaten me roundly when he had the opportunity to do so. Then he said something about Alice's injuries being entirely my fault. I knew it was untrue, but I couldn't contain myself. I felt no fear of his bluster, nor awe at his status. A strange emptiness seemed to pervade the room. I was oblivious to all its inhabitants save one: Robert Montfort. I turned back and hit him with all my force.

Chapter Twenty-eight

My dear Alice,

At last I've discovered from Fetherby (who else?) the reason for your silence. He tells me you went away with your brother to take the waters at Bath and convalesce from the injuries you suffered, that the remedies of that city have worked their wonders, and that you've returned restored to health.

To apprise you briefly of what has passed since my last chapter: the madness that made me attack Robert Montfort got me thrown into prison like a common criminal, till Foley paid to have me released. I returned to London without Chippendale's drawings, which Foley refused to hand me despite his earlier promises. He said that since I had yet to take up the matter of Partridge with Chippendale he was taking it upon himself to make a stand. It was no more punishment than Chippendale deserved to be deprived of the designs, and since Elizabeth and Robert Montfort expressed no interest in having them back, and he, Foley, valued them highly, he thought it only just that he should hold on to them.

On discovering I'd come back empty-handed, my master was

true to his threats. He flew into a terrible rage (which reminded me somewhat of Robert Montfort and his father) and without further ado dismissed me. In two respects his gesture was fortuitous. First, it gave me time to compose my account for you of all that had happened. Second, it prompted me to tell Chippendale what I thought of him for the way he treated Partridge. I no longer feared losing my job since I'd already lost it. During our exchange he seemed entirely unabashed. "You are judging a matter you don't begin to comprehend," he declared, lofty as ever, "and your ignorance gives you no right at all to pronounce a verdict."

"If I am ignorant it's because you've failed to explain yourself," I said. "I can only judge by what I see and learn. Partridge's and your sister Dorothy's letters have taught me all I need to know of your cruelty. I saw you outside Madame Trenti's boudoir when there was no reason for such a call. Did she hold some malicious sway over you? Was that why you supplied her with so many furnishings?"

But he refused to answer me, saying only that the truth didn't arrive to those who simply sat there and asked for it like a beggar with his hand out. Truth, like everything else in God's world, had to be earned.

So to the real purpose of the letter. The thousand pardons I owe you. I trust that with the passage of time you've forgiven me the harm I allowed to befall you. I curse myself still for my clumsiness, though I confess it strikes me as strangely curious that the same ham-fistedness that began these events concluded them too.

I must tell you here that through all my recent troubles an unlikely source of comfort has been Foley. Putting aside his awkwardness over the drawings, the man who once irritated me beyond description has turned out to be a patron I might almost describe as benevolent. You know that it was his carriage and his wife that took you so speedily to Cambridge, where Lady Foley ensured that Townes attended to your injuries. When Foley discovered I'd been dismissed, he offered to advance me sufficient funds to begin my own enterprise. When I asked him why he was being so philanthropic, he told me, a little sharply, it was only shrewd investing that allowed him to lead a life of indolence and that I might take or leave his offer as I chose. I take this to mean he feels a little pang of remorse for holding on to the drawings and losing me my employment. But now I'm gone, I'm glad to be free of Chippendale. I think I shall accept the offer.

Thus, Alice, I take my bow with the fervent hope that if you've not done so already this letter might spur you to forgive me enough to read my history of our adventure. Should you do so, I beg you to write and let me know what you make of it.

I am yours, affectionate as ever,

Nathaniel

Chapter Twenty-nine

When Alice arrived, she was the last person I expected to see. It was midafternoon on a Sunday, two weeks since I'd dispatched my last letter and sent her my account of all that had passed. I was alone, whistling a tune I'd heard at the playhouse, sifting through mounds of furniture components in search of a missing saw. Had she arrived a few moments earlier, she'd have found Chippendale hanging at my heels. Since my dismissal he'd barred me from the premises and refused adamantly to allow me to retrieve my toolbox. It was only after I suggested I might let slip to his friend the justice that his account of the day Madame Trenti died wasn't as accurate as it might have been that he'd been persuaded to let me take it.

When I'd entered his premises, he'd glowered over my every move. But after a short time he grew impatient; he hadn't succeeded in intimidating me in the least, and there were things he must attend to in his office. So he'd left me to my own devices. He would examine my boxes once they were packed. If I dared help myself to anything that wasn't mine, he'd summon the watch and make sure I was transported for it.

So there I was, crouching with chisel in one hand, two-foot rule in the other, gawking idiotically at a graveyard of furniture. Mahogany feet carved with claws, deal bed heads, oak tabletops, and panels of veneer. Would I ever amass such a heap of parts, I wondered.

"It is not often I come upon you and find you whistling a tune, and with no pretty companion in your lap."

I recognized the clear tone instantly. She was standing in the doorway holding a package wrapped in brown paper. I felt myself flush to the roots of my hair. How long had she observed me?

Nonchalantly as I could, I stood up and bowed. "I cannot think what you mean," I replied, at once annoyed to find she still had the power to disturb me and relieved to see her looking so well.

"I feared I'd be too late," she said, artlessly proffering her hand.

Forgetting that I was covered with grime, I stumbled eagerly to kiss it, leaving a black imprint on her flawless kid glove. "Are you quite recovered? Late for what?"

She ignored the reference to her health as if it was a matter of little consequence. "I feared that you might have gone."

"How did you know?"

"The carter Fetherby mentioned you'd be returning today, but he was uncertain when exactly."

"His garrulousness has at last worked in my favor."

She stared at me levelly, mysterious as ever. "I am glad you believe so. But he didn't know where you were going, nor for what you were exchanging all of this." Here she waved at the disorderly surroundings, as if to imply I were quitting a palace rather than a dust-strewn garret that stank of turpentine, linseed, and boiled animal bones.

"I've taken Foley's offer of assistance and found premises in St. Martin's Lane. I open them tomorrow."

"A new beginning?"

"Indeed. But Chippendale is here ... if you wish to speak with him."

"Have I not already made it clear it's *you* I've come to see?"

There was silence as I shuffled uncomfortably in the wood shavings, wondering at the purpose of her visit and what I should say and do. The weather had grown warm in recent days, and I cursed myself for not choosing my coat more wisely. My hair felt damp in its ribbon, and perspiration began to prickle my brow. I thought I read disapproval in her glance, a suggestion she was waiting for me to say something more. An instant later it seemed I was mistaken and that she'd sensed my discomposure and taken pity on me, for she asked me to take her somewhere we might talk.

The downstairs shop was unlocked, and I led her back across the empty cobbled yard to a silent showroom furnished as a saloon of the grandest proportions. She wove her way among sofas, chaises, daybeds, and commodes, gliding a hand over damask upholstery and carved and gilded backs, brilliant polish and marble tops. When she spoke it was not at all what I expected.

"And what will you fabricate in your new premises? Will you attempt anything as sumptuous as this?" By now she had traversed the room and, having placed the package on a table, stood looking up at the gargantuan writing cabinet Chippendale had designed for Madame Trenti.

Since Madame Trenti's death and the cabinet's completion it had been placed in the shop: a striking advertisement of the skill and refinement of which Chippendale's establishment was capable. I looked at the cabinet and then back to Alice. Set against its daunting scale, she seemed smaller than she really was, and for some reason its florid design repulsed me even more than usual.

I still didn't fully understand what had been the purpose of Chippendale's visit to Madame Trenti's on the morning of her death, or the reason he had planned to supply her with the most spectacular object he'd ever created when she clearly didn't have the means to pay for it. I still supposed she must have had some secret hold over him, although what that might have been I hadn't fathomed.

"I don't know if I will ever aspire to such extravagant heights. But simpler pieces may bring equal satisfaction and to greater numbers. Do you not agree?" I said.

She stared thoughtfully at the cabinet and then threw a challenging smile at me. "I agree your appetite for dispute is undiminished."

"And you haven't lost your directness," I retorted.

"I'm sad to find you so unfeeling."

There was a playfulness in her tone, but I chose to ignore it. "For what reason am I so cruelly accused?" I demanded peevishly.

"Your expression suggests either I or the cabinet displease you greatly."

Without pausing to reflect, I fell straight in her snare. "You've never displeased me, Alice. As for the cabinet, I confess when I look at it I cannot help thinking of Chippendale, and the thought disturbs me. You already know my antipathy towards him is well founded." I paused, met her eyes directly, and screwed up courage to continue. "As for my feelings towards you—the silence between us for the last weeks has been of *your* instigation, not mine. I sent you letters and my history of all that had happened; I was sure that, having played such a significant part in it, you'd be curious to hear of its conclusion, even if you were angry with me for causing you hurt. Yet you have never responded. It is I who should accuse you of coldness."

Her reaction to my outburst was curious. "I have come to return your account in person," she said, reddening slightly. "That is what the package contains. And I was never angry at you. Far from it: I'd be a half-wit not to realize how closely I brushed with death, how you saved my life. I owe you my heartfelt thanks." As she said this, for a moment I thought I saw an expression of something warmer than mere conviviality flicker in her eyes. Then, like a moth drawn away from a candle stub by the superior light of a chandelier, she settled herself in a chair, returned her gaze to the cabinet, and switched tack completely.

"Is it not fascinating how ordinary wood can be transformed to such an extraordinary object? It is hard for me to have any conception of what the skill and imagination of craftsmen can make of the logs and deals and blocks I sell them," she said.

I was baffled but wanted to see where this would lead. "Without the woods you supply we would be as helpless as an artist without his palette."

She smiled witheringly at my flattery, as if this was not at all what she wanted to hear. "Do you ever wonder, Nathaniel, what secrets a piece such as this might witness during its existence? How long will it endure? Will the unborn descendants of your patrons regard this cabinet with similar esteem? Or will it grow outmoded and stand in some forgotten corner as no more than a curious relic of our insignificant age?"

Was this digression intended to provoke me? Was it some kind of test? If so, for what role was I being challenged?

"You will think me very dull," I said hesitantly, "but I confess I've never troubled myself with such matters. What concerns me most is that the patron is content with his commission and that he might return to order more."

She shook her head impatiently. "Ever the pragmatist, Nathaniel. Then tell me something about this piece. What thoughts shaped its design? How was it crafted?"

Although she was now deferring to my knowledge, the tone of her voice implied a criticism which galled me. I was naturally tempted to show off my expertise, to convince her I was more than the shallow character she believed me to be, but a small voice somewhere inside my head told me that would be pointless. She was too sharp-witted to be hoodwinked by boastfulness. If anything, modesty would beguile her more easily. I composed my face to convey a message of professional detachment.

"It is constructed in three parts from a variety of tropical timbers: chiefly mahogany, ebony, and padauk. The most eye-catching decorations are the mounts made from gilt brass, but there are also morsels of mother-of-pearl and ivory; I believe Chippendale has based them on engravings from Goltzius and Berain," I said solemnly.

She gazed on gilded decorations formed as Nereid masks, cascading water, clusters of seashells, tied ribbons, and fronded scrolls; surfaces inlaid with wood and brass, and meticulously engraved to depict sea monsters, dolphins, temples, trailing vines and acanthus, and birds. A cabinet more decoration than structure, more gold than wood.

"What makes the piece doubly remarkable—apart from its lavishness—is the complexity of its design. There is scarcely a straight side anywhere, and to make such a shape the structure had to be laid in pieces. The minutest drawers inside are formed from boards cut no thicker than a baby's fingernail, with joints of similar delicacy rebated or dovetailed to hold them."

I looked at her again; she was sitting up in her chair, listening intently. Was she putting on a purposeful act of girlishness? Or was she as nervous to see me as I her? She was wearing a new gown of dark amethyst, which enhanced the fieriness of her hair and pallor of her complexion. No shawl or cloak, despite the time of year, as if she'd come out in a hurry. I remembered how she'd looked that day on the tower, when I'd picked her up from the roof and carried her half unconscious with pain through the park to Foley's carriage. She had seemed docile then, so much easier to handle than this unreadable character. And yet the unpredictable has ever drawn me.

Tiring of my knowledgeable dissertation, I concluded abruptly. "And finally there is the veneering to embellish the oak and deal beneath. You see the lively pattern the figuring brings. Each piece reflects the other, bringing balance and symmetry to the form. To create such a repeating effect, the craftsman must cut the veneers as finely as possible from a single block of wood. Of course I don't need to tell you that the more figured the wood, the more brittle it will be, thus this too involves great skill and dexterity." I paused and swallowed uncomfortably. My mouth was growing dry from so much explaining. I wanted her to say something so I might judge her reaction, but she remained silent. "I will not tire you with more details. Far better instead that you should admire the result for yourself." I gestured her forward as, with the flourish of a magician, I swung back the massive outer doors to reveal the interior.

She gasped at the profusion of niches and pigeonholes before her.

"That is not all," I said, enjoying her sudden loss of composure. I handed her a key. "Take this and open the door of the central compartment." She went to do as I instructed but turned back to me.

"There's no lock."

"Another marvel," I said, grinning at her confusion. "The keyholes are hidden in the inlays and can only be opened by touching a particular spot to activate a pressure point." I touched a cherub's hand; the keyhole opened. I inserted the key into the lock and opened the door of the interior compartment. A small cavity was now revealed. "In here alone, Chippendale says, are a dozen more hidden compartments that may be opened only if you know how to release the catches holding the sliding panels. At our last meeting, when he dismissed me, he challenged me to find them before I go."

"Did you try?"

"I confess I did not."

"And yet I would have thought you of all people would know where his secret compartments will be hidden."

"It is not the challenge that daunts me," I said, "for I've no doubt I'd find every space easily enough. What holds me back is knowing that if I accepted the challenge, Chippendale would view it as a tacit admission of his supremacy and be gratified. After all that has gone on, I see no reason to humor him."

She murmured some inaudible response, but she was hardly listening, for she had turned her attention to the inlay on the tiny inner compartments and was bending low to scrutinize them at close quarters. "Here's a curious thing," she said, squinting at one drawer front after another.

"What is curious?" I said, a little annoyed that she'd grown so quickly distracted and turned away from me.

She stood up straight and caught my gaze. "Have you not remarked the wood bandings?"

I shrugged my shoulders before reluctantly stepping forward and bending down to look as she had done.

"It's partridge wood," she said without waiting for me to speak.

Our eyes locked in mutual comprehension and puzzlement. "That is indeed unexpected," I conceded.

"There have been no consignments in recent months. None that I recall since I have taken over the business."

"Then he must have kept some in store." My eyes still held hers.

"Do you not think, bearing in mind the significance of this timber, you should accept Chippendale's challenge after all, and see what secrets his cabinet contains?" she said.

I am, as I've said, expert in divining where even the most artful craftsman might conceal a hidden space. I took out every drawer of the central section and ran my fingers over the aperture beneath, feeling for a bump or a join which might indicate a sliding panel. It took me nearly half an hour to find all the ingenious mechanisms and hidden catches, and to release them with the aid of a cluster of small spiked instruments and keys attached to the fob. At length I'd extracted twelve small drawers from the center and laid them out on the nearby table, leaving a hollow like a mouth behind. We looked at the drawers spread before us. All of them were lined with scarlet velvet as if they were intended to hold medals or coins or jewels. All were empty save one. It contained half a plain gold ring.

As I picked it up and held it in my hand, I felt chilled to the marrow. Removed from its luxurious bed of velvet, held up before the sumptuous golden cabinet, the ring seemed somehow diminished in luster, oddly dull and small.

"What is it?" said Alice.

"Unless I'm mistaken, it is the other half of the ring Foley and I discovered when we opened Partridge's grenadillo box. I don't believe you ever saw it."

I turned the crescent of metal over in my hand. It was inscribed, as the other portion had been, on the inner surface.

"And now I wish only that I had the other piece so I could read the entire inscription properly. From what I remember, the other piece read 'To C'; this reads 'from T. C.'" Alice had turned her attentions to the tiny drawers I'd retracted. She was picking up each one from where I'd laid them to examine the wood.

"A considerable quantity of timber would be required to band such a quantity of drawers."

I was hardly listening, for something else was troubling me. My knowledge of my master's virtuoso skill, together with some vague inkling in my gut, told me finding the ring had been too easy. Chippendale wouldn't place every secret cavity in a single area and provide the instruments to open them, for then they'd be no more than sham secrets, cavities you were meant to discover to stop you from looking elsewhere. With this thought came the conviction that there was something I still hadn't unearthed, something more to find.

I turned my attention to the area behind the writing flap, which was divided into a plethora of pigeonholes, and applied the same careful examination to the panels dividing each compartment. I was halfway up the second space when my forefinger touched on a minute but discernible ridge. I peered into the desk. A line no heavier than one inscribed with a pin dissected the panel. The wood had been joined on this side, while on the other there was nothing. I pressed my finger at each end near to the join, and then at each corner in turn. On my third attempt there was a small click, a catch yielded, and the panel came away. Tucked inside, so far back it was all but invisible, was a small slender box, about the length of my little finger.

"What is it?" Alice said.

I gently pulled out the box and opened it. Inside lay a fragment of paper, covered in writing. But as if it had once been drenched in water, the words were blurred and in some parts illegible. I screwed up my eyes to focus them. The script seemed vaguely familiar, but I couldn't think where I'd seen it before.

"It's almost impossible to decipher," I said, as she peered over my shoulder. Falteringly at first I read out the few phrases I could.

" . . . extremely uneasy at your lengthy silence . . . I have hardly the strength to hold a pen after illness that overcomes . . . very weak still, almost to death. I expect every hour . . . a good woman here has told me of a place . . . they will care tolerably . . . if you remember me, remember also our son . . . will suffer most severely . . . have sent him with the . . . recognize him. The block and this . . ."

I halted. Even as I uttered the words, their significance had struck me. I looked at Alice. She was slumped inert in her chair, apparently lost in thought, hardly listening to me.

"Do you not realize what this is?" I cried, waving the paper under her nose like a flag. "Proof positive of something we never considered."

She took the letter, looked at it hard, and then grew pale. "And what might that be?" she asked quietly.

"Partridge was Chippendale's son." I paused theatrically, expecting her to cry out in astonishment. She said nothing.

I persisted in a louder tone. "Do you not see, this letter can only have been written by Partridge's unfortunate mother on her deathbed? It's here because she sent it to *Chippendale*. That was why Chippendale couldn't allow Partridge to marry Dorothy, his sister. Dorothy was his aunt. That was what he meant when he said they were 'too close.'"

Still Alice was silent. She sat bolt upright in the chair, letter in her lap, staring dead ahead, as expressionless as if I'd said nothing.

"Alice, do you not comprehend me?" I repeated. "Partridge was Chippendale's child. The letter here proves it. The wood is another link, and the initials T. C. in the ring must refer to Thomas Chippendale—"

Suddenly she stood and held up her hand to halt my tirade. "I heard you, Nathaniel," she said almost wearily. "I'd reached the same conclusion. And, what is more, I believe I know who the unfortunate mother was."

Chapter Thirty

Alice explained then that the handwriting was that of her aunt Charlotte, the same relative who'd made the mirror hanging in her parlor. I realized then why the writing had seemed familiar. I'd seen it before on the design we'd consulted to identify the wood from which the temple box was made.

Alice had never known the reason for her aunt Charlotte's sudden departure from London. She had been an infant of scarcely two years when it took place. Afterwards, whenever her aunt's name was mentioned, it was said she'd acted against the advice of her family, left home under a cloud of disgrace, and died soon after from consumption. The whereabouts of her grave and the identity of her fickle betrothed were never discussed, nor, and here Alice was quite adamant, had any mention of a child ever been made.

Now she came to think on it, however, Alice recalled that as soon as Chippendale established his business and began to thrive, her father had manifested a curious antipathy towards him. This first showed itself in the unusually sharp tone of his voice when Chippendale came to buy wood, then in a marked reluctance to provide him with supplies unless it was stock of inferior quality—worm-eaten or rotten or poorly seasoned—that he couldn't sell elsewhere. He had never offered any reason for this dislike, and once Chippendale realized the poor service he was receiving, he took his trade elsewhere. It was only after her father had left on his travels and she learned of the flourishing Chippendale concern that she'd taken it upon herself to reestablish a rapport with his workshop. Now she regretted her actions.

"You cannot blame yourself for your ignorance," I said.

"Had I known, though, I would have felt exactly the same as he. I should never have courted Chippendale's trade." She hesitated. "I only wonder why my father never took care of the child after his sister died."

"Perhaps he knew nothing of it. Your aunt may have been so shamed by her situation that she was unwilling to confide in anyone after Chippendale rejected her. Or perhaps when she was dying and wrote to Chippendale, telling him of the child's existence, he assured her he'd take care of the child and she believed it would be unnecessary to bring further disgrace on her own family."

Alice sighed heavily, as if she couldn't quite convince herself. "Could my father have rejected his own sister, Nathaniel? I shudder to believe it of him. Yet if he did not, why was her name so rarely mentioned? Surely being jilted and falling ill would not be sufficient to have made him shy from speaking of her?"

The confusion in her face made me see she was facing disillusionment in the same way I had on learning of Chippendale's deception. I loved the way her expressions changed so rapidly and reflected her thoughts so frankly. Watching her now, the realization that, just occasionally, I *could* understand her spurred me to do my utmost to distract her.

"We cannot know for certain why Chippendale took on Partridge as an apprentice. Let us view it in the best possible light and believe that he did so deliberately, knowing this talented youth was his son. The fact that he kept Charlotte's ring and letter for all those years and secreted them in the writing cabinet bears out this theory, does it not? It proves he did feel some pang of remorse."

Alice thought about this for a moment. "How can you speak of remorse, bearing in mind the way he treated Partridge? He never viewed him in the same way as his legitimate children. Chippendale may have decided to rid himself of Partridge because he wanted to marry Dorothy, but that was merely an excuse he'd been searching for for some time. Quite simply, he was jealous of Partridge's talent and worried that if Partridge stayed in his workshop his own position, and later that of his legitimate offspring, would be usurped."

"As jealous of his talented son as Daedalus was of Talos?" I said wryly.

"Perhaps. Though I still hold the relevance of that story to be no more than a strange coincidence. If you deal a pack of cards on a table or roll a pair of dice, sequences may repeat themselves. Is it destiny, or God, or merely blind chance if a pair of sixes appears twice?"

Suddenly I didn't disagree. "You may be right, for there's another reason that might explain it."

"What's that?"

"Madame Trenti. She was prepared to blackmail Montfort on the subject of his illegitimate child. Who's to say she didn't uncover the truth about Partridge and try the same with Chippendale? Perhaps on her visit to the Foundling Hospital she found evidence linking Partridge to Chippendale. She removed the evidence, fearing that if it remained her story that Partridge was Montfort's son would be ruined. But she used the discovery nonetheless. Knowing how Chippendale's reputation was of paramount importance to him, she threatened him with the scandal of his illicit liaison. And that would explain his reason for creating for her such a lavish piece of furniture, would it not?"

I had scarcely finished speaking when I heard the creak of an upstairs door and the slow thud of Chippendale's boots descending the stair.

"Hopson, is that your voice I hear? Who's with you? What are you about? Not thieving my stock, I trust."

Instead of calling out to him, I fixed my eyes on Alice's, held a finger to my lips, and gestured towards the door. She nodded back at me, round-eyed and docile. Taking her hand, I led her out through the side door to the street. "Wait here," I whispered. "I shan't keep you long."

I stepped back inside and came face-to-face with Chippendale. He was looking down at the writing cabinet's drawers still spread over the table, and back at the gaping hole from where we'd removed them.

"So now you've dismantled my masterpiece and got at the truth," he said quietly. "Perhaps you'll rest easier than I."

But in place of the fury I might have expected to cloud his face, I saw a flash of something else. I still do not know what to call it precisely. Remorse? Satisfaction? Triumph? A mixture of all three? Whatever it was, I knew I'd no need to feel trepidation. It was only later that I began to understand that my finding the letter was thanks as much to his skillful manipulation as to my own clumsy efforts. It was his challenge that made me search the cabinet. He had granted me permission to find the truth; he was still a master of his craft.

But that realization came only with hindsight. At the time I foolishly believed it was I who'd gained the upper hand. "As you see, sir," I said firmly, "I've examined your handiwork, admired its ingenuity, comprehended how you constructed it. For my taste there is a surfeit of novelty here. I prefer my furniture simpler, more straightforward, more honest.

"Now, by your leave, I must ask you to replace it all, for I have urgent business to which I must attend. My boxes are packed and ready in the workshop; you may look at them when you will. I trust you'll find nothing concealed and will let the carter take them away when I send him in the morning."

With these words I bowed curtly and left him standing before his dismantled cabinet, fitting the delicate pieces back together. My final glimpse as I closed the door behind me was of him holding in his hands the compartments from which the letter and the half ring had been removed. He must have known both were in my pocket, but he'd resolved that was how it should be and did nothing to prevent me from leaving.

Alice stood outside in the sunshine, her hair a mass of ruby light. I could see from a slight tightness in her lips and a glimmer of a frown that she was growing impatient, but her crossness only underlined her beauty and made my spirits soar.

"I find I'm suddenly consumed by hunger. Let's dine together at Lucy's Chophouse, and you can tell me how well you've recovered from your injuries and what you made of the history I wrote."

She smiled, a rainbow after the tempest. "Very well, Nathaniel. I accept your offer. And while we're on the subject of injuries, I'll tell you of a curious coincidence that's come to my notice."

"What's that?"

"In Bath I chanced to meet a silversmith by the name of Samuel Harling. He claimed to know of you, and moreover to know how you came by the mark on your head. He made mention of a certain brass candlestick hurled from his wife's bedroom window . . ."

I put a playful arm about her waist and kissed her cheek softly. "That man is famous for his histories," I declared. "I should warn you it's a grave mistake to give them much credence."

She flashed me the drollest of glances, but she didn't push me away.

ABOUT THE AUTHOR

JANET GLEESON was born in Sri Lanka and has worked for Sotheby's London. She is the author of *The Arcanum* and *Millionaire*. This is her first novel. She and her family live in London.